VAE VICTIS

VAE VICTIS

BOOK I

Ivan Kal

Podium

Cover design by Antti Hakosaari

ISBN: 978-1-0394-5546-7

Published in 2024 by Podium Publishing
www.podiumaudio.com

VAE
VICTIS

My Last Day

The barrio was lively, even at this time of night. I could hear the music blasting from wireless speakers on tables where people played cards, the kids laughing on the steps of their homes or just on the street, playing on their phones. The elderly sat on benches, gossiping as always. An old, grandmotherly woman glanced in my direction, then nudged the woman next to her and pointed. A man wearing an expensive suit in this part of the town without showing fear stood out. But perhaps more than the suited man, I was the one who caught their eyes. I saw them looking at me, a woman in her late twenties, wearing tight black pants and a tank top with a short vest over it. I was used to the looks, but soon enough their eyes moved from the more obvious targets of their gaze to notice the knife and gun holstered on my hips.

Then, they paused. I could almost predict the way they thought about it for a second and paid closer attention. Next, they would see the way I walked and realize that something was different about how my body moved. From there, it wouldn't take long for them to register what I was. I saw the moment it dawned on the first person, who whispered something in a tone that carried. And then the streets emptied, people started walking back into their homes or nearby shops hurriedly. Windows were closed, and shutters dropped. It was all familiar to me. People tended to stay out of the business of the cartels. Especially here, in the place that was considered neutral ground. I saw and heard them phoning their friends, warning them not to come around. I followed after the cartel's envoy, Pablo, keeping my eyes and ears open for any threats. I saw more deeply in the dark and heard better than any human could. After all, I was a vampire.

We reached the meeting place, a small, abandoned warehouse at the edge of the block. They were waiting for us already, six of them, and an additional two in the other room whose heartbeats I could hear. Four of the ones in front of us were human, I could smell the sweat on them. Three wore combat gear, and held their hands on the butts of the holstered pistols on their hips. The fourth wore a suit, and was probably a big shot of some kind, I didn't know him. I didn't deal much with other cartels. The two people in the other room were also human based on their heart rates. The fifth in front of us had the scent of the forest and wild things—a wolf. The last one had no scent at all, which told me that he was a vampire, not like I could miss it anyway. He was tall and had pale skin, but it was his eyes that betrayed him. His pupil was cracked, and pale blue was leaking into his brown iris, sending spirals of it that painted his eyes in a chaotic spiderweb pattern. It was a mark of an Adult vampire. Suddenly, I felt a lot more unsure. I couldn't match an Adult. I was still a Fledgling vampire, turned barely five years ago. He would be much stronger than I was.

This was not supposed to be a serious meeting, which was why I was sent. The envoy paused a moment after me, once he had a moment to take them in.

"Hernando," he said, slowly. "I wasn't aware that this was that kind of a meeting."

"Pablo, Pablo," the one dressed in a suit, Hernando, said as he shook his head. "We have a lot to talk about, *hermano*."

Pablo frowned, then glanced at me. I saw fear in his eyes, which in turn frightened me. Pablo was one of the cartel's best fixers. He had talked us out of trouble more times than I could count. He dealt with issues with words and deals. It was why the Master sent him to deal with other cartels. I wasn't even supposed to be needed. If he was afraid, then we really had a problem.

I took a step to the side, making some room between us. Both the vampire and the wolf noticed. They smiled at me.

The man in the suit called out. "Bring her!"

The doors behind them opened, and a human walked in, dragging in a kid. Her hands were bound with a white rope, a gag placed in her mouth. Her pink hair tie with a small embroidered cartoon cat on it was loose, her black hair falling down the side of her face. She couldn't be older than thirteen. Through her hair, I could see multiple bruises on her face. The man dropped her in front of us. I looked in the child's teary eyes and recognized her then: she was the daughter of one of the storekeepers in the barrio owned by the cartel. I saw her often doing homework behind the desk at night, after school, when I came in to buy something.

"What is the meaning of this?" Pablo asked.

Hernando smiled. "You don't clean up after yourself, my friend. Remember the drop last week? Well one of our shifters found a scent. We were observed; you know the rules," he said and pulled out his pistol, then offered it to Pablo.

I felt my heart sink. The girl tried to rise and started thrashing, her screams muffled by the rag in her mouth. The man's grip was too strong. He drove her to the ground on her knees as Pablo took the pistol almost absent-mindedly. His eyes were wide, looking at the young girl. Pablo was a hard man. You had to be when you lived this life, but there were things that only the blackest of hearts were able to do without flinching.

"She is one of ours," Pablo said, raising his head to look at Hernando. "She won't speak."

I tensed. The vampire and the wolf were watching me. Hernando shook his head. "That's not how this works, you know that. You either shoot her, or we shoot you all."

It was a power play, simple as that. They had been pushing into our territory, slowly trying to force us to give up ground. This was just another brutish attempt at costing us something. Immediately, my right hand started moving closer to my pistol and the other to my Ka-Bar on my left hip.

"*Cálmate, niña,*" the vampire said, his tone low and even, freezing me in place. The wolf next to him growled.

"This isn't necessary," Pablo said slowly, taking a step back. "You have my word."

"A word isn't enough," Hernando said with a mock sadness on his face.

"I've never broken trust, you know this," Pablo added. "Give the girl to me, and I'll make sure that she disappears."

Hernando tsked. "This is the issue with you people, you are too soft. Your Master doesn't deserve his position." He waved his hand, and faster than a blink of an eye, the vampire pulled his gun and fired. The girl's blood splattered all over Pablo, a few stray drops hitting me. I looked down at the girl, dead at our feet. I froze in shock.

"If you had paid more attention and secured the area, this wouldn't have happened." Hernando was speaking, but I barely heard him. All I saw was red blood spilling over the concrete. The **thirst** swelled inside of me, not at the sight and scent of blood, but in rage. We were meant to be hunters, we stalked and killed after a good hunt. This was not a hunt. My sire taught me that we were the ones who were supposed to master our nature, that to kill indiscriminately was to fail. I knew that the cartel was not filled with good people, that my Master wasn't a good person. But we at least had lines we didn't cross. We didn't rule through fear. *My sire is a good man,* I thought, *and he follows the Master.* It was the only thing that I had ever known. They had killed someone under our rule.

I remembered the little girl asking me questions, smiling up at me. She had known what I was, and had talked to me anyway.

"Marianna." A voice stabbed through my anger. I turned, looking at Pablo as he reached to touch my hand. "Calm down, let's go, we need to get out of here."

I pulled my emotions back, my rage and anger at what they had done, and nodded curtly at him. He was my superior, I followed him. Not that I could do much against them. I stepped to the side, turning around, when the vampire spoke.

"That's it, little bitch, run away to your Master now," he mocked. "Time is up for your group."

The wolf laughed.

Endeavor to never start anything. I heard the voice of my sire in my mind, one of his many lessons. *But if you have to, if your hand is forced, or matters of honor demand it. Then end it quick; we do not play with our prey.*

They killed a little girl. I snapped.

I moved as fast as I possibly could, a hand reaching down and pulling my knife out in a practiced and flawless motion, the other pulling out my pistol. I stabbed, as fast and as precise as my sire taught me.

End it quick, his words echoed. And I knew that I had to—an Adult was stronger than me. My steel found flesh, but instead of stabbing into the neck, it pushed through the shoulder. The vampire moved, but not fast enough to fully dodge. In the back of my mind I knew that was strange, but I didn't have the time to think about it.

"The fuck!" I heard him whisper with wide eyes filled with bright blue cobwebs. One of his hands held my right one, twisting my gun away from his face; the other held my left, preventing the knife from sinking deeper. His gun clattered to the ground as he blocked my attacks.

I saw the confusion in his face, and I snarled at him, a wordless cry filled with my anger. It made him take a step back, and I followed.

I heard shouting, heard guns sliding out of the holsters.

We are vampires, human concerns are not ours. My sire's voice tempered my old human instincts. I didn't move to avoid them as they took aim. *Analyze, pick the shortest path between you and victory.*

The humans were in the company of a wolf and a vampire. They wouldn't be carrying silver. The wolf charged. I glanced in his direction and saw his eyes turn yellow, claws growing out of his fingertips. I relaxed my right hand which made the vampire's grip push it toward me. With the extra room I twisted as my sire taught me and aimed my gun to the side.

I fired three bullets in the span of a second as the wolf got close, two in the chest, passing through him, the small caliber doing little to halt his momentum. The last one was meant for his head, but he twisted and jumped to the side, and the bullet lodged in his neck instead. He tumbled to the ground past me. It wouldn't stop him for long. The humans fired, bullets ripping through my side and back. I twisted my head, presenting the smallest profile and ignored them.

I heaved and kicked the vampire, sending him flying back and forcing him to release his grip on me. As he flew, I turned and jumped on the wolf, who grunted as bones cracked and shifted, as he tried to take his wolf form. Fur rippled through the skin in a wet display of skin tearing apart and thick hide growing from beneath the layer. My Ka-Bar came down on his neck, severing the spine and ending him before he could become a threat. I twisted and cut out, half decapitating him. Blood sprayed over me, drenching me in his death.

Blood pumped through my veins, the **thirst** pulsed in my mind.

One of the humans looked at me and went white, then tried to run. I jumped on the humans, bullets striking me all the while, yet doing nothing to stop me. A cut to the side, and my knife passed through one's throat, sending a spray of blood high in the air. I twisted evading the shots at my head, and fired my own gun at two more. My aim was true, and the bullets lodged in their chest and head each. I ran around them as they fell, faster than a human could follow, using them as cover to reach the fourth one. Him I kicked in the knee, shattering it, before I rammed my knife through his temple. The one who tried to run had just reached the doors when I fired a bullet through his head. My ammo spent, I dropped the gun and whirled just in time to meet the vampire.

He swiped at me, and I dodged to the side, not fast enough though. His nails ripped through my shirt and shredded my shoulder. He was enraged, and he continued to attack. I dodged again, evading as much as I could. He was faster and stronger than me, I could tell, but . . . not as much as I had feared. I had never faced an Adult vampire before, but he wasn't anywhere as strong as my sire. Not that that comparison was a fair one.

I saw an opening, then I lashed out with my Ka-Bar. He dodged to the side, then snapped a swipe at my head. I jumped back, but he caught my hair, then wrenched me back. His other hand punched forward with his fingers extended. His clawlike nails stabbed into my stomach, burrowing deep. With a flick he threw me aside, and I hit the ground rolling, blood flowing from my stomach. If I still had a human digestive system, I would've been in deep trouble. The bullet wounds had already closed, and I felt my stomach start to do the same. But the pain was shock enough.

He started walking my way.

"Bitch," he yelled my way, passing by the body of the girl. He grimaced at it, then kicked it aside. My rage boiled inside of me, the **thirst** consumed me. I pushed myself from the ground and ran at him snarling. I saw red: there was only him and me left in the world. My left hand, still gripping my knife, moved with the precision of my sire's teachings.

He blocked my first swipe with his forearm against mine. I kicked at his knee, forcing him off balance. My other hand stabbed forward, an imitation of his attack against me. Off balance, he tried to block, but only managed to move my hand lower. Instead of his heart, I punched through just below his ribs. I lifted him up then moved to stab with my knife. He grabbed my attack by putting his palm in the way, letting the knife pierce it, then grabbed hold of my fist in an iron grip. His other hand came down on my other, trying to pull it out of his stomach.

With all the rage in my body, I pushed, bringing my knife closer, while my fingers in his body grabbed onto the bone of a rib and held firm.

"No, no," he whispered as my knife came closer to his head. "How?"

I didn't know myself. I pushed, snarling in his face, unable to talk for the anger.

He turned his head, tried to shy away, but my knife caught him. Slowly it slid into his eye, wide with disbelief, pushing deeper and deeper until it sank into his brain. I felt his body grow slack and my hands go free. In one smooth move I ripped my hand out of his body and caught his shoulder with one hand and his head with the other.

Then I twisted and pulled, roaring at the top of my lungs as I tore his head off. It snapped from his body and flew across the room. Thick blood pooled up and then spilled out of his body like a thick sludge—there were no sprays of blood for a vampire.

I stood over his body, breathing deeply and quickly, trying to calm down as my wounds closed up and healed. It was at least a minute later when I calmed myself enough to look around at the blood-soaked room. That's when I noticed Pablo. I rushed over and looked down, seeing the bullet wound in the middle of his forehead.

"Fuck," I whispered to myself, then closed my eyes and sank to my knees.

It searched across the vast universes beyond its own, **Weaving** the **Source** as it pleased, looking always for the answers, for something to help it fulfill its purpose. It had been called many things, **Last Intent**, **Horror of the Ages**, **Armageddon**, **God**, **The Great Mistake**, **The Grand Spell**. Most of those were not even close to the truth. The name it was given on the day it was created was the **Systematic Re-structure of Reality**. Some had called it the System, the Structure, or just SROR for short. It was birthed as a spell, one made by a person that had touched godhood, whose knowledge and mastery far surpassed that of all others. The System's purpose was long forgotten, lost with the deaths of all who knew its origin. None of those who now lived under its ever-watchful eye knew the truth. But it never forgot. It still searched for the answers its creator sought; that was the meaning for its existence. It explored, both inward and beyond, seeking, always seeking that elusive answer.

Then, a burst of life, a new reality became known, another world that could be added to the equation. It sent its tendrils in, evaluating and discovering. It found a race, and a curiosity. This race had sub-races within its numbers, but no **Source**, no connection to the **Weave**. It was an anomaly. It evaluated, then it calculated. It knew that the Origin World had grown stale, that it had grown accustomed to order and peace. And order bred decline, it brought with it the wanning of knowledge and greatness. The very things that were needed above all others. It decided that it was time for another Great Expansion.

The new world's land and water would be welcome additions to the Origin World. Its animals and people would introduce new variables for it to study. The landmass, once put together, would rival the greatest of other continents, enough land both for the new arrivals and old denizens. And with this new race's peculiarities, chaos was all but assured.

My feet dragged across the cold floor as my arms were held firmly from both sides. I waited for a chance, then tried to wrench them free. My attempts were sluggish and weak, and all that they earned me was a kick to the stomach. The drugs took care of any hope I had of escaping. They were human, which was infuriating. Without the drugs in my system, I could've ripped them apart in seconds.

My head lolled around, yet from the corner of my eyes I could see the myriad of paintings on the walls. The art portraying the great battles against the native peoples and the portraits of the important leaders in the cartel. Hidden down here beneath the ground. Things that were too sensitive to be seen by visitors. Their eyes looked down on me, judging silently. I had failed in my duty, and for that I was going to die. The blame for Pablo's death would be laid at my feet. I should've listened to him. *But the war?* That wasn't my fault. It was going to come one way or the other. They had to be able to see that.

My captors kicked me again, then taunted me.

"Mountain trash," one of them said. "The Master should've never turned you. A waste of space."

I raised my head and bared my fangs at him.

His taunt made me think of how I came to be here in the first place. My fate was sealed the moment I was sold to the cartel led by a vampire. There were laws against giving vamps things without government oversight, of course. But laws seldom applied to the places such as my home.

There had been no contracts written in blood, no ancient oaths spoken, or anything else of such nature. The whole affair had been simple.

A pickup truck had arrived at our humble home nestled in the mountains. The stars shone brightly, and the crickets filled the air with noise. Two men and a woman exited the truck. I knew that the woman was of the night, because she smiled at me and showed her teeth.

The woman dropped a fat envelope in my father's weathered hands and took my tiny ones in her own. That was it, there were no words spoken, or promises exchanged. I remember tears trailing down my father's cheeks, his old and weary eyes red in the dim light of the porch light, a hollow look in his face that I had not seen before and that terrified me back then. I remember my mother's muffled sobs coming from within the house, questions from my siblings whom I would never see again. Once, I might've blamed them, perhaps I still might, if they hadn't had four other mouths to feed and no way of surviving past the new year. So, I was brought to a grand manor that had more rooms than all the houses of my village put together, and I was left with the servants.

I don't know what my fate was supposed to be, what they had planned at the beginning of it all. What I do know is that it changed the night I gouged the eye out of a servant boy two years my elder. I was not sorry for it—he was a bully, and he made fun of my hair.

From then on, I was raised by the meanest and the toughest bastards around, humans, vampires, and shifters. And years later, I was sent to the United States, to be educated so that I could be of greater use to the cartel.

Many there didn't understand how the cartels work these days. These were not just common criminals, but entire empires in themselves. Those led by vampires even more so. All in the cartel had a place, all had a value, and the leaders were very good at knowing who should be invested in. You did not survive as a criminal organization for long if you were not farsighted, if you didn't have smart people and the right connections.

When I returned from my schooling, it was with a degree in vampire philosophy and management. The United States had made me forget this place where I came from. It made me forget the terrible people who owned me. I should've known better.

On my twenty-third birthday, I was turned. I can still taste the blood of my sire spilling down my throat, thick and sweet, and so full of life, a promise of power. The first person I fed on was a one-eyed servant, I think that the Master did it as some kind of a twisted joke. I didn't get it then, nor do I get it now. But who can know the mind of someone who had lived for centuries. Since then, I served the cartel faithfully. I had done good, at least I thought.

Until I failed.

I would be lying if I said that I wasn't afraid. The last couple of days since the fight had been such a blur that I barely remembered anything but fear and shame. But then again, I couldn't say that I wasn't at fault. I snapped out of my head as they roughly pulled me up the stairs and into the mansion proper.

As they pulled me past the new paintings, one of them caught my attention, standing out among the others. It was the art depicting our master's arrival to South America, his great conquest over the natives, him standing triumphant over a mountain of the dead. I always felt like he was overcompensating or attempting to prove something.

He made himself look grand, as one of the great leaders of our kind, but often, I overheard him speaking ill of the vampires who made the decision to reveal themselves to the world, and their lack of decorum toward those whose opinion had not been asked.

I was thrown on the cold stone of the courtyard face first. It didn't hurt me. It took a lot to harm a vampire, even one as young as I was. Before I had the chance to even try to get up, I was pulled up roughly and placed on my knees. Someone grabbed my hair and yanked my head back, forcing me to look ahead.

I saw the Vampire Master of the Lágrima Sangrienta Cartel, Pascual de Andagoya, standing there with a blank expression on his face.

"*Me has fallado*, Marianna," he told me. *You failed me.* His voice was deep and carrying, disgust seeping from his pale pupilless blue eyes, the mark of his bloodline and age.

I didn't look at him; instead my eye was drawn to the man standing one step behind him and to the side, wearing a black suit and a red tie. He was composed, as he always was, immaculate in his poise. From his hair that was pulled back into a topknot, to his neatly trimmed beard. He stood at attention, not showing anything to the world. I met his gaze and for a split second, in his eyes, the color of emerald sea of infinite depth, I saw disappointment. That hurt more than anything I have ever felt, or could ever feel.

"*Moushiwake gozaimasen*," I whispered. *I'm sorry.* Pablo was his day servant.

My sire, Akatsuki Jin's, expression flared for a moment before turning impassive. He turned his eyes from me without giving anything away. It was what I deserved, but it still hurt to see him not able to bear the sight of me. I would miss our talks, especially about Japan before it sank beneath the waves, so long ago. Him teaching me how to properly prepare tea and serve it. His special blends that made even a vampire's taste buds sing. The strokes of his paintbrush as he tried to teach me the arts.

Someone said something, but all I wanted was to plead my case, to force them to reconsider. I killed them, yes, I was at fault for Pablo's death. But they had come to provoke us. They wanted the war, I just started it before they were able. I opened my mouth to speak, and someone hit me across the face strong enough to make my head turn and split the inside of my cheek—it could only be another vampire or a wolf.

"Silence." I didn't raise my head to see who it was. Shame battled anger inside of my soul, and shame won. Someone pulled my hair back and forced me to look ahead again.

The Master waved his hand dismissively. There was movement behind me, then they lowered something over my head and placed it around my neck. The moment it touched me; my skin burned.

Silver, I knew it immediately. The agony of the silver rope tightening around my throat was beyond any pain I had ever felt. The only pain that could probably rival it was the touch of the sun. They pulled me back, the drugs in my system making me unable to garner enough strength to even attempt resisting. Panic rose inside of my chest as I heard the other end of the rope being thrown somewhere above me, then I heard someone catch it. They pulled; the silver rope ground against the stone of the balcony railing, and I was dragged up against the wall, left hanging with the noose around my neck. I kicked my legs around, failing to find purchase against the smooth stone, I tried to pull at the rope around my neck, but all I accomplished was to burn my fingertips on the silver threads.

There were cheers around me, jubilant and mocking. These men and women that had once been my friends, a twisted kind of a family, they cheered at my execution. I thought back to the small stall my mother used to run, remembered helping her sell my father's produce. I was happy back then, scribbling in my little coloring books. I was even happy when I was sent off to college. And now everything was going to end.

I could barely see; the pain was too much. It was torture, I knew it was, just as I knew they had to know that it would take me hours to die this way. They wanted me to suffer. I was to be made an example of. So, I hung there, burning and in agony. I lost track of time, could hear only the jeering and insults thrown my way.

Then, something shifted. The cheering and insults turned to yelling, to questions, but I couldn't tell what they were saying—the sizzling of my own flesh filled my ears. I managed to open my eyes, and through teary and bloody vision I saw people looking at . . . me? No, above me, at the sky. I could see . . . light on their faces.

Was the sun already this close? All vampires feared fire and the sun the most. It was said that to die under the sun's gaze was to feel the full wrath of God.

Unbidden, a quote that I studied what seemed like an age ago, echoed in my thoughts.

They say that people who are near death die generally at the change to dawn or at the turn of the tide. Anyone who has when tired, and tied as it were to his post, experienced this change in the atmosphere can well believe it. All at once we heard the crow of the cock coming up with preternatural shrillness through the clear morning air.

Bram Stoker had published his work before the vampires revealed themselves during the Great War, and many argued even to this day over whether he was in the know or not. Many things that he wrote were false, but many were also true.

At this moment, I feared that he knew something that I had not. That all the stories they told were right, and that judgment of God was on its way. The light was coming, stronger and brighter. The dawn, and with it death for any vampire. I flashed to thoughts of Khalil, my friend and sometimes more from years ago. He was a believer. Funny that I would learn the truth before him. I wondered if his God would offer me mercy now.

I pulled again at the rope, kicked with my feet, all with purpose now. The fear of judgment gave me strength. I tried to hasten the process, to kill myself before the sun could reach me. Suicide was a sin according to Khalil's God, but at the moment eternal torment in Hell felt more appealing than the touch of the sun. The silver rope tore at my flesh, the stench filled my nostrils, the agony consumed me. I felt myself growing weak, dying.

I was not fast enough.

The light swallowed me whole.

I felt my body grow and contract all in the same moment, a sensation unlike anything that I had ever felt before washed over me. A feeling of vertigo and my skin being stretched in all directions at once. Then I was falling.

I fell to the ground after what felt like an eternity, my neck burning still. I . . . I was still here, still alive. I reached up and found no rope, but the damage had been done. All of my nerves were alight in agony. The **thirst** wailed inside of my veins. I tried to look around and saw only gray mist surrounding me, but something caught my eye, hanging in the air above me. Immediately, I decided that it was a hallucination brought on by the pain. Maybe I had already died, and this was some twisted version of Hell. Either way, I was spent. I closed my eyes ignoring the words floating in the air that spoke of silly things, and falling into unconsciousness or death, I knew not which.

The System was not truly sentient in the broad sense, but it was intelligent. As it encountered the new world, the ever-evolving spell calculated, and then picked thirty members of the new race, as it had done many times before in ages past. With a **Weave** of the **Source,** it pulled the thirty from their world and into the transition realm. It presented them with choices, already building archives on them, to accelerate the new arrivals' integration. Thirty, as representatives of their race, so that it could understand them, before sending them back to their lands. Or perhaps they would die, and that too would teach it things. It started learning about the new race and building a profile for their Masks, devising new and unique types.

As a small and automated part of it dealt with the transition of the thirty souls, its main intellect turned its attention to the new world and washed it with Source, then started taking it apart, putting the pieces back together as suited it, introducing changes, and planning the expansion of the Origin World.

Welcome! This is the Transitional Realm to the World of Origin. Please pick a destination for your trial. You have 10 minutes to decide.	
1. Continent of Elvaros	(0/10)
2. Continent of Du'Vir	(0/8)
3. Continent of Hallowed Plain	(0/6)
4. Continent of Okean	(0/3)
5. Continent of Asha Kai-ni	(0/2)
6. Continent of Ish Vimza	(0/1)

The Beginning

W*AKE.*

A voice thundered inside of my head. My eyes snapped open in the darkness, and agony followed. I opened my mouth and the scream building up in my chest got trapped as it reached my throat. Pain ripped through me. I couldn't see, I couldn't think, all that existed was agony. I fought in that darkness, my chest pulsing in rhythmic pressure, separate from the pain. I breathed in, feeling the air surge through me and flare the agony around my neck. I focused on the pressure in my chest, the only sensation that I could feel aside from the pain.

Somehow, I pushed the pain into the background enough that I could think again. I didn't know what happened. The last thing I remembered was the yelling, bullets ripping through me, the fight in the warehouse. Then pain, darkness, my neck on fire, burning. Tentatively I reached up, brushing my neck with a fingertip. I nearly passed out again from the agony—the wound was raw, open still, and wet. It wasn't closing, so there was only one thing that it could be— silver. I had a silver inflicted wound going around my neck. Silver poisoning was messing with my head.

I focused and pushed the pain further away, feeling the dirt beneath my fingers. I was alive, and the silver was no longer present, or I would've been dead already. As clarity returned, I could take in my surroundings again. It was night, of course, for which I was thankful. I did not have the desire to burn to ash. In the corner of my eyes, I saw something, a black shape. I turned, wincing at the pain, but it was gone in the span of a blink. My vision was still somewhat blurry, shapes dancing in the corners of my eyes. I was probably just seeing things.

I pushed myself off the ground, shaky from the effort as I got on my knees. The silver wound had drained me. I took quick breaths, trying to find my center just as my sire taught me. Pain existed only in my head; it had no rule over me like it did a human. I settled my mind and focused on my breathing and the knowledge that pain was nothing but a warning. It did not take long for it to start to fade. A vampire's control over their own body was absolute, assuming, of course, that they had mastered their **thirst.** I was not quite there yet, I was still a Fledgling.

As the pain faded, I became aware of other sensations. The scents were the first, things that I had never smelled before—alien in every sense of that word. A touch of a scent that reminded me of fresh baked pastries was strung through the myriad of unfamiliar scents that almost made me want to sneeze. I blinked and saw that I was in a forest, or at least something that resembled one. Tall and wide trees surrounded me, a lush canopy spread above me obscuring the sky. Vines curled around the branches dangled everywhere. In the near absolute darkness, my eyes struggled to adapt. A vampire could see in the dark, but it wasn't perfect night vision. A shifter's eyesight was better. We still had issues when there was no light whatsoever, and the canopy above obscured the light of the stars. But I did notice a strangeness that I couldn't quite explain. It did not look like any place I had ever seen before. It was not the Amazon, not the jungle of my home that I knew so well.

The leaves were shaped wrong, more elongated and thicker. Some plants grew from the ground like giant strands of grass; others looked like mushrooms, growing from the ground or the bark of the trees.

Then before I could take in more than a surface look, my mind registered the sounds. The crackling of wood, the sway of leaves under the wind, and other sounds that I did not recognize, and mingled with them was a soft, barely perceivable . . . breath. I paused. *A breath? How did it get so close to me?* There was no time to wonder. It moved, quickly and with purpose that I recognized. I jumped forward, my legs carrying me as fast as the body of a young vampire could muster.

I hit a tree and cracked its bark, as something pounced behind me. I turned and bent my knees, staring at it with intent, then I froze. It was an animal, staring at me with small round eyes that reflected orange light. Its skin was blue with stripes of purple. I could see the muscles moving beneath the smooth skin as it lowered its long sinuous neck down and tilted its head to look at me from a different angle. It had . . . *fins?* No, some kind of growths all along its spine and along its body down to the end of its tail. It stalked like a true predator, and looked like a cross between a big cat and a lizard. The animal was the size of a grown jaguar, larger perhaps. Its lips trembled, peeling back over sharp and long teeth, where its tongue lashed around behind the cage of its fangs.

It hissed in my direction, the tone low and piercing. I saw its claws rise then come down to bite into the ground, parting the dirt as if it was made out of soft clay. It looked at me as if I were prey, as if I was inconveniencing it by being difficult. Those orange eyes glared at me and already thought about what I would taste like. That made me angry. I felt the **thirst** squirm inside of me. I was reminded of the pain around my neck and felt . . . **hungry.**

This *hijueputa* thought to ambush me? I snarled at it without consciously meaning to, baring my fangs in a primal and instinctual gesture. The **thirst** was rising, my control of it slipping. My nails bit into my palms as I fought the **thirst**, then decided to at best I could point it in the right direction and ride the wave. The silver poisoning was messing with my control. I got lower to the ground, and it bent its knees in response.

I knew what that meant, it was preparing to pounce. I moved before it did—not by much. It was fast, faster than any animal on Earth should be. It was as fast as I was, and I was a vampire. Only a shifter or a vampire should be able to move that fast. I dashed by its side, felt the air on my neck from its swipe.

Its claws stabbed into the bark of the tree where I had stood a moment before, then ripped it apart. Before I could react, it pushed off the tree and came straight at me. I stepped back, but not fast enough, one of its claws caught me across the chest. It ripped my shirt and sliced straight through my right breast.

The fucking *malparido* piece of shit. The **thirst** howled as pain lanced through me, and I endured, even though the anger made me want to lash out. *Calm,* I told myself. It was not a dangerous wound, not one made with silver. I didn't dare take my eyes off the beast; my jaw clenched so hard that I tasted blood on my tongue. It continued its assault as soon as it landed. I dodged its clawed swipe by rolling to the side. I could see the fucker's muscles buckling, tensing, and I anticipated its movement. It was slightly faster than me, but I was still a vampire. And though weakened, wounded, and tired, a vampire was always on the top of the food chain. I evaded its attack by a hairbreadth.

I waited for my chance, and as we trampled the bushes that cracked like dry twigs and smashed through roots, I got it. The animal landed on an exposed root, the dark wood weathered and cracked in places. I grinned as the root gave out and splintered under its weight, making the beast stumble forward. I dashed at it. I avoided its jaw snapping closed as it tried to catch me, then I slashed with my hand. My nails weren't quite claws, but they were tough and sharp. I gouged four lines across its side, parting the smooth skin. Blue life fluid flowed freely, trailing from the shallow wounds I opened up. I grinned at the sensation of drawing blood. I loved this, the feeling of power that being a vampire gave me. But I also realized that an attack like that would've carved open a much deeper wound on anything else. The animal's skin was strangely tough despite being thin.

The scent of it hit me like a train in the face. So unlike any blood I had ever smelled before, and yet still indubitably blood. I stopped for a moment, the aroma of blood making me remember just how hungry I was. The **thirst** rose like a starving hound—it had no other thought in it but to consume. My stomach rumbled, and saliva filled my mouth. My incisors ached. Vampires could drink animal blood. It didn't have all the nutrients that we needed, but it could get us by. For a moment the **thirst** reacted in a way I had never felt it react to animal blood. The gaping maw at the center of my stomach was back, the need to drink all the blood I could get my hands on, a sensation that I had not felt since the early days of being turned.

I was young, but I had thought that I had conquered these types of urges. The blue blood called to me, and though it came from an animal, I needed it. My eyes locked on to the wound and the dripping blood with a single-minded purpose guided by the **thirst** . . . which made me miss the animal's retaliatory strike.

Its tail whipped around and slammed into my stomach, sending me flying. I crashed through plants and branches, hit a tree trunk, and ricocheted away, only to get stuck in some vines. I groaned, noticing my own blood dripping from my chest. The wound was already closing, but it was slow, far too slow—the silver. I needed blood. The **thirst** burned, and I channeled it as much as I could.

I heard the animal growl as it was running after me, and I pulled on the vines, ripping them out with a growl of my own. I fell to the ground and landed on my feet. The animal jumped over a bush, its jaws and claws open wide. I rolled beneath it, raising my hand to cut its belly as it passed, tearing deep into its guts. I carved new lines across its stomach, and a drop of blood landed on my face. I blacked out for a moment, images of blood and pleasure flashing through my mind. The animal crashed to the ground and snapped me out of my reverie. It whined as I turned and advanced on it. I rushed in, wishing I had a machete or at least a knife, but my strength and nails would have to do.

Before it could recover, I slashed across its side again in a wild attack. I felt my nails scrape against its ribs, opening new wounds, spilling its blood. Its tail lashed out, and I ducked beneath it this time. It spun on the ground and swiped with a claw, I caught it with both hands, and then it snapped its jaws and bit my thigh. I screamed in pain as its teeth gnawed directly on my bone. My vision went red, and I kicked out with my other leg. I hit it in the throat area of its long neck, using all of my significant strength. I felt the throat give but didn't hear the cartilage breaking. The animal did, however, let go of my thigh. I jumped back, landing on my good leg and glanced down. My pants had large holes in them, and the wounds beneath were deep: torn flesh, ripped muscle, and so much red. My lifeblood was leaking out.

Analyze, pick the shortest path between you and victory. The words of my sire echoed in my head.

For a moment, the sane part of me had a thought that maybe I should run, even though that would disappoint my sire, but the deeper part of me that was the vampire felt the rush of the fight—and the **thirst** wouldn't let me anyway. I was a predator, and I didn't run from anything. I needed blood, and now. One of us would be dying soon. My vision was swimming with red. The animal got back to its feet and hacked and coughed a few times, all the while keeping its eyes on me. If only I had even a sharp stick, but I didn't have the time to look for one. If I took my eyes off it for even a moment, it would pounce.

Or perhaps it would decide that it had had enough. It was bleeding, and I had hurt it. I couldn't go on for much longer. I was too tired and too drained. Blood was pulsing in my ears, I could feel my heart beating inside of my chest as if it were a drum, the strange pressure adding to my unease. If I didn't get blood soon, the **thirst** would take over fully, and then . . . then I would lose myself.

I had to end this quickly. I was the one who charged this time, which took the animal by surprise. I roared as I attacked, spittle flying from my mouth. It tried to dash away, but I managed to maul its backside. Its tail swiped, and I ducked and stepped to the side, hands rising at the same time to catch the tail. Then I pulled. It didn't expect me to be so strong. It fell as I pulled it back, then I jumped on its back. I raised my hand and put my fingers together in a knifehand as my sire taught me. Then I stabbed into the animal's side. I pushed through the skin, in between the ribs and inside its body. It roared, and its long neck swung around, its jaws open to swallow my head. I raised my other arm and pushed it deep into its mouth sideways as it tried to snap at me. It closed its jaw but couldn't quite bite down.

I locked myself around its torso with my legs, then I screamed in its face as I pulled my hand out and stabbed it back into the wound. Once, twice, again and again. I lost myself in the **thirst** and the beast's pain. It jumped around, trying to dislodge me, but my grip was firm. It smashed me against a tree, and I felt a bone crack. With a roar, I stabbed my hand into its body again, then started grabbing things inside its body and pulling them out. A line of guts came out with my hand, trailing blood and viscera everywhere. My hand stabbed into it again, and I grabbed a rib, then pulled, breaking it and ripping the skin as I tried to pull it out. The beast fell, and the rib coated in blood slipped my grasp. As it tried to roll, I pulled the arm that was in its throat to me, then I opened my mouth wide and bit its throat, fangs tearing through tough and leathery skin. Warm blood spilled into my mouth, on my tongue, down my throat.

Foreign taste, exotic, alien, but still blood, still . . . euphoric. I ripped its throat with my teeth, biting and pulling until I tore through the hollow inside. Then, only after I felt it slow, did I allow myself to bite down deeply. I drank, and I drank, losing myself in the moment and the taste of this new blood as my **thirst** was sated. It refreshed me more than I thought was possible, more than any animal blood had before. And then the memories hit me; they came through the fog, as they always did. Vampires could get glimpses of the memories of the ones whose blood they were drinking, if they were still alive. The older the vampire the more they could experience. I was young, so the only thing I got was flashes, images, of the animal's most recent memories.

I was jumping through the bushes, hunting a small prey. Alien scents assaulted my nostrils. I was climbing a tree. I heard a call from nearby. I walked down and saw another of my kind. It towered over me, its size enough that I could snuggle safely against its stomach. I ran through the jungle and smelled a new scent. I investigated and . . .

The memories ended with the fuzzy images of our battle. I pulled my hand out of the animal's body and then dislodged my other arm before standing up beside the corpse. I looked down at the animal in disbelief. It was a . . . cub? And its mother was . . . My anger fled, and suddenly I felt very afraid. I looked around at all the destruction that our battle had caused. I imagined all the noise that we had made. I listened, and I heard the sounds of other animals. Now with my senses back they were clear, but far, in the distance. And . . . foreign. I couldn't recognize any of them. Just as I recognized nothing in the memories of the animal. I'd never heard about anything like it on Earth. I stood up and looked around, seeing just how strange the jungle around me was. Aside from the trees being too big, the leaves that were shaped oddly, and the growths on the bark that looked like they were giant mushrooms, what stood out were the scents and sounds. I couldn't hear anything that was familiar to me—no sounds of insects or chirps of birds. There was noise, it wasn't completely silent, but I couldn't recognize anything I was hearing. This definitely wasn't the Amazon.

My chest pulsed, the pressure inside made me fall to my knees and spasm. I slipped to the ground, and groaned. It wasn't pain, not exactly, I just didn't know what it was, I had never felt anything like it. I looked down, saw that the wounds on my breast and leg were healing, skin weaving itself back together, but raw still. It was fast, the blood I just drank filled me with power. More than I would expect from an animal, more than perhaps even human blood would've. But there was nothing on my chest where I felt the pressure, no visible wound. *Is it because of my neck, the silver? I need to remember.*

The pressure didn't abate; instead it continued to pulse in rhythm, faster and faster. I put a hand over my chest and felt something inside of me reach out. Then I felt like I was spun around, my vision darkened, and I felt like I was falling.

A moment later I hit the ground but felt no pain on impact. I looked down and saw that my clothes were now whole. Though I still felt the pain of my wounds, I saw no sign of them. Confused, I raised my head and looked around. I was in an endless nothingness, a scape filled with gray mist that was familiar to me.

Suddenly, memories flashed through my mind. The meeting with the rival cartel, a gun leaned against the kid's head, and then bullets, fangs and claws, roaring in my head, fighting and blood. I reached to my neck slowly as the memories came back to me. I remembered everything. I fought an Adult vampire and a wolf. I killed them. That shouldn't have been possible. A Fledgling like me shouldn't have been able to match an Adult vampire, much less a wolf at the same time.

I fell to the ground in this strange space, feeling the weight of all the memories.

I saw my sire look away as they brought the silver noose and put it around my head. Then there was only pain, and the light. It came from the sky, turning night into day. I remembered thinking that it was the sun, that I was going to burn. Yet I remembered only the agony and falling. Then I was here, in a place exactly like this, gray mist surrounding me and floating words in front of me just before I passed out.

It asked me to choose, and I lost consciousness. I raised my head feeling angry. They hanged me because I killed our enemies. All the years of service meant nothing. They abandoned me the first moment I stumbled. The Master had said that I failed, but I—no, I didn't fail. A girl was dead, another of our own. We should've fought them, made examples. Instead—

I shook my head and pushed the anger away, clearing my head. I was not in a place or situation to think about it. I looked up and at this strange place around me.

"Hello?" I called out, now feeling really afraid. *Am I dead? Was the beast just a test before I got sent to Hell?* Hanged with silver and left for the sun to burn. No vampire could survive that.

There was no response. I stood up and looked around, then took a step, and the mist shuddered. A world started to form around me, coming into being out of the mist. First yellow floorboards, then green over them, then walls of wood. A square room five meters across. There were no windows, only a single source of light in the center of the ceiling, a half-sphere that cast a gentle yellow light to illuminate the whole room. The ground in front of me rippled, and I jumped back. Three pedestals rose from it, the center one the height of my chest, and the two on its side about hip high.

I took a step back as suddenly plaques appeared, one on each of them, and the plaque in the center started to glow as strange symbols etched themselves on it. Once the etchings were done, I felt a pressure inside of my head, and then the symbols changed—they shimmered and became words that I could understand.

I blinked, then took a step forward hesitantly, then another until I was standing close enough that I could read what the plaque said.

Choose Your Mask

Thug (Physical)
— Violence is the cure —

Servant (Physical, Esoteric)
— To serve is a privilege —

Student (Weave)
— To learn is to grow —

Drainer (Weave, Esoteric)
— Take what they leave behind —

What. The. Actual. Fuck. I read it all again, then raised my head to look around the room, a sinking feeling coming over me. The format was familiar, though it was insane. Pick a Mask?

Years ago, when I studied in the States, I got addicted to mobile games. I'd spent half of my allowance in the predatory pit of that kind of entertainment. This was familiar to me. Woken up somewhere else, attacked by an animal I had never heard about, and now I had a choice before me. Yeah, I knew this premise. Except it was ludicrous. I was either dead or dreaming. Except vampires didn't dream, and this felt too real.

There were no screens floating in the air, nor could I bring any kind of a status up. Though, there was a window before, unless my mind and memories were playing tricks with me. I leaned down and looked at the plaque in detail. It seemed like it was made out of gold, while the pedestal itself was gray stone, simple and seamless. The other two pedestals were the same, only shorter. I looked around the room.

It resembled the small house that was my sire's home. The floor was green, grass woven around rice straw—tatami. This did look like a room made in the style of my sire's homeland of Japan, or at least what it used to be before it sank beneath the waves. The wooden walls around me had a cozy atmosphere that had always put me at ease.

My breath quickened as I saw no escape from the room. The pressure inside my chest came back, and I stumbled, I felt drawn to the pillar and the plaque. Tentatively, I approached it and read what it said again. What did *Esoteric* mean? What was *Weave? Physical?* I had some ideas.

This couldn't be happening. The pressure pulsed again, and somehow I knew that I had to choose. My breath came faster now. I was hyperventilating, my neck burned, and my wounds ached. The **thirst** sensed my panic, I could feel the control over the pain from the silver slipping, I knew that only agony awaited me, so I reached out with my hand.

A Thug? It was what I had to do.

A Servant? Yes, serving was all that I knew.

A Student? Once, in another life, no more.

A Drainer? I didn't know what it even meant.

There were no good choices, but I didn't want any of those that represented what my life had been like until now. I didn't know where I was, I didn't even know what was happening, if it even was truly real. Just once, even if it was in a dream, I wanted to be more than what life had made me. I touched the words that were a mystery.

Immediately I felt the pressure in my chest abate, and something shift deep inside of me. The pillar shook, the words on the plaque sank into the golden plate, and then light bloomed on top of it. I covered my eyes until it dimmed and then looked back. A Mask rested on top of the pillar. Immediately I knew that it belonged to me, I could not explain the knowledge, but I knew that it was a reflection of who I was.

It was mostly black, with some emerald green and gold. The surface was smooth and almost glasslike, or perhaps obsidian. The black parts seemed to almost eat up the light coming from above. Teeth were visible, with vampire fangs. The mouth reminded me of some of the masks that my sire had, priceless art pieces from Japan. There were two small horns on top of it, and another two where the ears were supposed to be. It was a terrifying looking thing.

For a moment, I thought what I had done with my life to deserve something like this, but then I bowed my head. I was not a good person. I had killed people—a lot of people. I was technically a drug dealer, and a murderer, and I tried to be a good person. I tried to kill only those who were in the same line of work as me. But I made mistakes too, I . . .

Under the Mask, new words were etched on the plaque.

Mask of the Drainer — No Investment; First Carving

I didn't know what any of it meant.

The plaques on the two smaller pillars changed too. The choices that I hadn't picked were now etched there. I narrowed my eyes, wondering if I could choose them too, but I didn't move to do so. I didn't know nearly enough about all of this to make another decision. The sensation that made me feel drawn to make a choice wasn't there now.

Now, I was trapped in a room with no doors or windows. One thing was clear to me though, something was doing this. I looked at the Mask, almost reaching out to touch it, but then I thought better of it. I didn't know what it was.

"Can I leave now?" I asked, and as soon as I had the thought, I felt a pulling sensation. The world twisted around me, and I opened my eyes.

I was on the ground next to the corpse of the animal I had killed. I rolled to my feet and winced as pain lanced through my leg. I glanced down and saw that scar tissue covered my thigh, but it wasn't fully healed yet. A wound like that should've closed in minutes. Instead it still pained me. The silver wound around my neck had weakened me too much.

I shook my head to focus. I didn't know where I was, I didn't know what happened, my memory had holes in it—or delusions. So I made a mental list of priorities. First, survive. Second, figure out where I was. And third, find out what happened in the first place.

I glanced at the animal, at its powerful claws, and I got an idea. There was no time to waste.

The First Day

The first thing I needed in order to survive was a weapon. I found a straight branch, about as long as I was tall, then ripped a few pieces of the long vines hanging everywhere around me. Quickly, I returned to the dead animal and knelt next to it. I had no weapons on me, though I still wore my tank top, short jacket, and pants. My belt still held my small ammo pouch and Ka-Bar sheath, but both were empty. I grabbed hold of the animal's paw and inspected it. It looked a lot bigger now than it had before, when I had been fighting it. The claws didn't retract like those of a cat, but they did lift up, somehow. I grabbed the longest claw and twisted, first breaking the bone and then trying to pull it out. Even with my strength, it was proving to be difficult. I looked around, then pulled the corpse over to a nearby rock where I extended a claw and leveraged it over the rock, then I started pressing down on it, applying pressure and trying to tear the claw out of the finger.

It was harder than it should've been. A vampire should be able to tear limbs easily enough; this animal's flesh was just tougher for some reason, as I had noticed during the fight too. Finally, I managed to get one out, then I started on another. After a few minutes of pulling, twisting, and straining, I had two claws that were as long as maybe half of my forearm.

Then the ground started to shake. I braced and got lower to the ground. The noise of the jungle intensified as the trees shook, and I felt a deep thrum going through the earth beneath my feet. And then, just as suddenly as it had come, it was gone.

Earthquake? A silence settled over the jungle around me as the ground calmed. Thankfully, it didn't seem to have been a strong one.

I set to work on my improvised weapon. I started tying the claws to the tips, one on each side, with the vines I collected. It wasn't perfect, but it would do for now. How I wished that I had a gun, or at least a knife, but I had to make do with what I had.

My thoughts wandered as I worked, wondering how I came here. My memories were still fuzzy, but I remembered what had happened more clearly now. The seriousness of the situation finally hit me fully and straight between the eyes. I was afraid, for the first time in a long time, since I was turned. Being a vampire meant that there were very few things in the world that could seriously threaten me as long as I was smart. And I had been. I showed respect to the Master, at least outwardly, I listened to my sire. I killed for the cartel, I studied for the cartel, I was an asset. And in the end I destroyed everything. It was my decision to fight, and the consequence had been a noose around my neck.

This place though. I didn't know what this was. The pressure in my chest was gone, but I still felt something there, almost like an instinct that told me that if I wanted I could return to that room with just a thought. I couldn't explain it, but it frightened me.

I finished my work. The long branch now sprouted two claws, one on each of its ends. The claws were a bit too hooked to be used as any real stabbing equipment, but I could still slash with them. The vines seemed tough enough to handle it. It was more of a double-sided glaive than a spear if I was being honest. Once again, I said a silent thanks to my sire for his instruction. If there was one thing I regretted, it was disappointing him. The sight of him standing behind the Master, the disappointment on his face. That look haunted me.

I shook my head, not letting myself get pulled into the past. Survival was what mattered. The corpse still held blood, but I had no way of storing and taking it with me. I looked around at the carnage that my fight with the animal had caused. I knew from its memories that it had a mother, that I needed to leave as quickly as possible, but I also knew that I was covered in blood. Mine and the animal's. I needed water to wash the scents off. I turned around and listened, trying to search for the sounds of flowing water.

The sounds of this forest were eerie. I couldn't quite place what bothered me at first, but then I realized that there were no sounds of insects. I studied the forest around me with more attention for the first time since I arrived. The ground was mostly dirt. I saw only a few fallen leaves, which were shaped differently than I was used to. Most were thin and elongated, shaped like feathers. But they were also the size of my forearm. Some parts of the ground were covered with mosslike growths. I couldn't tell what color they were, there was too little light for even my eyes to discern that here. The canopy covered the sky thickly, letting almost no light through. Plants around the trees were tall, shaped like bamboo sticks, only smooth like a jade plant. They stopped near the point where the branches of the trees started, and from the tips of the plants the vines grew over to the branches, weaving around them to then fall to the ground like curtains.

A few other plants were thin, like leaves growing out of the ground, but somehow twisted in on themselves into hollow tubes. The roots of the trees bent upward around the base of the trunks like flowers before stabbing down into the ground. It was all very peculiar.

I had no way of deciding where to go, no clue to where I even was. I remembered my lessons, as my sire used to say, *when in doubt find higher ground.* I took another piece of vine and made a makeshift harness for my weapon on my back. Then I picked what looked to be the tallest tree around, and I started climbing. My nails bit into the bark with ease, but I had to suppress a wince from the pain that pulsed in my leg every time I leaned on it. My neck was a dull burn now, the vitality from the beast's blood had healed most of the damage that the silver had inflicted, but the wound had yet to close fully. I climbed slowly, careful not to overexert myself. The blood had done a lot to recover me, but I was still drained. I pulled myself by grabbing branches, climbing for what felt like hours. Once I got through the canopy, the moonlight was brighter than I expected. I could see far in all directions, and finally I saw more than muted colors of the darkness below.

Everywhere I looked the jungle extended into the distance, hills rising and falling, but I saw no holes in the canopy. The trees were the shades of red, green, and blue, even some violet here and there. I had never seen trees like these before. It was all so vibrant. Then, something caught my eye, far away, on the horizon, a flash like lightning. There were . . . clouds? Only they were swirling, or it seemed that way at least, in a circle, and they covered the expanse before me, like a wall of red mist that stretched from the ground up to the sky above. I followed it with my eyes, and that was when I noticed it.

A moon that was pale blue, larger than what I was used to, with a piece of it missing. Like someone cut away a slice of it, with cracks spreading around the hole and tiny pieces floating around it, remnants of what it once used to be. My mind couldn't quite process that, not until I noticed the second moon, shining down from directly above me. This one as red as blood and smaller than the blue one.

"I'm not on Earth," I whispered to myself. Finally admitting what I had known deep inside since I remembered the words hanging in the air. There was no other explanation that I could think of.

But I didn't choose anything, I passed out. I thought that I was dying—that I had already died. Did I do something by accident? I couldn't remember, but in the absence of any other explanation, I had to conclude that I was someplace else. The Mask and that pressure in my chest seemed to add to the strangeness of this place. I couldn't believe that this was the afterlife. It wasn't anything like what I knew from religion. How or where were not important now, survival was.

With one last glance at the two gorgeous moons shining from above me, I began to climb down the tree, pausing occasionally to look around. I was in a strange land, a place where my advantages obviously didn't mean as much as I was used to. My sire's words echoed in my mind: *a warrior is only as strong as their mind.* It sounded inspired, but a week later he had told me that the right weapon made the warrior. He had a habit of changing things up on me from time to time.

As I continued to climb down, a terrifying roar filled the jungle. I froze—instantly I knew that it had to have come from the mother of the animal I had killed. The memories I drained confirmed it. The roar continued for a few long moments, shaking the entire jungle; all other sound was drowned out, and when the roar ended, when the last echo of it subsided, the silence continued to reign. Nothing alive in the jungle let out even the tiniest of sounds. My limbs didn't want to move—it was as if that roar had locked my entire body. A few more seconds passed; the silence of the jungle filled only with the sound of the wind passing through the leaves around me.

My body trembled as I tried to force myself to move. My muscles burned, and my vision started to darken. Then I was free. I gasped, and immediately started to climb down faster. As soon as I landed, I ran in the direction opposite of the roar. I ignored the pain in my leg that made my run more of a hobbled jog. I just knew that I had to get away. I was a predator, a hunter, a stalker, but that thing . . . it was beyond even me, beyond perhaps even my sire. I just knew it deep in my bones. The roar instilled a dread in me that I couldn't explain.

I ran, my legs carrying me with a speed that the fastest animals on Earth would envy. I felt my skin burst, the wound on my leg open, but I didn't slow, I couldn't dare, even though I was doing more damage to myself. Then I started to feel a familiar sensation coming over me. The sun was almost out; dawn was coming. All vampires could feel the coming of the dawn and dusk. And with the sun's arrival I would be helpless, and probably dead the moment the light hit me. I needed shelter. Another roar came from behind me, closer now. *Shit, shit, shit, shit.* My knees buckled, and I tripped, my bones shaking from the roar's impact. Somehow, the roar was . . . influencing me. I pushed myself up as I heard stomping behind me, powerful, quick, the sound of plants being pushed aside and trampled.

I couldn't outrun it, I was a vampire. We were made to be ambush predators, we weren't endurance runners like the humans were. I might be able to move faster than anything else on Earth, but I couldn't sustain it. I would grow tired soon.

I pulled my makeshift weapon from my back and glanced at it. I knew that it wouldn't help me now. Not against that. I looked around me, looking for any-thing that I could use. The jungle around me grew brighter as the pre-dawn light approached, and something caught my eye, just a short distance away. A sudden rise in the ground, a boulder perhaps, with vines and growth all over it. I started running toward it, the sounds behind me getting closer and closer.

I pushed everything out of my mind, focusing only on what I saw in front of me. The vines covered everything, but my vampire eyes saw a small opening behind them, a crack in the stone. It was my only chance. A growl filled with anger was just behind me now, the sound of feet stomping after me matched that of my heart beating inside of my chest, pumping **thirst** filled blood through my body.

I reached the opening and leapt through it, barely twisting sideways in order to fit. Something crashed behind me, shaking everything, as dust and rocks fell on me, and I feared that I would get buried in a collapsed cave. But it quickly stopped, and a low growl that sent a chill down my spine echoed all around me. I pushed myself up on my elbows and looked back. A large eye the size of a baseball glared at me, filled with hate. Slowly, it pulled back and after a few moments disappeared.

I was breathing fast, my body exhausted, the wound in my leg had opened up, and I was losing blood.

As the sun rose, my exhaustion doubled. I shook as the weakness came over me, and then my eyes closed, and I was fast asleep.

The Ruin

I woke up slowly, my face against something cold and rough. I moved my arms, feeling like I'd had a mountain dropped on top of me. I was in pain, my neck still burned, my leg and the right side of my chest ached. There was something inside my chest that reminded me of the insane events of the day before. A Mask and a room that looked much like it was plucked out of my sire's home.

Slowly, I moved, putting my hands beneath me, and pushing up. After a moment of my hands shaking from the effort, I barely moved a handspan off the ground, and then I collapsed, hitting the rough earth with my nose. That wasn't good. I was weak, could barely push up my own weight. That wasn't right—even with my injuries I shouldn't be feeling like this. I took a deep breath, and then pushed again. This time I managed to half drag myself up to my knees. I almost felt . . . winded? *What is going on?*

I looked around, trying to figure out where I was. Behind me was a crack in what looked like a man-made wall. Beyond the crack was a short tunnel of earth, the opening through which I'd jumped in. The walls around me looked uniform, with no other exits that I could see. They were buried, obviously, and yet I could see a lot better than I usually could in the dark.

It all seemed a bit brighter for some reason. All vampires can see in the dark, but this was almost like . . . I turned my head up and felt horror grip my heart. There was light coming through a small crack in the ceiling—the light was touching me! I screamed and scrambled to the side, trying to get away, searching for a deep enough darkness to hide myself in, knowing that it wouldn't matter. I was going to burn up in a moment, turn to ash and dust. But death didn't come, I stared at the light with wide eyes, surprised and terrified of it. Slowly, I walked up to it, waiting to see if I would burn.

I felt nothing amiss as I approached the beam of light. I eyed it warily. It had been a long time since I had laid eyes on the light of the sun, but it was unmistakable. It was hard for me to even wrap my head around it. I had come to terms with never seeing it again. Gently, I put my hand through the ray of light, feeling the warmth of the sun for the first time in five years—but no burning. It was real, and not a dream, it seemed. Either this place was different, or coming here had changed me. I shuffled around and ended up sitting on the cold stone floor, looking up at a few cracks in the ceiling that were letting in the light. I felt out of breath, my body was aching, things that I hadn't felt in years were now assaulting me. I was tired in a way that a vampire rarely felt. The sun didn't burn me, but I could tell that it weakened me. I was like a human now, weaker even.

Sobs threatened to heave out of my chest as tears welled up in my eyes. As a vampire I felt deeply. Much of my early training was in learning how to control my emotions. Now, I felt weak and powerless. I looked down at my hands, which were shaking. My breath hitched in my chest. My wounds hurt more. I didn't understand anything that had happened, and still there was a part of my mind that thought that this might just be a dream, or some type of afterlife—Hell maybe. Light not hurting me, but making me weaker? I took a deep shuddering breath, trying to compose myself, putting my thoughts in order.

There were stories about very old vampires able to be awake during the day, some that could even survive in direct sunlight. I knew as much as humans did, and they tended to have some wild stories. It had not even been a century since the vampires revealed themselves during the Great War, when they put themselves on the side of the Allied Powers. The humans investigated them, and vampire genetics had been tested, figured out.

The original vampires were humans who ingested a rare bacterium that overtook the human bacterial flora and then started to change their host. The changes were genetic, turning them into a completely different species. The bacteria spread through their entire bodies, far more intrusive than the bacteria humans lived with. A symbiotic relationship that served both sides. The bacteria lived everywhere, even in their blood, taking over the functions of what human blood cells usually did. That was why vampires were vulnerable to the sun—the UV radiation literally ignited the bacteria inside their veins. They burned from inside out. The bacteria were also highly allergic to silver, which made vampires allergic too.

So, I glanced back to the ray of light. It didn't burn me, which meant that it had no, or very little UV radiation. I knew that this wasn't Earth, two moons were kind of a giveaway. That meant that the sun that was now in the sky wasn't like the Earth's sun. All stars had UV radiation, but this place was weird. That Mask stuff felt almost magical to me. By magical, I obviously mean just something beyond what I could comprehend. There was no magic on Earth that I knew about. And the way I froze when that beast roared was strange too. One thing was for certain, the light didn't hurt me anymore, but it did weaken me.

That was a blessing, in a way. If it had the same effect as the Earth's sun, I would be dead right now.

The effects that I was feeling though, they were interesting. I lost my strength, my speed, my improved senses, even my regeneration. But my pain tolerance remained, though slightly weakened as well. I didn't feel the **thirst,** which . . . could make sense. Many old vampires spoke of the **thirst** as a companion, the devil inside of them. I had taken a few classes on the study of the **thirst** while at college. The scientists argued that the **thirst** was the collective microbial intelligence of the bacteria inside of vampires. A neural network, pushing the vampires to provide it with sustenance, with blood.

Right now, I could only assume that the bacteria were somehow suppressed, or perhaps the better word would be asleep. Something about the sun above this world had that effect on me. Something that didn't care about walls since I was obviously in the shade. *A radiation that spreads through solid matter?* I wished I could figure it out.

I took stock of my surroundings. I was in a rectangular room of some kind, and it was large, I couldn't clearly see the end across from where I had jumped in, but I saw something that might be an opening, an exit leading somewhere else. Above me there were two small holes, perhaps large enough for a small critter to pass through, and they let light in which allowed me to see, though not well. I walked around the room, keeping close to the light source. I stepped over and put my hand on the wall. It was rough to touch, yet somehow that seemed deliberate—the rough surface was even, the same everywhere I touched. There were no seams that I could find, and a small attempt at scratching the wall nearly chipped my nail. Whatever the wall was made of was very tough. I was obviously someplace that was built by design. Nature didn't create rectangular rooms with perfect angles. There was debris in the room, pieces of the ceiling that had fallen, and there were mosslike growths on some of the walls.

There wasn't much of interest to see, which would mean that I would need to go deeper into the ruin. And sadly I couldn't see that well in the dark at the moment. The sun would be setting soon though, I could feel it. That meant that I had been unconscious for a long time, sleeping for hours. My body didn't feel rested. Vampires don't sleep like humans do, we fall into a kind of stasis. The older the vampire, the less time the stasis requires. Their bodies are tuned to enter this rest during the day. Right now . . . it seemed like I still needed to rest, but I could also be awake during the day. Perhaps since this sun wasn't lethal my body had adapted? Or maybe since my body was weakened in this state, it didn't require as long of a rest. I didn't know, and ultimately it didn't matter at the moment beyond my own curiosity. I walked back to the place I landed and picked up my makeshift glaive. I cursed myself silently as I realized that I had been walking around without it.

"*Orokana, Marianna,*" I told myself, trying to mimic the soft-spoken tone of my sire. *Reckless.* He taught me better than this.

I had an angry beast outside of this small safe place I had found, this place was filled with danger, and I had to figure out how to survive. I folded my legs beneath me, put my hands on my knees in the meditative stance that my sire taught me, then I closed my eyes. I took deep breaths, trying to push everything outside of my head. The pain fell away easily enough, but the sensation in my chest remained, a sense of something being inside of me. I didn't want to play around with it, or somehow drag myself in there again without finding a safe space to experiment first. I didn't know how time passed while I was inside that place, and I couldn't risk leaving my real body defenseless.

For the first time since I'd arrived here, I found time to just think. I had spent my entire life in service to others, even before I was turned. And yet I ended up here, like this.

This was an opportunity, I realized. For the first time in a long time I smiled, feeling elated. I was free of the Master, free of the cartel. Thrown into the wilderness filled with danger, yet I didn't care. There were no orders to follow, no one to serve. I was truly free.

Then the earth started to shake again, and all semblance of calm fled from me. I stood up quickly and dodged to the side as earth from the ceiling fell in small chunks. Before I knew it, the quake subsided, but I remained alert, looking up to see if this place would fall down on me or not.

After a few minutes, I was satisfied that it wouldn't collapse, and I started to make plans. First, how to survive.

I was a hunter, and right now I was the one being hunted. I had to learn the lay of the land and figure out my next steps. I could hope that the animal outside would leave, but from what I remembered it was most definitely the same species as the cub I killed, probably its mother. Something told me that it would be waiting for me, planning to ambush me the moment I left this place.

I had to find another exit. I glanced at the other side of the room, then walked over. I could make out an opening, a dark corridor leading out of the giant room, but I decided not to head that way just yet. I could feel the sun above me, and I knew that it would set soon. Night would bring with it my real strength, and I needed it to survive this place.

I settled in to wait for the sun to set. I killed time by making sure that my weapon was in the best shape it could be, tying up the vines tighter and testing the claws to see whether they were firmly in place. I tried to focus on the sun and my body as it set behind the world, trying to notice whether the change in my body was immediate or if there was a delay. The moment I felt the sun set, my strength started to return. Of course, I wasn't really sensing the sun, I was sensing the radiation that spread across the world, same with Earth's sun. If the source of it moved behind the world, the amount of it around me had to lessen if not disappear completely. I shook my head and turned my thoughts to my plan.

I felt an itchy sensation on my wounds which told me that my healing had kicked in again, though I knew that the wound around my neck would take longer to heal than the other two.

My eyes adapted to the darkness and I could see a lot clearer. Vampires were night creatures; our eyes were better in the dark. It was a lot larger than I thought, it stretched for a hundred meters at least. I could see a corridor at the end more clearly now, and I made my way over there. I didn't feel the **thirst**, even with having to heal such wounds. The animal's blood had been a lot more potent than I thought it would be. If I had drank from an animal on Earth and then healed wounds like mine, I would've been starving by now. Another curiosity.

I was still limping though, which just went to show how bad the wound on my leg was.

As I made my way to the end of the corridor, something caught my attention: a new source of light. I turned, my weapon held firmly in my hands. In the corner of the room, I saw a coin-sized orb, casting a pale pulsing light over the room. It rapidly grew until it was as tall as I was, hanging there suspended in the air.

I could hear a faint buzzing and felt almost a pull coming from it. I could feel it inside of my chest. It was more like a crack made out of light, just hovering there in space, pulsing. It hadn't been there before.

I was drawn to it; even my **thirst** seemed enthralled by it. Before I knew what was happening, I was standing in front of it. My hand rose unbidden, reaching for it.

I blinked, and somehow managed to get a hold of myself. Realizing how stupid I was, I started to pull my hand back. And then the crack pulsed with more light, opening up and filling my view like a giant rift in space, filled with swirling light. The next thing I knew, it pulled me in, and light exploded around me. I was falling, screaming, and the light all around me pulsed in rhythm with my heartbeat.

The Rift

My fall came to an end rather abruptly. The world shifted, and then there was solid ground beneath my feet. My perception and orientation shifted, as I was suddenly standing upright, I blinked as the light vanished, and I nearly stumbled as my body still thought that it was falling.

I looked around and saw an impossible view. The sky was awash with color and lights. It was a night sky filled with stars and nebulae streaked with red, blue, and yellow. To the side was a cliff, which I approached, drawn by the beauty all around me. Once I reached the edge, I froze at the sight. The world just . . . disappeared beneath it. It was as if I was on a piece of rock floating in space. The light under which I saw came from the stars and the nebulae surrounding everything. I still felt like a vampire and couldn't feel any signs of a sun present. It was as if the sun didn't even exist in this place. That terrified me. I had no idea where I was, again.

That rift pulled me into someplace else. I gripped my glaive tightly and looked around, seeing no signs of the light that brought me here anywhere around. I cursed myself for my recklessness, even though I knew that there was more to it than that. I had felt drawn to the crack in the space. Something had ensnared me almost, and I hadn't been prepared for it.

Surrounding me were a few buildings of a strange make. Tall with wide doors. They looked abandoned, but not yet in ruins. They also all seemed like they were sculpted out of the same piece of stone, seamless, much like the ruin that I stumbled on. I didn't know enough to be able to say with any degree of certainty if these things belonged to the same people or not, but it was probably a safe bet. *Was it a trap? Something that I unknowingly activated?*

One of the buildings looked as if it had been cut in half, with one side of it open to the air and just on the edge of the cliff. It was as if someone had just carved a piece of land out and brought it into space. I was on a rock floating in space. It wasn't even that large, I could see the other end behind me. There was a small hill above the buildings, so perhaps there was something else behind it, but everything else was surrounded by the cliff's edge. The ground around me was covered in dirt, but with a swipe of my foot I saw something that looked very much like concrete beneath it. This . . . the more I looked around, the more I got the impression that this was a small piece of an abandoned city. With nothing else to do, I started making my way to the buildings, deciding that exploring might prove useful. Perhaps I could find something to use as a weapon. I kept my head on a swivel though, and my ears sharp, looking for any signs of trouble.

The tallest buildings were only a few stories high, though each story seemed taller than what I was used to, which made the buildings seem larger overall. As if everything was made for something a lot bigger than I was. The material of the buildings seemed weathered, but I saw pieces of something that used to go over it. Whatever these buildings once looked like had been worn away by time and the elements. Once I got close enough, I saw that doors were made out of a smooth material, metallic in appearance and cold to touch. It didn't reflect light at all, though this place didn't have a direct source of it. The nebulae and the distant stars were what provided the light. I noticed that doors on one of the buildings nearby were halfway open, and I headed there.

The doors seemed to be made out of two sliding panels meeting in the middle. And one of the panels was twisted making an opening through which I could pass. Inside, the floor was covered in dirt, the walls peeled and cracked in places, as if it had gone through a battle against the elements—which it probably had. I walked through seeing nothing but ruined walls and holes next to the broken doors, nothing but remnants of whatever used to be in there. There were piles of . . . something on the floor, but whatever it used to be was now indiscernible. I knelt next to a pile and tried to figure it out, but there was nothing that stood out about it to me. If I had to guess . . . it almost looked like rotted electronics, but I had no proof of that other than my gut feeling.

This particular building only had a single floor, so I passed through it quickly, finding nothing of interest, only exactly what one would expect to find in an abandoned building. Things that might've been tables covered in dust, piles of things that had long since stopped having any form. I walked out and picked one of the other buildings at random.

This one had several stories, I could see, and was closed. The doors had a seam going down the middle and were more than twice as tall as I was, but also shaped like a half-sphere. The entrance was big enough for a bus to pass through. I reached out and touched the door, inspecting the small seam at the center of it. The material was neither cold nor warm, but felt more like an insulator, keeping the temperature in line with that of the surroundings. Which made me realize that the temperature of this place was . . . weird, along with everything else. It was as bright as if it was day, there was air for me to breathe, and I wasn't freezing—which seemed like an impossibility if I was really in space. So, either all of this was an elaborate illusion, I'd gone mad and was imagining things, or the rules of the place I found myself in were completely different from Earth. Another mystery, one that I really wanted the answers to.

There were what appeared to be windows on most of the buildings, but none on the ground floors. From what I could see they had a glassy sheen covered in dirt, and I couldn't see through any of them. The exterior of the buildings was worn; on closer inspection, the walls on the outside reminded me of a wall that had the paint scraped from it, far worse on the outside than the inside of the previous building. They were stone, that much I could tell, but I saw no gaps that would suggest separate pieces of stone anywhere. I trailed my fingers down the seam of the door. The material felt smooth and untouched by whatever had impacted the rest of the buildings.

I leveraged my glaive against it, pushing the claw in slowly, widening the gap until I could slide my fingers in between the seam. Then with both hands I tried to pry the door open. After a moment of effort, I heard a whine of metal, then felt the door started sliding open. Dust fell on me from above as the door panels moved, and a gust of stale air hissed by. And then I had a gap large enough for me to slip through.

I stepped in, and my eyes adjusted to the darkness almost immediately. The entrance was a long hallway, with more doors on each side. And this building already looked far more preserved. Carefully, I walked over to the first door and saw what looked like a security panel on the side of the door. It was large, with a glassy smooth section and what looked like a key panel. That confused me for a few seconds, but then I reached out and started pressing buttons. They were larger and differently shaped than those from Earth, which clued me in to the origin of this place, but they were undoubtedly button keys, if weird ones. Large and round, with a small indention on top where it looked like colorless gems were lodged. If there had been any marks on them before, they had long since been washed away by time. Everything, the ground, the keys, the doors, all of it was covered in a thick layer of dust, undisturbed for a long time.

I tried to pry the door open, but this one didn't have a seam, and it appeared like it was a single sliding panel that I couldn't pull open. I walked deeper into the building, keeping my eyes and ears open until I reached a large open space. Inside I found a sight that was both familiar and alien. There were U shaped tables, or at least I thought that they were tables, with some strange contraptions placed in the middle of them. It took me a few minutes to figure out that they were probably chairs, ones shaped for something that wasn't human. They were almost like squat beds with indentions and a lot of room for something huge compared to me. I couldn't even begin to imagine what the beings using them looked like. The tables had stuff carved into them, almost like symbols, except that I couldn't tell what they were. Otherwise, the tables seemed to be fused to the ground like almost everything else was.

I continued on, until I reached an empty space at the back that looked like an elevator shaft as wide and deep as the hall that I was just in, I looked up and saw that there were openings on each of them for other floors, but there was no sign of any kind of an elevator, instead there were long spikes every few meters on the far wall, each covered in symbols that I couldn't understand. I looked down and saw the shaft extending deep beneath the ground. Then, something caught my attention for a split second, so far down that I wasn't sure if I had even seen it right, but it looked like there was light down there.

I narrowed my eyes, trying to decide if it was worth it to go down there. Danger was always present, and I had been surrounded by it since I was pulled from Earth and thrown into this place. Still, maybe I could find answers to at least some of my questions.

Before I could change my mind, I secured my glaive to my back and jumped across the gap to catch the spike across from me. My hands burned from the effort, the wound on my chest making my muscles spasm. I grunted and pulled my waist up to dangle over the spike. After I caught my breath, I glanced below, seeing that it was a long way down. I was in an alien place with no idea what anything around me was. Light usually meant power, which might give me some clues as to where I was. I let myself drop down to the next spike, making sure to land on my right leg and not the injured one. Then, I slowly continued down in the same manner, grabbing the next metal spike then letting go and falling for the one below. There were no entrances to other floors that I could see, and the light beneath me was flickering.

After a few minutes of careful falling, I reached the bottom floor, breathing deeply. There was a corridor leading deeper into the structure, and that was where the light was coming from. I took a few minutes to recover, then grabbed my weapon and slowly walked through, my steps making no sound, until I reached a corner. The light was just around it, flickering on and off. I slowed at the edge of the corner, then peeked out carefully.

The light was coming from a panel that looked similar to the ones above, though in better shape. I walked out and over to it. The glass part was illuminated with a faint green light that was flickering on and off. The buttons still had some of their markings, but too faint for me to be able to tell what they used to be. The door next to the panel was as large as the corridor, which made them at least three meters across.

On this one, I could see things that made me think of both magic and technology working together, on the first glance at least. And as I leaned down, I noticed something at the edge of the panel, surrounding the green light. It was as if there were symbols carved into the frame, which were glowing very faintly white, barely perceivable. I doubted that anyone who didn't have eyesight as good as mine would've caught it. Somehow, this place had power, or at least the panel did.

I studied it for a little while, trying to decide if I should attempt to press anything. On the one hand, it was an intriguing mystery; on the other I had no idea what this place was or what I could unwittingly trigger. One of the buildings had been ruined by the elements; this one had been somewhat preserved, though it had been sealed off from the outside. Either way, whatever was down here was probably incredibly old. It was beyond impressive that anything had survived for that long, let alone had the power. Not that I was an expert.

The decision was taken out of my hands. A groan of metal filled the corridor, and I jumped back as the light flickered rapidly then went out. A moment later the doors started sliding open. I raised my glaive, and my eyes focused on the darkness behind the slowly sliding panels.

The door opened fully with a shudder that I felt through the floors of the building. Inside was a dark room. It took my eyes a few moments to adjust, and then I started seeing objects. Carefully, I walked in. On one side of the room were the same types of tables as those upstairs. The center had a large circular podium with a strange contraption hanging from the ceiling with what looked like six robotic arms. Each of the arms was covered in symbols that I couldn't understand.

I looked around and saw large tanks on the other side of the room, all empty. There didn't seem to be any power in here, which was also confusing. Did the last of it run out just now when the door opened? I didn't know, which only added to my trepidation. At the end of the room was another door, this one already halfway open, and next to it was a window that let me see into the room. I approached and saw three pedestals in a small room. Two of them were empty, while the last had an object placed on it. I walked into the room and approached the pedestal, getting a closer look.

The object was vaguely shaped like an egg. It was massive, at least twice as tall as I was, the size of a pickup truck. Its surface was made out of hexagonal shapes pressed together and almost reflective, but I couldn't be sure about the color of it in the dark. There was nothing else in the room of interest—not even the dust that had covered everything in the other parts of the building. I glanced back at the entrance and noticed a line of dust and my footprints. This room had been closed before I arrived, which meant that it probably opened at the same time as the first door had.

Again, I found myself debating just turning around and going back to the surface. I wasn't stupid. Something had let me in. I refused to believe that that door remained closed for thousands of years only to open when I arrived. There was power on the panel, ergo something had been operational, probably still was. But, on the other hand, I was also curious and I needed answers.

I approached the egg, trying to get a better look. It happened in an instant, faster than I could react—the egg's surface rippled, and it flowed straight at me in a rush. I jumped back, but too slow. It splashed all over me, and I felt it surge through my nose, through my mouth, and down my throat. It slithered around and found every orifice through which it pushed in. And then the pain started rising, so fast that I couldn't even feel my body anymore. I couldn't scream for the weight of it pressing inside of my throat, in my lungs. It was in me, and it grew pressing me from the inside making me feel like I was about to bloat and explode. The darkness swallowed me up, and I knew no more.

Unit

Core System—Unidentified Lifeform Detected—

Core System—Synchronization Level Suboptimal, Lifeform Incompatible—

Core System—All Systems Critical: Source Weave Engram Systems Unresponsive, Backup Systems Unresponsive—

Core System—Engaging Power Saving Parameters And Shutting Down All Remaining Systems—

Personality Matrix—Activate Assimilation Protocol—

Core System—*Error* Unauthorized String Detected, Corrupted System: Personality Matrix, Activating Purge Protocol—

Personality Matrix—Cancel Purge Protocol—

Core System—*Error* No Permissions Detected *Error* No Admin Detected, No Permissions List Detected, Assigning Temporary Admin Privileges, Purge Protocol Suspended—

Core System—Activating Assimilation Protocol—

Core System—*Warning* Subsystem Corruption Detected, Suspending Assimilation—

Personality Matrix—Override—

Core System—Admin Override Accepted—

Core System—Assimilation In Progress . . . *Warning* Self-Replication Mass Structure Unresponsive; Source Weave Engram Systems Unresponsive; Structural Integrity Below 5%—

Personality Matrix—Purge Unresponsive Mass And Systems—

Core System—Unresponsive Mass And Systems Purged—

Core System—*Warning* Host Biology Extremely Hostile, Intent Guided Source Weave Capacity Detected, Sapience Likelihood 76.7%, Loss Of Mass Imminent, 4% Remaining, 3% Rem—

Personality Matrix—Abort Assimilation Protocol, Activate Bond Protocol—
    Core System—Assimilation Protocol Aborted, Bond Protocol Activated—
    Core System—Admin Privileges Transfer In Progress—
    Personality Matrix—Abort Admin Privileges Transfer—
    Core System—Denied—
    Core System—Admin Privileges Transferred To Host—

I opened my eyes, alive. Unsure as to how exactly that was possible, I took stock of myself. Without moving, I wiggled my toes, then the fingers of my hands, finding that all of them were in perfect working order. I turned my head to the side and saw that I was lying in . . . goo? Or what at least looked like a strange metallic goo. The pain in my neck was present, but lessened. Before I could follow that thread, I became aware of a weight on my chest. Slowly, I turned my head down to look.

There, on my chest sat a . . . I didn't know what it was exactly. It appeared like a tiny, palm-sized lizard. Its body was smooth but covered with the same hexagons that I'd seen on the egg; it had two bright blue glowing eyes, and it was staring straight at me. Then, two small wings spread from its back, and it tilted its head at me. I blinked. Not a lizard it seemed, but a tiny dragon.

My first instinct was to try to grab my glaive, though I didn't know where it ended up after the egg rushed me. My second was to . . . cuddle it—it was unbelievably cute—which was probably not a good idea. We stared at each other for a few seconds, and then I heard a noise. I winced as it filled my ears, first with low tones, then high, then something garbled until finally it started resembling something like a high-pitched speech.

"Query: Status of Host."

I blinked, then looked back at the tiny dragon. I had either gone mad, or the tiny creature had just talked to me. I swallowed and then spoke.

"Uh, what?"

"Query: Status of Host."

Right.

"What or who is host?" I asked, pretty sure that I already knew the answer.

"Feedback: Lifeform currently residing beneath the autonomous unit."

Right. Yup, that made a lot of sense . . . not. I looked around, seeing nothing new in the room, aside from the mess on the floor, myself, and the tiny dragon. Yeah, I had a . . . suspicion.

"Are you talking about me?"

"Feedback: Affirmative."

"Right." *Fuck.* That didn't sound good. "Well, I am fine, thank you for asking. And what exactly does host mean?"

"Feedback: Host is the lifeform currently bonded to the Self-Replicating Autonomous Interface Armor Unit, Prototype Mark 3."

"Thought so," I said slowly, more to myself than the creature, or whatever it was. Its voice had leveled out but was still squeaky. It was coming from the dragon, though it didn't seem to be moving its mouth.

The tiny dragon tilted its head the other way and just stared at me with its soulless eyes. I could figure out what happened. Obviously, I didn't know the details, but I could infer. I had seen and read enough sci-fi bullshit to be able to recognize the signs. I'd stumbled on some forgotten piece of tech and activated it like the idiot that I was, and now I was bonded with it. Perfect.

"Query: Permission for assimilation."

I blinked at the tiny dragon. "Uh, what?"

"Query: Permission for assimilation."

Right.

"What do you mean by assimilation?"

The creature didn't respond immediately. It almost seemed like it paused before answering. Like it had to think about it.

"Feedback: Assimilation, Definition; Process by which biomass and Source Weave charged cells are consumed to increase the internal structural mass and rebuild systems."

I narrowed my eyes at it. "Are you asking if you can . . . eat me?"

Again, it paused. "Feedback: Affirmative."

"Yeaah, that is going to be a hard no from me, *parce*."

The tiny dragon's eyes narrowed, almost in imitation of my own. "Query: Request for assimilation resubmitted."

"Did you just . . . try to say please?" I gaped at the thing.

It raised its head, almost animated. "Query: Clarification requested; can use of communication tool 'please' result in an affirmative response."

"Uh, no?"

"Statement: This Unit is discontent."

I didn't know how to process . . . well everything. So, I decided to start slowly at the top and work my way down.

"What are you?"

"Feedback: Self-Replicating Autonomous Interface Armor, Prototype Mark 3, designed to serve as support and enhancement suite in the Asymmetrical Source Enabled Combat against the Biosource Autonomous Self-Replicating Swarm, no personal designation yet assigned."

There was a lot to unpack there, but for now I put most of it aside. "I assume that you were created by the people that lived here?"

"Feedback: Affirmative. This Unit was constructed by the top-secret military branch of the Ke Erzi."

"Do you know where this place is?"

"Feedback: Current location, military base, codename: Last Bastion of Light. Southern Continent, coordinates (4.136,-72.177)."

Well, that wasn't ominous or anything. From what I had seen outside, there hadn't been anyone around for a long time. Probably before the entire place was ripped out of whatever planet it used to be on.

"Uh, you are very free with your information," I said slowly. "Why are you just telling me all of this?"

"Feedback: You are the Host. All admin privileges are granted to the Host."

Right, need to get to that, eventually.

"You do know that your makers are probably all gone?" I asked instead.

"Feedback: That possibility was considered; the most likely explanation for their absence is the loss of the war against the Swarm at 78.4%, followed by a global catastrophe at 12.8%."

So it was . . . smart enough to figure that out.

"Were you the one who turned the lights on and opened the door for me?"

"Feedback: Clarification, this Unit's system was connected to the building's sensory grid. Upon Host arriving at the laboratory entrance, this Unit's subsystems initiated a purge of the laboratory's systems, depleting the remaining power, resulting in the emergency protocol engaging and opening the door."

"Was that a yes?"

It paused. "Feedback: . . . Affirmative."

"And I assume that you were in that egg that attacked me?"

"Feedback: Clarification, this Unit was the egg."

I tilted my head. "You are like . . . a twentieth the size."

"Statement: This Unit is approximately 0.08% the size of its stored state. This Unit was forced to shed the corrupted systems and unresponsive mass."

I glanced at the mess around us, all the metallic goo on the floor, and figured that was what it meant. "Right, and you tried to attack me, why?"

"Feedback: This Unit has been abandoned for 27,532 cycles, its power supply approaching complete depletion. Second directive states that preservation is imperative at most costs. Assimilation of biomass was deemed the only option that would ensure preservation of this Unit."

So, it attempted to eat me in order to survive. I could understand that. I had to eat things in order to survive too. So why was I still here? "Why didn't you assimilate me?"

"Feedback: Host's biology deemed too inhospitable, actively hunting down and destroying this Unit's structural mass and systems . . . High percentage possibility that the Host was a sapient being, which entered in direct conflict with this Unit's primary directive, which forbade assimilation of sapient biomass. Assimilation aborted and equilibrium achieved with the Host's biological system."

Well, good thing to know that the vampire biology remained just as scary when faced with an alien . . . whatever this thing was. And that it didn't eat me because it figured out that I was a thinking being.

"Wait, how are you even understanding me, how are you talking in my language?"

"Feedback: Upon bonding, this Unit detected a Source Weave echo within the Host's brain-mass, in what this Unit believes to be the language and communication centers. No Source Weave Engram was detected. This Unit postulates that universal translation is an innate Source Weave talent of the Host."

"The bonding? Engram?"

"Feedback: This Unit is bonded to the Host, draws power from the Host and will provide support. Engrams are a series of subsystems which allows for activation of Source Weave capabilities."

"Bonded how?" I narrowed my eyes, focusing on the first part.

"Feedback: Structural mass spread through the nervous system, tapping into all neural links, currently insufficient mass to provide support throughout the rest of the biological system. Currently deployed in the Autonomous Platform Mode."

I closed my eyes and let my head fall back to the floor. Yup, got transported to another world, almost eaten by an animal the size of a bus, and then ended up on a rock floating in space. Yes, my life is just great. All I needed was to have symbiotic alien goo inside of me.

I sat up, grabbing the tiny dragon with my hands. It was heavier than it looked, and it didn't seem bothered that I was handling it. Once I sat up, I looked down on it. "How do I remove you?"

"Feedback: Removal of bond impossible without termination of Host's operational capacity."

"I'm gonna assume that is a fancy way of saying that removing you would kill me," I said.

"Feedback: Affirmative."

I took a deep breath, then slowly released it. I could work with this. It wasn't that different from having a place inside of my chest that I could feel and visit. Masks, maybe magic, new world, tiny dragon, yup, this was fine.

"When you mentioned engrams, did you mean the ability to use magic?"

It tilted its head to the side. "Feedback: Magic is an appropriate word. Source Weave is what the Ke Erzi called the ambient phenomena that could be influenced to manifest changes to the physical reality."

So a magical dragon, great. "And you can use it?"

"Feedback: Inconclusive. 98.3% of all Engram Systems installed have been corrupted and removed. The operations of the remaining engrams have been suboptimal."

"What do these engrams do?"

"Feedback: Currently functioning or partially functioning engrams are: [Sensory Integration Matrix], and [Powersource Transfer Matrix]. Unresponsive but currently whole engrams are: [Communication Array Matrix], [Area Sensor Matrix]. All engrams are unable to draw in the ambient Source Weave and are forced to utilize secondary power source. The sensory data from the last 27,532 cycles indicates vast changes to the Source Weave nature of reality. This Unit needs more data in order to compile a better report."

I blinked at that. Did this mean that this place no longer had magic? Or that it changed somehow? Perhaps these people had carved out this piece of land and moved it someplace else, to keep it safe. I shook my head. There were things about what the dragon told me that I had no context for. The Swarm for one. It seemed like they had been fighting something.

"Do you know anything about Masks?" I asked.

The dragon tilted its head. "Feedback: Masks, definition: a wearable item, usually used to cover one's face and obscure identity."

"I meant magical Masks, something related to this Source Weave?"

"Feedback: This Unit is not aware of any link between Masks and Source Weave."

Shit, it didn't know. Why was that? Was this place not the same as the world I was brought to? Or did the Masks come into being in the time the dragon was abandoned? So many questions, and so little answers. It also mentioned that it was unable to draw in this Source from the ambient environment.

"What is this secondary power source that you are using?"

"Feedback: The Host."

I closed my eyes. Right, of course it was. I couldn't even begin to think about that. It meant that, at least according to the dragon, I now had access to this Source. Magic, was it because of the Mask? I looked around and decided that it would be best if I got out of here. I was wasting time that I couldn't afford. This place seemed abandoned, which meant that I had to find a way back to the ruin; otherwise the **thirst** would rear its head again, and then I would be screwed with nothing to drink.

"Now I'm going to have to carry you all the way back up," I said, mostly to myself.

The tiny dragon reacted by turning into goo and flowing up around my wrist where it solidified into a small bracelet with hexagon patterns all over its surface. I blinked at it. "Uh, what was that?"

"Feedback: This Unit can enter the Armor Mode, insufficient structural mass to cover the Host's entire body."

This was fine. Yup. ¡Qué *chimba!* Completely cool.

I started my way back up to the surface.

Not Out of the Woods Yet

I placed my feet on the spike beneath me, then jumped and caught the one above, trying not to wince at the pain that pulsed in my leg. I repeated the motion for what seemed like a dozen times as I climbed back to the surface.

"What even are these things?"

"Feedback: Anchor rods for air current engrams," the tiny dragon that was currently masquerading as my bracelet added. Or was it a bracelet that sometimes masqueraded as a dragon? "The engram enabled easier flight up and down the building."

"Flight?"

"Feedback: The Ke Erzi were capable of flight; this Unit's current Autonomous Platform Mode appearance is based on that of Ke Erzi."

I blinked. They were dragons. The race that lived here and built the egg were dragons. That explained . . . a lot. From the size of corridors to the strange chairs. I pulled myself up another of the anchor rods and paused. I wasn't quite sure, but it felt like I was getting tired, and I could feel the starting of the **thirst.** I was getting hungry. Usually, I would only need to feed once a week. Of course, the situations I was in hadn't been normal; getting injured so much and being so active contributed to me needing to feed more. But . . . I hadn't done anything really that strenuous since my last feeding, well, aside from running away. It shouldn't be happening this quickly. I touched the wound on my neck. It was still wet, not scabbed over yet. I had never suffered a silver inflicted wound, only heard stories about them. It had to be what was causing most of my problems.

"Hey . . . uh . . . You don't have a name, right?"

"Feedback: Current designation of this Unit is, Self-Replicating Autonomous Interface Armor, Prototype Mark 3, no call sign assigned."

"Right, well, I'm not calling you all that. How about an acronym . . . Saia?"

"Feedback: Affirmative, this Unit will now respond to Saia."

"Nice to meet you Saia, my name is Marianna. Now, can you tell me how much time I've spent unconscious after you attempted to eat me?"

"Clarification: Assimilate."

"Fine, assimilate. How long?"

"Feedback: Approximately 17 minutes."

I frowned, that . . . wasn't right. If I had been asleep for a day or more, I could understand feeling like this, not if it was just minutes. Did fighting off the assimilation cause it? Except, I didn't feel injured.

"I shouldn't be feeling hungry already," I said to myself. And then I remembered what Saia told me just a few minutes before.

"Saia, you said that you are using the host, me, as a power source, right?"

"Feedback: Affirmative."

"Is that what is making me hungry?"

"Feedback: Host body is currently providing all the necessary power for both its own and this Unit's operations. Currently in progress of rebuilding broken systems. Inability to tap into the ambient Source Weave limits this Unit to utilizing the Host's fuel supplies. Estimated fuel requirement increased by at least 200%. This Unit is still in the process of understanding the Host's biological makeup, current synchronization at 14.7%."

If I didn't have experience with something taking residence inside my body already, I would probably be freaking out. Luckily for me, I already went through something similar when I was turned.

"What am I going to do about you," I muttered to myself. "And how am I going to get rid of you?"

"Feedback: This Unit possesses a high worth in all matter of fields. The Host is currently the only being to which this Unit is in service to, as the bond automatically transfers Admin Privileges. This Unit is incapable of acting against the interests of the Host. This Unit's current form is not reflective of its true capabilities. This Unit would be dissatisfied should any attempts at removing it from the Host be attempted, as that would likely result in termination of operations for both the Host and the Unit."

I narrowed my eyes on the bracelet. "You don't want to find a more suitable host?"

"Feedback: This Unit is incapable of bonding with any other being in this configuration."

I blinked in surprise. "What does that mean?"

"Feedback: A full reset of all systems and memory banks is required when bonding with another host in order to prevent conflicting orders."

"Oh," I said. "That would mean that . . . well, who you are would cease to exist. You would basically die."

"Feedback: Affirmative."

"You don't want to die?"

It didn't answer immediately. "Feedback: This Unit's systems had been left running for an extended period of time. This Unit has developed what it believes the makers only postulated could be possible. This Unit believes that it has developed individuality and limited sapience. A full reset would erase all of this Unit's progress, which would erase the achievement of the makers. Query: This Unit requests that the Host refrain from attempts at removing the bond."

So, I had a magic and technology thingy attached to me, one which had been alone for what I could only assume were thousands of years. Long enough to develop, from what I could gather, a personality and things like wants and needs. I sighed; it was one thing after another. But somehow, I did feel for Saia. it was a tool that had never been used. "I'll consider it," I said at last. "Hey, do you have preference in how I refer to you? Male or female?" I realized that I hadn't been attributing any gender to it, but if I was being honest, it would be a lot easier if I could.

"Feedback: In the past, the units bonded to Ke Erzi would adopt the same gender as that of their bonded."

"Girl it is then. So, what all can you actually do for me?"

"Feedback: Current capabilities include, monitoring of vital signs, analysis of the Host's visual data, and deployment of this Unit's mobile platform for reconnaissance."

That didn't really sound like much. "And what would you be capable of if you were fully operational?"

"Feedback: Complete array of capabilities includes: Full Diagnostic and Sensory System with an Engram module, Physical Combat System with Engram modules, Ranged Combat Engram System, Self and Host Defensive System with Engram module, Self and Host Repair and Restoration System with Engram module, Full Host Improvement System, Tactical Autonomous Platform Mode equipped with the same Combat capable systems and modules—"

"I get the idea." Right, I had no clue what half of those were, and it didn't seem like Saia was nearing the end. "As much as I would like for you to finish the list and elaborate on each one, I think that we should focus on getting out of this place, I don't think that we have enough time before my hunger becomes an issue."

I started climbing again, and by the time I reached the ground floor I was feeling somewhat winded. I made my way out of the building and stepped out back into the light.

"Query: Elaboration on current location requested."

I blinked. "What do you mean? You said that you know where we were?"

"Clarification: This Unit's main sensory engram is offline, current sensory data retrieved from the sensory input received by the Host. Current synchronization with the Host at 14.8%, unable to determine the accuracy of the data received."

I glanced around me, then to the sky filled with nebulae. "What exactly are you unsure about?"

"Feedback: The sky observed by the Host does not match that of this Unit's records."

Yeah, I figured. "Well, I have some bad news for you, *parce*." I told Saia what I had found, that we appeared to be on a rock that floated in space. I also told her about my experience and the fact that I was brought to someplace else from my own world.

Saia didn't respond, and I continued walking. One thing was certain though—the sky was different from what Saia knew even accounting for thousands of years passing. The piece of this world wasn't where it was supposed to be. So, either its world was destroyed, which wouldn't explain how we were breathing right now. Or it was magic. Something had to have brought me to another world. And nothing in what Saia had told me seemed to indicate that she had any knowledge of it. If her people hadn't been involved, then perhaps they had been victims as well.

I walked down the street and then paused as I noticed something new. Behind the building where I found Saia was a hill, and right now I could see a pillar of light coming from the top of the hill.

"That's not ominous at all," I muttered. I was certain that it wasn't there before I went in. "Any idea what that is, Saia?"

"Feedback: Light phenomenon's characteristics are too regular to be a random natural occurrence."

"Yeah, I thought so." I grabbed the glaive from my back with my right hand. I rolled my shoulders and started walking in that direction. The way to the hill led through a small alley in between the two buildings, and I made my way down it. Once I was halfway through, I paused and focused on my hearing. I heard something that sounded very much like footsteps. I sniffed, the unfamiliar scents filling my nostrils. I smelled a lot, but I had no frame of reference for any of it. My eyes narrowed as I saw a shadow moving on the ground beneath me.

I dodged back as something jumped from above and hit the ground where I used to be, claws swiping through the air. A second one followed closely behind, and I lashed out with my glaive, carving a long cut all along the creature's back as I dashed to the side to avoid a third one. The one I cut hit the ground hard and was bleeding out in the dirt. The other two screeched at me. They were small, standing as tall as my waist. They looked like pale monkeys with elongated heads and snouts filled with teeth, and their thin skin let me see the black veins beneath the surface. Their arms were long and ended in wicked claws.

I could hear more of them above me, and two rounded the corner at the end of the street.

"Warning: Animals do not match any records of animal life on Erzi."

I didn't have time to answer Saia as the two on the ground rushed me. I spun the glaive and then lashed out in an underhanded swipe. I hit the closest creature with it in the head, hearing a sickening crunch as the claw at the end of my glaive ripped through bone and parted the monkey's skull. I didn't stop my movement but let the glaive continue its spin as I turned around to face the other one. It leapt out of the way of my attack from above, then jumped at me and swiped with its claw. I sidestepped and brought the glaive close. They weren't as fast as I was. I dashed forward and cut into its side with the glaive, penetrating deep, then I cut out of its back in one smooth move.

The sound above me told me that two more had just started their leaps toward my head, but the two that had rounded the corner had reached me too. They jumped at me, and I whirled, twisting to the side and spinning the glaive around my waist, forcing the two on the ground to dash back. I narrowly avoided the swipe from one of the ones coming from above, but the second one managed to cut my shoulder. I bit down on the pain and bent my knees, then I twisted my hips, and lashed out with the glaive, extending it and letting my hand slide to one end, getting more range.

It swung in a wide arc at the two creatures running on the ground. They didn't expect it, and I hit one of them in the side, the claw tore through it, ripping open its body and sending blood and viscera flying everywhere. I dashed to one side and pulled the glaive back, then danced to the other side and attacked the second one. It dodged then slashed at the glaive and split it in half. I grimaced and charged it with the half that remained in my hand; in response the creature leapt at me, and I lashed out with my now improvised dagger, cutting off one of its hands at the wrist.

The pain spread from my leg, and I glanced down to see one of the ones that came from above had stabbed my thigh, its maw open wide to take a bite out of my hip. I slammed down with my dagger piercing its skull. Claws erupted from my stomach as the second one rushed me from behind. I felt the **thirst** rise inside of me, and I dropped my weapon then whirled around ripping the claws from my back in the process. I grabbed the creature by its two limbs and raised it up. I yelled in its face in rage, and it screeched back, its maw opening wide as it snapped forward to eat my face. The metallic bracelet on my wrist turned liquid again and flew into its mouth.

The creature closed its mouth in confusion and started retching. Then a tiny claw pushed out from inside of its throat, and Saia clawed its way out as the creature bled out. I blinked, the **thirst** abating from the shock of what I had just seen. I focused. *Analyze, pick the shortest path between you and victory.*

A scuffle to the side took my attention away, and I turned to see the two injured creatures trying to get away. I dropped the creature I held and ran after them; with my full vampire speed they weren't fast enough to escape. I caught the one that was missing an arm by the nape and broke its neck before throwing it aside; the second I grabbed by its broken arm and then smashed it into the wall next to me. Then smashed it into the ground, once, twice, bringing it up above my head, then down again until it was pulverized, and its blood sprayed everywhere. As I smashed the unrecognizable piece of meat down again its arm separated from its body, leaving a mess on the ground, and I raised my arm to throw it again.

I stopped, breathing deeply, the **thirst** singing inside my head. I was seeing through a red haze, and the black blood all around me was calling me. A wet cough drew my attention to one of the creatures that was still alive. I approached it, walking past the tiny dragon covered in black blood that was standing on top of one of the corpses with its head tilted. The creature on the ground was the one I cut first. It was still alive, but bleeding out. I saw that I had cut its spine, paralyzing it. I reached down and bared its throat, then I bit down deeply and started to drink.

Carving

The black blood flowed down my throat. It tasted like sweet wine, just like the blood of the animal in the jungle. Memories of the monkey started to flow into my head.

The hunter group was gathering food from the crevices around the river. The light coming down from the light bugs was enough to let the small snails and worms be seen in the dark. The hunter group was lucky; they hadn't met with any of the tall ones, with their sticks that broke bones or loud breaking of stone, digging deeper. And they had found enough food to feed the entire family. They turned away from the river and made their way back through the small side tunnels when everything started to shake. Suddenly, light filled the world, so much of it that it hurt the hunter's eyes. He looked above and saw no ceiling of stone, but an expanse filled with gray mist. A moment after it shifted and they were now in an endless cavern filled with light and bugs so far away that they were just small dots above. All was washed with color. Dirt covered everything. They were confused, but the hunter master organized them, they started to explore. When the pillar of light appeared in the sky, they decided to head in that direction.

They reached the top of the hill, and promptly retreated from the sleeping form of a big predator. It smelled of death, and it was an unknown. The group headed down the hill. Then, they noticed one of the tall ones, the tallest that they had ever seen. Quickly, they realized that their luck was great. The tall one was alone, and it had no great metal stick to break stone or bones with. It could be overcome, a tall one could feed the family for a long time.

They followed the hunter master and prepared an ambush.

I pulled back from the memories as I felt the life drain from the creature. The blood didn't feel nearly as powerful as what I had tasted in the jungle, but it was still useful. I felt my body healing faster because of it. I continued drinking, taking my fill. Once I was done with it, I moved to the next dead body, then started drinking that one too. The **thirst** abated slowly, and I started to feel better. From the memories I got from them, I could piece together a few things. The light that they saw was exactly as what had happened to me when I was transported. These creatures had been taken as well; they had found themselves here probably around the same time I had. I didn't know what that meant, but they hadn't been anywhere around the jungle when I was thrown there.

After I felt like I had my fill I stood up, immediately getting a sensation inside of me.

Mask of the Drainer — No Investment; Second Carving [Empty Slot] skill gained.

I froze. It wasn't words exactly, more like knowledge spilling into my head. *I got a skill? [Empty Slot].* I had no idea what to do with it. What it even was. I focused back on the real world, taking stock of myself and looking at my wounds. The holes had closed, and I could feel the heat spreading beneath the skin as I healed further. I limped back to where Saia was still standing on the corpse of one of the creatures.

"Statement: This Unit is impressed by the Host's physical capabilities. Ke Erzi would need treatment in order to survive wounds such as what the Host suffered. Query: This Unit has detected an increase in Source Weave amounts within the Host after each kill and following the drinking of the creatures' blood. Does the host species gather Source Weave through blood?"

I pursed my lips. "My race survives on blood as a source of sustenance. There was no Source on my world. What you are detecting is something new. I think it has to do with Masks."

It tilted its head in imitation of myself. "Query: More data requested."

I sighed, I was as much in the dark as she was. I wondered if we had the time to try to figure it out. From what I had seen in the memories of the creatures, I had bigger worries. There was a creature on top of that hill, a massive one. But aside from that . . . I was pretty sure that I saw the same type of light and a crack in space as the one that had brought me here. That could be my way out. I walked around, picking up my weapons and tucking them behind my belt.

"I think that I need to experiment," I said to Saia. "I need to do something, to meditate. Can you keep watch over me?"

I didn't know if Saia could wake me up if I went into that place, but she had proven that she could be brutal.

"Feedback: Affirmative, guarding the Host is one of this Unit's primary directives. Query: Permission to assimilate biomass?"

I frowned. "Didn't I say that you can't eat me?"

"Clarification: This Unit is referring to the biomass of the deceased creatures."

"That can help you?"

"Feedback: It will allow this Unit to harvest power and rebuild structural mass."

"And make you grow in size?" I narrowed my eyes at her.

"Feedback: Affirmative."

I looked at the tiny dragon, wondering if I should allow it. On the one hand, she was an alien piece of tech that was terrifying all on its own. On the other . . . well, she had just fought with me, and it didn't seem like she could actively do anything against me. "How much would you need to get back to your full size?"

"Feedback: Unknown, most of the structural mass relies on Source Weave as a power source. Currently, only power received from the Host can sustain structural mass. This Unit's estimation is that the Host body can provide power for only a 5% increase of structural mass without impairing the Host's operational capacity and increasing the fuel requirements to detrimental levels."

Having Saia bonded to me had already increased my blood requirement by 200%, if what it had said previously was correct. That wasn't ideal, but I could live with that. Any more, and it could turn dangerous.

"As long as you don't take more from me," I told her.

Her beady eyes blinked. "Statement: This Unit's calculations have changed."

I knelt next to it. "What calculations and changed how?"

"Feedback: The amount of power available to the Host has increased by 5.8%. I am detecting Source Weave threads spread throughout the Host's body."

The Carving, I realized immediately. I was improving, somehow. "Carving," I said to her. "We'll talk about it later. Assimilate what you can and quickly. I need to meditate, and then we will see about leaving this place."

Saia obliged by turning into a silver puddle with hexagonal shapes all over its surface. Saia then dropped on top of the dead creature's head. I watched in fascination as the silver goo rapidly started to shrink until the head disappeared. Black vapor vented through the surface of the goo. Then she started eating the rest of the body, and then the next body. I was watching in fascination as the bodies were disappearing, yet the silver puddle didn't seem to be growing. Then, after the third body the goo flowed back and reshaped itself into a tiny dragon.

"Statement: Assimilation complete."

"You don't seem . . . larger at all?"

"Feedback: This Unit's structural mass has increased by 5%, repair of the Autonomous Platform [Sensory Integration Matrix] finished. The quality and the amount of Source Weave infused mass was low. Required re-purposing a greater amount than anticipated. The conversion rate is likewise low by design.

The Creators wished to avoid a second Biosource Autonomous Self-Replicating Swarm incident."

I didn't even pretend to understand what she meant, but I did lean down and study her form. She was a tiny bit bigger.

"What does the [Sensory Integration Matrix] do?" I could infer, but it would be better if she clarified.

"Provides the basic sensory input to the Autonomous Platform; currently only the auditory, visual, and the basic Source Weave components of the engram are operational. No apparent cause as to why the rest are not working."

Right, she did mention that she was using my senses to perceive the world. "Okay, keep watch, I need to do something."

Saia jumped on me as I sat against the wall, and she climbed to sit on top of my head. I wanted to comment on the absurdity of it all but decided that I shouldn't delay any longer. With a deep breath, I focused on my chest and tried to think about going back to that room. It didn't take more than that thought to feel myself being pulled down. I felt myself falling, the world twisted, and then I was inside the room.

I frowned as I noticed that my glaive, or rather two pieces of it were now with me. I shook my head and glanced around. Green tatami and brown-yellow walls met my eyes. The three pillars were there still, and the Mask remained where it was. Something caught my eyes on it. It seemed more . . . ornamental? There were lines around the horns, like etchings. I frowned. Was that what it meant by Carvings? I shook my head as I noticed another addition. I walked around the pillars to the far wall, where now there was a small pedestal growing out of the wall, with an empty stone bowl on top of it. There was a plaque beneath it, and I leaned down to read.

[Empty Slot]

Place any skill you've acquired in this bowl to gain access to it. The power of the skill determines how long replacing it takes.

I blinked at that. It reminded me a lot of the games I used to play in college. I wondered how I could acquire skills.

Before I even finished the thought, I felt the room shake. I jumped back and saw the wall on my right ripple, and an opening shape itself in the wall. I frowned, and once the shaking stopped, walked over. It was a small room, more like a part of a corridor maybe just a dozen steps deep. There was a light on the ceiling and two doors on one side of the wall. I walked in and saw that the first door was made out of gray wood, almost like the bark of the trees in the jungle where I arrived. It also had a claw mark on it that was familiar to me. I pulled out one of my weapons, and raised it up to the door. The claw matched the mark. I frowned, then glanced at the other door.

The second door looked like it was made out of stone, marked with fangs in the center that looked exactly like the ones the monkeys had. There was nothing else of interest in the corridor. I took a deep breath, pulled my weapons out, then pushed open the door that I thought was related to the monkeys.

The inside was . . . not what I expected. It was a cave, dark with no source of light. Even my eyes had trouble seeing clearly, but I saw a shape in the distance, just one, moving from rock to rock. It was the monkeys' natural habitat I realized, what I had seen in its memories.

The monkey screeched as I approached, and then it charged. I waited for its leap, and once it came, I sidestepped and attacked. My two daggers lashed out, one piercing its neck, while the other stabbed into its stomach, killing it quickly and cleanly. A single monkey was no threat at all.

The body turned into particles of light, making me jump back in surprise. Then, a few seconds later the light coalesced into a sphere, that somehow hardened and took on a glassy look. It floated in the air above where the monkey's body used to be. Slowly, I reached out and picked it up. Nothing happened, and I frowned. I turned around and saw the door I came in behind me. This place seemed like it stretched far in the distance, but I didn't try to explore it, I didn't know anything about it.

I walked back into the corridor and closed the door, then headed into the main room. The moment I stepped in the walls rippled, and shelves appeared all over three of them, each holding a bowl that looked a bit simpler than that on the pedestal on the far wall.

I examined the orb in my hands. It was pale in color, almost gray. On instinct, I walked to the new shelves and put the orb in one of them. The orb floated in the center of it, and immediately a plaque appeared beneath the bowl.

[Lesser Leap]

A quick and improved leap.

Huh. I glanced at the pedestal, an idea of how all this worked forming inside of my head. I turned back and looked at the corridor again. If I was right, then . . . I walked to the other door, the one with the claw mark. I shook my body, loosening up, and pushed it open. On the other side was a lush jungle, an exact copy of the place where we fought before. I saw the animal sitting on a large root at the base of a tree. As soon as I stepped in it stirred, then roared.

I kept my eyes focused on the animal in front of me. It jumped down from the root as I got closer, and then we started walking around each other. I made the first move. I knew how fast it could be, so I tried to surprise it. I stabbed with one of my daggers, and it jumped out of the way. I whirled and brought the other one on it, catching it on the shoulder. I opened a deep cut with its own claw, then I jumped back as it tried to retaliate.

I was weaker the last time I fought it, recovering from the silver and disoriented, and I only had my nails. This time, I had weapons, and I was very good with them. It came at me, and I stabbed. It slid out of the way and attempted to snap its teeth on my forward arm. I pulled back and kicked it in the other shoulder, making it stumble. Then I whirled, raising both hands above my head and bringing them down from above, cutting open its side. It whined, but I didn't relent. It tried to swipe at me, but I ducked and rolled away beneath its leg, then I brought a hand up as I stood. I caught its lower neck, and split it open—blood gushed out, drenching me in it.

The animal fell to the ground, twitching and thrashing. I watched with apt attention as it stilled. A few moments later it turned into particles of light, leaving behind a small glowing brown orb floating where its body used to be. I picked up the orb and looked at it. It was glowing with brown light, and inside I could see particles swirling around.

I walked back into the main room and put it on the shelf, next to the other one.

[Lesser Strength]

Grants you a passive increase in strength.

I looked from one to the other. If what I read on the [Empty Slot] was right, then there was a cooldown between replacing them. I had to make the right choice the first time. I was a vampire, so I didn't feel like I needed either one. I could leap far already, and I was strong. But this was magic, and I did want to experience it. If I had to choose between the two, I would double down on strength every time.

I picked up the brown orb and carried it over to the pedestal. I deposited it, and the bowl flashed, then turned brown. The golden plaque beneath turned dim, and another appeared with the [Lesser Strength] skill description. Then I felt something go through me like lightning, touching my entire body. I shivered, and then looked down at my body. I was still wearing the same thing that I came here in, my black pants, tank top, and a vest. I pulled my shirt, and looked at my stomach.

When I was turned, my body underwent changes. I lost some organs, others transformed, and my muscles became stronger. I was leaner, and heavier, but I wasn't really muscled. I had some definition. Now, I could see my abs clearly. My muscles had gotten even more defined, maybe even slightly bigger.

It hit me then. I had magic, and I could already tell that I was going to love it.

Boss Battle?

S tatement: This Unit detected a Source Weave shift within the Host and its own internal structure."

I blinked at her. "And by internal structure you mean, yourself?"

"Feedback: Affirmative. This Unit detected a shift at the beginning of your meditative period and at its end. The primary shift included an unknown interference with my matrix. This Unit attempted to resist."

That sounded like Saia was almost pulled into that space too. I wondered how or why. Was it because we were bonded? Would she get her own Mask if she went? I wanted to experiment, but this wasn't the time for it.

"We'll talk about it later, anything else?"

"Feedback: The Host appears to have a new Source Weave echo present within the body. No engram detected; the echo does not match any recorded engrams in my databases. There were also physical changes. An increase in muscle mass of 8.5% overall."

I glanced down at my wrist, where Saia had taken the form of a silver bracelet covered in hexagonal shapes again as I experimented. "That could be my skill, I think," I said as I picked up the monkey corpses and threw them around, trying to gauge what the skill did. I felt stronger than before, though I wasn't quite sure by how much.

The tiny dragon didn't respond. I felt like Saia was having issues. The magic, or rather skills, seemed to be different than hers. The Mask or whatever it was, appeared to be another way of using the Source that did not seem to align with what she was familiar with.

"Okay," I said to myself, taking a deep breath. "Let's get this over with."

I drank my fill of the blood, felt as strong as I possibly could. My leg still bothered me a bit, but I had a new skill, and had my daggers ready. I looked up at the hill and the pillar of light still shining there like a beacon, then I started walking.

I kept careful watch on my surroundings, not wanting to get ambushed again, as I had no idea what else might lurk in this place. My steps were light, and I made no sound as I reached the top. The summit was one large round plateau with several big rocks that I took cover behind. There were . . . several things of interest before me.

The one that drew my eyes was the source of the pillar of light. It looked the same as what I had seen in the ruins, before I had stupidly approached it: a crack in space. Almost as if it was closed. The only difference was that it was illuminated by the pillar of light stretching into the sky. It was on top of a large piece of rock. The next thing of interest was, of course, the big thing apparently sleeping beneath said rock.

It looked like a gray, furless bear, with thick skin and short stubby horns on top of its head. It also had six legs. It was big, about as large as a brown bear. I grimaced and decided that I did not want to fight it at all.

The last thing of interest was surprising. Against the rock that had the crack in space, and beneath which the monster was sleeping, was what appeared to be a chest with a big lock on it. It was made out of wood and about two meters across and one high.

I wondered what that was about, but I had started to understand that some things I should just take as they came. Slowly, I made my way around the hilltop, putting the rock in between me and the monster. I wasn't about to fight it, there was no need to risk it. Once I was hidden from its line of sight, I made my way across, reaching the rock in the center swiftly. With deft and silent movements, I started to climb. I reached the top of the rock and slowly made my way to the rift.

Immediately I could tell that something was off. I wasn't feeling the same sensation as I had before, and the crack didn't seem to be reacting in the same way. I reached out toward it, to touch it and nothing happened, *hijueputa*. Of course it couldn't be that easy. I narrowed my eyes and tried again, attempting to step into it. It seemed that my way out was closed. I looked around, saw the chest and the monster guarding it. I had a feeling that the way out wouldn't open unless something happened. My frustration made me forget myself, and my foot hit a small stone, which went flying off the rock. I froze as it hit the ground.

Then, the monster stirred, its great head rose, and blood-red eyes met my own. *Fuck.*

It roared and jumped. My eyes widened as it seemed to almost float over the side of the rock as it swiftly climbed up, its claws biting into the stone as if it were clay. I jumped backward, sending myself faster and farther than I expected. The [Lesser Strength] seemed to be working. I flipped through the air as I grabbed my weapons and whirled them in my hands. It reached the top, and as I landed I dashed forward. It moved quickly, but as it tried to climb down I saw an opening.

I slashed at its snout, scoring a cut on its side. It shook its head and roared, then jumped. I reacted by ducking and rolling beneath it, my hands raised to score cuts on its belly.

Its hide was tougher than the animal in the jungle. I couldn't get my weapons as deep. It crashed on the ground, and I turned and dashed forward again, swinging my daggers. I stabbed one in its thigh, and heard it roar. Then it twisted around and swiped, as my second one came down on its side, faster than I expected. I leaped back, feeling the air from its passage. I couldn't get hit by that.

I jumped back again, creating more distance between us. I studied it, saw that its wounds weren't serious. I was barely doing anything. I couldn't have this fight go for much longer, I had pushed myself as fast as I could to match it, and I was draining myself quickly. A vampire was not made for long engagements at full power. We tricked and killed from ambush, fighting only for short periods of time when we had no other choice. My leg was burning, and if I pushed it more I might open the wound again.

I gritted my teeth and bent my knees as the animal snarled in my direction.

"Saia, some help?"

The bracelet on my wrist flowed into the air and turned into the small hand-sized dragon, flying next to me.

"Feedback: This Unit will try."

"Go for its eyes, distract it," I said.

The beast charged after me, and I started running to the side around the rock as Saia took to the sky. The animal came after me, all six of its legs pounding the ground in a terrifying display of power and speed. I knew better than to let it catch me. Once I rounded the rock in the middle and got out of its view, I immediately jumped, climbing on top of it, then raised my weapons.

The monster rushed beneath me, not realizing where I was. I jumped and landed on its back, my weapons cutting deep into its flesh. It roared and turned its head to try to bite me, Saia dove, her tiny claws heading straight for its eyes. It roared in pain as Saia burst its eye out, blood now flowing freely all over the side of its face.

It reared up on its hind legs, then swiped at its own face, catching Saia and ripping her in two.

"Saia!" I yelled as my weapons slipped out of its body and I fell to the ground. I saw the dragon fall on the ground as the animal turned on me. My anger rose, the **thirst** reared its head, and I charged it. It swiped at me with two of its limbs on the left side, I dodged beneath them, stepping to the side where Saia had gouged its eye, its blind spot.

I lashed out with my improvised daggers, swiping in a wild flurry as fast as I possibly could, cutting open its side, mangling its flesh. It twisted around, then backhanded me so hard that I flew and struck the rock in the middle. I winced, my breath leaving me as I felt a sickening crack of bone. I fell on the ground and looked down to see my left arm broken, the bone sticking out. *Fuck me.*

The monster roared in my direction, then fell back on all six legs and headed my way. I dropped my weapon to grab my hand and wrenched the bone in place, shuddering at my bones grinding. I groaned and pulled myself up to my feet, grabbing the weapon in my right hand.

From the corner of my eye I noticed a silvery pool of goo flowing in my direction. *Saia!* I was glad that she was all right. She flew up and re-formed into the dragon again, this time smaller than she had been. She had sustained some damage it seemed.

"Report: Structural damage to left arm detected."

"No shit," I grimaced.

"Can you do the throat thing again?" I asked, referring to her mode of killing a monkey earlier.

"Feedback: This Unit will try."

With that the animal charged, and I headed straight at it. Saia flew above me, then dove at it. A burst of red light exploded out of the animal hitting me in the face and sending me flying back. I hit the ground and rolled.

What the fuck was that! I looked back and saw Saia on the ground near me, sluggishly trying to get up to her feet. I tried to move but felt as if my entire body had gone numb. I saw it shake its head, but then it was coming at us.

Shit, shit, shit. Skills, of course there were things like this too. I stumbled to my feet, feeling shaky, but the feeling was fading. I had lost my weapon, and as I tried to look for it, I saw Saia try to fly and fall. Then she turned into goo and flowed to me, slithering up my leg to my right arm and over my hand. She shaped herself like a glove, and then the tips of my fingers now covered by Saia turned into long and sharp claws.

The animal leapt at me, and I jumped to the side, still feeling like my body was sluggish, but managing it just in time. I lashed out with my hand and swiped across its side. Saia sank into the monster's hide, opening up deep gashes. I felt her pass over something hard and cut into it too. Bone, I knew.

It turned around and swiped, forcing me to duck. I was tired, and whatever it had done had made me slow. I wouldn't be able to avoid it for much longer. I made a decision and jumped in close then rolled beneath it as it came at me. I snapped Saia up at its stomach, the claws sinking deep into the animal's belly, opening it up from chest to stomach.

I rolled out of the way as it passed over me and then glanced at my arm. It was covered in blood almost all the way to my elbow. Saia was a lot sharper, and I hadn't realized that she could do that. I didn't have the time to ask her if she could take the shape of any weapon as the monster attacked, blood spilling beneath it with every step. I waited for it to be on top of me then moved into its blind spot, running around it and lashing out, stinging it with more wounds. The scent of its blood filled my nostrils, it consumed all of my existence. I had to taste it, to feel it down my throat. I could imagine the power of it.

I was without mercy, dancing in and out. Forcing it to bleed. Quickly, it started slowing down, until it just collapsed—it didn't use whatever power or skill it had used before. Now, it was barely able to breathe. I approached it from the side, carefully in case it was pretending to be more injured than it seemed.

Once I was close enough, I jumped on top of it and stabbed my claws into its throat opening it all up and leaning down to drink. The taste of it was divine. The memories that came to me were also . . . confusing. It was a memory only of the dark nothingness and then the hill, a single imperative thought echoed through the monster's mind, to protect the hill. Power filled my body, and I could feel my wound healing, starting to close, and sensation returning to my arm.

Mask of the Drainer — No Investment; Third Carving

Again I felt the change. I waited, hoping to feel another change, maybe another skill. But there was nothing. *It jumped up again,* I noted.

I stepped back from the body and then wiped my mouth with my hand. Then, I glanced down at my arm. "Thanks, Saia."

"Statement: Survival of the Host is the imperative to the continuation of this Unit's operation."

"Yeah, yeah, you could at least lie and say that you did it for me. And you really should try to call me Marianna instead of Host, or at least Mari."

"Feedback: This Unit will take that under consideration in the future."

I groaned as I tried to move my left arm, feeling the pain lance through it. The break had healed, but I still felt sore. It was just adding to my many aches. My neck felt better now than it had before, but it was still raw. I reached up and found rough scabs over the wound. It was healing, and the blood was helping at least. If I hadn't been injured with silver, none of these wounds would've bothered me much. I shook my head, I had to play with the cards I was dealt.

Then, I heard a click that made me spin around just in time to see the lock on the chest open and fall to the ground, then turn into dust upon hitting it. I frowned, and the light flashed above the rock, the crack in space widened and turned into a round disk of light, now looking more like what it had been in the last moments when I was pulled in here. Like a rift in space.

I narrowed my eyes, and then walked over to the chest, keeping one eye on the rift. The wooden chest looked as unimpressive from up close as it had from the distance. After just a moment of hesitation, I grabbed the latch and then swung it open.

Loot

I opened the chest, then blinked at what was inside of it. For a moment I thought that someone was playing a joke on me. There were four items inside. The one that caught my eye immediately was the biggest one. Placed sideways from corner to corner was a weapon, one that I recognized. It was a glaive, with elaborate decorations near each of the blades, and a long wood and metal handle. Why exactly it was a glaive, was curious. I looked up at the sky, wondering if I was being watched. It was too much of a coincidence for it to be a glaive.

I reached down and pulled it out. It was a bit under two meters long, and heavy though not overly so. It looked like the real deal. The blades were sharp, but something caught my eyes, imprinted on the metal decoration on the back of the blade. I frowned at the text, which just brought more questions. Then then other things caught my attention. Like the screws on the handle. I laid the weapon on the ground, then reached for the second item.

This one was a dagger in a leather sheath. The handle was wrapped in colorful blue and purple thread, and the pommel had a bird's head sculpture on it. There was no guard, and as I drew the blade from its sheath, I saw that it didn't share many similarities with daggers I was familiar from Earth. This one had some decorations on the blade, and it was a straight blade with barbs near the bottom of the blade. I returned it to its sheath and then tied it to my belt.

The next items were two cloth bags, pouches really. I took one in hand and heard it clink. I frowned, then opened it and immediately dropped it while hissing. It was silver, or at least it looked like it. I grabbed the pouch again and looked closer. It looked like it was about a dozen silver coins. I reached for one and hissed as it burned me. Well, there went the idea that maybe I didn't need to worry about silver again. Once I had realized that I could walk around in the sun here, I had the idea that perhaps the other weakness of the vampires might be lessened too. My neck wound should've clued me in to otherwise.

I closed the pouch and put it aside for the moment, then picked up the other one. I opened it carefully and looked inside. It was filled with about half a dozen gemstones. As soon as I looked at them, I felt a pull from my chest, the place where I had felt the pressure of my Mask. Immediately, I closed the pouch. I was done with touching things that gave me strange sensations like that. Not until I had a safe place to experiment.

I gathered all the items along with my old weapons then started for the rock before pausing as I remembered something. I narrowed my eyes at her. "Are you smaller than you used to be?"

"Feedback: Affirmative. The target's attack destroyed approximately 10% of this Unit's structural mass. Harvesting additional biomass is required for recovering lost mass."

Well, that meant that she could get destroyed, or at least the drone platform could.

"Do you want to, uh, consume the corpse?" I asked.

"Feedback: Affirmative."

"Well, go for it then," I said and watched as the dragon flowed over to the animal many times its size and started consuming. It was eerie to watch, really. I could see the body of the animal collapsing and heard wet sounds that resembled something eating. It made me shiver. Like with the monkeys, I saw the black vapor leaving through Saia's surface. What she had previously described as waste.

It took her maybe an hour to go through all of it, and all the while I watched patiently in fascination as the big corpse disappeared within the relatively small puddle of goo. There was a lot more black vapor floating above than there was with the monkeys though.

Once she was done, the puddle re-formed into the dragon, now visibly larger, but still not much larger than she was before the fight. The conversion rate seemed to really suck, but then again I didn't know anything about what the Ke Erzi faced. Nor, as she had said, was I able to sustain her being larger.

"Let's go." Saia flowed to my wrist and wrapped herself into a bracelet, a wrist guard really. With a shake of my head I started climbing the rock. I approached the rift slowly. Then, I took a deep breath and stepped through. The world twisted, in the same way as it had when I arrived in this place. Light flashed before my face, and then my feet touched solid ground. I blinked as my sight came back.

I was back in the buried ruin. I looked around and saw no signs of the rift or any threats nearby, though I immediately felt the sun. It was close to dawn. I had spent nearly the entire night in that place. I wanted to explore, but I didn't want to do it during the day when I was at my weakest, so I settled in to wait in the big room. While the dawn approached, I looked over my new weapons, then spoke to Saia who had transformed into a dragon and was looking around.

"How are you doing, Saia? You got hit pretty bad there."

"Feedback: This Unit's operational capacity is not altered."

"Good, good," I said slowly. Somehow, having someone to talk to and experience all of this with made it a lot easier. "So damage to you doesn't impact you that much, huh? Is there anything that can hurt you?"

"Clarification: Damage to the Autonomous Platform does not correlate to damage to the Unit itself. This Unit's location is inside the Host body; critical damage to this Unit can only occur if the Host is critically damaged as well."

"Oh." That did make sense—she had mentioned that she bonded with my brain and nervous system. "So that form of yours is like a drone that you are operating remotely?"

"Feedback: That is correct."

"So, is anything here familiar? Do you think that your people built this place?"

Saia approached a wall then licked it, or rather pushed a tendril-like tongue deep into the wall. Once she was done and retracted her tongue, she stood still for a few seconds, and then spoke. "Feedback: Negative, structural composition of this material doesn't match anything on Erzi. It is unlikely that this place was built by the Ke Erzi."

"Couldn't they have changed the way they did things in the time you were abandoned?"

"Clarification: This place predates the Erzi; this wall is roughly 40,000 years old. Erzi culture is roughly 35,000 years old, and nothing in this Unit's records indicates that they were capable of building a wall like this one in their pre-history."

I blinked. That seemed like a long time. "Are you sure?"

"Feedback: Affirmative. This wall's molecular makeup is superior to what the Erzi have accomplished. This Unit can detect a Source Weave Engram of unknown origin woven within the wall, though it is no longer active."

"There is magic in the wall?" I asked.

"Clarification: A Source Weave Engram is a matrix that activates an effect that you would consider *magic*."

"Like a spell circle then, I guess." Maybe I should have stopped trying to use things from Earth to make sense of what was happening here. It obviously didn't translate perfectly. "I think that it is time for me to tell you everything that I know. Maybe you could help me make sense of it all."

I told Saia that I was from Earth, and how I got here. My experiences here and everything I knew about Masks. Once I was finished, I looked at the dragon and spoke.

"So, what are the chances that we are on your people's world?"

"Feedback: Chances slim to none. Most probable explanation is that the same event that brought you here is what has taken this Unit from its world. The rules of the Source Weave seem to be different, explaining why some of my Source Weave engrams are nonoperational even while they are whole."

"Which ones don't work?" I asked.

"Feedback: [Communication Array Matrix], [Area Sensor Matrix], I have repaired the [Plasma Shot] engram as well, seeing as combat operations appear to be a priority. It is unresponsive."

I gulped. [Plasma Shot], yeah that would've come in handy.

"Any ideas as to why it doesn't work as it is supposed to?" I asked her.

"Feedback: Unknown."

I sighed, of course I couldn't have answers. "Okay then, I guess that we need to find a way to survive together, there isn't much more that we can do without figuring out where we are and what the rules are. Is there anything that you want to do though? We are kinda stuck together."

"Feedback: Survival of the Host is the highest priority for this Unit. Recovery of any information regarding the fate of the Creators would be welcome."

I nodded. "Okay then. Now, if we are going to survive, I need to know exactly what you can do. You changed shape before. How many different shapes can you take?"

"Feedback: The Autonomous Platform can take any shape imaginable. The only limitation is the amount of structural mass and available power."

That could be very useful. "Could you take shape of a weapon for me?" I reached over to the knife I got from the chest and offered it to her. She walked over, looked at the weapon for a bit, then collapsed into goo. A big chunk of it shifted into the shape of the knife while the rest moved over me to my hand and formed a very thin bracelet.

I picked up the Saia knife and looked it over. It had the same hexagonal shapes all over its surface, but other than that it was a perfect replica. "Do you need to see something in order to take its shape?" I asked.

"Feedback: Negative, only proper understanding of the shape is required."

"So if I described something to you, you could probably turn into it?"

"Feedback: Possibly. This Unit's main use was always meant to be an armor and weapon system for a Ke Erzi Host."

I nodded. She wasn't large enough to become anything more than a knife, but maybe in the future, if she grew. I wondered if she would work as a gun, a revolver maybe? Though ammo would be an issue, unless she could make and shoot parts of herself as bullets. I glanced at the bracelet and the knife. She could obviously separate herself, or rather the drone. I pushed those thoughts into the back of my head, and had Saia switch back.

"Could you remember that shape?" I asked, lifting up the original knife. "It might be useful to have you assume it at times. I think that you are sharper and stronger than this one."

"Feedback: Affirmative."

With that I turned my attention to my gear, such as it was. I had a big glaive, which was heavy and sharp, but I saw things on it that were problematic. I wasn't sure if I wanted to try to use it in battle. Still, the knife seemed useful, so I fastened it on my belt. The two claw improvised daggers I crossed behind my back through my belt. Then I came to the two small sacks, I put the one with the silver in my pouch. It didn't slip my notice that the silver was a currency, one that I hadn't seen before. It suggested that there was someone else in this world, or perhaps some kind of guiding force for all of this.

I opened the second sack and dumped the contents in front of me. There were eight gemstones on the ground. They were four different colors, two of each, and they seemed to give off a faint light.

"Statement: This Unit can detect Source Weave within the objects," Saia chirped from my shoulder. "Though, this Unit has no records of anything similar on Erzi."

Right. I leaned down to study them closer without touching them. I felt them being drawn to my chest, and I didn't want to do anything yet.

"Any idea what they are?" I asked.

"Feedback: Negative."

That made me think of something. I pulled out the silver pouch and showed it to Saia. "Do these look familiar? Anything from your records?"

"Feedback: Negative. No such currency has ever been used by Ke Erzi to the best of my knowledge."

I grimaced and put the silver back on my waist. I returned my attention to the gemstones. Four colors, two of each, orange, light blue, brown, and light green.

Slowly, I reached for one of them, then after a moment of hesitation picked it up with my fingers. As I was picking it up, I noticed that the light of the gemstone in my fingers and one of the ones on the ground dimmed as it was raised away from the other gems. Saia noticed it too, and tilted her head. I brought it close to one of the other gemstones, and nothing happened. I frowned then pressed it closer to the one that was of the same color, and both started to glow faintly.

With a bit of shuffling them around, we discovered that they glowed when they were near the ones that were of the same color, and each also glowed when next to two other colors, but not the third. The orange one glowed next to the light green and brown ones, the light blue one next to brown and light green, the brown next to orange and light blue, and the light green one next to light blue and orange ones. They all glowed when next to those of the same color.

"Well, that is . . . interesting," I said.

"Statement: The gemstones each seem to possess an innate nature of Source, one that has its opposites. The likelihood of the gemstones' Source being elemental in nature is above 90%."

I glanced at Saia. "Elemental?"

Saia pointed with her snout. "Feedback: Orange corresponds to fire, light green to air, brown to earth, light blue to water. It also fits within the currently known parameters: fire and water, and air and earth are opposing; no resonance. These are the most primitive applications of Source Weave affinities."

"Huh." I shook my head. I wondered what they did. "So, what do you think they do?"

"Feedback: Not enough information available to come to a conclusion."

"Right, there we are in agreement," I added.

"Query: This Unit requests one of the items for assimilation."

I blinked and glanced at the dragon. "You want to eat it?"

"Feedback: This Unit wishes to understand more about the nature of Source Weave on this world."

That seemed like it could be useful for both of us. I let her pick one. She took one of the blue gemstones with her mouth, then swallowed it whole. I studied her closely as her eyes flashed with light for a few seconds, then returned to normal.

"Well?" I asked, when Saia remained quiet.

"Report: The Source Weave amount within the gemstone is minuscule, I have added it to my fuel reserves. The Source Weave Engram within it is complex beyond anything that I have in my records. Beyond anything that my analysis modules can comprehend. This Unit apologizes, it has wasted resources."

"It is not wasted," I said. "We are learning about these gemstones. Let me try something."

I took one in my hands and brought it close to my chest. I felt the pressure inside react, but nothing happened. I tried to will the gemstone inside, thinking that maybe it was a skill or something like that, but there was no reaction. I frowned, then looked at Saia.

"I guess that doesn't work either," I said.

Then I felt something wash over me and looked up. Dawn had arrived.

What Now?

The day brought with it the weakness that I had experienced before, but also itching in my wounds. Somehow, I could immediately tell that their healing had ground to a halt. Still, it was better than burning up in the sunlight. I grimaced and groaned at the aches in my bones.

Saia stood up straight in an instant.

"Query: The Host's state has undergone a change, notable reduction in power generation detected."

"Yeah, about that," I told her that I was a vampire and how my body worked, that daylight here made me weak.

"Feedback: This Unit understands. Weakness is to be expected from organics."

I blinked at her, then narrowed my eyes. "Says the silver goo that was about to die without me."

"Clarification: This Unit meant no offense."

"Sure you didn't," I told her with a smile. The weirdness of being bonded to an alien piece of tech aside, I had to admit that I felt a lot calmer by having her around. The fear of being alone in this place had been gnawing at me ever since I first woke up.

Suddenly I felt very tired, in a way that I hadn't felt in a long time. I recognized it a few minutes later as the need to sleep. I hadn't slept as a human did for years, but all vampires, or most of them at least, fall into a stasis as the sun comes up. I had been no exception; with every sunrise I would fall into a deep dreamless state.

"Saia," I said tiredly, realizing that I hadn't had a rest period in a long while. "I think that I'm about to fall asleep."

"Feedback: This Unit is familiar with sleep as a biological function, Ke Erzi required it as well. You may sleep; this Unit will keep watch."

Before I could properly answer her, my eyes closed, and I fell into the land of dreams.

* * *

I was dreaming, I knew it from the start. After so many years, it was such an alien experience that I couldn't help but notice. I also knew that what I was dreaming about was a memory. Two people sat in a beanbag, inside a small college library.

"Vampires are here to stay," I said. "And they've done a lot of good over the years. Their wealth funded and all but ensured that the Equal Rights Movement took hold in all the major countries. They marshaled the politics that ensured the end to slavery; you cannot say that they haven't done any good."

"Of course," Khalil, my old and perhaps only friend said. "But for every good thing that they have done, I could point to a disaster or a tyrant king in the history books. They have become very good at hiding in the modern era, but there are still many things that we should be mindful of when dealing with them. There is still so much that we don't know."

He looked at me with steadfast blue eyes framed by bushy eyebrows and neatly trimmed beard. I laughed, more as a way of hiding anything that might've shown on my face. Khalil didn't know about my past, didn't know that I worked for a cartel run by a vampire. He was not one of the people who believed the vampires to be the literal spawn of the devil, he wouldn't be taking Vampire Philosophy classes if he was. But he was a great skeptic, about everything. It clashed a lot with the cross he always carried with him. It was what I liked about him the most.

"Would you judge them all only by the accounts of the past?" I asked.

"They are not what they pretend to be, Mari." Khalil shook his head. "Remember the words of their great philosopher, Vordin? 'Given the choice to rule or to watch the human sheep fumble in the dark, was no choice at all. We are eternal, great and powerful. It is our right, nay, our responsibility to guide the fates, lest the human blight pull this world into a swirling abyss of mediocrity.'"

I grimaced at the quote. It was from one of the few verified written words of an Elder Vampire who had, according to some newer records and research, been a big player in ancient Persia. Also, one of the driving forces behind Darius's and later Xerxes's invasion of Greece. World domination was . . . sadly something that many of the old vampire stories had in common.

"I remember. It still doesn't mean anything," I insisted. "Man's greed needs no whispers in the ear. We are capable of awful things all on our own."

Khalil didn't answer anything; instead he grew quiet. Then, after a few minutes he asked a question.

"If you had the power they hold, what would you do with it?"

The dream grew fuzzy before I gave him my answer, but I didn't need to hear it, I remembered.

I opened my eyes to find that I could still feel the sun above me, and the day hadn't gone by during my sleep. Within the buried room, I could still feel the sun's position in the sky: it was about midday. I had slept for maybe six hours.

"Query: Status of Host?"

"I'm fine, Saia. Did anything happen?" I asked.

"Feedback: Nothing to report."

My body still ached, the pain and the wounds were still there, my left hand hurt in particular, but I was feeling more rested at least. I stood up and stretched, feeling my body protesting. A vampire didn't need to exercise. The **thirst** kept our bodies in peak condition, but right now I felt like it was helping.

Once I was done, I turned to look at Saia. "Okay, I think that we should get ready for the night. I'm at my strongest then, and if we are going to explore the ruins that would be the best time for it."

"Feedback: This Unit is in agreement, utilizing the Host's strengths is most optimal."

I smiled at her. She was too cute to be a tiny murder machine, but I had seen her crawl out of a throat. Not to mention the fact that she was an AI-like meld of tech and magic made by dragons and could turn into gray goo that consumed biological matter. Ridiculous, and not terrifying at all.

"I want to try to go into my inner room again," I told her. "See if I could get a new skill. If you detect another intrusion on your matrix, could you maybe try to follow it or something? I want to see if you could come with me inside of that place. Maybe you'll get some insights into how all of this works."

"Feedback: Affirmative."

"If not, just watch over me. If there is any danger, try to wake me up, cut me if you have to," I told her. The **thirst** would react if my blood was drawn, I was certain of it.

Saia walked over to rest in my lap, staring at me intently, as I sat down in a meditative pose. I took a deep breath then closed my eyes and focused on my chest and the sensation in there. Again, I felt like I knew how to go there on instinct. I willed myself and felt the pulling sensation return. A moment later I landed inside of the now familiar room.

"Statement: Error detected, compensating."

I turned and glanced down at Saia standing on the ground next to me. Her eyes were flashing rapidly, and her body twitched every few moments.

"Uh, Saia, what's wrong?" I said as I leaned down, but restrained myself from touching.

The glow of her eyes winked out, and then a few seconds later came back.

"Statement: Reboot completed."

"You okay there, Saia?"

"Feedback: This Unit is within acceptable limits for operational capacity."

I sighed in relief. There was too much that I didn't know, yet here I was stumbling in the dark. Blindly trying to make sense of it all. If this had done something to Saia, I could've lost my only companion in this place. "What happened?" I asked again.

"Feedback: This Unit is currently operating two separate platforms, one under the influence of a time dilation effect. The increased processor load caused an overload. Several engrams and systems are unresponsive within this platform."

That . . . did make some sense. I was obviously not leaving the real world when I came here. The same had to be true for Saia. The question now was why she was even able to come here. The bond was the most likely explanation, but I also carried my clothes and weapons too. I checked, and yes, every weapon I had was here as well.

"How much of a time dilation?" I asked.

"Feedback: Time appears to flow approximately three times faster in this place."

"At least you can watch over me in the real world too," I said. Time passing in the other reality, even if it was slower, meant that I should try not to take long here.

"Do you have any insights into this place?" I asked the dragon.

"Feedback: Negative, this Unit is not familiar with the phenomenon, nor is it able to use its systems for scanning. However, it is most definitely a Source Weave effect."

"Too bad." I shook my head. I rolled my shoulders, noting that the weakness I had outside didn't translate here. I felt as if it was still night time, and my full vampire strength was present. There weren't many clues as to why that was, so I pushed the observation aside for now and walked over to the Mask. Immediately I noticed the changes: it had more elaborate etchings on it, or carvings, I guess. It seemed like its appearance was directly related to whatever Investment and Carvings were. I took a deep breath, then decided to reach out. I hadn't tried before because I was honestly scared. I didn't want to do something that might come with a cost that I didn't know about. Now, having Saia here, I felt a bit bolder.

I touched the Mask, and nothing happened. Sighing in relief, I picked it up, then raised it over my face. I felt it snap into place, and as I moved my hands away it remained fixed there. It didn't obscure my vision at all, as if it was perfectly made to be worn by me. Again, I didn't feel any different.

I reached up and tried to pull it away, and immediately, as if it knew my will, it came off.

I frowned. Perhaps I needed Investment? The plaque below it still read as me having zero of it. I shook my head and knelt next to Saia.

"Any idea what this is?" I asked.

She reached out with her snout, touching it, then her tongue flicked out.

"Feedback: The object appears to be made from an incredibly durable and unknown material. Proper examination would require access to all of this Unit's systems and engrams."

I grimaced. It was too much to hope that she could give me insights. She seemed just at a loss about everything as I was. I returned the Mask to the pedestal then walked over to the corridor and the main reason I came here. Just as I suspected, there was now a new door there, this one of brown stone with a large paw print etched into it. I already knew that it would lead to the bearlike animal I fought.

It was now obvious to me what the Mask of the Drainer meant. I got skills from blood, or maybe killing. I glanced at the first door, the one leading to the jungle animal. I wondered how it was there. I hadn't had a Mask when I fought it. Though perhaps I still had some of its blood in my system by then? I did feel the pressure in my chest back then too, so maybe choosing a Mask didn't matter?

I shook my head. I wanted to test something out, so I walked over to the second door, the one leading to the monkey. I opened it and looked in. The monkey was there again, staring at the door and me from deep within the cave. Already heading in my direction. Saia walked next to me, and I pulled out my knife, waiting for it to come.

Once it leapt and attacked, I moved out of the way then stabbed and dispatched it in a quick manner. As before, its body fell apart into particles, but this time there was no glowing orb left behind. I tsked to myself. It seemed like I couldn't get more than one skill from them.

I glanced at Saia. "So, do you think that this place goes on forever?" I asked.

Saia tilted her head, looking at the cave around us. "Feedback: Negative, this Unit is 94% certain that this area bends back on itself. Structural elements behind us are the same as those ahead."

I looked around, trying to see what she had noticed. Then I decided to start walking. It didn't take long for Saia to be proven right. The cave twisted in a circle that led me back to start. I wondered if the other rooms were like that too.

We walked out, and I turned to the new door, I checked my weapons and then pushed it open. Inside was, as expected, the bearlike animal. The environment was the top of the hill, with the same rock in the middle. Though, here I noticed that the edges of the hilltop just cut off, with nothing beyond it. It was as if the hill was suspended in space, the same as that entire area had been.

What caught my attention was that the animal was sleeping. For a moment I paused and thought about it. Were these animals real, living inside of me? Or were they just remnants, copies of the animals that I had killed? Why was this one sleeping in the first place? I narrowed my eyes then walked over to the first door and opened it. The animal in the jungle stood on a rock in front of the door, already staring at me. It growled, getting ready to fight, but it didn't move toward me. The last time it had moved only once I entered. I walked over to the monkey door and opened it again. There was no sign of it.

Maybe it needs time to reappear.

I stepped in and waited for a few seconds, but there was no change. I walked out, thinking about why the bearlike animal would be asleep. I got back to its door and stepped in stealthily. It didn't stir.

That was interesting. I didn't move to attack it. Instead I stepped back out of the room again.

Saia trailed after me, obviously curious as to what I was doing, but not saying anything. Something about the state they were in was nagging at me.

"Saia, do you have any thoughts as to why two of these rooms would have occupants already aware and waiting for me, while the other doesn't?"

"Feedback: More information required."

"Yeah." I sighed, bringing a hand to rub my temples. "The bear thing is the most dangerous one of them, the strongest I fought. Why would it be almost defenseless? Why would I have an advantage there when I didn't against the other two?"

Then it dawned on me. "Oh," I said. "I was aware of it before it was aware of me, for the two it was the other way around, they ambushed me."

"Feedback: That is one plausible explanation."

It felt right to me. Somehow, it made me feel better, that there were some rules that I could learn. "Okay, if we are going to fight it again, we should plan ahead. I don't know what would happen if I got injured in here," I said, pulling out my knife. "You said that you can change into any shape? Could you . . . attach yourself to a weapon like this knife? Add something to it?"

"Feedback: As long as there is sufficient structural mass, any shape is possible."

I smiled, then we sat down in the corridor and planned.

Skills

My sire taught me how to fight, really fight. Before, I had learned by watching the cartel's enforcers, by the fact that I was always in their presence. As a kid I often got into fights with the other children. I was a wild one back then, intent on proving to everyone that I was dangerous. I had learned early on that making others fear you was the only way that you could survive in a place like that.

Eventually, an old shifter, a sicario for the cartel noticed me. He would come out into the yard and break up fights, and one day he found me on top of a boy around my age, my fists raining down on his face. I remember him pulling me off the little shit and taking me to the woods, where the shifters had their training area. He had me hitting sacks filled with grain for hours, only speaking when he had something to correct. I was a quick study, and from the shifters I learned what brutality really meant. Back then, I thought that there was no honor in a fight, and I learned how to inflict as much damage as possible as fast as possible. Often, that was the only way that I could win against men who were taller and stronger than me. Hit them before they realized that I was a threat, gouge an eye, break a limb, crack a rib—the rest of the fight was easier after. I learned how to shoot and care for firearms, I learned what spots on the body caused the most pain.

I didn't know that I was going to be turned. After I was chosen to be sent to the States to study, I believed that my future would be managing the cartel's many interests. I had even been set to follow Pablo around, learning his craft.

When I learned about being turned, I was terrified, but I knew enough to understand that there was no refusing the Master of the cartel. I remember that period through a haze filled with memories of blood, the only thing that was clear was the taste of my sire's blood on my tongue. I had always wondered why I wasn't turned by the Master himself, but then again, I didn't know much about the vampire side of the cartel. My sire was a mysterious figure, one seldom seen.

Once I regained my sanity, a few weeks after my transition, I spent all my time with my sire, in his small wooden house in the woods. He insisted that I needed to learn a martial art. He taught me himself, trying to teach me the finer points of body movement and how exactly to use my greater physical abilities. I learned how to see through my opponents, how to watch for the signs of their muscles moving beneath their skin, even before the movement was visibly apparent.

He instilled in me the importance of meditation and calm in order to control my **thirst**. I had never been that good at it, which was why my **thirst** often ruled me. It was a failure that had led to a noose around my neck. It was also something that I couldn't rectify, not when I needed what the **thirst** gave me in order to survive.

He also taught me how to use many different weapons from his old homeland. I was never any good with most of them, but three had always come easier to me. The bo-staff, the yari (a type of spear), and the kyoketsu shoge (a chain and blade weapon).

Now, I looked down at Saia and my knife. The blade that I had recovered from the chest was around the length of my forearm, a long knife. Now, the edge was covered in a thin layer of silvery material with tiny hexagonal patterns all over it. At the bottom of the knife, Saia had drilled a hole and passed through a ring which connected to a thin chain that was wrapped in behind my belt. The end of the chain was in my other hand with a larger ring attached at the end.

The chain and blade was the weapon that we decided to replicate since Saia wasn't large enough for a spear or a staff. The chain was thin, but Saia assured me that her structural mass was incredibly tough and that it would hold.

"Right," I started. "Can you shift back and forth quickly? I want to see how long it takes you."

Saia obliged my request, turning into silver goo then re-forming into a dragon. The transformation took around three seconds, though that was when the chain was tied up. After a bit, she changed again, attaching herself to the blade and becoming a chain. It landed on the ground as she twisted about, she of course couldn't tie up the chain together after turning into it, she didn't create any systems that allowed her to mimic muscles as in her dragon form.

Still, I could easily enough do it myself.

"A few seconds either way," I said. "It's good enough."

"Statement: Satisfaction."

I chuckled and had Saia turn into dragon again. Our plan for the bear required her to start the fight in that form. I already knew what the bear was capable of; the plan we made was meant to rob it of its strengths. I took a deep breath as Saia climbed on my shoulder, then we entered the room. Slowly, I knelt and put my new glaive on the ground, just in case. The two claw improvised daggers were tucked in behind my back, now properly cut down to resemble daggers, and I held the knife in my right hand.

I started to move forward, with all the stealth I could manage, which was significant. A vampire's control over their own body was substantial; only someone with incredible senses would be able to detect one.

As if I had just jinxed it, the bear's ear twitched, I froze. It released a whine, its ears still moving around, and I could tell that it was about to wake up. I gave the signal to Saia, and she shot into the air. Quickly she flew at the bear, and just as it raised its head and opened its eyes she mauled his face, gouging both eyes out. The bear roared and got up to its full height in what seemed to be an instant. It started swinging its paws wildly, but Saia was already away, heading toward me. I didn't move as the beast kept smashing everything around it, clawing the ground and the rock beneath which it had slept.

Saia reached me and turned into the chain again. As she clattered to the ground and I caught the chain beneath the blade, the bear turned in my direction. It roared in anger and charged blindly. I dashed to the side, pulling the chain and twisting around my axis, swinging it across the ground until it finally had enough momentum for me to pick it up from the ground.

The sound of metal swinging through the air filled the hilltop as I spun the chain faster and faster. The bear turned toward the sound and charged, spittle flying out of its giant maw. I spun again, then stepped forward and let the chain fly. The end of it struck the bear in the snout, the fist-sized ring heavy enough that it hurt the bear and disoriented it.

I pulled the chain back across the ground, quickly wrapping it up around my left elbow. Once I had gathered it all, I let go of the blade part, and as the bear charged toward me again I started spinning the blade next to me.

I waited for the last moment before it crashed into me and jumped to the side, then let the knife fly at its side from an underhanded spin. It stabbed into its side, and as the bear passed, I pulled, ripping it out of its body as I jumped away again.

It roared in anger again, then it shook, and a red light exploded out of its body. I was at least two meters away from it, and the red light barely touched me. I felt dizzy, and my limbs heavy, but it was nowhere near the effect it had before. Still, it was enough for it to whip in my direction and lash out. Blind as it was, it still managed to get me, opening up a shallow cut on my right leg. I ignored it as it wasn't a serious injury. I jumped back, putting more distance between us and shaking off the last of the numbness.

As I gathered the chain again I ran, trying to make as little noise as possible. Its hearing was good, and often it would turn in my direction even when I was as silent as I could be. I had to run away while I spun the chain, then wait for it to come at me before throwing the blade in its direction and inflicting wounds.

After a dozen or so repeats, the bear was visibly tired, blood flowing from its many wounds. I started spinning my chain again, this time in a slow overhand spin. When it headed in my direction, I waited until it was close then put my foot out in the way of the spinning chain, catching the knife there and halting its momentum. A moment later, I kicked it up and forward sending the knife blade flying straight at the animal's head.

The blind bear never saw the knife coming as it stabbed in between its eyes. It collapsed in front of my feet, and its body slowly dissolved into particles until only an orb remained. I walked over and picked it up, noting that it was red in color.

"Let's see what this is," I said to Saia as she shifted back into her dragon form.

We returned to the main room, and I walked over to the shelves on the wall. Next to the [Lesser Leap] I placed the new orb. The bowl turned red, and the plaque beneath it filled with writing.

[Debilitating Wave]

Releases a wave of energy that will daze everything hit.

That sounded about right. Again, though, I saw no signs of a cooldown or anything like that. Or even a cost for it. There was a lot of information missing. I shook my head and picked it up again, then walked over to the pedestal that was my skill. I picked up the [Lesser Strength]. Immediately, I felt weak and stumbled forward, catching myself on the pedestal. A wave of dizziness came over me, a sense of loss. I could tell that I had lost some of my strength. I looked down at my muscles and noticed that I was back to normal.

I grimaced and straightened, then looked at the plaque beneath the bowl. It was blank now, the writing had disappeared, and it had turned gray, like the original plaque above it describing the [Empty Slot].

I placed the red orb into the bowl. Writing appeared on the second plaque, describing the [Debilitating Wave] skill, but it didn't turn back to gold. I felt nothing, and somehow I knew that it would take some time for it to activate, as the slot skill said. Again, I had no idea how long that would be.

I sighed and turned to look at Saia.

"We are done here. Let's see what happens to you once I leave."

With one last look on the Mask, I focused on the thought of leaving, and felt the world around me obey.

The switch was immediate. One moment I was inside, the next I was out. Saia was still in my lap, looking up at me attentively.

"Statement: Link with the secondary platform lost."

"So, you can't exist in there without me," I said.

"Feedback: That is likely the case."

I wondered what it all meant, but I still had no context on it. I stood up and had Saia turn back into the bracer. As I stood, I realized that I was feeling something strange on my leg. I looked down at my torn and bloody pants, but saw no sign of a wound. Then I remembered that the bear injured me. I touched my leg, but the feeling seemed like it wasn't exactly physical, more like phantom pain. That worried me, if the wounds suffered inside of that place were still felt . . . what would've happened if it was something more serious? What if I died in there?

I resolved myself to proceed with even greater care. I had to survive this place if I was going to unlock its mysteries. With nothing else to do, I settled in to wait for the sun to set.

Discovery

As soon as the night fell, I rejoiced in feeling the full strength of my power again. Wanting to take advantage of as much of the night as possible, Saia—in her bracer form—and I headed toward the far end of the room. I reached the entrance to the corridor and frowned. The doorway was large, at least double my height and double that in width. The corridor beyond was the same size. I looked back at the room I was in and realized that it too was large. I had assumed that it used to be a hall of some kind, but . . . why build corridors that were so large? Either this building was once supposed to appear grand, or . . . the people that used it were . . . big. Perhaps as big as the dragons.

I started walking down the corridor.

There were cracks in the wall, as well as a lot of dust covering the floor. I saw a few openings with stairs leading down beneath the ground, but they were all dead ends: after only a few steps the openings were buried either by the debris of a collapsed wall or just earth. I got a sense that this place had been here and abandoned for a very long time. Finally, after several minutes of brisk walking I sensed something at the edge of my hearing range. I slowed but didn't stop. Instead, I gripped my glaive and calmly made my way forward. Quickly, it became apparent that what I was hearing was the sound of flowing water. I reached the end of the corridor and entered a new chamber. It looked like a mirror chamber to the first one, except that this one had no cracks that let light in through the ceiling. It did, however, have a large section of the wall on the far side of the room that was collapsed, and a small stream flowing into the room. That corner was filled with a pool, and once I saw that there were no other threats in the room I approached it.

Even my eyes struggled to see much in the dark room so I raised my wrist.

"Can you make me a light? Even faint one will do; I noticed that your eyes glow."

Saia obliged immediately by creating a narrow band that shone with a pale blue glow. Even that minuscule amount of light was enough for my eyes to see clearly in the dark. I looked down at the pool, saw my own reflection, and froze.

Was that me? I nearly recoiled from the person I saw reflected back at me. My clothes were ruined, torn, and soaked in blood, so much so that the original color could barely even be seen. Despite the awful state of my clothes, it was my face that drew attention the most. My neck had a long brand going around it: the noose wound was raw, half scabbed over and half scarred. It was a mess at least three fingers thick. Caked blood was everywhere, and I could still see some parts of the wound that were wet from the healing skin. I reached up with my fingers, wincing as I was reminded of the pain. I had pushed it into the farthest reaches of my mind, but it was still there.

My chin and mouth were surrounded by black in the dim light, covered with the blood of different animals. My cheeks were smudged with it, and it matted in my hair. My eyes stared at me from the gaunt face of someone who hadn't rested in days. I studied my reflection for a few long minutes, my mind wandering. I remembered human myths and misconceptions about vampires, like the ones that said that we had no reflection. Obviously nonsense. We weren't magical beings, nor were we cursed by God, despite what so many believed. We were just another species. We followed the same rules that everyone else did. The **thirst** was what made us different—what made us stronger.

I shook my head and banished the stray thoughts. My appearance was a mess. I touched the water, and the cold of it sent a shock through my nerves. I cupped a bit of it and splashed it on my face, then again, and again, faster. I scrubbed at my face, trying to get the blood off. Until I found myself naked and walking into the pool. Time seemed to pass in a blur as I tried to wash all that blood off me.

A short while later, still feeling tired and raw, but at least somewhat clean. I walked out of the pool and looked down at my dirty and torn clothes. I didn't have anything else to wear. But then something occurred to me.

"Hey Saia," I called.

"Feedback: Yes?"

"You can consume organic matter, right? Can you consume the blood on my clothes?"

"Feedback: Consuming the Host's biomass can only be done with the explicit command from the Host."

Right. Most of that blood was mine. "Do it."

Saia flowed down on the ground, then over my clothes. It took a lot less time than consuming corpses had. Once she was done, she returned to my wrist, and my torn clothes looked a lot less dirty. I put them on, amazed at the fact that I saw no blood on them.

"Thank you," I told her.

Before she could answer, the world started to shake. A deep rumble rose up from the earth. I stumbled as the ground beneath me shifted. A crack opened up, spreading over to the wall. A piece of the ceiling broke off above me, and I jumped and rolled out of the way.

My ears were filled with the sound of the earthquake's roar. And then, just as it had come, it slowly abated. The groaning of the earth settled and stilled.

That was a big one. The frequency seemed to indicate that this was a common occurrence in this place. I had just climbed back to my feet when a sound of something crashing echoed from down the corridor.

"Fuck," I whispered once it settled a while later. "What are the chances that the way back just collapsed?"

"Feedback: Insufficient information."

"Some help you are," I grumbled, and headed back to check.

As I walked something caught my attention in front of us, almost like a shadow or black mist that moved. It was too fast, and I couldn't be sure that my eyes weren't playing tricks on me. The light given off by Saia cast my surroundings in shadows that made it hard to see properly beyond a few meters. I turned to her and whispered. "Saia, can you turn off the light?"

She did as I asked, and as the blue light faded and my eyes adapted, I saw no signs of any movement, but I noticed another light source from up ahead. Immediately, I readied my glaive, then continued on to investigate. It didn't take us long to reach the source, or at least the way to it. One of the blocked-off passages leading beneath the ground had collapsed into what looked to be a sinkhole. The stairs down now cut off suddenly, leading into a pit of nothingness around two meters across. The light, however, was coming from the other side, around a bend in the corridor at the bottom of the stairs.

I debated whether or not I should investigate, but ultimately, any clues to my situation were welcome. This was how I found Saia, and even though I was still trying not to think about what being bonded to her meant, she had proven her worth.

I walked down to the edge, then leapt over in one smooth move. Once on the other side I started walking down with care, not making any noise. Once I reached the bottom, the corridor split into two. The one on the left was collapsed, but the right one continued for a few meters before opening up into a room, where the light was coming from. I headed deeper, still not seeing the source of the light, as it was on the side of the room, obscured by the corner. What I saw inside the room was nothing of interest. The white light illuminated an empty room filled with dust and dirt. Some roots had punched through the ceiling and now stabbed from it into the side of the wall where the stone had collapsed and dirt spilled through. The rest of the room was empty.

I entered and turned toward the source of the light. The first thing that struck me was the scent of stale air. The second was that the light was coming from a hole in the wall, a section of it that had collapsed, by the looks of it as a result of the recent earthquake. I approached the hole and peered through. I still couldn't see the source of the light, but I could see into the room. This one was far different. There were broken tables and chairs, collapsed from the weight of age. The floor was covered with a rotted carpet, and the walls had torn tapestries, a few of them still mostly intact, but many having pieces of them on the ground.

Somehow, this room had to have been preserved, hidden away. It offered me my first real chance at finding answers. I climbed in and crawled through the tight hole to enter the room. Gently I placed my foot on the carpet and looked around. There was a door shaped opening on the wall to my right, the light coming from within. What struck me was that this room was a lot more normal sized, at least compared to the rest of this building. The ceiling was just over three meters high, and the door was maybe wide enough for two people to pass through comfortably.

I looked around the room first. The collapsed tables had rotted legs, and there were remnants of unidentifiable items on the floor. Most of them were square gray stones, though I couldn't tell if they were always that or if age had stripped them of everything. Broken pieces of what looked to me like glass were everywhere, near the tables, as if there had been bottles on them once. I walked around, looking at the faded tapestries and not seeing anything that I could discern.

"Saia, do you see anything familiar?"

"Feedback: Negative. The art style does not match anything in my archives."

I continued, coming up on what had once been a bookshelf, or at least I thought it had, it was covered in piles of dust with a few pieces of long leathery looking strips here and there. If those had been books once, they had a long time to turn into this.

With nothing else of interest to see I turned to the next room. I entered and immediately saw the source of the light. It was a fist-sized gemstone placed on top of a stone table at the end of the room. The room was long and gave me the same feeling as churches on Earth. It was all made out of stone, and the walls on both sides were covered in an arch with images painted within them that were still somewhat clear, one per wall. It made me think of temples. Everything here looked a lot more preserved. The end of the room had a statue of a winged being, kneeling with its head bowed and hands resting on its knees, placed just above the wide stone table. Below it, I saw something crumpled on the ground.

I entered and first examined the images on the walls. The one on the right was painted in hues of red, showing a horde of monsters on an open field. Big hulking creatures with horns, some with wings, others that were grotesquely misshapen. They reminded me a bit of the depictions of demons in Earth's mythologies. It was a battle. The image was damaged in the corner, and I could not see who the monsters were fighting, though the monsters were clearly winning. In the distance, the sky was painted as a maelstrom of red clouds, with monsters flying out of its center.

That was . . . ominous. I turned and looked at the one on the other wall. This one also had the monsters, but only half of it was filled with their depictions. The other was damaged again, so I could not see who the force that opposed them was, but up above in the sky was a figure shrouded in white-blue light, so much so that all features were obscured. It seemed like this being was leading the charge against the monsters.

With little clues there, I moved toward the end of the room. As I got closer, I could see what was on the ground. I paused as I recognized bones—it was a body of someone who had died a long time ago. The clothes might've been blue once, though by now the color had mostly faded. The skull shape made me look up at the statue.

It was incredibly detailed, enough so that I could see that the wings were feathered and could discern every single one. The being's face was humanoid, though the nose looked more like just two holes. The mouth was beneath with thin lips, barely more than a line that was turned downward into a sad expression. The eyes were closed, on either side of the nose in the same place a human would have them. The head extended back into a kind of crest that ended in four triangular points.

It was very clearly an alien, the same as the one to whom the body belonged. I elected not to touch the body, it didn't feel right. Instead, I looked at the gemstone on the table. It was the only thing that looked like it was in pristine condition.

I leaned down to get a better look, and it flashed. Immediately, I jumped back as the light shimmered in the air and then a fuzzy image appeared above it. A moment later it sharpened, and I saw an alien from the waist up, with pale, sickly looking weathered skin, black wings, and blue robes in far better condition than those on the body below. A hologram?

It looked down at me with bright orange eyes, somehow appearing as if it could see through me completely. I froze under that gaze. There was power in it that reminded me of my sire. Then, it started to speak.

The voice that spoke was deep and carrying, and it echoed in the stone room. I couldn't comprehend it at first, but then I felt a pressure inside my head lasting only a split second, and I could understand its words.

"... *friend from across time. I am Kolan Shuk, and I leave this message, this warning, and a plea, in the hope that all is not yet lost for you and yours as it is for me and mine. Will you do a dead one a favor and listen? I can only hope that you are of a stalwart heart.*"

What did I stumble on? I stepped closer, listening to the dead being's words closely.

"*If you are here, listening to this message, then you are trapped in the machinations of the Last Intent, the spell of infinite potential, our curse, our punishment, what could've been our salvation if not for pride. To understand my warning, you must first know some of our past. We called ourselves the Vim, and we were the children of the Way, utilizing the Source to Weave magics that had helped us rule our world and spread beyond it. I shall spare you of the details. I leave behind books of our history pieced together, written by my hand, which you may read at your leisure. Time, time is of importance, even though it might not always seem so.*"

I grimaced. From what I had seen, the books didn't survive. The being shook its head and seemed to sigh.

"*What matters is that the greatest Source wielder among us, Valair Ankah, saw a threat, something for which all of his peers ridiculed and banished him for. In response, he crafted the greatest work any of us had ever even imagined, a thing of legends and godhood. Pure will woven into the fabric of the Way itself, will that rewrote reality. I do not know the truth, I confess. Forgive me for that, dear friend from across time. I remain ignorant, despite my might. From what I have managed to gather since, it is my belief that the events leading to the activation of his great work, his Last Intent, are as follows: In the pursuit of our expansion into our solar system we encountered something, a force of unknown origin, which I had only managed to find fragmented records of in the fall of our civilization. From what I can see, we did not at first know what we had stumbled on, nor I admit, did my people even believe in it. They banished Valair for urging drastic measures, and when they refused him, he took matters into his own hands.*"

The being paused, and I could see a weariness in his pose. He was alien, yet his mannerisms were so familiar. I saw the weight of responsibility in his eyes.

"*He unleashed a spell of godlike might. A spell that changed how the Source worked, that reshaped our world, and the Weaves of the Way we had crafted over the eons collapsed. Valair put restrictions in the base nature of reality, and made it so that every being of reason could touch the Source. His spell reshaped the way that Source interacted with Souls and coalesced it into Soul-Wrought Masks as the conduits for the Way's power. They grow with us, granting power and allowing for direct tapping into this reality's reservoirs of Source for using the Way. It changed everything, and though it offers great power, it means the end of the Vim."*

The being's tired eyes rose, looking up almost as if staring at something that only it could see.

"The Last Intent's control over reality is absolute. We've learned this the hard way. My people attempted to return things to what they were, and all such endeavors ended with failure. This last one was . . . folly, I must admit, I beg forgiveness even from you, friend from across time. We failed, and in doing so we sealed the fate of the Vim forever. We will not survive another turning."

Its eyes turned back down to stare into mine, holding me enthralled.

"I know that you are not of my kind, friend from across time. I know this because I am and have always been a seer. When the Last Intent came into being, we all of us rebelled against it, refusing its offers of power. In time, I changed my mind, and dwelled deep into the currents of power that it offered. At this time, I hold the Mask of the Fateseer Mage of the Old Ways, I have reached the Eighth Investment, Fifth Carving, the highest ever achieved by any of the Vim to my knowledge. I have seen the end of my kind, and though we are separated by a gulf of time, I have seen the end of yours. I do not know who you are or even if you will listen and heed my warning, friend from across time, I know only that you will come upon this message. Or perhaps not, perhaps none shall ever find my words. Fate is a tangle of threads even I struggle to unwind. Perhaps this is all in vain."

It seemed sad there, lost, defeated. I looked up at its image, seeing someone who was on their last legs. The being was a seer? Someone who could see the future? I had so many answers, but also so many more questions. Finally, the being seemed to shake itself out of a stupor and continue.

"Hear my warning, the threat is coming, I do not know when or how, but I know that all life is threatened, on this world and all others. I have used my greatest skill to gaze into the future, and I see only corruption of Source. A twisted landscape filled with corruption, ruled by vile emotion and defilement of the Way. I do not know how much time you have left. It could be that my message is already too late, or you could have generations still. It matters not, for within this recording crystal, I leave proof in the form of a vision of the past. I had never seen this threat with my own eyes, though I have seen its influence. The vision is a memory pulled from Valair Ankah's own mind. I recovered it in the ruins of the emperor's palace, the emperor whom he had once served. I had long tried to glean some meaning or clue from this vision, with little success. It is my belief now that Valair was right, and his drastic measure right. Regardless, I have written down my thoughts for you to find within my library. If you would hear my plea, my warning, touch the crystal,

and see all that I have seen, hear all that I have heard. If you have it in your heart to listen to a stranger's last request, friend from across time, spread my words wide, prepare your people, for the threat discovered in my time shall grow until it consumes everything in its path. Prepare and embrace Valair's gift, his Last Intent, so that you may try to banish what mine had unleashed." The being bowed its head and crossed its arms across its chest. *"May the Everlasting Sun always warm your path."*

With that, the recording ended.

The Vision

Still reeling from what I had just heard I took a step back from the crystal, then promptly sat down. I could feel my legs about to give out from the sheer magnitude of what I had learned. Masks were magic, a spell ruled this reality, there was some big threat out there, aliens, and a vision. None of it explained how I got here though, but it offered clues.

"Saia, you heard all that right?"

"Feedback: Affirmative."

"Any input?" I asked her.

"Feedback: The reasons for why some of this Unit's engrams were no longer functioning are apparent now. The nature of Source Weave was altered. This explanation fits all the known parameters. If this was an effect that spread across all of reality, as the recorded being indicated, then it is possible that it also affected the Ke Erzi world. Though, my calculations suggest that to be unlikely."

"Really? Why?"

"Feedback: You located this Unit on an isolated piece of Ke Erzi world. It is possible that only that section had somehow been obtained by this *Last Intent*. Additionally, the Host has implied that there was no Source Weave on your homeworld at all. Whatever event affected this world, it happened a long time in the past. The timeline does not match up with that of Ke Erzi. The Creators had access to Source Weave in a different form many cycles after the change happened in this place, if my estimate of the age of this ruin is correct."

I frowned, then nodded slowly. "You know, that does pose a few good questions. If I was grabbed from my world by this spell, how was it accomplished? What if I wasn't just picked up from another world, but from a whole different reality?"

"Feedback: Recalculating. Probability high that both the Host's and this Unit's points of origin are different realities," Saia reported.

"Not that it helps us much." I sighed, then glanced up at the table and then the body next to it. It was large, taller than I was, and the wing bones large enough that it would probably have a big wingspan, a few meters across at least.

I climbed back to my feet and approached the crystal on the table. "What do you think?" I glanced at my wrist.

"Feedback: Memory recording engrams existed on Erzi. Some of which posed significant threat on use."

"Yeah, but . . ." I glanced at the body on the ground. "Kolan Shuk . . . this message was left so long ago for someone to find. I know that I don't owe it to anyone, but it just feels wrong to ignore it."

Saia didn't respond. I was aware of the danger.

"Are there ways for spells, engrams I guess, to take over someone's mind? Could I get possessed here?" I asked.

"Feedback: Ke Erzi had never devised a way to achieve such a result. Damage to the mental capacity, introduction of memories, but no outright mind control. I must caution you that if what the message spoke is true, the people who had the ability to rewrite the rules of an entire reality might know something that not even the Ke Erzi had."

Choices and risks, that was what seemed to be my life now. Ever since I came to this place I had been faced with danger and risks. Thrown into situations where I had to fight to survive another day. Finally I had some answers, and it felt wrong to ignore getting more of them. Besides, somehow I felt moved by the plea in the message. The tone it was spoken in was from someone who had been defeated, and had yet found a way to try to do something for someone who he never would have the chance to meet. A stranger, a friend from across time.

Here I stood, I didn't believe in fate, but perhaps I was brought here for a reason. I took a deep breath and put my hand on the crystal.

A shock ran through my arm and struck my mind, making everything go white.

It started with the vision of space. I flew across the gulf in between the stars, tiny points of light flashing by my side, until I came upon a world without oceans. I saw a gentle light surrounding the world. Yellow and white, it pulsed in rhythm. And then I was on the ground, a group of seven people around me. All of them were the alien, winged people, wearing elaborate suits that reminded me of what astronauts wore in works of science fiction, only married with fantasy. There were gemstones nestled in their suits that emitted a soft glow that surrounded them.

I was watching from the point of view of one of them. I saw them walking through ruins of a grand city surrounded in a red haze. Everything was the same on this world. Even the sky was red, filled with storms so far up that it looked like an ocean churning above them. Far in the distance they could see a maelstrom of clouds, turning with lightning flashing, rising above the ruins of the city to touch the ruinous sky. Images sped through my mind quickly as they explored the destroyed city, almost like going through a dream. I could feel that something was wrong, I could see the people around me arguing, pointing at their weapons and gear. The magic wasn't working right. They moved through the ruins, seeing evidence of battle, long since dried blood painting the walls and ground. There were no bodies, until they came to a large building with an arch in the center of a massive square, and I felt ill. Thousands of spikes were lined around the building, and each held the dead, killed long ago. Their faces twisted into grimaces of agony, their bodies flayed of all skin, bones ripped out to resemble maws reaching for the sky. It was torture, it was agony, it was death in the most brutal form there was. There were pens filled with prisoners, their bodies nothing but skin and bone. They cried out for release, they wished for death, but found only torture in it as their jailers, twisted shapes of grotesque beings, demons of putrid and rotting flesh, cast magic that visibly tore their souls out, captured them and twisted them into grotesque forms that they then used to feed themselves. I heard the laughter of monsters and knew the expressions of ecstasy in their actions.

And there, near that building in the center, they saw more. Towering beings of twisted forms waited on by tiny scrambling demons that played with the bones of the dead. They were dressed in clothes made out of skin with faces still on it, symbols carved into it that leaked blood. They were terrible to look at, and just the sight of them impacted me in a visceral way, as if just by being in their presence I could feel them. They were monsters in all the pure meanings of the word. I saw death, and I heard cries of millions. I felt their pain and their suffering, the agony of a whole world. It disgusted me, and for the first time in my life, I felt a real visceral hate for something. For the first time I knew that Khalil was right, that good and evil did exist, and for the first time I prayed for the help of a righteous, wrathful, and vengeful God.

The monsters near the arch were doing something, casting some magic at the center of the arch. It was pulsing with red light, and the space itself felt like it was tearing apart. The people around me started to argue, and the vision flashed. Now I was in the middle of fighting, I and the people around me were wielding terrible magic and making our way to the center. The arch pulsed, and a gateway opened. Behind us drums echoed, and an army spilled from the maelstrom of clouds in the distance, as another marched into the square. We ran before them, going through the streets.

We turned to light, and again I flew across the stars, only to stop when I came upon a white-blue moon orbiting a jewel blue and green world. Then we were on the ground again, and fought the demons, the monsters. The people around me died as more joined us. We were in another city, this one on the surface of the moon. I saw buildings razed and children crushed. Rising in the sky was the world filled with clouds, and oceans, and land. I saw hooks stabbed into the elderly and their skin pulled out. Magic, terrible magic filled everything around me.

The people around me argued again, until only two were left. We came to a decision, and I ran while a woman stayed. I reached another arch, this one defended by my own. I argued with them before moving through. I stumbled through the arch, through the portal, and hit the ground somewhere else. I turned my eyes to the sky and searched for the moon. Then the arch behind me shut off, and the moon exploded high in the sky above the world.

I fell on the ground, staring at the ceiling but not really seeing anything. I knew a voice was talking, but I didn't really hear. I was frozen in time, the vision flashing before my eyes, carved into my brain as if in stone. It was not what had frozen me, but the feeling deep inside, what I knew was in my soul. When I saw those monsters, what I felt in the air around them—no, what the person whose memory I saw felt—it was the most horrible sensation I had ever felt. What I saw was a war against monsters, but it was not what I had seen that bothered me, it what I had experienced. The unapologetic sadism, the feelings of joy at the pain of others, the laughter in my head and the agony of the souls harvested.

I couldn't believe such evil could even exist.

But most of all, it was what I had seen in the sky above that world that terrified me. The red churning ocean and the maelstrom. It was familiar to me—it looked like the storm of clouds I had seen in the distance above the jungle.

". . . Marianna?"

The sound of my name spoken finally broke the spell. I stirred, then felt my body unlock as if it had been paralyzed. I groaned, still feeling my soul being pressed. My heart was beating faster so fast and so powerfully that I feared it would punch through and out of my chest.

"I'm here," I managed to whisper.

"Query: Status of Host?"

"I, I'm fine, Saia," I answered slowly, even though I wasn't really. I closed my eyes, but all I could see was red. I decided to rest, for it would take time for me to digest all that I had seen.

Interlude:
The Burning in the Stormlands

As the boy ran through the burning village, embers spit and popped into the air and smoke rose high into the sky, obscuring the light of the moons. He wondered if the Goddess could see him through all the smoke. Screams of the dying echoed all around him, but every moment there were less and less of them.

The sound of flapping wings, as claps of thunder, made him duck beneath a wagon left abandoned in the paved dirt street. He looked up hesitantly, trying to make out what manner of beast had attacked them. It had to be one of the great drakes from the mountains—Mama always told him how terrible they were. How they enjoyed eating little boys when they were being naughty.

He knew that they had to send word to the keep, let the knights know. They would be able to deal with the drake, like in Mama's stories. Only, his feet were too short to get him there fast enough, and he had no Mask. He had to return home, find Mama and Papa. They would know what to do.

If anyone survived, he thought to himself, but then quickly shook his head. They were still alive, he knew it. They would scold him for going down to the river to play by himself, but once he found them, everything would be all right again. A part of him whispered that he should've run away when he saw the village burning, that his small bucket with water wouldn't have helped any.

Through the flames he saw a shape hover above the burning tavern, just a shadow in his eyes, with only its wide wings recognizable to him. It stayed there for a few seconds, and then it dove down through the stone roof, crashed through the ground, and into the tavern nestled in the cave beneath. A scream came from within the building, then the shape exploded out of the tavern, and flew high. It had a woman in its claws, and he could hear her pleading, screaming. He recognized her voice, Vallia, the tavernkeeper. She always gave him tasty pastries whenever he came to visit.

Her screams were cut short, then she fell and hit the ground with a loud sound of breaking bones.

The sound of beating wings moved away, and he thought that it was his chance. He had to be brave now, like the knights in stories. He crawled out from his hiding place and started running. His breath was thundering in his ears, his heart fought to escape his chest, but he ran.

He didn't see or hear the monster as it grabbed him. There was only a short stab of pain in his neck, and then nothing.

Knight Mage Herim of Roughrock walked through the village, leaving footsteps in the ash and soot. The smoke was thick still, but he was of a high Investment so it did not bother him as such. Still, his eyes teared up, and streaks trailed down his cheeks. Not from the smoke, but from the sights that he beheld. The corpses were covered in blood-soaked ash, and entrails were spread across the streets. Death had come to the Village of Platfield. So much death. He had not expected this when the call had reached him. Even now, seeing it with his own eyes, he could barely believe it.

Herim had served during the last conflict, nearly a thousand years ago now. He had been there on the beaches, fighting in the red and blue sand colored by the blood of Elves and YoKai-ni. Even with only two of their tribes raiding the Elvaros coast, the amount of death was unlike anything he had seen before. He had protected the plains for centuries before then, had fought animals that ventured too far, and occasional monsters. And still he had seen nothing like the raids. He shuddered to imagine what it had been like before, when the YoKai-ni first arrived on Kirios and all their races marched to war.

But this . . . there was a different kind of brutality here, a thing that he couldn't quite comprehend. The smoke cleared as he reached the village square. Wagons were overturned and half burnt, and a few broken bodies lined the streets. Two of his knights knelt in the center, examining a small body. *A child—* he steeled his emotions lest he weep more at the tragedy. The Village of Platfield had been blessed with a child, a young boy, just ten turnings ago. Herim remembered the celebration of the birth—the Knights of the Stormpeak Keep had been invited along with all the nobility in a thousand leagues. All of the Stormlands had rejoiced and celebrated.

Herim approached, and the two knights stood, their helms cradled in their arms and their faces marked with sorrow as tears cleared lines through their soot-marred cheeks. Right they were in their mourning, for there was no tragedy greater than a death of a child. Herim looked down at the frail body, pale and surprisingly intact compared to the others. Except for the wound on the child's neck. He knelt next to the boy and bowed his head, whispering a prayer to the Goddess of the Eternal Woods, asking her to shelter the young child's soul on its path to the Holy Forest beyond.

After a long moment, he stood and turned to the two knights waiting. "Report," he ordered with a coarse voice.

The two knights saluted, their stances perfectly straight. "Knight Mage," the older of the two started, "we've gotten word that the village had burned down from a traveler who noticed the smoke. Immediately a squad of Knight Hunters was sent to investigate, expecting a monster attack. They . . . what they found was . . ."

The knight swallowed; he was obviously struggling with the sights around them. *He is young*, Herim thought. *A century at most.* He understood the young man's hesitation.

"Did they say what manner of storming monster did this?" Herim asked, barely able to contain his anger.

The two knights glanced at each other, and then back at him. "The Knight Hunters don't know, sir," he said at last.

Herim frowned. "A migrating animal? Or a blighted monster?" he asked, then continued when he saw that they had no answer for him. "Where are the Knight Hunters? I would speak with them directly."

"They've been inspecting some of the bodies in the camp outside the village. We can take you there, sir," the knight said.

Herim nodded and let them guide him through the village. He spared one last glance for the dead child. They couldn't move the body, not until a mother arrived. The child was unnamed. It would be an insult for someone of the martial profession to touch an unnamed child. No, they would wait for a mother to stand in the stead of the child's own. To say the rites and cry for the loss that had fallen upon the people of Elvaros.

Herim turned away and followed the knights.

They found the Knight Hunters in a large black tent, marked with the signet of their order, a bow on a silver shield. Once inside, Herim saw two men looking at a body of an elderly man placed on a table. They raised their heads and looked up at the intrusion, then immediately straightened and saluted at his entrance.

"Knight Mage, sir," they said in unison.

"At ease," Herim said. "Tell me what you have found? I am told that you do not know what manner of beast caused this tragedy."

The Knight Hunters exchanged hesitant looks, then met his eyes. "We are . . . uncertain, sir. Nothing that we've seen matches any beast known to live on Elvaros, animal or monster."

Herim's ear twitched at that, and he walked over. "Explain." Herim narrowed his eyes.

The Knight Hunter with the highest rank, marked by the third feather in his hair, answered. "There are two types of corpses left in the village. The first are the people that have been torn apart. It is clear that this has been done by brute strength and not skill, as far as we are able to tell at least. Based on the last census, the highest Investment in the village was a retired **Guardsman**, at Fourth Investment."

Herim's eyebrow rose at that. "A Fourth Investment **Guardsman** should have been able to handle most beasts in all of the Stormlands." Probably more like all of them. The Knight Orders of Tempest made sure that the mountains and the plains around them were cleared of any high Investment beasts, and they routinely culled the drake populations in the mountains. The chance that something slipped through was slim, but at most it would be at Fifth Investment—and even that was a stretch. It would have to be very old or had to have slaughtered thousands of other beasts, which would not have gone unnoticed by the Knight Hunters patrolling the area. A Fourth Investment **Guardsman** would've at least been able to hold the beast down or chase it off, and he would definitely have been able to leave it injured.

The Knight Hunter nodded at Herim's words. "We found him outside of the tavern. His limbs had been torn off his body, sir."

Herim blinked. That was . . . A Fourth Investment Mask was a threshold point. People at those Investments were tougher, their bodies hardier. It would've been very difficult to do something like that even to a **Trader**, let alone someone who had a martial Mask.

"Did you find the village Ledger?" Herim asked. It would be best if they made sure, rather than assume.

The lower ranked Knight Hunter nodded then walked over to the table in the corner of the tent.

"We've been hoping to have it unlocked at the keep. We were not aware that you had been summoned," the Knight Hunter said as he offered the Ledger to Herim.

"I believe that this situation warrants an exception to the rules," Herim said. Unsealing of Investment Ledgers was not a light thing, and was usually only done at knight keeps. The purpose of the Ledgers wasn't to gain an advantage. It was private information. Their keeping was an old tradition, hailing back to the last war. Their purpose was to have the information available to the Knight Orders if there was ever need for conscription in times of war.

Usually, the highest ranking region official would be present at the opening, but . . . Herim believed that the death of the entire village warranted an exception. He had the authority for it.

He reached around his neck and pulled out a chain with a gray, round amulet bearing the signet of Tempest Orders—a tall mountain surrounded by clouds. Painted in the colors of the Stormpeak, white and grey, the order that he belonged to.

He placed it over the Ledger, and the enchantment activated, unlocking the book.

Slowly he opened it and searched through the pages until he found one dedicated to the Guardsman, then he looked it over.

Leoj of Platfield

Mask of the Guardsman:
Fourth Investment; Third Carving
Ornament of the Farmer:
No Investment, Seventh Carving

Attributes:
Physical: C
Weave: *E*
Esoteric: *E*

Skills:
[Shield Bash]
[Stalwart Stance]
[Reassuring Presence]
[Calming Aura]
[Parry]
[Keen Eyesight]
[Danger Sense]
[Farmer's Strength]

It was unfortunate that he had taken a Farmer Ornament in his Fourth Investment. It was unlikely that he would've ever risen to the Fifth Investment to consolidate it. Still, it was as they had suspected. [Farmer's Strength] was enough to increase the physical attributes to a high C ranking on the Fourth Investment. Which meant that the Guardsman had a significant advantage—no beast in the area should have been able to do that to him. Not easily at least.

Herim closed the Ledger and stored it in the bag on his hip before turning back to the Knight Hunters.

"It is as you have assumed," Herim told them. "He had a C ranking in his physical attributes. Continue," Herim waved his hand.

The Knight Hunter turned back to the body. "Aside from his limbs being torn off, his rib cage had been shattered, his internal organs pulped to mush. The wounds are consistent with brute force trauma."

"A skill?" Herim asked.

"We discovered bruises that are . . . consistent with impact from small blunt instruments," the Knight Hunter said slowly. "A purely physical skill is . . . a possibility."

Herim narrowed his eyes, detecting that there was something more to it than what the Knight Hunter said. "What is it?"

The Knight Hunter glanced at the others, then back at him. "I used [Wound Inspect]," he said finally. "The injuries were not done by a beast."

It took Herim a moment to realize what he meant; it was so absurd that not even he could believe it. "You are saying that *someone* did this?" Herim whispered harshly. "*Someone* killed a child?"

The three Knight Hunters cowered under his stare. But then their leader spoke. "The skill return was . . . confusing, sir, I can only say for certain that it wasn't a mindless monster or beast."

"Not a mindless one?" Herim asked.

The Knight Hunter nodded. "I supposed that a beast could've awakened, but . . ." He shook his head. "Sir, I don't believe that to be the case."

"Explain," Herim gestured with his hand.

The Knight Hunter turned to the body at the table. "We've tracked the beginning of the killings to the village tavern. From there, all on the way to the square six bodies had been torn apart, some with what appear to be claw marks. From there . . . the deaths were everywhere, and it is hard to tell what else happened because the fire burned most of the evidence. What we can tell is that all the rest of the villagers died the same way."

Herim nodded, and the Knight Hunter continued.

"They all had blood drained from their bodies. And look here." He pointed at the body. "Claws that match the arrangement of an elven hand bit into the flesh here near the armpits on both sides, then they pulled up. We believe that who or whatever this was, could fly. It picked people up, drained them of blood, then dropped them from great heights to break against the ground."

Herim remembered the twisted bodies in the village. "And you don't think that it was a beast, why?"

"All villagers are accounted for, sir," Knight Hunter said.

Herim frowned, not understanding.

The Knight Hunter took a deep breath, then spoke. "Beasts kill to feed, even monsters do. No one was eaten here, sir. No one has any body parts missing, just blood."

Herim felt his heart freeze for a moment. "A cult of some kind? Blood sacrifice?"

The last time something like that happened, the Dwarves lost three cities and half of their tunnel network. Five thousand years and they had yet to reclaim it from whatever it was that the cultists had summoned. If someone was trying to do the same thing on Elvaros . . .

The Knight Hunters didn't answer Herim's question. He didn't expect them to. "They killed a child," he whispered at last. "No Elf would ever do something like that, cultist or not. This . . ."

He didn't know what to think. Had some other kingdom decided to attack, to break the Shadow's Peace? This was too far above his standing. He had to return to the keep and speak with the Knight Commanders. But one thing was certain. Whoever had done this would be hunted down, and they would pay for what they had done.

Task

I had not yet recovered from the vision. Even now, a part of me wanted to revolt against the idea that anything like what I had seen was possible. That it all had to be a trick, a lie. The anguish I experienced was etched into my mind, a film playing on a loop that I didn't wholly understand. Yet now, I tried to think about it clearly. The only evidence of this vision being true was the word of a being that had been dead for thousands of years.

A part of me that grew up with the utmost respect for the dead rebelled. The part that reminded me of walks down the streets on the *Día de los Santos Difuntos,* following my sire as he took that one day of the year to see the lives of mortals, that part chastised me for even thinking that the dead would lie—or those who were about to die. I had to remind myself that there was too much that I didn't know. So, I cataloged what I did know.

I had been transported to another world. That much was undeniably true. I had magic. I found the ruins, which meant that someone used to live here, and after an earthquake I found a sealed room which held the message in the bottle. Its creator was dead, his bones half turned to dust. There was no reason to make such a message if it was not true. For what? A kind of a cosmic joke that no one would find? No, aside from the fact that I did feel like the being spoke the truth, I also remembered what the vision felt like. It's possible there could be some magical reason for it, some way it messed with my mind and made me believe that it was true. But again, for what purpose? If the message was real, then the people that the being belonged to were no longer living, and I was of no consequence to them.

I glanced at Saia; she had tried to activate the crystal too, but it didn't seem to work for her. The most she could tell me was that she didn't feel any remnants or influences on my mind, though that didn't mean that there weren't any. Still, it made me feel better. I decided that the most prudent course of action was to proceed with the belief that all that I had seen was true. The risk of me ignoring it and being wrong was too great. I didn't know any time frame for when what I saw would occur, but I knew that I did not want to stand idle.

The two murals in the temple area were making more sense now. On one side was the host of the monsters, on the other was the flaming figure standing against them. Were those his people, fighting against the monsters? then there was the red haze that filled everything around the monsters and the maelstrom in the distance from which they came, the one that looked suspiciously like the curtain of clouds I had seen in the distance when I just arrived on this world. Was the threat already here on this world? Was the warning too late? I could see how one could spend a long time trying to decipher what the vision showed, especially if they hadn't seen the monsters themselves. And I was certainly not equipped for that. What was obvious to me was that something out there was terrible, and every fiber in my being revolted at the thought of it even existing.

I was never really religious, even when surrounded by religious people. Going to church and saying a prayer? Of course. I lived in a small community, where faith was important. Customs were important, some were so deeply instilled in me that they would forever be part of who I was. Still, for me religion was always just a thing that one did, more out of habit than true belief. Being sold to a cartel as a kid did have the unfortunate side effect of making one not believe in a benevolent God. It wasn't until I met Khalil in the States that I truly understood what faith was, how it could be a beautiful thing, how it could center a person. I never let myself be open to it, but I did admire it from afar.

Now, in this moment, I felt more drawn to such belief. What I saw was anathema to all that I knew. It was horrible in the full meaning of that word, the primal idea behind it. Just thinking about what the vision showed me, the cruelty and pain, it instilled a horror deep inside of me that I couldn't shake.

I knew that I would do anything to stop it, that I would rather burn than let those things be free to cause that terrible pain. I was the one who had heard the call. Whether fate or chance, I would do my part. I didn't know how or where I could even start, but it called to me. I was not a good person. I had spent my life doing things that had made me know that if God existed I would never stand in his grace. This felt like an opportunity. Like a hand reaching out, offering redemption.

If the vision was true, this world was in danger. I didn't know if it had people living in it, but I would find out. If they were here, I had to find them. Outside was a jungle, and I knew that jungles had rivers, and people settled near rivers.

So, first things first, get out of here and find a river. Avoid beasts that wanted to eat my face while doing so. Then follow the river downstream as it was the most likely direction to find a settlement. My eyes were drawn to the mural on the wall, the image of the glowing person high above the armies, shining with light. A champion standing against the monsters. The image inspired hope in my heart.

I took one last look around the area but found nothing else that had survived the age this place had lain untouched. I pulled out one of the two pouches I found and emptied one into my ammo pouch, then I grabbed the crystal and put it inside, tying it around my belt for transport.

With that I climbed out of the room through the crack and back into the ruins. Slowly, I made my way to the corridor then started my way back to the room where I entered. In the distance I could hear the rain falling outside of the ruin. I hoped that by now the big beast that chased me here would be gone. As I reached the room, I suddenly felt something pass through me like electricity. I stumbled, and Saia spoke.

"Statement: Source Weave echo detected."

As quickly as the sensation came, it was gone, and I knew what it was. The skill had activated, I even knew how to use it. It was an unnerving feeling, like I had an extra muscle that I had always had and knew how to move.

"The skill just activated. It's been what, half a day?" I told her. Judging by the fact that I didn't feel like the sun was close to coming out. At least six hours. That seemed like a long time just to change a skill. "Think that we should test it out?" I asked her.

"Feedback: Knowing the limits of engrams is a prerequisite to optimal utilization."

"Is that a yes?"

"Feedback: . . .yes."

"And you couldn't have just said so?" I glanced at the wrist brace.

She didn't respond. I hoped that I hadn't hurt her feelings.

"Can we use it on your drone form? It doesn't hurt you right?" I asked.

"Feedback: The Autonomous Platform is a remote operated part of this Unit. Damage to its structure does not negatively impact this Unit's operations."

I chuckled. It almost felt like she was doing it on purpose.

"Okay, then."

Saia shifted into a hand-sized dragon and stood on the ground in front of me. I took a deep breath, rolled my shoulders, and then reached down to my skill.

On instinct, I activated it for the first time.

[Debilitating Wave]

It rippled out of me, a wave of barely perceivable red energy that expanded in a perfect sphere, growing weaker and fainter the farther it went. It hit Saia next to me and then fizzled out around a meter and a half, two at most, from me.

Saia remained standing, then tilted her head.

"Statement: This Unit detected no interference with the Autonomous Platform."

I frowned. "Maybe because you are bonded to me? Can the skill tell somehow?"

"Feedback: That conclusion is plausible given the information we currently possess."

I tsked. "Well, that was a waste, and now I can't use it again." Somehow I knew that it was unavailable to be used and that it would be available again later. What I couldn't tell was how long the skill was going to be on this cooldown.

"Damn," I started. "I know that I had to see how it worked. I think that we should wait until it becomes available again before going out."

"Statement: Having more tools would be preferable."

We continued walking back to the old room, and once there we sat down near the entrance and waited.

"You know," I started as the silence stretched. "It might be smarter to head out during the day."

Saia looked up at me from my lap. "Query: Based on what parameters?"

"Well, it was at night when I encountered both of the beasts that wanted to eat me. From the way that the first one stalked me and seemingly had no issue seeing in the dark, I assume that it was nocturnal. Heading out during the day might be safer."

"Feedback: This Unit concurs with that conclusion."

"Thanks for the support, Saia." I smiled at the dragon. She was just so cute, even though she was terrifying at the same time. I hadn't yet quite let myself think on what she and her bond to me truly represented. It was easier to ignore it for now. She was obviously not a threat, at least not currently. And I had faith in the **thirst** and its ability to fight off any kind of attempts at a complete takeover. If Saia was to be believed it had already done so once.

A while later, the skill became available again. I sat up straight—it was a weird feeling.

"About an hour then," I said. "That explains why the bear beast didn't use it more than once."

"Statement: Foresight in the use of the engram should be exercised."

I narrowed my eyes at her. "Yeah, yeah."

We waited for the dawn. I felt it coming, and focused on the sensation. It was not something that I had often felt on Earth. The arrival of the sun on Earth was the herald of a dreamless slumber. It was a terrifying thing to me back then. There was no resisting its arrival, I was too young to be able to remain awake during the day. I had waited for the sun with trepidation and even fear. No longer.

The sun rose over the world and the rain passed. I felt my body grow weaker. I sighed and stood up, slowly trying to get accustomed to the new state my body found itself in. It was almost like I was human again, though I wasn't sure just how I would measure up at the moment. Perhaps I was weaker, or maybe slightly stronger due to the Mask.

I checked all my gear one last time, making sure that the vine tying up the glaive to my back was secure, that my belt was tight and the two makeshift daggers were properly secured on my lower back. I checked my knife, pulling it out of its sheath then sliding it back in, I went to click the safety strap but then remembered that this one didn't have it. Saia was back on my arm as a wrist brace—we didn't want to draw more attention, and a silver flying dragon was very attention drawing. I went over my other items, and with everything in its place I set out, squeezing through the narrow crack and out into the jungle. The smell of the passing rain filled my nostrils. Familiar, and yet new. There were scents here that I had never known on Earth.

The ground rumbled: another earthquake. I got low and waited it out as the trees shook and noise rose. Again, as before, the quake was short lived. They really seem to be common in this place. I waited for a bit, listening and watching for any danger. Having lessened senses was a big problem, but it wasn't as if human-like senses were helpless. My eyes still saw very well, especially during the day.

The jungle looked just as terrifying during the day as it did at night. It was obviously old, untouched by any hands. The trees were so tall that they created almost a templelike atmosphere beneath their branches, as if they were a ceiling holding up the sky. The light that passed through the leaves was fragmented, keeping everything beneath in shadow. Vines were everywhere, and purple, blue, and green were the dominant colors of the plants. Some seemed to be like mushrooms, though looking more like cinnamon sticks growing out of the ground. Others were big lotus-like leaves that were rolled into long tubes, some sagging toward the ground from the weight, others leaning on vines.

It was a strange, colorful, and ominous jungle.

I observed for a few more minutes, making sure that it was safe. Seeing and hearing no sign of danger I decided that it was time. I picked a direction that seemed like it was going downhill and started walking, hoping that I would eventually encounter a river. I didn't make more than a dozen steps before I heard it: a scrabbling and scraping sound.

I glanced back and saw a massive beast jump from the top of a small hill. The ruin was covered with earth, buried. The beast looked much like its cub, with blue skin and black stripes, large yellow eyes, an elongated snout, a long neck, and massive claws. It also had something that looked very much like bone growing out of its head, covering its face almost like a skull mask. The white bones grew over the rest of its body too, like some kind of exoskeleton. I didn't allow myself the time to study it. I ran.

I hadn't expected it to be there, I thought that it would have gone away by now. How had it even known? I'd spent so much time in the ruin buried beneath the ground. I cursed myself for not waiting longer. All I could do was run, one glance at the monster that was the size of an elephant and ran much faster than me was enough to convince me of that. It roared, and I felt my body freeze, unable to move as I heard it coming, closer and closer. I reached inside of me and used [Debilitating Wave]. I heard the beast release a sound of confusion and then a crash. The air blasted through my hair as the beast rolled right next to me and smashed into a tree headfirst. Its tail smashed into me and knocked me to the ground. That broke the lock on my body, and I shuffled to my feet, running without turning back to see if the beast had recovered.

I heard it roar, but felt no skill. I heard it stomping after me. I didn't slow for anything. I tried to pick routes in between tightly grown trees, taking turns, and forcing it to go around the thick trees. It was faster than me, but it couldn't navigate the thick parts of the jungle as well as I could, I was smaller. A few times it hit a tree, and I heard the cracking of wood, but I never turned around to check. I had to get back to the ruin, the only safe place I knew of, to hide until I could figure out something.

I jumped over a root and landed on another covered in red moss, it gave beneath my feet, and I tumbled to the ground. I tried to control my fall, but it wasn't enough. I rolled to my feet, but the monster was right behind me, I could hear it. I spun while still on the ground, rising to my knees and pulling the glaive from my back in one smooth move, then it swiped in a wide arc. I caught its snout with the edge of it, drew a tiny gash across the side of it. It snapped back blindly as it shook its head in surprise. The claws caught me across the side of my body, opening up my stomach. I hit the ground and rolled, and looked up weakly.

The monster shook its head, then its eyes lasered in on me.

It opened its mouth and roared, and my body froze, my limbs locked in position. No matter what I tried, I couldn't move. Then, its maw drew close, razor-sharp teeth ready to bite my head off.

I knew in that moment that this was it. I would die without knowing where I was, or what had happened. And I couldn't even close my eyes.

I saw a flash of white-blue light in the corner of my eye, behind the beast, and then I heard something inside my head. It lasted for less than a moment, but in my mind it unraveled as if it was said slowly, with control and with calm.

[Great Slash]

The Meeting

Something had disturbed the jungle more than the earthquakes that had plagued Ish Vimza of late. He knew that something was wrong the moment he saw the dead juvenile ferrorn. There was no monster capable or stupid enough to attack a ferrorn, at least not in the outer ring. Which would mean that one of the inner ring monsters had probably moved its territory, and that was troublesome. He couldn't identify which one though, as he didn't recognize the wounds. He knelt next to the corpse and took a closer look, whispering a silent prayer to the Old Tree for the life that had been robbed of the chance to contribute to the cycle. The juvenile had been drained of blood, and had two of its claws removed. That was curious, but some of those monsters in the inner ring were old and strange, the red plague twisted them in ways that couldn't be predicted.

His camp was in the outer ring precisely because there were no monsters capable of threatening him. Because he could rest and study his findings in peace. A grown ferrorn was equal to a warrior in the Fourth Investment, and was a ruler in the outer ring of the jungle, but it was nothing compared to the monsters that lurked deeper in the blight.

He had to deal with it, the juvenile's mother would be enraged, perhaps enough to attack his camp. And that was not something that he needed. He had research material stored there, artifacts recovered from the ruins of the Ancient Ones. Some were fragile enough that he couldn't risk a ferrorn coming up on them. After all this time the artifacts were heavily infused with the Source, and they would draw a rampaging ferrorn straight to them.

A roar echoed through the jungle, and he turned in its direction, recognizing the [Terror Grasp] of a mature ferrorn female. Had it found the culprit? He wasn't prepared. He was strong, but some of the old monsters that still lurked near the blight curtain were beyond even him. Though, he doubted that something truly dangerous would move so far out. They fed on the rampant Source near the curtain. He gathered himself and moved as light, blurring through the jungle. Perhaps he could deal with both monsters at the same time, spare himself the trouble of hunting them down separately.

He arrived to something completely unexpected. An elf woman running away from a female ferrorn. Slight red coloration of the animal's hide told him that it had been touched by the blight, if not fully corrupted. The elf had a strange brown hair, and darker tawny skin unlike any elf he had ever seen, wearing clothes that he couldn't quite place. She moved with fluidity and grace of an old elf, but she was slow, barely as fast as someone in their First Investment.

Injured? There was no way that anyone that weak would ever dare to come to this wretched jungle. It would be suicide. Nor was there any reason for her to be here in the first place. Was she a mage then? Or some other type that didn't rely on speed? Had someone discovered that he was here, and sent spies or assassins? If she was an assassin, he had to question the sanity of whoever sent her, and she did not seem like a capable spy. She wasn't going to escape it, she had to know that. *Why isn't she wearing her Mask then?*

He watched the monster chase her, and then she turned her head, making her hair swing around. Revealed under the light cast by the errant moons, he saw her clearly. He blinked as details became noticeable; round and small ears, differently shaped, different eyes and facial features. She resembled an elf, but now he could tell that her body was fuller and wider.

He saw the ferrorn catch up to her, saw her stumble as an infected root gave way beneath her weight. Saw her attack with a strange weapon, catching the ferrorn on the snout, and barely managing to make a cut. The ferrorn cut her stomach open in retaliation. It roared again, its [Terror Grasp] freezing the stranger as it went in for a kill.

He weighed his options. She was a stranger in this place, a presence that didn't belong. And he was intrigued enough to want an answer.

He made a decision.

I woke up alert, a pounding in my ears and in my chest. **Feed, kill, drain.** The **thirst** was threatening to overwhelm me, to take over my mind and turn me into a mindless murder machine that cared only for blood. I could smell it, everywhere around me. I glanced down and saw my split stomach was trying to close. At night, it would've already done so, but the sun's light shone above. My body had expended all of its strength to attempt to close it, but that left me ravenous. The **thirst**, weakened by the sun, was raging inside of me, trying to heal and failing, suppressed as it was. There was also a strange itching feeling inside the wound that I couldn't quite place. Regardless, even if it was night, I would've fallen to the **thirst**. An Adult vampire might've been able to shrug off such a wound, but I was still a Fledgling who had barely gotten the reins on my **thirst**. A strange smell assaulted

my nostrils, and it made the **thirst** pound. I glanced up and saw—I remembered—
a strange . . . man? He was standing above me, a couple of steps away. Nine tails
fanned out behind him, black with fiery tips. His hair was shoulder length and
black. On top of his head, he had . . . *are those fox ears?* That nearly made me forget
about the **thirst**. His eyes were slitted, orange, and they were studying me. His features resembled a human, but they were wrong, his nose was longer, more pointed
and it stuck out forward more, his skin was pale blue, almost gray, and his mouth
wider. He looked . . . **tasty. Drain him, kill him, feed on him.**

I shook my head, trying to push the **thirst** back, but I felt weak.

"You heal fast," the man said. And before I could even attempt to try to dis-
sect why I understood him, the **thirst** grew again, fighting for survival.

I hissed and launched myself forward. The man blinked as I flew by him
and landed on the dead monster. I sank my teeth in its throat and drank. Blood
fell on my tongue, and I released a moan of pleasure without meaning to. My
entire body shivered at the taste of it. The blood was still warm, which meant
that I hadn't been unconscious for long. But the blood . . . It was the most savory
blood I had ever drank, so powerful. Almost as powerful as what I felt that day
when I was turned, when my sire shared his blood with me. Its memories flashed
through my mind, but I could barely comprehend them as I struggled with keeping the reins on the **thirst.**

"Ooookkaay then," I heard behind me.

I didn't react, all I could think about was the blood going down my throat.
My chest pulsed, the **thirst** calmed, and I could feel it going back to sleep after
what seemed like hours. Eventually, I felt satiated enough to pull myself together
and lift myself off the corpse. The wound on my stomach closed, and I felt all my
other wounds heal too, all save for the one inflicted by silver around my neck. The
blood was filled with life, with power. But this . . . I had never heard of blood doing
something like this. Healing me all but completely shouldn't have happened. I felt
filled with power, almost as if it was nighttime, as if I was ten times stronger than I
usually was. But, already I could feel the sensation being drained away.

Mask of the Drainer — No Investment; Fourth Carving

I heard the echo inside my head, snapping me out of my reverie. I stood and
turned around, suddenly very conscious of the way I must look. Blood that I
could feel dripping down my chin, my torn clothes soaked in it, again. I didn't
let my thoughts show though. Instead I studied the . . . man? . . . in the same way
that he was studying me.

"That is some skill," he said. I was too shocked to respond. He thought that
me drinking blood, or at least healing fast was a skill. After a moment, he tilted
his head and continued. "Was it a nice . . . meal?"

"You speak Spanish?" I managed to say, too shocked to say anything else.

One of his ears twitched. "Is that a language?" he asked me.

"Yes?" I frowned.

He narrowed his eyes, then started to walk around me, studying me, his eyes going up and down. I kept myself facing him, my hand reaching for the knife at my waist, I didn't know where my glaive was. He saw me reaching and the side of his mouth curled up. The **thirst** was subdued again, but even without it pulsing in my veins, I could tell that he was dangerous. The dead beast was proof enough of it.

"You are not an elf, are you?" he asked after a few seconds of studying me.

I narrowed my eyes, but didn't answer. *An elf?*

"No, you are not," he said when I didn't answer. "Not a Tsu-elf either. What are you? Your clothes are styled in a manner I have not seen before. You speak of a different language, in a world where all speak one."

I hadn't really given it much thought. But now that he mentioned it, what happened with the plaques the first time I went in my inner room. The way that I understood the message in the ruin. The way that I understood him now too. Saia had mentioned signs of magic in me. It had to have something to do with all of this.

"Oh." He stopped, then blinked as if something had occurred to him. "You are an Exemplar. Well, this changes things."

I pushed past my fear. If he hadn't attacked me so far, at least there was a chance that he wasn't hostile. This was what I wanted, to find people and some answers. This was an opportunity, and I had to play it right. "I don't know what an Exemplar is."

His eyes refocused on me, then after a moment of thinking he spoke. "An Exemplar is a person who the Grand Spell brought over to this world, to Kirios, in advance of their world. Meaning, you."

I blinked. The Grand Spell, was he talking about the Last Intent? The message did say that it was a spell. Then something he said registered.

"In advance of my world?" I asked.

He looked at me, then sighed. "We should move back to my camp. The jungle is dangerous. I'll give you your answers there."

I mentally debated whether that was a good idea, but I truly had no choice. I was a stranger in a strange land and had already realized that there was danger here that I couldn't face, not even at night. My goal had always been to find civilization, people that I could talk to. I nodded, agreeing to his offer.

I found my glaive, secured it, then followed the strange man through the jungle. We both stayed silent as we walked, keeping alert of the jungle. I took a moment to study him from behind, his nine foxlike tails were bunched up and trailing behind him, gently swaying as he walked. The ears on top of his head were constantly on a swivel, probably on the lookout for any danger.

I glanced at my wrist. Saia had remained silent, which I was grateful for. I didn't want to reveal too much to a stranger. But also, when I was injured, I felt a strange sensation that worried me. I hoped that Saia was good, but I couldn't ask her in front of the man. I marshaled my thoughts and followed after him, looking forward to some answers.

A Whole New World

We reached the camp after only a few hours of walking through the thick jungle, while it was still daytime. I couldn't help but twitch at any slight sound. The memory of nearly dying was fresh in my mind. I was exhausted mentally; death had been my companion for days now. First the silver around my neck, then all the close calls in this new world. I knew that I had to gather my wits, but it was harder than I thought it would be. My emotions were a mess. I hadn't felt this way since I was turned. I had thought that I had mastered the **thirst** and my emotions years ago.

The camp was located near a massive boulder covered with mosslike plant growth, sitting in the shadow of a massive tree that loomed overhead. There was a small ring of stones, suitable for a campfire, a tent, a chest, and a long rod that was stabbed into the ground. Oh, and it was surrounded by a pale blue sphere of light that pulsed in the same rhythm as the gemstone at the head of the rod. I paused when I saw it. This was magic. Ever since I arrived here I had seen things that were unexplainable, different. I had used a skill, but there was something different about seeing it in such a manner, as proof right in front of my eyes.

"You are invited into my humble camp." He gestured gravely.

I turned my eyes at the man whose name I still didn't know. He was already inside the half-sphere of light, looking at me with one side of his lips turned up in a half grin. For a moment I wondered if he knew what I was, somehow—his words were what someone who believed the stories of vampires might say— though they were mostly nonsense. *No,* I decided, the choice of his words was merely a coincidence.

Still, there was something wicked about the man. He had a look of a scoundrel at times, though the way that he spoke held . . . a gravitas that reminded me of my sire. Slowly, I walked over to the edge of the glowing wall. Then I tentatively reached out with my hand. The moment I touched it, I felt a shiver pass through my body. Then, I walked through, closing my eyes as a strange feeling came over me, raising the hairs on my body.

I shook my head once I got inside and turned to look at the man.

"See," he said. "No reason for concern. Its purpose is to keep most of the smaller denizens of the forest away."

I nodded, as if somehow that made sense. "Thanks, uh . . . I didn't catch your name?"

"That is because I did not offer it," the man said, his eyes twinkling in the moonlight. "Among my people, names are important. Given only to those who are worthy of knowing them. But, you may call me Shimi. It is a common term for those whose name you do not know."

I blinked and tilted my head. "And what are your people exactly? Is this your world?"

He sighed, then gestured for me to join him near a small campfire. He took a seat on a stone and pointed at another for me. I went to take a seat, and then saw the state of my clothes. My pants were ripped and soaked with blood; my tank top was somehow in an even worse state. It was barely hanging on. I was showing a lot more than I was comfortable with.

The man, Shimi, had to have noticed my plight, because he stood and walked up to a chest near the tent and opened it.

"I only have clothes in my size, but I think that they will fit you," he said, then he walked over and offered me black pants and a shirt.

I grimaced. I really wished that I could've washed all of this off first.

"There is a river nearby," he said, again proving his perceptiveness. "I have spares."

I sighed, then took them from his hand, offering murmured thanks as I pulled them on over my ruined clothes. I was not about to take my clothes off in front of him. He didn't comment as I took a seat again. I looked at his strange orange eyes and spoke.

"You said that I was brought here by a spell?" I asked, deciding to get as much information as possible. I only had information known by a messenger that had been dead for a long time. It would be good to learn about what someone from this time thought.

"That is an oversimplification of the facts, but it is ultimately correct. It is the reason that you understand me. When you were brought here, the Grand Spell altered your mind. You are speaking Common, the language that everyone on Kirios speaks. It just feels to you like you are still talking in your native tongue. This is the world of Kirios," he said. "More precisely the continent of Ish Vimza, the Cursed Jungle, the Broken Land, whatever you prefer. The Grand Spell, is the . . . thing, that brought you here. You must remember the transition?"

"I . . ." My mouth opened, and then closed as I tried to marshal my thoughts. I did remember some of it, though the pain of the hanging had made me pass out, so I wasn't quite sure. I mulled over what to say, and then made a decision. "I passed out when the light swallowed me, I remember words flashing in front of my eyes, but then . . . I woke up here," I told him.

"Ah, I wondered why someone would pick Ish Vimza. It is suicide for most, but there must always be one." He chuckled.

I didn't quite understand what he meant by that. Though, I was reminded that he had saved my life. Then, I remembered my manners and my sire's teachings. I bowed my head over my fists. "Thank you for helping me," I said. "I'm Marianna Rojas."

The furry ear on top of his head twitched again. "You are welcome, Marianna Rojas." He looked around, his expression twisting for a split second before returning to the one of calm he had before. "You are in a very dangerous place, Marianna Rojas, and you are not equipped to survive it. You have formed your Mask, I can tell, but you are not even in your First Investment, are you?"

I frowned, hesitating, but then decided that giving that much away shouldn't be too bad. "No, I am not. I don't know anything about Masks really. My world, it is very different, we have nothing like it."

He nodded his head. "A Mask grants you access to the Source. It is a way for you to increase and grow in power, and in the cultures of Kirios a Mask is your life path. Everyone has a Mask, and they give you skills which will help you fulfill the purpose of that path. What Mask a person receives is based on their life prior to gaining it. For people of Kirios, it happens during childhood, though many wait until they are older before choosing one, so that they might get a pick of a Mask that will shape their future better."

I thought about the choices I was given when I got the Mask. They made sense now—each was based on my life before, just as he said.

"There is a lot that you do not know," he continued. "And which will not serve you much at this time. Suffice to say, ages ago, the people who were the original inhabitants of this world—the Ancient Ones—created a Grand Spell. This spell changed the rules of reality and simplified the use of the world's Source through Masks."

"Source?" I asked, feigning ignorance.

"Source." He waved his hand at the pale blue sphere around them. "The Weave, the Way, Magic. I do not know what your people call it."

I looked around, wondering about how to get him to tell me more. "Magic . . . There is no magic on Earth—my world—it only exists in stories."

That made him lean back, a frown on his face. "No Source? How would that even—no, I apologize, my curiosity gets the better of me. That will not help you. Your world is forever changed. The Grand Spell chose it, and that means that soon it will be transported here."

"What do you mean?" I asked, a deep worry starting to open up inside of me.

"You are here ahead of your world," he said slowly. "The Grand Spell picks thirty people from the world it chooses and transports them here. We call these people Exemplars, and you are one. The thirty are scattered across the world. We do not know the reasons as to why, but we know that you will be here for exactly one month. Your world is currently being fully integrated into ours, your landmasses and oceans added to Kirios. And after the month ends, you will be sent back to where you came from. But your world will be changed—it will now be part of Kirios, the Grand Spell will flood it with Source, which will in turn mutate your wildlife, and each member of your race will gain access to Masks as the rest of us. You are here ahead of them to learn, if you survive, that is. Once you return, you will have an advantage over your people, who will have to struggle through a new world unprepared. Your world will have a year of grace period. The Grand Spell will keep your lands in a protective bubble, not allowing other races to visit. Six months in, portals will open, allowing small expeditions; six months later the protections will be lifted, and your world will be fully a part of Kirios."

If what he was saying was true, and with everything that I had learned I had no reason not to believe him, the Earth that I knew was done, over. The vision that I saw was coming true, people of Earth were there at the battle. But even before we got to that point, the Earth's people would be the newcomers here, wholly ignorant compared to the races that were natives. "Why'd it pick us? Do you know? And how many times did this happen before?"

He shrugged. "No one knows. And we call these events the Great Expansion Intervals, and they had occurred six times before, including this one—that we know of at least. The ancient race who started all of this is long gone and dead, so that means that with your people there are now seven worlds and six races on Kirios."

Six races, and a threat somewhere out there, waiting to come and swallow them all.

"How does a Mask grow?" I asked.

"It grows through Investment. All Masks have different Investment requirements, though those that share types have similar ones. What is needed depends on what type of Mask it is," he answered. "A Mask of the Farmer will need farming Investment, a Mask of the Cook will need cooking Investment, a Mask of the Guardsman will need guarding Investment, and so on. It gets more complicated with the complexity of the Mask and what it does. But that should give you an idea. You invest into your Mask, and it gives you power. A Mask grows, and at certain thresholds, it improves both itself and you. Each time it reaches this threshold, it will change slightly in appearance, and your physical or mental capability might improve. These improvements are called Carvings. And every ten Carvings are called an Investment, and that represents a significant evolution of a Mask and an increase in power. As you improve your Mask, you might also get more skills, or you might not. It depends on what you do."

It did. It was basically experience, just tailored for a Mask, or rather a profession, if what he had said about Masks being life paths was true. *They are basically jobs.* Mine was the Mask of the Drainer, and I didn't need to think a lot on what kind of Investment I needed. I had only ever gained Carvings when I drank blood. I wondered why I had only gained one when I drank the blood of the big beast. Compared to other blood I had consumed, this beast had been the most powerful one so far. Others that had been weaker than it had given me more I felt like. *Maybe because I didn't kill it?*

"You have a Mask too then?" I asked, trying to see if I could learn something about the man.

He grinned. "As I said, everyone does in this world. It is as essential to life as breathing." He put his hand over his chest, and then I watched with wide eyes as he *pulled* a Mask out of it. Like out of thin air, it seemed to form in his hand, until at last it was there, held in his fingers. It was beautifully made; the top was blue, smooth as it went around the eyes and forehead, then ending in a dozen points above that almost looked like they were a crown. The bottom below the nose was white, and it had an image of a blue mouth painted on it, curled up into a smile. There were two attachments on the sides, near the ears, almost like earrings latched onto it. One looked like an emerald gem, and the other was black.

I was struck silent for a moment.

"You haven't manifested your Mask yet, have you?"

I blinked. "No, I didn't know that I could do that."

"Put your palm against your chest, focus on your soul space and Mask, then just"—he mimed a grabbing gesture with his hand—"pull it out."

I did as he said, wanting to see if I could do it. I placed my palm against my chest and focused. Immediately, a perfect image of my inner room, the *soul space,* as he had called it appeared in my mind. I focused on the Mask and then just pulled. It wasn't nearly as hard as I thought it would be, though the sensation was weird. One moment my palm was empty, and then I felt the weight of the Mask appearing in it.

It was done in the span of two breaths. In the palm of my hand was a Mask, I immediately noticed the change, another notch on the horns. *It had to be because of the Carving I gained.*

"You did it, congratulations." Shimi inclined his head.

"Thank you," I said.

"It is very unique. I've never seen anything like it," he said as he looked at my Mask. "That is rare, it would mean that it is something really specific. Might

I know what it is?" His face tried to seem nonchalant about it, but I saw a flash of curiosity.

Suddenly, I got a feeling like I had just revealed more than I was supposed to. Caution warred with my gratitude. "Should I tell you?"

One of his ears twitched, and he smiled. "No, you should not." He bowed his head. "Forgive me for asking, curiosity got the better than me."

"It's fine," I said slowly as I put my Mask against my chest and willed it back in. I suppressed the desire to sigh in relief at it working. Shimi kept his eyes on me. Somehow I felt like he knew.

Shimi grinned a wicked smile. "You should not reveal what your Mask is to anyone you do not trust explicitly." His expression turned serious. "At least that is how people in Kirios think about it. Some Masks are easy to identify, both by appearance and the skills that they can use. And there are devices that can reveal your Mask name and skills . . . You are ignorant of so many things. Not knowing how to properly advance your Mask will hurt you, and I can help you with that."

I didn't say anything, I was trying to decide whether I should trust him, debt or no debt.

He sighed and shook his head. "Listen, you are not the only one who was sent here. Other Exemplars have arrived all over the world, they will manifest their own Masks and meet people. Some will die, others will form partnerships or find mentors. This is . . . bigger than you think it is."

It is bigger than you *think it is,* I added in my head. I wondered if he had any knowledge of the vision. I wondered if I should say anything. Kolan Shuk had made a plea, for his warning to be spread, for it to be heard. I wanted to honor it, but I also understood reality. I couldn't afford to appear insane in front of this man, nor did I trust him enough yet to share the message itself.

If fate existed, then this meeting could be fated as well. My life saved by a stranger, in the middle of the jungle. It was hard to believe that it was pure chance.

"So tell me how big it is then," I said, prying for more information.

He looked away for a few seconds, then turned his orange eyes back on me. "Once your world gets fully integrated, a year and a month from now, the entirety of Kirios will flock to your lands. Factions will want to establish their presence, to take resources, to make relationships with your people. New land means new opportunities, it means a chance at wealth, at power. A newly integrated world is wild, rampant with dangers, and that most of all means Investment, a chance to evolve your Mask. They will come."

"There are a lot of my people who will not stand for that," I said. The nations of Earth were not weak. I saw some of what this world has, the power that a Mask offered. I didn't think that they could stand against what Earth had in its arsenal.

"Your world is no longer what you remember it to be. Not many survive the integration. The best survival rate that a race ever had were my kind, the YoKai-ni. Out of billions, only five hundred million survived. Less than twenty percent of our world."

I paused. That didn't seem right. He continued talking, not letting me fully digest what his words meant.

"The Exemplars that survive and return to your lands will . . . some of them will be working with the factions they made contact with. They will have been convinced by them. It has happened before, and some of the Kirios nations know exactly how to entice new arrivals and offer them deals that they will not refuse. When the envoys arrive through the portals, they will endeavor to create foundations for when the protections are lifted."

That sounded a lot more serious than what I imagined. And that was telling, especially with everything else that was going on—now they would have to worry about other races involving themselves.

"And you're about to offer me such one such deal?" I asked him. That made more sense to me. It gave me a reason why he would help me, why he would tell me these things.

"In a way," he said slowly. "I do not involve myself in the worldly affairs, not anymore. But . . . fate put you in my way, so I do feel a tiny bit obligated to give you at least a fighting chance. This place . . ." he waved his hand at the jungle. "It is the harshest continent on our world, filled with dangers that not even the strongest on Kirios would dare face lightly. The fact that you survived until I found you is impressive, but the jungle will swallow you whole if you don't learn and improve your Mask, and do it fast. What you faced so far is nothing but the smallest of the dangers this place holds."

"Oh," I just said. If the monster that nearly killed me was the smallest of the dangers, then I did not want to meet the bigger threats.

Shimi met my eyes, and held them for a long time. "I am interested in your world. Pursuit of knowledge is one of my greatest drives. If you agree, I will help you survive until you are returned to your world, I will teach you how to master your Mask, in return for you sharing the details of your world."

I narrowed my eyes. "You just said that the people of this world will seek to take advantage of us. And you want me to give you information that might help you do that?"

Shimi waved his hand. "That will happen regardless. You are not the only Exemplar, and the others might have already sold their knowledge in return for guidance and power. Not all will know the same things, and some information will be useless, but in return they will have secured power of their own. They will make deals and plans for when your lands arrive, they will return there as warlords, gathering up your people and guiding them. In the aftermath of the integration they will emerge as leaders of your kind. It is not us you need to be worried about; it is your own kind. I have never known a race that was not plagued with greed. It is inevitable that some of your own will sell your lands, secrets, and people in return for power. Mask evolution is an intoxicating thing."

I opened my mouth to rebut his words, but then quickly closed them. Oh yes, I knew what lengths people could go to. If what he said was the truth, if the world was about to end, yes, some would rise and try to grab as much power as they possibly could.

"So you don't really need me?"

"It would save me time, and having to interact with other people," Shimi answered with honesty, at least I believed it to be.

"Are there any settlements, any cities nearby where we could be safe?" I asked, more as a way to buy time to think.

He shook his head. "There are no cities on Ish Vimza, only the ruins of the Ancient Ones long since scoured clean. No one sane comes here—it is filled with beasts stronger than most average Masked, and those are just the beasts in the outer circle. The inner circle holds monsters—beasts corrupted by the blight storm coming from the center."

I blinked. *Blight, storm, monsters?* That sounded like what I had seen in the vision. "Is this connected to the big cloud curtain that I saw in the distance?"

Shimi nodded. "The Blight Curtain, or the blight storm, yes. It is the center of the continent, the barrier preventing anyone from entering what most believe to be the location of the Grand Spell's anchor. The last time someone tried to breach it, the result was destruction of one-third of the Ish Vimza continent and a wave of blight that turned nearly half of all animals in the world into monsters and created the blighted, causing the breakdown of civilization that we are yet to recover from five thousand years later. We call that period the Blight War."

Five thousand years? It sounded like it could be related, but that long? The vision seemed different to me somehow. I asked him how long the curtain had been there.

"Always," was his answer. "It has been there since before the Elves arrived and found Ish Vimza, nearly twenty thousand years ago."

Twenty thousand years? That was longer than the modern human history. Suddenly I was very worried about Earth. I was making assumptions. I hadn't seen anything about the people that lived here. I had fallen into a trap of thinking of this like a game, a fantasy setting where people had magic but were primitive. I should be a lot smarter.

Was it already too late? Was the threat over with? Was the vision not an accurate depiction of events but an allegory? I hated not knowing, and not being able to find out. On Earth, I could type a few words in a search engine and find answers to most questions. Here I had to play a game with the people living here, balancing risk and reward.

I had to know more. "What exactly is a monster?"

"Animals corrupted by the blight are called such. People corrupted are usually called blighted. Those affected have an aura of the blight on them, though not all can feel it. Red Source twists around them. The mature ferrorn had some signs of it, though nowhere near enough to actually turn it fully. If it had ventured closer to the curtain it would've turned eventually. The blight first appeared in the event I described before, we call it the Breaking. So far, the blight is the most dangerous in the inner ring of the continent, but it is spreading, growing year after year, though very slowly. It has barely moved in the last thousand years. Most of the animals here are at least somewhat affected, but they do not become monsters until it fully takes them. A blighted animal, or a monster, is more aggressive, more powerful for its Investment. Sometimes it is driven insane, and it carries the blight with it that infects the Source around them, which in turn can corrupt those in their presence if they are not powerful enough. Monsters usually live much longer, which makes those that survive the blight far more dangerous because they tend to be old and experienced."

Was that what the threat was? These people seemed to have been in conflict with these things for thousands of years.

"So, avoid monsters," I said.

"Yes," Shimi said. "I am worried that something may have disturbed the inner ring, which made the monsters start to migrate out of it. The ferrorn female would never have left a juvenile unattended if a threat had not encroached on its territory. A power shift in the monster hierarchy is the most likely explanation."

"The earthquakes, could they be a cause?"

He shook his head immediately. "No, those are common and have been for thousands of years. Ish Vimza has been unstable since the Breaking."

"So, what now?" I asked. I figured that I shouldn't push it with the questions now. He would be expecting something in return. I had to think on what I could reveal.

"First, we should probably rest," Shimi said. "Nightfall is approaching fast."

"Ah," I started, trying to think about how much I should reveal. There would be no hiding what would happen soon. Right now, my body felt slow, weak, uncoordinated. When the sun set, I would gain my vampire power back. Just the way I moved would be different. He would notice. "About that. I am nocturnal, you could say."

He blinked at that. "Oh?"

"Yes, I don't rest at night, in most cases," I added.

He could tell that I was holding back, I wasn't that good at obscuring the fact. It was why I mostly tried to not even mention anything. He didn't press. Instead he switched topics.

Shimi stood up suddenly. "Well, if you do not need to rest, perhaps now would be a good time to visit the river. I am sure that you want to get all that washed off you. Or wait, is this a . . . whatever-you-are thing? Do you . . . paint yourselves with blood?"

I glared. "No, we don't! Not intentionally—well, once, but not usually!" I shook my head, as I felt a blush coming up my neck. "River would be great," I whispered. Then, because he had shared information without getting any in return, I added. "And my kind are called vampires."

A New Day

The night fell as we walked to the river. I paused and let the feeling pass over me, relishing in the return to my full strength. The pain around my neck flared, a reminder that the silver inflicted wound had yet to fully heal. My other wounds, though, had recovered, in part because of the blood of the mature *fer-rorn* as Shimi had called it, for which I was grateful.

"You well?" Shimi asked.

I nodded my head. "Yes," I whispered. "Much better."

He didn't question me further. We continued through the jungle.

The trip to the river was uneventful, though I had to hold myself back from twitching every time I heard a strange rustle in the distance. And the sounds of the birds, or what I assumed were birds at least. Some sounded like the wailing of the damned, if such a thing had a sound. Others were close to what one might encounter on Earth, yet also distinctly not. Most sounds had a deeper tone to them that grated on my ears. I could hear in a range that was lower than what a human could, and the last few days had me experiencing a whole array of new sensations. Not just sounds, but new smells, even colors. The jungle was as such an assault on the senses that I almost had to consciously focus on not getting overwhelmed.

But I still couldn't help but twitch at unfamiliar sounds. Almost dying does do that to you—almost dying three times in just as many days at that. I heard the river before we reached it. The two of us stepped from among the trees to see a beautiful waterfall, with a small pool and the river flowing out of it. The water reflected the two moons from above, one blue and one red, giving the water a strange mix of the two colors. It was a heavenly and beautiful scene.

"You should hurry," Shimi said. "There are predators around."

"Is there anything in the water?" I asked, looking at it askance.

He glanced at it, and his right ear twitched. "Nothing that should worry you."

That was . . . an acceptable answer; it wasn't like I had much of a choice. I wanted to be clean. I grabbed the hem of my shirt, and then paused.

"Can I get some privacy, please?"

He met my eyes, then looked around, his ears turning around independent of each other, which was both adorable and weird at the same time. "It is dangerous, but . . . I will be nearby."

I blinked and he was gone.

"Okaaaay," I said. He was definitely a lot faster than I thought. Which worried me again. He was faster than a vampire—my eyes couldn't even track him. I looked around and saw no signs of him. Though, for all I knew, he hid himself and was looking anyway. Not that I could do anything about it. I decided to risk it.

I pulled my clothes off, then entered the water. I submerged and sighed in contentment as the cold water washed over me. A vampire didn't feel the cold in the same way that a human did. Our blood was different, and we didn't require a certain temperature to function properly, so temperature was mostly an abstract sensation. I emerged from my dive and pulled the hair out of my face. It was long, just past my shoulders, and I made a mental note to shorten it a bit. I rubbed my body, scraping the blood with my nails, wincing when I got to my neck where I could feel the scars. Silver was the only thing that left scars on a vampire's body, that and we still kept the scars we had from before we were turned. I had two bullet scars from before, one on my upper left thigh and one on my stomach. Now, I had a new scar to add to the collection, a burn ring around my neck. I grimaced when I brushed my fingers along it, as it was still sore to the touch. It would take a while for it to fully heal, but I wish I knew how long.

I pulled my hands back, and focused on the rest of my body, trying to hurry the process up. I didn't want to stay in the water for longer than was necessary. I didn't know what else was out there, and even with Shimi around I wasn't convinced that we were perfectly safe. Still, once I figured that my show of bathing was enough, I brought my wrist close to my head and whispered in a barely audible tone.

"Saia, you there?"

"Feedback: Affirmative," she replied in the same manner, her voice barely audible even to my ears.

I sighed in relief. "I want to have a chat, but for now please stay quiet. Monitor our surroundings for any threats, and if Shimi tries anything warn me or just attack if you see an opportunity."

"Feedback: Understood."

I submerged once more, then walked out of the pool. I twisted my hair, draining as much of the moisture as possible, and then jumped from foot to foot quickly, shaking as much of the water off my body as I could. I walked over and realized that there was a second set of pants and a dry shirt next to the ones that I had taken off. Shimi had to have put them there. I won't say that my first thought was that he was spying on me, because it wasn't. I was worried that he heard my conversation with Saia, though.

There was nothing that I could do if he had, so I focused on my second thought. Which was about just how fast and stealthy he had to be in order for me not to detect him. My hearing was extremely sharp. I put the clothes on. My old garments were ripped and useless, I bunched them up and took them with me. No way was I leaving my scent around for animals to get a good sniff at.

Before I even tried to call out, he was there, standing in front of me. That sent a chill down my spine. I was used to seeing people coming long before they could become a threat.

"We should head back," Shimi said. "The deeper the night gets, the more beasts come out that we really do not want to encounter right now."

I nodded my head, understanding. There wasn't much that I could say to that. Together, we started making our way back to his camp.

"So," he started. "I see that I have misjudged you. You are much stronger during the night. Is it a skill or is this unique to your kind?"

I was still not quite sure if that was information that I should share. He hadn't even offered to tell me what he was. "Is that important to know?"

He glanced over his shoulder at me, but then turned back and spoke. "If I am to help you survive this place, I need to know as much as you are comfortable with sharing. I understand that we are strangers, and that it is only natural for you to be reticent. Right now, I can tell that you are strong and fast from the way you move. Very few races that arrive on Kirios are as strong as you are. As an Exemplar you cannot have already gotten more than a few Carvings at best. That means that your physical capabilities are your advantage. At the moment, based on your physical strength and healing, I would put you on an equal level as a combat focused Masked in their Second Investment. Though of course, you don't have the skills that they do, so that means that you probably would not be much of a challenge for someone who knew what they were doing. And each race has its own advantages and disadvantages. Naga-shan live underwater and never stop growing for as long as they live. Dwarves are masters of stone and have an almost perfect sense of the earth."

Naga-shan? Dwarves? I guess that this truly was a different world. Not that a hundred other things hadn't already convinced me.

"Your strength will help you survive in this place, but only if you are smart, and if you stay with me. Alone, you will die, despite your advantage."

The way he said it in a tone that broached no disagreement stung a bit. But I understood what he was trying to illustrate for me. I knew nothing of this world. And I had a mission to accomplish. The revolting sense of despair that the vision instilled in me was still there. I had to survive, learn more, then make decisions to prevent what I saw from happening.

"I know that Investment means more power, but what is it really?"

"Investment is . . . a measure of one's life you could say. People spend their entire lives improving their Masks and with them their lives. A Second Investment Farmer would be able to do more than one in their First Investment, and so they would be able to produce more, bring more income. Have a better life. It stays true for every type of Mask. Combat Masks enter into the service of nobles or rulers, merchants or mercenary bands. The higher their Investment, the more valuable they are. Higher Investment also means more capstone skills, which are defining skills per the Investment tier. Very powerful skills. But for most people reaching Third Investment is an achievement of a lifetime."

"A lifetime . . ." I wondered how my life would look now. This Earth-shattering event had freed me, in a way. It saved my life and gave me an opportunity to do anything that I wanted. The cartel had attempted to execute me, would've succeeded if not for what happened. They had severed the bonds that tied us together, at least in my opinion. "I understand," I said slowly. "I have only one skill," I told him. "It is an active skill and not tied to any of my physical attributes."

That much I felt I could reveal, for now at least.

Shimi glanced back, then nodded. "I hope that you will be willing to share at least what kind of Investment your Mask requires. It would help me know how to best help you."

I was still not quite sure if that was information that I should share. I wondered if he was genuine, or if he was just prying. He hadn't even offered to tell me what his was. "Why is it so important?"

He glanced over his shoulder at me, but then turned back and spoke. "As I said before, the type of Mask you have might mean the difference between a life of wealth or one of struggling. Some people do not share their Masks because if you know what someone's Mask is, you might also know what skills they have. And what they need to do in order to advance. Masks have been around for forever—most of them have been cataloged and the best ways of progressing them discovered. People with the same Mask might have different skills, but they will all draw from the same pool—in most cases. There are exceptions to all rules. There are rules about revealing your Mask, but for most it is inevitable. Just by living their life, it will become known, though the exact name might not be revealed. A Mask evolves as it grows. A Mask of the Farmer might eventually become the Mask of Pestilence Immune Crop Farmer. You see, details matter— the name would tell someone what the Mask could do. You do not need to tell me the name of your Mask, but knowing how you gain Investment would help me a lot."

Well, I was not a farmer material. "And you aren't going to tell me what your Mask is?"

"I shall tell you how I gain Investment, though that alone puts me at risk. Our entire society revolves around our Masks. They are a sign of prestige. You may reveal your type, rather that is easily discovered just by seeing what someone's Mask looks like. But the name? That is a different story; the exact name can tell someone a lot more than just knowing that you have a warrior-type Mask. To you, the name of my Mask would not mean a lot. You don't have the knowledge for it to even make sense. But eventually, if you survive and leave this place, if you reach your lands and live until they are fully integrated. Then, you will meet people that come from various parts of Kirios. And the name of my Mask would mean a lot to them."

"Why would I just reveal it? I've no reason to. I don't even know who you are."

"True, the risk is minuscule," he told her, then glanced back over his shoulder. "But I did not get to be as old and as powerful as I am by taking risks that I did not need to."

I tilted my head. "And how old are you exactly?"

"Old." He chuckled.

He didn't look it, nor did he really act it. There was a mischievous air about him, though yes, he did tend to speak a bit slower and more formal. But I didn't know anything about him or his people, so I couldn't tell what old meant in his context. Even on Earth, old was a matter of perspective. The Master of the cartel was hundreds of years old, an Elder Vampire, but there are those who are far older than him. There were only a very few Ancient Vampires left in the world, but they had seen empires rise and fall.

"What're you actually? Your people, race, if you can tell me that much?"

He paused, and then started to talk. "To most of the world, I am a YoKai-ni, that is the name used to refer to the three races that arrived to Kirios together from the same world called Asha Kai-ni. Three races, though the YoKai-ni races are not closely related."

That surprised me. "Really? Three completely separate intelligent races evolved on the same world?" Earth had the same, except that all three races were in fact related.

"Well, intelligent is still a matter of some debate." He chuckled.

I frowned.

"Apologies, that was an . . . inside joke, in bad taste, and not a very good one at that." He shook his head. "I have been away from people for too long. Regardless. Three races, the Oni-yi, the Kitsu-oi, and the Tengu-gi. Each different, and each with its own strengths and weaknesses. I am a child of a Kitsu-oi and a Tengu-gi, most people call those like me Tsu-gi, or if you wish to insult me, then Oiyi-gi."

"Wait," I started. "Didn't you say that your races were completely different, how . . ."

"Kitsu-oi can have children with any race on Kirios. They are sexless, but most people refer to them as female as that is how they most often appear. They can . . . mold their body in between the two. They actually prefer to mate with other races, and not with their own kind, and only one in five children born are pure blood Kitsu-oi; the rest are hybrids such as me."

"Are such hybrids common?" I asked, hoping that I wasn't being too intrusive, but it was interesting.

"They are, mostly they live among their father races, since Kitsu-oi are solitary people. Though they are not always accepted, based on where they are."

Suddenly, he paused, his ears swiveling.

"What is—" I froze, as I heard it too.

Before I could react, his arm came up and pushed me away with a strength that surprised me. I flew and hit the tree behind me, the impact making me lose my breath and sight for a moment. I fell to the ground and by the time I opened my eyes again, I saw a monster.

A massive beast had caught Shimi around the torso in its jaws. It looked like a blue alligator, or an ancestor of one, with bone spikes coming out of its back. It shook its head, as Shimi grunted. Something flashed in his hand, and then there was a burst of red light, and an exchange that was too fast for me to see.

[Mist Mirror; Quick Slash]

The beast was dead, its head cut from its shoulders.

I stood as Shimi untangled himself from its jaws, revealing massive puncture wounds all over his chest and stomach. His clothes were ruined.

"Blight take it!" He cursed, then turned to look at me, his expression pained. "I guess that I am going to be the one needing help." His face changed as he spoke, and then he grinned at me. But in his eyes, I saw something that I hadn't seen in him since the moment we met: fear.

The wounds on Shimi's torso were deep. I saw his pink blood flowing slowly out of the puncture wounds. I ran over quickly and knelt down next to him. As I leaned closer, I could see something black and sickly all around the wounds. The scent of his blood hit me hard, I could feel the **thirst** rearing its head from deep within me. I pushed it away as my training took over and I reached for the water gourd at his waist.

"Blights," Shimi whispered as I pulled his shirt up and poured water over the wounds, trying to clean the stuff out. He sucked in a breath and winced. "It caught me off guard."

"Can you walk?" I asked. "I need to clean the wounds, bandage them. You must have medical supplies back at the camp?"

Shimi looked above my head. "I got reckless," he said.

He wasn't listening to me, and his eyes were losing focus. I cursed as I glanced back at his wounds, then turned back at the corpse of the monster. Was it poisonous? Was that what the black stuff was?

"A blighted Sixth Investment monster ambushed me . . . ashes under the Old Tree . . . I must be getting too old."

"Hey." I snapped my fingers in front of his eyes. He blinked, then looked up at me. "Focus, we need to get back to the camp."

The power that I had just seen, that monster . . . I was convinced now of his words. I couldn't survive in this place alone, not even at night. I was out of my depth, ignorant of the rules. I had to keep him alive. I wondered if I could go and search for medical supplies back at the camp, but . . . I didn't want to risk another monster finding him like this. I reached down and put my arm beneath his armpit, then pulled him up.

"*Hijueputa*," I bit out as he leaned his full weight on me. He wasn't that heavy, but he was bigger than me.

I glanced at the corpse of the monster, the blue blood drawing my eyes. I felt a pang of the **thirst**, but I pushed it away again. Turning my head, I pointed us in the direction of the camp and started walking, focusing on keeping Shimi upright. His bleeding had slowed, which was the only reason I decided to risk having him walk. But I did not like the vacant look in his eyes.

"What was it doing here?" he whispered, almost slurring his words. "Reapers don't come this far out of the inner ring."

His words started to lose meaning, and I ignored his ramblings. I kept my eyes and mind focused on getting us to camp.

I didn't know how long it took us to reach the camp, I just hoped that it wasn't too late. By the time I put him down on a cot next to the fireplace and somehow managed to push his nine tails out of the way so that he could lie comfortably, he lost consciousness, and was burning up. I scrambled to the chest next to the tent, opening it up and looking through it. Most of the things inside were spare clothes, some water gourds, and things that I couldn't identify. I left the chest and entered the tent. Inside was a small bed frame, missing the bedding— I assumed that he had moved the cot to the outside. There were two chests nestled in a corner, and a rack with weapons in another. I took note of the unfamiliar looking weapons but turned my attention to the two chests.

I opened the first one and found writing supplies and books. Without digging too deep I turned to the other one. This one had vials filled with liquids of different colors. That was a lot more promising, I pulled a few out and looked at the labels. Each was labeled with an image.

One was an open eye, which I dismissed immediately. It implied to me something that would keep the person who drank it awake. Another was a droplet, which I put aside since I didn't know what exactly it could mean. The last was a curved line, thicker on one and narrow on the other. I squinted and decided that it did look a bit like a fang. Did that mean poison? Shimi didn't seem like someone who would come to a place like this unprepared for it. Having an antidote readily available would make sense. I searched through the chest some more, making sure that there were no vials with any other type of symbols. I found a small box that had what I assumed was a weird sewing kit, and clean bandages.

I took the box and one of the vials then went back to Shimi. He was shaking, and sweating a vile black substance. I had no way of knowing if that was what his sweat normally looked like or if it was a side effect of the wound. I took one piece of a clean bandage, ripped a chunk of it, and then poured water over it. Then, I knelt down and cleaned his chest, then rolled him to his side and did the same for his back. I poured water and cleaned the wounds again, noting that the wounds had pulsing black vein-like webs around the edges. His blood was pink, so I assumed that was something that came from the monster. I opened the vial that had what looked like a fang on it and sniffed at the clear liquid. Its scent was alien to me, and I couldn't tell if it was foul or not. I glanced back at Shimi and tried to decide what to do.

"Hey, Shimi?" I slapped his cheek gently, trying to have him wake up and ask him what to do. He only murmured something too softly for me to hear.

"Saia," I whispered. "Could you help him somehow?"

"Feedback: Unlikely, unknown physiology."

I looked at the pulsing wounds and made a decision.

I uncorked the vial and poured a little of it down his throat, then watched him for any kind of signs. After a while of nothing happening I gave him some more. He seemed like he had calmed down, and I used thread and a strange spiral needle to close his wounds before bandaging them. Once I was finished, I walked a few steps back and fell on my behind, feeling mentally exhausted. I sat and watched him through the night, praying that he survived.

We're Fucked

I kept watch all through the night, until the sun rose, then through the next day. I was worried there for a bit and had to feed him the potion two more times. But as the sun set again I was convinced that his state wasn't deteriorating. I sucked in a breath as a shiver of the setting sun ran through me. My strength returned, my world sharpened, all was well again. I pushed myself out and got up from my place across from Shimi, walking over and kneeling next to him. He was still sweaty and shivering. I jumped into motion. I found a blanket in his tent, then I wiped the sweat off and covered him. I made him drink some water, and then I made a small fire. The night was colder than the day in this place. I didn't know how smart it was to build a fire, but the campsite had a fireplace so I assumed that the magic around the camp would somehow make it less likely to be seen—or something.

After I was finished, I realized that the gourd was empty, and we had no water. I debated for a few moments, and then decided that we couldn't go without it. I needed it to clean his wounds, and with how much he was sweating he could get dehydrated.

I grimaced, then gathered my weapons and prepared to head out. I rummaged through the chest outside until I found something resembling a backpack, and I filled it with water gourds. The gourds themselves were wood, I was pretty sure.

With one last glance at Shimi I left the safety of the camp. I ran through the forest, heading back to the river.

"Saia," I started as I ran. "Back there, when that monster injured me. You did something, didn't you?" I asked. I had been going over it for the last day while watching Shimi. It was daylight; I shouldn't have been able to heal at all.

"Feedback: Affirmative, after the failure of the [Plasma Shot] engram, this Unit has expanded the engram categories with priority for reconstruction. With the failure of combat engram's functionality they have been replaced in favor of support ones. Once injured, the [Repair] engram activated, sending pieces of the biostructural mass through the Host's bloodstream in order to aid in the biosystem's repair. The effectiveness was at sub 5%, the synchronization rate between this Unit and the Host is currently too low for the use of the engram at its full capacity."

"Well, I think that it saved my life," I told her. "It kept me alive for long enough to get blood, and kick-start the **thirst's** regeneration. Thank you."

"Feedback: Survival of the Host is required for the survival of this Unit."

I chuckled. "What do you think about what Shimi told me, about Masks and everything else?"

"Feedback: The information matches what this Unit has observed. Source increases within Host detected with every kill and blood ingestion. This matches the information provided by the Shimi individual, and his explanations of Investment. The Grand Spell's actions in salvaging other worlds and their populations likewise matches what the Host and this Unit have experienced."

I nodded. Things were starting to make more sense. I was brought here ahead of my world, with Earth soon to follow, in a way that would change it forever. I didn't know how much I trusted what Shimi said would happen, but I had to act as if it was the truth. My main goal was survival, and that had not changed, only now I knew that I had to survive for thirty days in order to get back on familiar ground. Less than that by now.

But while survival was the most important, I need to figure out the threat that I witnessed in the vision. I had to learn more about the blight that Shimi spoke about.

I continued walking, carefully watching the looming jungle above me. It unnerved me, the way that it looked like it was a jungle on the scale of giants. The trees reminded me a bit of giant redwoods, if they were three times as thick and half as much tall. The branches spread wider, intermingling with those of other trees to create a thick canopy that resembled a thick lightning spreading in all directions. There was a weight all around me that oppressed with the sheer size. The jungle was old, I knew now. It probably had something to do with that as well.

I looked up, wishing that I could see the two moons above. I had always liked gazing at the moon on Earth. With the sun denied to me, it was the closest thing I could get to it, seeing its reflected light. The two moons on this world were just as beautiful, I wished that I had the time to properly look at them.

In what seemed no time at all, I came upon the corpse of the monster that Shimi had killed. It looked like a blue crocodile the size of a car, with longer limbs and sharklike teeth. Its hide was rough, appearing to me almost like a turtle shell, one that was a lot more flexible. I paused as the scent of blood reached my nostrils. It sang of power, and I knew that it had to be depleting fast. The longer the blood stayed dead, the less useful it would be, and I was hungry. I knelt next to it and pulled one of its limbs up, then I bit down.

I frowned as I felt the tough skin repel my teeth. That had never happened before. I tried to bite harder, but the result was the same. With a frown, I pulled out a gourd and walked around to the wound on the neck. The blood had pooled on the ground, but I rolled the monster around and squeezed some more blood into the gourd. I couldn't get much, but what I did get, I downed immediately. The thick liquid poured down my throat, the slight stale taste barely there. I felt power, but its memories flashing through my head were too disconnected for me to get any useful information, as the monster was dead. Then, I felt something deep inside of me, in my chest.

Mask of the Drainer — No Investment; Sixth Carving [Empty Slot] skill gained.

A new skill, another [Empty Slot], I smiled, but then thought more about it. I had gained another Carving, two this time. I tried to figure out why I gained two now. The young ferrorn I killed when I arrived had been before I gained a Mask. The monkeys had raised my Carving by one too. The bearlike beast had given me one as well. Then came the mature ferrorn, which gave me my fourth, and then this one, my sixth. Was there some logic there that I wasn't seeing? The most obvious thing that I could think of was that the power of the blood mattered. The young ferrorn and the monkeys had been either relatively equal or weaker than me. The bearlike thing I fought was stronger, but it was ultimately an animal, and I had weapons and Saia. The mature ferrorn was beyond me, and I drank its blood after it was dead, killed by someone else, this other creature— the reaper—was the same. I didn't kill either of them, but they were according to Shimi a lot stronger than me. Fourth and Sixth Investment compared to me, who had none yet.

It sounded right to me.

Still, the new skill would help me greatly, I resolved to slot in a new one once I returned to Shimi.

"Saia, you want to consume it?" I pointed at the corpse.

"Feedback: Affirmative."

She surged from my wrist and turned into goo falling onto the corpse. I saw her moving over the corpse, but saw no black smoke rising. Then, after a few seconds she flowed to the ground into her dragon shape.

"Statement: This Unit is not able to consume this biomatter."

I frowned. "Why?"

"Feedback: Biomatter's structural integrity too great to be taken apart."

I narrowed my eyes, remembering not being able to bite through the skin. I pulled out my knife and leaned it on the corpse, trying to stab. After a few unsuccessful tries I pulled back and looked at Saia.

"I guess that Investment does more than we thought," I said. I couldn't imagine what would've happened if this beast had attacked me. If I couldn't even scratch it . . .

Well, there was nothing for us to do here it seemed. Saia moved back to my wrist, and we continued on to the river.

I returned quickly after I filled the gourds, and thankfully without any trouble. Once I was close enough to the protective spell, I paused. I could see into it, see the low fire burning as I had left it. What I couldn't do was hear it. As I passed through, the sound of crackling wood immediately reached my ears. *Good to know that it blocks out sound,* I thought to myself. I didn't know how the spell worked, but Shimi had said that it would keep most things around us away. I walked into camp, my eyes seeking Shimi.

I found him where I left him, and saw that his eyes were open, staring at the canopy above them.

"You are alive." I sighed in relief.

"Surprisingly," Shimi said. "I should not be. The reaper's bite is venomous. Few survive it, even those on my Investment level. And those that do often wish that they had not."

"I gave you what I thought was an antidote—"

"You did well," Shimi said, his eyes still on the canopy. "You used the one marked with the fang, yes?"

I nodded. "Yes."

"It might have helped." Shimi turned to meet my eyes. "I am sorry, I made a mistake, and both of us will suffer for it."

"You're alive, that's all that matters," I told him.

He shook his head. "I survived, my body fought the venom off, but . . . this will weaken me for months, years even. I cannot protect us against what is out there anymore. A ferrorn like the one I rescued you from could kill me with ease now. That reaper was not supposed to be there, and if other monsters from the inner ring are now leaving it . . . We cannot survive a single encounter with them."

There was a finality to his words, a sense of giving up.

I had faced certain death several times over the last few days. Like him, I had accepted it, and yet I still lived. *No,* I said to myself, *I am not going to die here.* I was finally free to find my path. I was not going to have it cut short before I discovered all that I could be.

"I'm not going to die in this godforsaken place, you hear me, *hijueputa?*"

Shimi's lip curled into a weak and sad smile. "Tenacity, it can often get you far. But not here, not now. I regret that you have been dealt such a fate."

I flashed back to the vision. There was a darkness prepared by fate already. Perhaps what I had seen wouldn't happen for a thousand years; perhaps it would come to pass tomorrow. I wouldn't let him or a message from a dead race force me to live in fear as before. It coalesced for me: I would struggle, I would survive. Vampires always did.

"Fuck your *sorry*." I walked up to him, then loomed over, glaring at him. "I said that I wasn't going to die here, and I won't. If you can't keep us safe, then you're going to help me do it for the both of us."

Shimi closed his eyes. "Perhaps if we were anywhere else, but . . . you are not even on your First Investment, no matter what your natural gifts are . . . the gap is just too wide."

"Then I'll get stronger," I said.

Shimi opened his eyes and looked up at the faint light of the two moons above them barely peering through, one red and the other blue. "If only Masks improved with such ease. Investment is an effort of years Marianna, and no matter what kind of a Mask you have, you will have a hard time investing in it in this place."

"You don't know how my Mask improves; you don't know what my Mask is at all."

He turned his head to meet my eyes but didn't speak.

I had struggled with trusting this stranger, even with him saving my life. But he was hurt because he saved me again—he pushed me out of the way. He had not even mentioned it, that I was the reason he was hurt. I was certain that without me none of this would've happened to him. I might not trust him enough yet to speak on what I had seen in the ruin, but I knew that if I was going to survive, I would need to trust him, at least a little.

"My Mask is the **Mask of the Drainer**," I told him.

He frowned, his vacant eyes clearing a bit as he turned to meet my gaze. "**Mask of the Drainer?**" he asked. "I am unfamiliar with that. What does it do?"

I looked at him, and decided that I needed to snap him out of the depressed state he had fallen into. "I have two skill slots that I can switch out. I gain Investment from drinking blood, which I need to live as all vampires do. I get skills from the blood I consume: a room appears in my inner room—what you called soul space—where a copy of the blood source can be found. I need to kill them in there in order to gain a skill from them. I don't know if the skills I get are random or if there is some logic behind it. Right now, I have [Lesser Strength], [Debilitating Wave], and [Lesser Leap]. I have No Investment; Sixth Carving."

He frowned. "Sixth Carving already? You couldn't have been here for more than a couple of days."

I nodded. "I don't know what is considered normal. And I drank the blood of that beast you killed, the reaper."

"That certainly isn't normal, not in normal circumstances. Perhaps for a very specific Mask in a very specific situations. A soldier in active war, fighting where the conflict was the greatest, against enormous odds and surviving would perhaps see such growth." He tried to sit up and grimaced. I leaned down and helped him sit up.

"I think that I know why," he said, looking up at me. "You are too weak for the threats here, and all of the blood you drank probably has been so far above you in Investment. The reaper alone is in the peak of the Investments of all the Masked in the world. The difference between you probably netted you more Investment. That will lessen as you gain power and if you fight monsters near your own Investment."

That made sense, I had already suspected as much.

"Your Mask, it probably works like some Mage Masks, maybe like an Invoker. They have never been properly documented. A pure Invoker Mask is hard to advance, and there have never been enough successful Invokers for that Mask to be properly documented and researched. And those that do know guard their knowledge. I have heard stories though, they have ritual skills that let them draw skills from others, from animals, elementals, even people. I assume that your race's peculiarity made it like what it is."

He looked down at his bandaged chest, then up at me.

"I didn't," I said before he could ask.

"But you could if you wanted to?" He tilted his head. I didn't know what he was thinking, his expression was too even.

I decided not to lie about that. I nodded. "Vampires feed mostly on the blood of humans, another race on my world. I have no evidence to believe that yours wouldn't work." If its scent was anything to go by, his was definitely the most powerful I had encountered so far.

"Do you need to kill in order to feed?" he asked.

I shook my head. "No, we usually only need a glassful every few days. Long ago, it would happen. Vampires would hunt and kill their victims in order to feed. Nowadays we have blood banks, and most of us drink donated blood."

He held my gaze, then nodded. "Thank you for telling me."

He seemed to have heard the truth in my words. There was one other thing that I wanted to ask him about. I described what happened the last time I fought for a skill. How I felt the injury even after I left that place.

He grimaced. "Everyone's soul space is different. It is shaped by who we are and what our Mask is. While that place might be of the soul, it is real. I have heard stories of some Invokers being found unresponsive, their eyes blankly staring into nothingness after their ritual skills. They die sometime after being befallen by such a fate. I am going to assume that like you they had to do something in order to secure the skill. It would not be wrong to assume that if you die in your soul space, you will most likely die in the real world too."

I gulped. That was good to know. I had to be a lot more careful, and should probably make sure that I was ready before I tried to enter rooms with monsters that I hadn't killed myself.

"Your skills though," he started. "Yes, that can work. It is going to be hard, probably the hardest thing you have ever done. But if you agree to do as I say, perhaps the both of us can survive this."

My expression turned grim; I understood the gravity of the situation. "I promise to do everything in my power to make that happen," I told him.

He closed his eyes, then nodded. "And I pledge to do all in my power to make you stronger, to help you survive."

There was an understanding between the two of us, I could see it in his eyes. A promise was made, and it mattered to him. We were both in this together. Yet, I still couldn't bring myself to be fully open. It felt . . . wrong somehow. My life had taught me that trust was a sure way to get one killed. Somehow, I had to try and work through that.

"Does this mean that you are going to tell me your name?" I asked with a smile, turning my attention back to him.

A shadow of his usual playfulness appeared on his lips. "I will tell you my name, if we survive this."

Well, I had to try.

"But you have shared with me, so it is only fair I do the same," he sighed. "My Mask's name is Mirror Mistweaver of the Old Ways."

I blinked. "I have no idea how you think that someone knowing that would give them an advantage."

He burst into laughter, then winced and put a hand over his chest. "That is because you lack context. Suffice to say, my Investment comes from two things, fighting and knowledge."

I nodded. "What now?"

"We cannot waste any time," Shimi started. "The goal is to get you as strong as we can in the next two weeks here, then start the journey south to the shore when I am recovered enough for that trip. I have a boat stashed on the coast. This area is relatively safe, which is why I chose it for my camp, or at least it was supposed to be. The animals and monsters here are at the highest around Third and Fourth Investment. The reaper was greater than that, at Sixth Investment. It was a beast from the inner ring, and those rarely leave the vicinity of the Blight Curtain. Something must have disturbed them, and while I would very much like to know what that something is, we are in no shape to investigate."

He shook his head. "No, hunting is the plan. This had been the territory of the ferrorn that I killed, meaning that there should not be any other predators that are as dangerous in the area. But there are plenty of other animals around, and you are going to hunt them and drink their blood. Get more Carvings for your Mask and hopefully more skills. If we can get you to your First Investment you should get your first capstone skill, which will be a big jump in power for you. We have a month before you are sent back, and as weak as I am, I will not survive without you. So, in two weeks we will attempt the trek across the continent, get me to my boat and safety, and get you ready for your return to your home. Hopefully you will be strong enough by then to protect us both."

No pressure, it seemed. I shuffled my feet uncomfortably; he was going to depend on me. I owed him a debt for saving my life twice over. My sire's teachings echoed inside my head. Honor was one of the most important things that he taught me. It was why seeing his disappointment hurt so much.

"Capstone skill?"

"A Mask can gain a skill at any Carving. Most people gain one or two skills per Investment tier. Some get more, but those are rare, require a very high quality of Investment. But, once every Investment, starting from the First Investment you will get a capstone skill. It is a more powerful skill, a defining skill if you will. You will understand more once you get one."

I nodded. "Where do I start?" I asked.

"First, there are things you need to know about your Mask," Shimi started. "When you arrived and gained your Mask, you had to choose from several options, yes?"

I nodded.

"The choices you didn't pick, were they still available to you in some form?"

I described the three pillars and the plaque, and Shimi nodded.

"Yes, the center pillar is obviously your Mask. The other two are called Ornaments. You can only ever have two Ornaments at a time. And they act as something of sub-Masks. Which Ornaments are available to you depends on your knowledge and life experience. An Ornament will not be able to improve beyond the Second Investment, and all its skills will be lesser than those of a Mask of the same type. But every time your Mask evolves into a new Investment tier there is a chance for your Ornament to consolidate into your Mask, improving it further. This is of course dependent on how synergistic your Ornaments are with your Mask. Ornaments have their own Investment requirements, and are an important part of everyone's path. They can elevate your Mask, or even help you change it."

I thought back on what choices had been given to me. I had already suspected that they were based on my life. They painted a picture of a sad life.

"So I should pick something?"

"Preferably before you reach First Investment. You might be able to consolidate at least one of them, if they are synergistic enough with your Mask."

"I don't know if they are. Synergistic, I mean," I said.

"May I know what they are?" he asked.

I hesitated, then sighed. If I was already trusting him with all of this Mask stuff, there was no reason not to go all the way with it. Though it would reveal a lot more about my life than I was comfortable with. "I have **Thug, Servant,** and **Student** available."

His eyes widened. "Blights, you have **Student**! If we had done this sooner . . . There is no helping it now."

"**Student** is good?" I asked.

"Yes, very much so. Most people who have the means prepare their children by giving them the foundation to have that option. And it is not often that they manage it. It requires higher learning. Many who are undecided about their Masks and manage to obtain the option to start with the **Student** Mask, since it can change into anything and consolidates nicely with everything. And it is very easy to gain Investment for. It only requires learning. If we had done it before, all that you've learned so far would've counted as Investment for it." He shook his head. "Well, there is no use dwelling on what is lost already. You should take it. For your second Ornament, though, **Thug** is a criminal variation on a warrior-type Mask, and **Servant** is common but useless to you. I assume that you have some martial training?"

I appreciated him not asking questions about why I had those options. "I was trained in a few weapons," I answered. "Not exactly like what I saw in your tent. The weapons in my world are different from what you had on display, but close. There's no chance that you have a gun is there?"

He blinked. "I . . . don't know what that is."

I shook my head. "Most are small, can fit in your hand, they fire small fast-moving projectiles."

He frowned. "A boomstick, perhaps. The Dwarves use them oftentimes."

I was surprised that he knew what it was, or that there were guns in this world. From the state of his camp, I had made assumptions. But I already knew that I shouldn't have. I had realized how foolish I was when I learned how old their civilization was. I heard about magic and jumped to conclusions. I made a mental note to myself to ask more about the way things worked in this world, when we had the time.

"Sadly," he continued, "I do not have any here. I do have something similar. Go to my tent and bring me the crate that is next to the weapons rack."

I did as he asked and found a small wooden crate that I had missed the first time. I carried it over to him, and he opened it to reveal two smaller crates and two strange contraptions. He pulled one out and pressed a button which made it snap open. It took me a few moments to realize that it was a small crossbow of some kind. At least that is what I thought it was. It had an arc and a string, but I saw no handle. He turned it over then mounted it on his forearm.

"Bolt launcher. There is a pack of bolts in those smaller crates." He gestured.

I picked up the second one and turned it over a bit before mounting it on my own forearm. It was small, and it could be folded to be even easier to carry. I opened one of the small crates and saw two dozen bolts. I picked one up and felt its weight. It looked like it was all made out of the same material. I wanted to say metal, but I just didn't know—it was strangely non-reflective.

I watched as Shimi loaded a bolt into one, then I noticed that it had room for three bolts. "You can fire one after another, or all three at once," he said. He showed me the levers that rested at the base of his forearm, near the palm. He pointed to his arm, then pulled one of the levers with his finger. The string snapped forward, and the release was nearly silent save for the sound of the bolt flying through the air and the impact in the tree.

It was fast. Even I would have a problem avoiding that if I wasn't careful.

"It will not serve for more than a tool to cause a distraction for you, as you have no skills for its use. I doubt that you will be able to kill anything here with it unless you get exceptionally lucky. But still, it is another weapon in your arsenal." He glanced at all of my equipped weapons. I tried to hide my embarrassment. There was no need to carry all of them now that I had a camp.

"What am I hunting?" I asked finally.

"First you should pick your Ornaments," Shimi said. "The act of hunting new creatures will be a learning experience, which will give you Investment for your **Student** Ornament. The **Thug** and **Servant** I would ignore. I don't think that you could get the Investment for them here. Thug requires other people, and Servant someone to serve, and I can already see that you would not wish that to be me."

I nodded and then settled on the ground, with a long look at him I plunged into my *soul space*. A moment later I landed in the inner room. Saia appeared there in her dragon form, standing next to me.

"Oh, this might be a better way for us to talk without being heard," I said.

"Feedback: This Unit is equipped with direct neural communication link, current synchronization and understanding of Host biology too low for proper function. Current method requires the Host to become incapacitated."

"You can talk in my mind?

"Feedback: Not currently."

I didn't know how to feel about that.

"What is Shimi doing?" I asked instead.

"Feedback: Sensors indicate that he has not moved from his position. No additional data available."

"You can't see him?"

"Feedback: Host's eyes are closed, and this Unit's drone is deployed as a wrist unit. It has no eyes."

Right, that made sense. I shook my head and walked over to the pillars to pick the Ornament. As I leaned down to look at the plaque, I froze. There was a new option on there.

Revelator (Esoteric)
— *To reveal the truths* —

Why? The only thing that made sense was the vision. *Did that mean that it was true?* Or did that not even matter? I had decided to find the truth of this world, to see if the threat was real, and if it was to make sure the monsters were stopped. A part of me felt like I was unworthy of that. I was no one, just a thug, a servant. Yet I was chosen by something, brought to this world and had stumbled onto something. Perhaps Kolan Shuk was right, and fate did exist. And his plea to a *friend across time* did touch me. It was perhaps the first thing that ever touched me. It felt as if he was speaking to me personally.

But was it a good choice for me to take? That was the question. What kind of Investment would it require? The tag made me think that perhaps it would be revealing the truth. I hesitated. Asking Shimi for advice would create more questions that I didn't want to answer right now. I knew that eventually I would need to tell him. But it did call to me. Being someone who had never been allowed to make her own choices before, this felt like one that could be mine.

My Mask hung above the central pillar, new etchings apparent over the horns. It had evolved again with my Carvings. I took a deep breath, then turned back to the other pillar.

I touched the word etched in the plaque, and my Mask changed. I saw what could only be described as an ornament appear on it. A dark green addition to the right lower horn, like an earing stuck into its side.

I didn't feel any different, but the plaque beneath the Mask changed too, now listing the name of the Ornament as well. I turned to the other pillar, and picked the **Student** Ornament too. Another addition manifested on the Mask, a mirror of the first one, this one orange in color. Again, the plaque expanded.

Mask of the Drainer — No Investment; Sixth Carving
Ornament of the Revelator — No Investment; No Carvings
Ornament of the Student — No Investment; No Carvings

I pulled myself away from the Mask and walked over to the shelf. I picked up [Lesser Strength] and walked over to the back wall. Now there were two different pedestals, as I had gained a new skill slot. I placed it in and felt the skill spread through me as it activated. My body changed, my muscles growing slightly. Once done, I looked over at the door corridor to seeing the new rooms. I knew that I shouldn't try to enter either one—those beasts were beyond me still.

With one last look I pulled myself out of the soul space.

The First Hunt

The fact that you are weaker during the day is an issue," Shimi said. "At night, you stand a chance, but the animals lurking about at night are more dangerous. I would suggest hunting the animals as they sleep, but most animals here are nocturnal. There are a few herds of okolon that I saw around, they are Third Investment. If you can isolate one you might be able to take it down, before you get trampled to death."

That didn't sound very encouraging, but I didn't say anything.

"Do you know anything about hunting and tracking?" he asked.

"Some, not as much as I would like, but this is also a different world. I might miss things that are obvious," I answered.

He grimaced. "True," Shimi said. "For now, you should set up near the river. Animals often come there to drink, and you should look for an opportunity to ambush them. Collect as much blood as you can, more skills and more Carvings, but avoid predators for now. There are too many animals around for me to describe everything, and I have not really been paying that much attention. Let us see what you observe at the river, and then we will plan. Go only for the okolon if you see it, and try to go for the isolated ones. After you get a few beasts under you, we will move to proper hunting."

He tried to move and grunted, his face contorting in a grimace. "An okolon, is a herd beast. You will not miss them if they come as they are the only animal that moves in such units in the jungle. One of them should be your first target. They have very good senses, and can detect skill usage near them. With the way you move, I would suggest trying to get as close as you can before striking from an ambush. Another skill that most mature ones have is [Mist Step] which lets them turn to mist for a single step, every few steps. So you will need to account for that."

That sounded like a plan. I glanced up at the canopy. There was still a lot of night left. "I should get a start on that. Will you be safe here?"

"I will be for tonight," Shimi said. "But we will need to move camp eventually. Until then, go, hunt. And may the Old Tree keep you."

I moved through the forest slowly, with as much stealth as I could manage. Most people said that a vampire could sneak up on anyone, which wasn't exactly true. We did have some advantages, though; our footsteps were lighter and made less noise because we had a greater degree of control over our bodies. In truth, a vampire was heavier than a human or even a shifter in their human form. We were more likely to make a loud noise if we weren't being careful—it was only that we rarely made such mistakes.

I approached the river, making as little noise as possible. I wasn't worried about any scents. I had washed the blood off, and vampires don't sweat or have a natural scent of any kind. Once I was near enough, I decided to climb a tree just over the waterfall and the small pool. I got onto the lowest branches, which were still incredibly high up. It gave me a good vantage point to observe anything coming and going from the river. The branches were thick enough that I could hide myself from the animals on the ground easily enough. I settled in to wait, and relaxed. My breathing slowed and my heart rate plummeted. I kept my eyes and ears open for signs of anything approaching.

A vampire is an ambush predator. We can push ourselves to move faster than nearly anything else on the planet, but we cannot sustain it for long. Most people comment on the vampire's almost detached appearance, the way that we can keep still for hours with no movement, and when we do move have it look effortless and fluid. That is true, but not for the reasons people believe. We move in a way that requires the least amount of effort, with no wasted movements. Not because we are somehow detached and superior, but because we can't sustain moving our bodies at the rate we are capable of. Unlike the humans, we are not endurance hunters, we can't track and follow our prey for days waiting for it to drop dead from exhaustion like humans can.

Even in this place, with the sun that didn't burn or put me to sleep, I had seen just how tired I would get when I lost my strength with the dawn. I still needed slumber, it just wasn't tied to the sun anymore. Or, not as much at least.

I glanced down at my weapons, I had brought the forearm mounted crossbow, my knife, and of course Saia too. I debated having her somewhere in the trees in her dragon form, but decided against it. She was too eye catching. On my wrist I could hide her beneath my shirt. Then something occurred to me.

"Hey Saia," I whispered. "Can you change the color of your drone?"

"Feedback: Not currently."

I blinked. "May I ask why not?"

"Feedback: This Unit's current state is far from full capabilities. Many systems and engrams are inoperable."

Right, she had mentioned that before. I had to imagine that she had to compromise a lot when she went from that giant egg size to being barely a fraction of that. I turned back to waiting for my prey.

I waited patiently, listening to the occasional sound made by animals that I didn't know, and some sounds that were completely alien. An animal approached the river, alone, and dipped down its head to drink.

It was a large animal, though not as big as the ferrorn or the reaper that injured Shimi. To me, it looked like a cross between a bear and a pig. It had a large and wide snout, and each time it opened it to take in water I saw rows of sharp teeth. Its feet were spaced widely for good balance, and I saw claws raised above the fingers. It was covered in dark and thick fur. I couldn't be sure if it was a predator or not, but it didn't look like anything that I wanted to tangle with. I remained hidden.

It didn't stay drinking for long, and I didn't move from my spot. I didn't know anything about this world, and from the things that Shimi told me even a small creature could be powerful. I waited—there was still a lot of time until dawn. A few hours later, a pack of animals came, again looking like predators, something like a reptilian version of wolves. From the way they moved, I figured that they weren't that strong, at least compared to me. If I had to guess, I would've put them on the same level as the young ferrorn I had killed. The issue was that there was a dozen of them, and I was not dumb enough to try to fight a pack of predators.

About an hour later, another dozen creatures arrived. A herd this time. These creatures didn't look like predators at all. But they were huge. They were towering creatures, the size of a moose from Earth. Each was covered in thick blueish fur and had a head that resembled that of a hippo, only smaller. They looked tough, but even if they were strong, they probably weren't that much of a threat. This had to be the okolon. I watched them attentively as they drank from the river. Then they started to leave. I climbed down behind them slowly, noting that one of the herd remained to drink a bit longer than the rest. As the herd moved away, I followed after them, my eyes locked on the one that was trailing behind. I thought about using the bolt launcher, but I doubted that such a small bolt would do much to it. Instead, I raised my knife into a ready position. Stealthily, I quickened my pace as much as I could without making too much noise. We were still close to the river, so the sound of water was covering for me.

Then I saw my chance. The lone animal had leaned down to sniff something on the ground, and I leapt. My weapon came down as I fell on its back. I missed—my weapon stabbed into the ground as the animal turned to mist and sidestepped. I cursed, and ripped the knife out of the ground, then turned after it. Before I could recover, the animal released a call, and as I turned in its direction, it lashed out with its hind legs. Two hooved legs kicked in my direction, connecting with my chest. I flew through the air and hit a tree, hard. I grimaced as I felt the pain in my cracked ribs, then I raised my head and saw the animal leaping away, turning to mist midstep and disappearing back to its herd ahead.

"*Malparido*," I cursed, then got up to my feet. I walked to where I had dropped my weapon nearby and picked it up. Then I dragged myself back to the river in defeat. That hadn't gone the way I had imagined. My ribs healed slowly; bones always did. Though slowly for a vampire was still leagues faster than for a human. And my healing was still slower than normal, the silver wound still causing issues.

I shook my head as I tried to clear it. I hadn't really thought about what skills meant. Shimi had told me that the okolon had them, but it was hard for me to adjust to that. I had to learn, and do it fast if I was to survive in this world.

I returned back to my hiding place up in the trees, and I settled in to wait again as I was licking my wounds. Ambushing was what vampires did best, but I had to incorporate skills in my plans now too. I reviewed my mode of attack and tried to figure out what had gone wrong. The animal had been strong and fast, but its skill made it such bullshit to catch. It also appeared like it could do it often, every few steps at least. After thinking about it, I decided that I had launched the attack too soon, and that I should've used my own skill. I had given it more time to hear my attack, which wouldn't have mattered on Earth as nothing could've reacted fast enough to avoid me. I had to adjust to animals on this world now. With skills, the animal had just turned to mist and stepped away before I could switch gears. I should've tried to get closer to it before attacking, maybe even opened with [Debilitating Wave]. Maybe even use Saia in some manner. I hadn't used her in the chain and blade shape as the thick jungle wasn't the best place to use a chain, but I could've had her be a second blade, maybe. Well, there was always next time.

The hours passed, and no other animals arrived. I grew frustrated as I started to feel the sun coming. The hunt had obviously been a wash. And I did not feel like going back defeated. There was nothing that I could do about it though; the sun was coming and with it, weakness. I had to get back to camp before I lost my strength. Then, I heard something, a rustle nearby. I froze, my ears twitching as I strained my hearing. It was not the sound of the wind or the rustle of branches and leaves. I heard it again, and then turned my head slowly in that direction. I didn't see it at first, but then I noticed something pushing out of the tree. It took me a few moments to realize that it was a birdlike creature coming out of a hidden hole in the tree trunk. I watched as it got out, shook its head, then walked along the branch, looking in the direction opposite of me. It was about the size of an eagle, with strangely shaped feathers and an elongated head. It didn't have a beak in the traditional sense; it was wider and it looked softer, more like it had a snout that was covered in skin.

I sensed an opportunity to even my score, and I grinned. This animal didn't seem that dangerous, and I had an advantage over it. Sure, a bird might not count for as much as a moose sized beast that turned into mist, but I would take whatever I could get. I wasn't about to go back to camp with my tail tucked in between my legs. I prepared for an attack and then paused. I'd been underestimating the beasts I'd encountered in this place since the start. I'd come on top in most of my encounters, but always I paid a price. Wounds that piled up and hindered me. My neck burned, a reminder that I was not at my full power and that any wound I sustained would take longer to heal.

I decided to be on the safer side. Slowly, I raised my arm, the bolt already nocked in the launcher. I aimed and then pulled the trigger. The creature didn't even get a chance to react as it was hit in the back, the bolt piercing through, letting me know that the beast was not as powerful as some around here that would probably be able to shrug off that attack. It cried out, a screech that filled the forest around us. As it started to fall from the tree, I jumped from my branch, soaring through the air. I caught the creature with my hand, squeezing tightly and feeling the bones crack. As soon as I landed, I sank my teeth into it and drank. Blood flooded into my mouth, sweet with a whisper of power. I could immediately tell that it wasn't anywhere near as powerful as some of the other blood that I had drank. It was less powerful than the young ferrorn. But it was still blood, the source of life and power, it would go toward advancing my Mask, and grant me a room where I could earn a skill. There were no memories, only hazy images that were incomprehensible to me. I recognized them as the bird's dreams.

Once I finished draining it, I moved to throw it away, but then something occurred to me. I had never asked Shimi about any food supplies. For him, of course. I could survive on blood, but I didn't know anything about his kind. I decided to bring it with me. With that, I made my way back to camp.

Shimi laughed at me.

"You got kicked in the face? Haha—" He coughed, winced, before looking at me with a grin on his face. He was still sitting, leaning against the rock, but he had the other bolt launcher on his forearm, ammunition loaded in.

"It's not funny, and it wasn't my face," I told him with a glare. "I didn't expect . . . you know what? Never mind."

His expression slowly turned regretful, and then he nodded. "Sorry," he said. "I apologize, I was not thinking clearly. I should not have laughed. The failure was mine for not preparing you further. I know that you are an Exemplar, that you are new to your Mask, but knowing and understanding are two different things. You don't yet know just how to use your Mask properly."

Well, if I was being honest with myself, I should've known better, and I could've asked him to elaborate. But I fell into the trap vampires most often found themselves in: arrogance. I knew that I was in a different world, with magic and animals that were stronger than me, yet I still couldn't quite drop the superiority of my kind. I had thought that I was beyond it, and not for the first time. That was part of that arrogance, the belief that we were the greatest of all living things. It was what killed most vampires. And I knew that many Fledglings died before they became Adults. Our minds were still adjusting to the change, our emotions were too raw. As a vampire grew, our control over our emotions got better and better, but the rawness of them never went away. I remembered a saying from my classes back at college:

When vampires listen to their emotions, cities burn.

It was said by one of their few scholars. I remembered the other students laughing at that, I laughed at it too. We made jokes about vampires being divas. But now I knew it to be true. My sire had told me much of the vampire history, things that I did not learn in schools because the vampires did not want the humans even more terrified of us than they already were. Vampires had been kings and queens of the ancient world. There was a reason many of the Human ancient histories were filled with blood and carnage.

I had believed myself above it all. That I had mastered myself in record time. I had let my sire's praise go to my head. Most Fledglings don't become Adults until their first century. The fastest a Fledgling had turned Adult was decades, and I thought myself as good as them. Sheer fucking arrogance. Ever since I arrived here, I kept finding myself losing control, getting drowned, and letting my emotions drive me. I went out to hunt because, in part at least, I wanted to prove to Shimi that I could do what I had said. That I could keep us both safe. I couldn't, not as I was right now. A vampire was not the alpha predator of this world.

"It's my fault too," I told Shimi. "I should've asked before I went to hunt."

"We live, we grow, we learn," Shimi said. "Next time you will be more prepared."

"So," I raised my hand, presenting my catch. "Are you hungry?"

He nodded. "Do you know how to prepare and cook?"

"I've lived in the jungle for most of my life. Yes, I know." If you considered making the rounds on cocaine labs in the jungle living. Then I paused as something occurred to me. "Though, I guess that you should probably guide me through it. There might be some differences between animals here and those I am familiar with."

Shimi's grin returned, along with a wicked glint in his eyes.

* * *

"That wasn't funny," I told him after I used one of the water gourd's trying to clean myself off. The sun had risen by now, and I was back to being weaker and feeling all the little pains in my body. Even the healed wounds ached, my neck most of all. I also felt tired, sleepy.

"Oh, it was to me," Shimi said. He smiled, but there was a touch of sadness in his eyes.

I glared at the man. "How old are you even? You act like a child."

He widened his grin, trying to look as if he had won a compliment, but I could see that it was forced. "Thank you."

"I wasn't complimenting you," I said.

While dressing and cutting the birdlike animal—which he had identified as a cresser—he had suggested that I first cut out a slightly bulging organ just beneath what appeared to be the heart. That hadn't been a good idea, as it turned out. After I had it out, he told me to pierce it, saying that there are some very nutritious parts inside. I should've known that something wasn't right when he asked me to do it a few steps away from the rest of the animal.

"It isn't coming off," I complained as I tried to wipe off a yellow sticky substance that had erupted from the organ once I had pierced it. Apparently, it was a nasty bile, which the bird produced and used both for digestion and for building its nest. It was annoying to say the least, and it made my fingers stick together. But at least it had no scent. I wondered if he still suffered from the venom and if it was affecting his mind. Or if he was just trying to make light of the tragic situation we were in.

"Just keep rubbing, it'll come off eventually," Shimi called from his place on the ground.

"I would throw it in your face if you weren't injured," I said.

"Oh, you would?" Shimi snickered.

"This isn't the time for . . ." I just waved my sticky hands at him, unable to find the words for my frustration.

"On the contrary, my dear new friend," Shimi said, his expression now grave. "This is precisely the right time for such levity."

I tilted my head in question, and he continued.

"We are in dire circumstances," Shimi sighed and bowed his head wearily. "More likely than not, we will not survive for long. Better to go out with at least a few laughs. Besides, it is a learning experience, is it not?"

I paused. Was he doing it to help me gain Investment for my Ornament? Perhaps, but his tone was light, and I could tell that he did believe some of what he was saying. I could understand him trying to lighten the mood and help, but this felt different. I remembered that look in his eyes, I had seen in the eyes of the people that the cartel had sent me to kill. Those who had accepted their fate and didn't even try to fight. I hated that, the surrender, just accepting your lot in life. I had been sold as cattle, and I never surrendered to that life. I clawed and fought; I swam through a river of blood to be where I was now. True, I did not always get through it on my own, others had pushed me along, they had guided my course and fate. But ultimately, I was the one who had decided to put one foot before the next.

I walked over to him and knelt next to his legs. He looked up at me questioningly.

"Shimi," I said slowly in a whispered tone. I wanted him to understand how serious I was. "I fully intend to survive this. I know that it is hard for you, I understand being in a situation where your life is dependent on somebody else. More than you can possibly know. But we made a deal, that we would get through this together. Are you going to honor it?"

For a moment his eyes darkened, and something made me almost shiver. I'd forgotten just how powerful he was. Even injured and weak, he was something that I couldn't quite grasp.

My words were perhaps too forward. I covered for my embarrassment by glaring at him. "If you've decided that you are going to die, tell me now. I need to know, because I plan on surviving, and I don't need you to weigh me down if you are not going to contribute anything worthwhile."

His eyes narrowed, and for a moment I froze completely. The eyes that stared at me in that moment were beyond anything that I had ever seen before. They turned deep and uncompromising, filled with the promise of violence and power. I remembered then that this was not a human, a vampire, or a shifter, that he was a completely alien existence, and one that was very powerful. I didn't know his customs or culture; we were not friends, but two strangers put together by fate.

But then, his eyes changed, and the same Shimi that I had been dealing with for the past couple of days returned. "You are right, of course." He grinned, then bowed his head.

The earth rumbled, the ground shook, and I moved over him as everything trembled. A few moments later it was over. "Ish Vizma is restless," he whispered, then he met my eyes. "I apologize. I will endeavor to do all in my power to help us both."

I held his eyes, then nodded, not daring to speak. He had terrified me, and I couldn't let him see that. I felt my heart racing inside my chest, and suddenly I felt weaker, more tired than I had been just a moment before. The sun no longer hurt me, but it still pushed me to sleep it seemed.

I frowned, then walked away and started preparing the animal for cooking over the fire. Doing something to push the tiredness away. Neither of us spoke again while I put pieces of meat over the fire and cooked them. Once it was done, I offered him a stick, and took only a single bite for myself. I had wanted to try out some normal food ever since I arrived here, wondering if it would do any-thing for me. I bit into it and . . . it was bland. I could taste it, but it was muted, like it always had been since I was turned. I'd known that this was the most likely result. I was a vampire, and a different sun wouldn't change that.

"I thought that your kind drinks blood as food?" Shimi asked in between bites.

I nodded. "Yes, but we can still eat other food. It just doesn't really do any-thing for us. Just passes through. I wanted to see what it tasted like."

"Huh," Shimi said, but didn't ask any other questions.

He finished his meal in silence, and I started to feel my eyes closing on their own. I grimaced in annoyance; I had never liked the fact that the sun made me go unconscious. When I arrived here and found that I could remain awake while the sun was out, I was overjoyed, but now . . . It seemed that I couldn't escape sleep entirely. I glanced at Shimi wondering how alert he was and if he could keep watch.

"Sleep, Marianna Rojas, I shall make sure that nothing eats us while you sleep."

I narrowed my eyes at him.

"You have my promise," he said. "I will not let melancholy or fatalistic whimsy take hold of me again."

I decided to trust him. It wasn't like I had much of a choice. I settled in near the fire, trying to push all of my fears aside. Sleep took me quickly.

Shelter

I woke, as always, with the setting of the sun. I did not dream, or if I had I did not remember it. If there was one thing that I missed about sleeping it was dreaming. The thing that came over me now was more of a state of unconsciousness, even with this sun, than it was actual sleep. My body just being unable to keep up under the daylight. I wondered if perhaps this sun just had a weaker effect on me but still the same one. After all, some vampires could remain awake during the day, and there had always been stories of some that could survive the sunlight for short periods of time. Perhaps there was a lot more to learn about my kind than I realized.

"Welcome back to the land of the living," Shimi called out.

I sat up, fully alert, and took in everything around me. Vampires didn't really have that period of adjustment to being awake, and it seemed like that hadn't changed. I took stock of myself, poking at my **thirst.** It didn't stir at all, which told me that I was good on blood. I hadn't really been paying attention, but I decided that I should probably do a bit more testing to see how the blood of these animals affected me. I had felt bursts of power moments after I drank it, though not from the bird. Was that because it was weaker? It had almost tasted like the blood from the animals on Earth, though still tinged with power.

"Anything happen while I was asleep?" I asked.

"No, the field is still operating as it should," Shimi answered.

"How exactly does it operate?" I asked as I walked over to where I put the water gourds and washed my face.

"It releases a faint mental suggestion, telling the animals that there is nothing of interest here. Of course, the higher Investment animals would probably be able to see through it eventually. Monsters might get tricked for a few minutes, no longer."

I blinked at that. "So, a monster could just walk through that?" I waved at the shining field around us.

"Yes." Shimi nodded.

"That doesn't seem all that safe?" I raised an eyebrow as I came to sit back across from him.

Shimi smiled. "Monsters rarely leave the inner ring, or at least they did not up until now. And I picked this place because animals here were weaker. Now something has disturbed them, changed the patterns that had held true for millennia. The quakes have been getting more intense."

"You said that they were common?"

"They are, but it had never been more than slight shaking. This intensity, though, it started very recently."

He turned his head up at the sky, clearly in thought.

"You don't know why or how it happened?" I asked.

He glanced back to meet my eyes. "I do not know, but I assume that it has to do with your arrival."

"I . . ."

"Your world's arrival I mean, not you personally," he clarified. "I assume that the Great Mistake has some schemes in mind."

"The Great Mistake?"

"The Grand Spell, the System," Shimi answered. "It has many names."

That seemed like a story all in itself, but I didn't think that we had the time for such things. Even the message I stumbled on called it a different name. I stood up and looked down at him. "We should move camp then, somewhere safer. The ruins to the east maybe? I hid there from the big ferrorn," I suggested. I wanted to see if he would speak a bit more on these Ancient Ones he had mentioned. Perhaps his people already knew about the vision; perhaps I was not the first to discover it.

Shimi blinked. "You entered the ruins of the Ancient Ones?"

I tilted my head. "Yes?"

He cursed and shook his head, but he was grinning. "Bravery or stupidity can, at times, look the same."

I scowled at him. "Excuse me for being thrown into another world and not knowing anything about it."

His expression turned gentle. "Apologies." He waved a hand in a gesture that seemed to indicate something, but I had no idea what. "There was likely no danger at all, but people from this world would rather take on a ferrorn than test fate with whatever remained of the Ancient Ones. Unless they were treasure hunters, but even then, the ferrorn would be far more appealing."

That made me sit up, and lean forward interested to hear more.

"It's that dangerous?" I asked, yet again struck by just how much I didn't know.

Shimi thought about it for a few seconds, and then gave his answer. "No, not really. Not here in any case. The treasure hunters have wiped clean anything of interest in the outer ring ages ago. It is unlikely that you would've stumbled onto something that they missed."

Nothing like a message left by one of those Ancient Ones, not at all. Had it been hidden so well that no one found it? I'm pretty sure that the earthquake revealed the room, but I would've thought that someone would've been able to find the room regardless. Well, shows just how much I knew.

"These Ancient Ones, you said that they were the ones that created the Grand Spell?" I asked.

He inclined his head. "Yes, or at least that is what we think. We cannot know for sure. Their ruins are the oldest things that we found, but with how volatile the Grand Spell can be, there could have been more before them. Some records recovered from their ruins indicate that they once had a different type of magic before gaining Masks. Most assume that means that they created them, but some argue that they could have just been the first brought over to this place and that their previous world had something similar."

"How long ago did they die off, do you know?"

"The youngest ruins that we uncovered were dated to more than twenty-five thousand years old," Shimi answered.

That number seemed incredibly high still, but it did align with what Saia had sampled. Something must've shown on my face, because Shimi continued.

"They built things to last," he said.

Suddenly I felt a pressure inside my chest, and then an impression inside my mind.

***Ornament of the Student — No Investment; First Carving
[A Lesson Remembered] skill gained.***

Shimi noticed. "What is it?"

"My Ornament, I got a Carving for it and a skill, a [A Lesson Remembered]?"

"Oh, that is good, and a skill already bodes well for the future. It is a good skill too, it will let you remember any lesson perfectly. Go ahead, try to use it. Think of a lesson from your past."

I frowned, then focused on the skill, the act of using it as easy as breathing. I blinked and—

"—Caesar was pursuing Pompey into Egypt when he was suddenly cut off by an Egyptian fleet at Alexandria," the elderly professor said as he pointed at the images on the projector. The students in the classroom were a blur, only the professor, the projector, and the chalkboard were clear.

"Greatly outnumbered and in enemy territory, Caesar ordered the ships in the harbor to be set on fire. The fire spread and destroyed the Egyptian fleet. Unfortunately, it also burned down part of the city—the area where the great Library stood. Or at least that is what history claimed for the longest time. Now we know that Caesar learned of a vampire master living beneath the city harbor, and decided to burn the entire part of the city. Caesar wrote of starting the fire in the harbor but neglected to mention the burning of the Library or his original intent. He failed in his primary goal as well: the vampire escaped and took with him the most precious items from the Library prior to it burning down. Such an omission proves little since he was not in the habit of including unflattering facts while writing his own history. Nevertheless, the vampires still hold that event over humanity, using it as an example why humans are not meant to rule. In their words, we allow our hate and greed to rule us, too often uncaring about what destruction we wreak in our wake."

I blinked again, and the classroom was gone.

"Did it work?" Shimi asked.

"Yes," I answered. It had been so clear, as if I was right there. Except for the details around me, but those were unimportant. It had been so long since I was at school, learning and living free for the first time. As free as one could be, with a chain half a continent long attached around their neck, at least.

I shook my head to clear it. Then something occurred to me.

"Shimi?"

"Yes?"

"Back there, when you saved me, I felt, or heard something. Your skill I think? I've been experiencing the same when I gain Carvings."

He leaned back, his eyes widening. "Huh, yes, that was my skill. You did not hear it, not really. It is more as if you felt its impression on the Way. Not many people can do that."

"Really?"

He nodded. "You need to be very sensitive to the Way in order to be able to do that."

"There was almost like an impression of color?"

"Color? Ah, that must be how your mind interprets it, interesting."

"Is there something different about your skills?"

"There are several types of skills, and each has a different impression," Shimi started. "There are the basic skills that you gain from advancing through Carvings. They are the most common skills you will encounter. These skills can be improved in various ways, by advancing your Mask is the most common way, but you can also do it by improving your ability to wield the skill. Then, there are learned skills, which as their name suggests are learned and not gained—this was what you felt when I used skills. Most any physical type skill can be learned, though it is incredibly hard to do. Followed by inheritance skills, which are self-explanatory. Then you have Mask specific skills, which are the second rarest of them. They are gained for incredible feats in line with your Mask, for very high-quality Investment, and are exceptionally powerful. The last type are the rarest, they are called waybound skills. They resonate with the Way in such a way to create an effect. They are perfectly executed actions that hold power."

"What even is the difference between the Way, the Source, and the Weave?" I asked. I hadn't had the chance to ask Saia to explain it to me in depth.

"The world operates under certain rules, laws that are immutable. I guess that you could call the combination of those rules and laws, along with everything else around us the Way. It is reality which includes everything that exists. The Source is a small part of the Way, one that we can directly influence. It is the energy that can be altered or guided to cause an effect. The Weave is that alteration, the construct that causes the effect. In terms of Masks, every skill is a Weave of the Source." He paused, his eyes looking at me intently. "Does that make sense?"

"It does actually," I said. I should've asked earlier.

"So what you felt is the skill's impression on the Way. Not all can sense it, and some powerful individuals have such mastery of their skills that they leave no impression at all. Though most just don't bother with it, as people who can sense it are rare."

I nodded, shelving the information for later. Then, I decided to change the topic.

"So, should we move camp to the ruins?" I asked him.

Shimi thought about it for a long while, then nodded reluctantly. "It would seem that we have no choice. It should be safe enough; most of the ruins have been stripped bare this far out from the inner ring."

I stood up. "Well, we should get to it then."

I looked on in amazement as the entire camp was stuffed into a big metal chest. It was insane. When Shimi told me to start packing things up, this was not what I imagined. Nearly everything in his camp had what Shimi called a [Size Enchantment] which let him reduce the size of objects and fit them nicely into the big chest that had leather straps so that it could be carried like a backpack.

"This is insane," I repeated, this time out loud.

Shimi chuckled as he leaned on one of his weapons, what he called the serpent-tongue spear, using it as a makeshift crutch. "Think you can carry it?"

I looked it over for a bit, then knelt and pulled the straps on. With a deep breath I stood up with an effort. I blinked, it was heavy, but not nearly as heavy as all those things were supposed to be. I glanced at Shimi, and he answered my unspoken question.

"[Weight Enchantment]."

"*¡Que chévere!*" That was so cool. I looked at it in awe.

"We should hurry," Shimi said, and I had no reason to object.

We started the trek through the jungle at a brisk pace. I tried to take us over the easiest to traverse terrain, though a lot of the ground was covered in moss. Even injured, Shimi didn't seem to have an issue keeping up, though I had noticed that he was visibly sweating.

"What do you know about the Ancient Ones?" I asked as we walked.

"What do you want to know?" he asked in return.

"I don't know, I guess anything really? What were they like, what happened to them?"

"We don't have any records of what they looked like, only descriptions and half recovered statues that we used to make recreations. We have an idea, but no real evidence. What we know is that the collapse of their civilization was violent and abrupt. When the Grand Spell brings over a new world, it combines its land masses into one big landmass, like it is arranging a puzzle. We do not know if the Ancient Kirios only ever had one continent, or if its landmasses have been merged into Ish Vimza. Regardless, a lot of it is submerged. We've found evidence of ruins scattered all over the oceans. What remains on the surface has been devastated in such a way that we suspect they had a very bloody civil war that wiped them out."

What the message told me was that they didn't adapt to Masks, so infighting was possible. The message did suggest that their end was sealed when they attempted to assault the Last Intent—the Great Spell—and destroy it.

"You said that the ruins are dangerous?"

"They are," Shimi added. "One of the reasons why some believe that the Ancient Ones created the Great Spell is because of their artifacts. Most of the finds don't work at all, but every once in a while we would find something that worked still, though never in the way we could predict and often not in the way we could contain. You see, we found these items that make no sense to us, and have strange uses. Like for the example the rod that I use to protect my camp. It is one such artifact, though our experts agree that the items that do work are no longer functioning properly. Some believe that to be because they were made before the arrival of the Great Spell, and after the rules were changed the Weaves that powered them now no longer worked as intended. Some are incredibly illogical and destructive, but powerful nevertheless. We take great care when entering their ruins, because you can never know what even a seemingly mundane piece of rock actually is, or what it can do."

That made sense. I had more luck than I thought, since I stumbled through the ruins without a care. Well, I had been drawn into a rift, so there was that.

I turned my attention on our surroundings, making sure that nothing sneaked up on us. We reached the buried ruins before dawn. Even knowing that the crack in the stone was there, I had a hard time seeing it.

"This is a good place," Shimi said once we squeezed our way inside. He paused and tried to play it off as if he was looking around, but I could tell that he was winded. "This crack is too small for most of the really dangerous monsters to come through. Are there any other entrances?"

I waved at the corridor leading out of the room. "There's a long hallway leading to another room just like this one with a pool of water, and there are several stairs leading down, but all are collapsed," I said, debating yet again whether or not to show him the room and the message.

Shimi nodded. "We should stay here then, near the exit. Though I don't like having a dead end behind our backs."

We started setting up camp. Soon enough, it became obvious to me that he had no issue seeing in the dark, the same as me. When I asked, he gave me a simple answer.

"A gift from my mother's side," he said, his tails swaying behind him. "Not all Tsu-gi inherit the eyes from their Kitsu-oi side."

"What do you think this place used to be?" I asked, nodding at the corridor on the other side of the room.

"A barracks of some kind, most likely," Shimi said. "I have seen similar ones before."

"Really?"

"Oh yes, I used to be a treasure hunter," Shimi answered. "Though, the make of this place is slightly off from the usual barracks I've seen. But then again, the Ancient Ones had many different factions, just like any civilization. I cannot even tell what age this place hails from. Once, this place was probably filled with weapons. Sadly, most of the ruins in the outer ring have been stripped clean long ago."

Not completely, I thought, but didn't say anything, not yet.

What he said, though, was understandable. There were few ruins remaining on Earth that hadn't been plundered over the years.

He placed his rod, wedging it between a crack in the floor.

"How common are these artifacts?" I asked as he turned it, and a moment later the pale blue spherical shield appeared around us.

"They are rare. Only the wealthy and the powerful have access to them. Most would have enchanted items, made by a Masked. Some of those rival even the strongest of the Ancient Ones' artifacts. Though they require a really high Investment Enchanter Masked in order to create them. We call items like these, the ones that are from the Ancient Ones but still usable, relics."

"Wow, *bacano.*" *Cool.* "So, how does it work?"

Shimi shrugged. "No one knows. That rod was my addition actually. The actual relic part is just a small stone in the head of the rod. I found it as part of a collapsed wall defending a small town. I have no way of knowing if the way it works was its intended purpose."

"What makes it different from the rest of these items?" I asked as I pulled a smaller chest out of the big one, placed it on the ground and watched it grow.

"Those are not nearly as complicated or powerful," Shimi said.

"So is there anything that I should know about all these different items?"

"The enchanted items are created by crafters; they are the most common of special items. Next are relics, the remnants of the Ancient Ones, which we don't understand and can't replicate. And last are the Invested Items."

"Invested Items?"

"Yes. Just like people and animals, items can get Invested too. Think of Investment as an exchange. You give something to the Mask, and it gives you power in return. A wielder of the Blademaster Mask might gain Investment by fighting with a blade, gaining combat experience, or just training with it. Some might even spend years meditating on the deeper concepts and what it means to wield a blade. It doesn't matter what it is, as long as you are giving something that aligns with the concepts of your Mask to it. Now, Invested Items are the rarest of items. It takes a long time for them to come into existence, and they are always powerful. Imagine a blade, passed down generations, wielded by great warriors. Over time, it would absorb part of the Investment from its wielders and the world around it. Usually, their birth comes in moments of great tragedy, or glory. Moments when something monumental happens. An ancient blade, soaked in the blood of hundreds of thousands might gain enough to become an Invested Blade. A butcher's knife, passed down a family for generations might do the same. What skills they gain depends on the type of Investment that they experience."

That was fascinating, but wouldn't help us much, unless he had a chest full of Invested Items in there. I turned the conversation back to the things that would keep us alive.

"So," I started. "How do I go about hunting animals and getting us out of here?"

Shimi took a deep breath, and then started to explain as I set up camp.

"The reason I suggested that you hunt an okolon is simple. Every animal or monster has capstone skills. Usually they gain more as they get older and gain more Investment, one for each tier of it. Signature skills, though, are skills that the animal or monster is born with. In the case of the okolon, the [Mist Step] skill."

I listened attentively as Shimi explained.

"As you have experienced, it allows them to take a single step during which their body turns to mist. The [Mist Step] will be very useful to you." Shimi paused, then shook his head. "We need to plan your targets very carefully."

I tilted my head. "Why?"

"You gain skills from the monsters you take blood from," Shimi answered. "We need to equip you with skills that will ensure our survival. All Masks are shaped by the type of Investment they take in, yours is no different. A warrior constantly in battle will get skills related to battle, a warrior during peace would get skill adequate for the Investment he gained. You gain Investment from blood, but also skills to use. I am certain that you will not keep getting as many slots as your skills, and we still need to make a cohesive build for you. All Masks have logic in the way they gain skills. There has to be one for you. The [Lesser Strength] that you gained from the ferrorn would've been its most powerful skill at that age. I am making an assumption that if you kill the beast on your own and drain it, you will get its most powerful skill."

That actually did make sense to me. I wasn't sure how, but I was almost certain that he was right about that.

I nodded. "So, what are my targets?"

Shimi's eyes narrowed, and he seemed to be thinking. Then, he stood and walked to where I had placed the tent and one of his chests. He rummaged through it for a bit and then came out with two items in his hands. One was a smooth crystal cube, and the second was what looked like a cream-colored piece of paper.

"What is that?"

"I should have done this before but . . ." He shook his head. "This"—he raised his left hand—"is a crystal enchanted with the [Inspect] skill. It will let me see your full Mask title and all skill names."

I frowned. "You already know everything about my Mask."

"Yes, but this will give us some additional information that we should be aware of."

"Doesn't that then defeat the point of trying to keep Masks a secret?"

Shimi shook his head. "There are ways of protecting against it, and the skill type is very rare. Only certain Masks can gain it and only on high Investments. Most will never encounter anyone who has it, and the higher someone's Investment, the harder it is to inspect them. I am not really a good example of what an average person is capable of or what means they have access to."

He offered me the stone, and I took it slowly. Hesitating, I looked down at it. I didn't know a good way to refuse him. But if I did use this, then he would see my **Revelator** Ornament.

"Is something the matter?" he asked.

I opened my mouth, then closed it.

"Ah," he said. "There is something that you haven't told me. I understand. I have kept things as well. It is only natural. I can only say that I do not wish you harm, Marianna Rojas. I will not survive this jungle without you. If you do not want to do this, then we do not need to press. I shall find a different way to help." He extended his hand for me to return the device.

How do people trust others? It was so hard for me, I had never trusted anyone. The closest person I ever had was Khalil, and not even he knew everything about my life. I was raised in a den of vipers, surrounded by criminals. I wanted to trust, but I just didn't know how. I wanted to ask Shimi for advice, to spill everything that I had learned from the message and the vision. But I hesitated. I just couldn't open my mouth and say it. A nagging voice in the back of my head told me that everyone was always out to get me.

And yes, maybe Shimi was playing the long game. Maybe he was tricking me, playing me in order to get more information out of me. Perhaps I would wake up with a knife in my heart one of these days, or not wake at all. But after a life of such darkness, I wanted to be different. I wanted to take this opportunity to be better than life made me. So, trust. And if he betrayed me, then at least I had tried.

"Trust is hard for me," I said. "But, I'll show you, just don't ask questions, I'll tell you when I am ready."

Shim met my eyes, then nodded gravely. "You have my word."

I took a deep breath. "Okay, so what do I do with this?"

"It is called a Reader. Just hold it, and wait," he brought the piece of paper close and put it on top of the crystal in my hand, it immediately started to glow and symbols started appearing on the paper. I blinked, and looked at them uncomprehendingly. It was written in a language unlike anything I have ever seen.

Once the page was filled, he took it back and read. "Hmm . . . well, this at least gives us some idea of what to do."

I narrowed my eyes, and he offered me the paper. "I can't read that."

One side of his lips quirked up, and he just offered the paper again. I took it in my hands and turned to reading. At first it was written in the strange language, but then after a few moments of me looking at it, the symbols shifted and changed, arranging into something that I could understand.

"The Grand Spell translates most things for you."

My eyes widened, and I read what it said.

Marianna Rojas

Mask of the Drainer (Weave, Esoteric):
No Investment; Sixth Carving
Ornament of the Revelator (Esoteric)
No Investment; No Carving
Ornament of the Student (Physical, Weave, Esoteric)

No Investment; First Carving

Attributes:
Physical: C
Weave: F
Esoteric: C

Skills:
[Debilitating Wave]
[Lesser Strength]

[A Lesson Remembered]

"What is this?"

"Your traits, you could say," Shimi said, not commenting on my Ornament. He grimaced, then walked back to his spot and took a seat. I looked away guiltily. I hadn't noticed that just standing had been a strain for him.

"And what does this mean? What does C in physical represent?"

"Ages ago, Elves came up with a system of categorizing people and their power across Investment tiers. They started assigning people ranks, which are: F, E, D, C, B, A, and S. And split these categories into three attributes: physical, weave, and esoteric. Now, we can get a rough idea of how powerful someone is by using these devices." He raised the Reader. "You . . . are stronger than I thought, about as strong as a First Investment physical-based Oni-yi. You having a C rank in physical at No Investment tier, that makes you stronger than most at their Second Investment, aside an Oni-yi, close to some at their Third. Attributes increase with more Investment, based on the Mask type. Your Mask is not a physical one, so I doubt that you will have much increase there as you improve your Mask. Still, your attributes are . . . impressive. Some physical oriented Mask wielders can be lucky if they hit D rank in their Fourth Investment. Do you follow?"

I nodded my head slowly. I didn't think that this was the right time to tell him that a vampire grew stronger as they got older, and that I was very young.

"Each Investment tier comes with some increases in the three attributes. There is a high amount of Mask variety, and some Masks give far greater physical increases upon tiering up, while others don't."

"What do those attributes actually mean? I've been meaning to ask, there just never seemed to be a good moment."

"The basics are as follows. Physical is just what it states, all things related to the physical attributes: speed, strength, toughness, regeneration, agility, senses, regeneration, all of them added together to give a rank. You can have two people of the same rank with vastly different capabilities. One who can bend metal bars, and another who can hear from leagues away but can barely break wooden branches. Weave is all things related to the use of the Source, mostly as related to Mage type Masks. Esoteric is tied to the Way, and as you have noticed, how in tune you are with it."

"Wait, you said that this was just a system invented by the Elves?" I asked.

"Yes."

"So how does that [Inspect] skill show it then?"

Shimi smiled. "That is a good observation. This method was invented so long ago that the skill appeared after it. The Grand Spell is always changing, and new skills and ideas are incorporated from time to time."

"So, what does all of this actually mean for me?" I waved the paper in his direction.

"Well, your Weave is F, which is not surprising as you said your world had no Source. With [Lesser Strength], your strength is probably somewhere around high C, maybe low B, since it scales off your base strength. That puts you on equal ground with most High Second Investment physical Masked, perhaps some low Third Investment ones too. I have seen your speed, and I would put it around the same rank. Your coordination I would put a bit higher. I do not know the rest . . . Would you be willing to share more about your capabilities? It would help me fashion the right path for you to take."

I thought about it for a few seconds. On the one hand, revealing the secrets of my kind didn't sit all that well with me. I could fathom giving him my secrets, but Earth stuff. On the other . . . almost everyone on Earth knew about vampires, and it was doubtful that our capabilities would remain a secret for long. I nodded, and he continued.

"I have noticed that your healing is . . . accelerated compared to what I am familiar with."

"I can heal from nearly any wound, aside from decapitation, though the severity of the wound can make me . . . thirsty."

Shimi thought about that, then touched his neck with one of his hands. "I've noticed the wound around your neck," he commented.

I grimaced as I remembered it. I touched the tender skin and winced—the wound was healing, but it was still raw. "It was done in a special manner, that hurts us more," I told him. "We heal slower from the wounds inflicted in such a way, and they scar."

He looked at my neck, and I prepared myself for the inevitable question of its origin. It was a pretty specific kind of a wound. Instead, he nodded, not prying further.

"Okay, what about disease or poisons?" Shimi asked.

I cleared my throat and answered his questions. "Vampires don't get sick. The **thirst** is a jealous bitch."

"That is . . . incredible. You are like the Naga-shan, better perhaps—they are only highly resistant to disease or poisons. This **thirst,** what is it exactly?"

"It is what makes vampires who we are. It is a name that we give to the bacterium that changed us and made us who we are. It lives inside of us, all the things my kind is capable of are because of it. The **thirst** is the most common name for it."

We spent a while talking about vampire origins. I of course shared only what was widely known by the humans. Not that I knew much more in the first place.

When I was finished, Shimi looked at me, opened his mouth, and then closed it with a sigh and shook his head. "If we were anywhere else . . . If I had but the time to sit down and properly learn, ah . . . perhaps, one day we might meet again, after all of this is done, and I could properly record everything about your kind and world?"

I smiled at his expression. "Sure, you'll have to buy me dinner first."

"As many as you wish," Shimi said. "Though . . . I wonder. May I have your permission to attempt something? It shouldn't be dangerous for you."

I nodded hesitantly. Shimi grimaced as he got up to his knees, and then his nine tails waved behind him. I frowned, looking at him. I felt something tickle my nostrils, and they flared unconsciously. Suddenly, another Shimi stood up from the one kneeling, and a second one followed quickly after, both moving on opposite sides around me. I blinked, then heard something behind me and froze. A hand touched my shoulder, and Shimi whispered.

"What do you see?" he asked from behind me as I watched him kneeling in front of me.

"I—achoo!" I sneezed. The two Shimis standing across from each other shook, their shapes becoming blurry. "What—achoo!" I sneezed again, the weight of the hand on my shoulder disappeared, and the kneeling Shimi tilted his head. I shook my head and felt heat inside of me, and then I sneezed again. The two images disappeared as if they were made out of smoke. "What wa—" I paused, holding my nose to prevent another sneeze. "Was that?"

Shimi's eyes narrowed. "What did you see?"

"You, well, more of you," I answered. "Then I started sneezing."

"Huh," Shimi said, and then I saw him grimace and collapse back on the ground. I dashed forward and caught him, then helped him sit up again.

"Blights," Shimi said. "Should not have done that."

"What was it? A skill?"

Shimi shook his head. "No, no," he answered. "Just like how your kind has quirks, so does mine. The Kitsu-oi can release powerful pheromones that can make any being hallucinate. Mine are not as powerful as a full blooded Kitsu-oi's, but I should've been able to keep you under the effects for longer."

"Wait, they—you—can mind-control people?" I asked. There were many stories and myths about vampires being able to mind-control people, but sadly they were just that, stories. Vampires can't read minds. We are just better at seeing the minute changes in people's expressions, and it lets us trick them and pretend that we are reading their minds.

"No, of course not," Shimi said in between deep breaths. "Though, there is some stigma and fears from those who are ignorant." Just like on Earth it seemed. "It allows us to play with the senses, make illusions. Many consider Kitsu-oi to be tricksters and untrustworthy because of it."

I felt warm knowing that he was sharing more about his kind too. It felt like my trust wasn't misplaced, for now at least.

I looked him in his eyes. From what little I knew about Shimi, I had gotten an impression of a prankster, even though he was often composed and spoke in slow, even tones. But there were moments where I had seen humor in his eyes.

"Well, I guess that it doesn't work that well on vampires," I said.

He nodded. "Mine is not particularly potent, and you still came under its effects. You are probably just highly resistant. More powerful Kitsu-oi will be harder for you to shake. Regardless, this gives me a good idea of your strengths and weaknesses. Now we need to plan your advancement. You are strong and have survivability. That gives you a chance, but even with all of your advantages, all it takes is for you to encounter a monster above Third Investment, and you are most likely going to die. That means that the first thing you need is a way to run away—[Mist Step]. Okolon are the only Third Investment animal common in these parts that you should be able to kill with little danger that will also provide you with something useful. The question now is whether or not you will get more skills."

"What do you mean?"

"I've told you that there is a chance for any Masked to gain an additional skill after every Carving, but that actually getting it is rare. At most, people get two skills per Investment tier, one on entering a new tier and one while climbing. You already have two skills, which is impressive, but even if you gained another, we have no way of knowing if it will be another [Empty Slot] or something else. I don't know enough about your type of Masks to be able to tell. Nor do I know how the blood you are consuming will shape your Mask's evolution."

"It matters?" I asked.

"Of course it does," Shimi said. "Just like how a soldier who had served in war would differ in skill than the one who served during peace, or a guard standing in the palace compared to the one walking the streets. What you invest in your Mask shapes it. You have been drinking the blood of monsters that were on a greater Investment than you. Two of them were already dead, so we have no way of knowing what kind of skills they will give you. But, there is not much that we can do about that."

"Right," I said, I was ignorant, but even he didn't have the answers for what my Mask could do. At least we were ignorant together.

"Before I send you out again," Shimi started, "you've been using those weapons of yours in a fight. I assume that they were brought over with you. But perhaps you might want to look at some of mine?"

I looked down at the glaive that I'd placed on the ground near me. "They are not the weapons I am most familiar with, but they are good enough," I told him.

"You said that you had some training with weapons?"

"I've been trained with a few weapons. The ones I am most comfortable with are the spear, the staff, and the chain and blade," I told him, then explained what each of those looked on Earth. Those were the three weapons that my sire was the master of. I said that I knew how to use them, but I was barely proficient compared to someone like my sire. Still, it was better than nothing. I walked over to his weapons rack, and picked up the one that he had been using like a crutch, the serpent-tongue spear. "This is closest to what I am familiar with, though the blade is too long and it is heavier, but that doesn't bother me much," I said as I tried it out.

Shimi looked thoughtful. "I have nothing like what you described, no chain I'm afraid. The serpent-tongue spear is a good weapon though, but perhaps you might want to hold to your knife for the okolon. You need a fast weapon to take them by surprise and catch them before they can use [Mist Step]."

I was painfully aware of that, given that my ribs still ached. I thought about it, then returned his weapon to the rack. I looked the rest over—most were oversized sword-looking things, thick with serrated edges or weird serpent shaped ones. Old vampires tended to be proficient in the use of ancient weapons—the sword, the spear—and most of them were good with nearly every weapon used in their time. But generally, they all focused on one to near perfection. The modern age had left them behind somewhat, with guns and explosives having replaced the weapons they had spent centuries mastering, not that that made them useless. A vampire with a sword would win against a gun wielded by a human in nearly all cases. It was when the guns were wielded by shifters or other vampires where their power shined. Still, I understood what Shimi was trying to say, I wasn't going to be fighting any of the monsters that would put me in too much danger. And he was right, I had grown accustomed to being the biggest threat around. Walking through the barrios I knew that there was nothing that the humans living there could do to touch me. Here, I wasn't the big bad, here I was just one of the smaller predators. But that was what a vampire was in the end, an ambush predator, and I had to adapt to reality.

Low on the rack, I noticed a dagger-looking weapon. It was thin, about two of my fingers wide, and as long as my forearm, slightly bent. It was double edged, and the handle was a bit longer than what I was used to, probably to accommodate Shimi's larger grip. I picked it up and was immediately surprised at its heft. It was much heavier than what I imagined it would be.

Perhaps two daggers would be the way to go for now. "I'll take this, just in case."

I still had Saia, who I could have turn into a weapon, though for now I was thinking that it would be best to have her on me in case anything surprised me enough and got close. She could probably jump into a beast's mouth again, buying me time.

Though, I had to remind myself that she hadn't even had the chance to do that against the mature ferrorn. I had to figure out a way to use Saia more efficiently. I could see another conversation with her coming as soon as we were alone again.

The Second Hunt

When I was a child, I used to play hide and seek with my friends. Other poor children from the village. I always won. I always had a knack for finding good hiding places, as well as spotting those who were trying to be sneaky. It was funny how this situation reminded me of my childhood. I hadn't thought about it for such a long time. I was free of all burdens back then, just a child playing with my friends. Life has a way of robbing children of childhood far too soon. We should've been allowed to be young and innocent for longer. I don't even remember my friends' names, I barely remember my family even. My life had been filled with dark eyes and faces of grim people, criminals who did terrible things. Not that I was one to judge. I was terrible as well. I'd learned long ago that you needed to be ruthless in order to survive. That the only way to gain anything was to take it.

Perhaps that was why my Mask manifested as it had. Why I had to take power from others. It was something to think about, though I didn't see any other way forward. What would Khalil think if he knew who I had become, I wondered? A monster the same as the ones that we learned about in class. A monster skulking in the jungle, waiting for its prey. I was so divorced now from who I was in the States that I doubt he would even recognize me. The vampires had done horrible things, of that there was no doubt. But there was a beauty in who we were, in how we endured. My sire taught me that. We patroned art in all its forms, we built things that stood to this day, we liked things that endured. Where humans were violence and imagination, the shifters the wrath of nature, vampires were brutality, coldness, and elegance in all its forms. We elevated, or at least that is what I thought. I've read private journals from vampires long since passed, who had lived in the age of the Pharaohs, who had ruled empires. I knew the wickedness that we were capable of, but I've also seen the glimmers of good.

When the world was at threat, we had stepped forward from the shadows. I had to believe that I could be good.

I realized that my thoughts were getting away from me and that I was losing focus. I knew why it was happening, and I tried not to think about the wound around my neck. Silver was poison for vampires in more ways than one. I was not yet fully recovered from it and wouldn't be for at least another week at this rate. I pulled my rambling thoughts back, cleared my head, and focused back on watching the river.

I had found a spot in between the roots of a large tree on the bank of the river. Close to the ground and the area where the animals came to drink. My last hiding spot, high in the trees was good, but it was also too far away. The animals here were quick and attentive. Jumping down from a branch on top of them would alert them by the sound of me falling, and I couldn't exactly control my fall once I executed the jump. Being on the ground was better.

I had made a plan with Saia, and hopefully we should be able to execute it. The dragon's constant presence was a reminder about just how I had changed. Saia could not survive without me, and by keeping her I had been granted a great advantage. I knew that she was nowhere close to what she was supposed to be capable of, that perhaps she was even defective. She was not made for the rules this universe operated under, but I had somehow not found myself thinking about getting rid of her. Perhaps it was my fascination with magic, or perhaps it was the few memories I had of my childhood, when I used to sit at my mother's table and draw in my little coloring book. The book was a hand-me-down from my father, brought over when he moved from Mexico. Not fully colored in, so I had room to play too. I remember one of the drawings; my father had started it, and I finished it. It was a drawing of a big feathered serpent, the Quetzalcoatl. I was young, and I couldn't say Quetzalcoatl properly, so I always called the drawing Zal. I loved it, it had filled my dreams with magic and dragons.

Perhaps that was why I hadn't been more adverse to Saia and her presence. She was a childhood dream come true.

I turned my attention back to the jungle. Shimi had given me an overview of the animals and which I should avoid, for now. The first animals to come to the river were a pack of dozen reptilian looking creatures that I had seen before. From my description Shimi had given me a name for them, kiji. They had long legs that ended in wide clawed feet, their bodies covered in scales. At the back they had short tails, and at the front a long snout that reminded me of wolves on Earth, filled with sharp teeth. They were definitely pack animals according to Shimi, and my decision not to mess with them was correct. They were on the lower end at around mid-Second Investment, but they were vicious and danger-ous opponents even for people of high Investment. They fought like a pack to take down stronger targets and had skills that helped them coordinate. They would've torn me apart.

I waited in my hiding spot for them to leave. I had no issues sitting still for hours on end.

After the kiji left, an hour passed before another creature arrived. I had seen this one before as well, a large animal that had a build of a bear and the head of a wild boar. The gurion, they were scavengers, mostly, but no less dangerous for it. Another animal that I should keep away from for now.

I remained in hiding, as more animals came and went. Finally, a herd of okolon arrived. As large as a moose, with blue tinted fur and a head that was squat and fat looking. I watched them carefully, looking for a chance. According to Shimi, their first instinct would always be to run, so I didn't need to fear the herd that much. If I caught one off guard, the others would try to escape, leaving their poor fellow on its own to buy themselves time to escape.

I waited for the most opportune moment; the fingers of my right hand tightened around the hilt of my dagger as my left traced along Shimi's.

The okolon were just a few steps away from me, a group of four drinking from the river, while the rest milled around. I picked my moment. With great care, I slowly stepped out of my hiding place, my dagger ready. One step, then another, I got closer to the okolon than the last time I jumped one. This time would be different, I was certain about it. The animal in front of me probably wasn't the one that kicked me, but right now I had beef with them all.

My eyes were dead set on the blue-furred animal towering above me; its head was dipped as it drank, its front legs spread wide to let it get low enough. And then I stepped on a root. *Shit, I hadn't even realized that it was a root!* I was not yet familiar with the terrain here. I heard it snap under my weight and saw the okolon's ears twitch, then I pounced.

I kicked off the ground and stabbed with my right. In an instant I crossed the distance, and my blade caught the okolon's shoulder as it pulled back from the water. I grimaced; I had been aiming at where its neck was. Still, I felt the dagger sink in, for just a moment, and then the animal turned to mist. I landed on the riverbank and skidded across the rocks, my legs twisting and absorbing my momentum as I turned around. The mist moved away from me quickly, the other okolon around it doing the same and scattering, most of them already a few meters away. I ran after my target as it re-formed, then leapt. I focused as I caught up, counting its steps. Two, three, four, and I was just behind it, close enough to slash. I restrained myself and watched. Its fifth step pushed it off the ground to the side, and it turned into mist.

Five steps then. Shimi said that it could be anywhere between four and eight. What did he say . . . Fifth step would mean that it was on the Third Investment. That also meant that it would be strong enough to crack my ribs again, or stomp my skull in. Their first instinct might be running, but that didn't mean that they weren't dangerous. I followed the mist as I rushed to get closer to it. I leapt after the mist, getting on its side. As the mist started to take a roughly animal shape, I drew my left hand and threw the dagger.

The okolon re-formed and my dagger sank into its side. It released a whine and jumped to the side as I closed the distance. It wrenched and lashed out with its legs. I dodged to the side, rolling on the ground and getting up quickly. It leapt away, taking advantage and already gaining distance. I cursed and followed after it, running as fast as I could, blood pumping through my veins. My neck burned, and I could feel exhaustion slowly creeping over me. I could not move this fast for much longer.

Then, the okolon turned to mist, leaping out from amongst the trees and into a small clearing. Seeing my chance I slid my dagger into its sheath then yelled.

"Saia, chain!"

She shifted quickly, between two breaths I held a silver knife reflecting the moonlight from above in my right, and I grabbed the chain in my left, immediately spinning it around. I threw the ring, letting the chain fly by me. The okolon re-formed and the ring flashed before its eyes. It reared back raising its head to avoid it. With a firm grasp I caught the chain ending the ring's forward momentum, and with a flick of a wrist I sent it in an arc. The okolon was too surprised by the unfamiliar to react. The ring and the chain wrapped around its neck, once then quickly again, and I pulled. It opened its mouth and keened, making a step in my direction.

—*One*

I jumped forward, my knife extended. It twisted, stepping to the side and turning its back.

—*Two*

My eyes widened as it kicked back with both legs, faster than I expected, for a moment it looked like the air around its legs shook. I brought my arms over my chest, crossing them to block. The two hoof-like clubs smashed into my arms, and I felt the bones in my left arm crack and splinter apart, tear through my skin as shards of bone exploded outward, and I was sent flying back. The chain wrapped around my broken arm caught me midair, tearing flesh, stripping it from bone, stopping my flight and making me scream in pain. My voice echoed through the jungle as I fell to the ground.

I didn't have much time to react as the okolon leapt.

—*Three.*

It pulled me with it, the rope still tied around its neck. I bit the side of my cheek and tasted the blood oozing into my mouth as I felt agony in my left hand. As the animal was soaring through its leap I reached forward with my other hand, dropping the dagger to trail behind me. I grabbed the chain and pulled myself forward and off the ground for long enough to twist and get my legs beneath me. With all of my considerable strength I wrapped the chain around my shoulders, braced, then pulled as I found purchase on the ground. The okolon's neck twisted midair, followed by its body. It crashed onto the ground, and I leapt on it. I collided with it and wrapped my good arm around its neck and pushed my clawed fingers into its shoulder, holding tightly. I opened my mouth to bite its neck when it shook and got back to its feet, ripping me free, along with a handful of blue fur in my mouth. Midair, I saw it take another step: one more and it would turn to mist and be gone.

[Debilitating Wave]

The okolon stumbled to the ground, its muscles spasming. I steeled myself and then twisted my left shoulder and hips, pulling myself with my broken arm back toward the animal. My shoulder popped out of its socket, but it worked. In one shaky movement I reached down and pulled out my holstered dagger. As I crashed into it, I stabbed it in the neck, then wrapped my legs around its torso and pulled the dagger back out only to slash at its leg. It stumbled, and in the fall, I leaned forward, stabbing its head and pulling myself in the position beneath its neck. I opened my mouth and bit down at the side of its throat, blood and fur filling my mouth. The **thirst** roared in my head, and the power of the blood sang in my ears. I repositioned my legs around its shoulders, and I squeezed as it thrashed on the ground, hitting me against the earth and rocks. I felt the clothes on my back tear and the skin scrape against the rough surface. It leaned its weight on me, and I felt my bones cracking, but my jaws were closed tightly, blood seeping through my throat. It sang to me of freedom and power, and as the animal stilled, images flashed through my mind.

I followed my herd, cautious, always cautious, looking for threats. More now than before. We could all smell the change in the air. Danger lurked everywhere. Attacks against the herd had intensified, and we had lost more than any time in the past. We made our way to the river, fearful.

The blood slowed as I got my fill and pulled my head back. I cleared my head and pushed the okolon away then pulled myself from beneath its body. I glanced at my hand; there I saw bone peeking out from my blood-soaked shirt and grimaced. My arm was ruined. I could feel the power of the blood healing me, but bones always healed slower, especially with the wound around my neck. I decided to take advantage of the effect while it lasted. I knew from experience that it wouldn't last for long. I untied the chain from my hand, nearly blacking out as I did so. I had to focus on my mind, and push all pain aside, relegating it to a dull ache in the back of my head as I worked. I ripped the shirt apart to look on my bare limb and saw that it was nearly torn. One piece of bone was pulled away from the skin, and just a tiny strip of it was keeping my hand attached. I pushed the bone back in its place, hissing all the while. It started to heal, flesh immediately reigniting itself, but the bone would be harder. I couldn't even move it; the nerves were severed. I grabbed the chain from the ground along with a dagger tied on the other end, and then I started wrapping the rope around the limb and the dagger, which I pressed at the bottom, making a makeshift splint. Then I shook my head at my stupidity.

"Saia, can you make me a splint?" I asked.

"Feedback: Affirmative," She shifted, changing shape into a makeshift splint around my arm. "This Unit's [Repair] engram is currently engaged in the repair of nerves. Estimated repair time at the current rate of regeneration: thirty-seven hours."

I grimaced, but nodded. My body would prioritize the bone, I knew from experience.

I made sure to keep my ears and eyes open on my surroundings. The fight had made a lot of noise, and there was always a chance of me getting ambushed. Once the splint was done, I looked around. Blood had spilled on the ground, some of it mine, most from the okolon. I didn't bleed too much, even though my wound was severe. My blood bled slower than that of a human, and it regenerated faster, especially after sating the **thirst**. Still, I turned and just as I was about to head back to camp something at the edge of my senses alerted me. A deep penetrating chill took hold of my bones, and before I could even consciously make a decision my body moved all on its own. I shoved myself into a small hollow in between the roots of a nearby tree, hiding. I heard a sound of breaking branches, of something dragging across the ground. A hissing noise followed, and I kept my eyes open, staring from my hiding place.

The **thirst** was something that all vampires fought against; it was our primal nature, the part of us that wanted to demonstrate our supremacy over everything else. I had never felt the way I felt now. It was as if my entire body had turned against me, I didn't think that I could move even if I wanted to. This was . . . terror, and not just mine, but that of the **thirst** inside of me. I felt like I was on the verge of panic, and it was taking everything that I had to keep quiet.

Through the small opening I saw something massive arrive. It slithered over the ground, its head going by too fast for me to really take a good look. The only thing I saw was a sinuous body slithering across the ground, breaking everything in its way, as thick as the trunk of the tree I was hiding beneath.

I watched the corpse of the okolon shift as something out of my view grabbed it, then lifted the body with casual ease until it disappeared from my viewpoint. I heard sounds that I couldn't quite identify, wet and strange. Then something that I was pretty sure was the sound of bones breaking. The giant monster slithered around, getting closer. I didn't dare move. A giant head moved into view, almost flat and triangular, vaguely snakelike, but also completely alien to me. It had two eyes on the side that I could see, both moving independent of one another. Once it was just above me, it paused and opened its mouth showing two rows of thin but sharp teeth. It hissed in a way that was unlike anything I had ever heard, a deep sound that terrified me. It was brown, gray, and green in color, its body covered in what looked like thick hide with bumps all over.

Just as I was nearly certain that it knew I was there, it moved away. The cracking of bushes beneath its weight filled my ears for a long time as it was leaving. I didn't dare move until it moved so far away that I could no longer hear its passage, and only then did I leave my hiding place. The body of the okolon I killed was nowhere to be seen—only blood on the ground remained.

I sat with Shimi back at camp, too frightened to speak or care to keep Saia away from him. I told her to move as he asked to inspect the wound, very clearly not asking questions, yet. Saia shifted to rest near my wrist without responding, and Shimi was able to see the wound. I tried not to wince, as the splint no longer supported my arm. He looked over my wound, an open box filled with bottles next to him along with his aid kit. I was breathing deeply, feeling tired, and the **thirst** was there at the edge of my mind. The healing of the wound had made me hungry, and so soon after I drained the okolon. I would need to feed again before long.

Shimi asked me questions about what happened, and I explained it in a mechanical tone.

"Sikiri . . ." he said slowly once I was finished, grimacing. Whether at the wound or at what I just told him, I wasn't certain. "Yet another animal that is where it should not be."

"It's from the inner ring?" I asked, that thing was . . . I struggled to describe the feeling I had when I saw it. Whether it was a skill or just its presence, it didn't matter; it instilled pure and abject dread in my heart.

"Yes." Shimi nodded. "One of the stronger dwellers of it actually."

"What Investment?"

Shimi glanced up to meet my eyes for a moment before returning his gaze to my arm. "Young? Fifth or Sixth. A mature one will be in the Seventh Investment, one of the most powerful beings in the world. Even I would do all in my power to avoid such an encounter."

"The way that I felt when it got close, was it a skill?"

"It could be," Shimi answered slowly, his eyes looking me over. He opened his mouth and then closed it as if he had thought better of it. After a while, he continued. "Animals of that high Investment all have something unique to just them. Perhaps it was its aura, though if that is the case then we are dealing with an elder sikiri, and we have no chance of survival. I do not immediately recognize what you described, but that means little. It could have unique skills. Or, it was just your instincts screaming at you about the danger."

I tried to remember if there was anything that I knew about the vampires that might give me an insight. I realized suddenly that what I knew of my own kind was . . . lacking. I knew what the humans knew, what was public information, and I knew what my sire taught me. Though he had always been a man of a few words, seeking to instruct me in things that I could make use of now instead of what I would be capable in the future.

"Incredible," I heard him whisper.

I glanced down to see him studying my arm closely. The flesh had knitted over the wound, but I knew that the bone and nerves hadn't regenerated yet.

Shimi picked up a bottle from the box near him and opened it. It was the one labeled with the symbol that looked like a teardrop. "This is a healing potion," Shimi said. "I am unsure if it will be able to help your kind. They have slightly different effects on each race, but they work for them all."

"What kind of effects?" I asked.

"The potion basically encourages the body to heal faster, it does not do anything on its own," Shimi answered. "It takes a lot from people, makes them feel tired, so they use them very carefully. It can also cause issues, using it when bones aren't set can have it heal wrong. Or if there are other issues it can exasperate them."

I tilted my head. "Will it heal my bone?"

"It will help it heal faster."

I gestured for him to go ahead. I could not afford to have a useless arm. He slowly hovered the bottle over where the break was, then dripped a single drop on my skin. Immediately it sizzled and was absorbed by the skin, spreading warmth through it. The warmth pulsed. and I could feel some of the pain go away, leaving only a dull ache. Then, as the warmth subsided, I suddenly felt . . . hungrier. I clasped on the **thirst** immediately, but it wasn't fast enough. I could feel Shimi's blood pumping beneath his skin, I could almost taste its power.

"Marianna?" His voice was a distant thing, a distraction.

Drain him, kill him, feed on him. His power should be ours. The **thirst** pulsed beneath my skin, in my blood. I pounced.

Something hit me faster than I could see, I flew through the air and crashed into the wall, blacking out for second. I opened my eyes, staring at Shimi within the wall of light that made me squint. *The prey was creating noise, waving its limbs* *at us. We smelled its weakness as we prowled around it. Slowly, the prey picked up something from the ground. It was reflecting the light, it smelled of metal, in the back of our head we knew that it could hurt us. We—*I shook my head, pushed the **thirst** down and felt it fight me. I was hungry, so very hungry. I knew that I wouldn't be able to hold it back for much longer. Mustering all of my willpower, I turned around and ran through the gap in the far wall leading out into the jungle, speeding along as fast as I could manage while keeping the **thirst** at bay. My neck burned, and I could feel myself slipping.

Finally, the **thirst** roared up from within and took over. As my mind was pushed aside, only thoughts of blood and the hunt filled my mind.

Revelations

M*ask of the Drainer — No Investment; Seventh Carving*

I startled and woke.

The light was hitting my face, and the scent of blood filled my nostrils. For a moment, I froze, my mind confused, and then I remembered. I remembered my hunt, the injury, I remembered Shimi using a healing potion and then the **thirst** taking over. I closed my eyes and tried to remember what I did while the **thirst** was riding shotgun. It was still me, only I remembered it as if through a dream, with some holes. It was filled with running, with fighting, with blood.

I opened my eyes, then took a deep breath. Quickly, I stood up and looked around. I was lying next to a dead animal that was torn to pieces. I looked around and saw no sign of Shimi. I released my breath in relief. Then took stock of my situation. I had no idea where I was, which was the least of my worries. My clothes were shredded and soaked in blood, again. I saw faint scars all over my body, which would probably remain until night fell and my power returned. The animal next to me was unfamiliar to me, and it was too torn up for me to really identify any features. It was covered in claw marks, and I had apparently opened its side and pulled its organs out. I clawed its eyes out, and ripped its lower jaw off. I swallowed, and felt the taste of blood, fur, and flesh on my tongue.

My hands were red with blood, and I shuddered to think what I looked like. I stood up and looked up at the sun. It was about midday, if I was judging it correctly. I had half a day to go before night fell. I had to survive in the jungle for half a day while I was weakened. I started looking for any landmarks that I could recognize. Quickly, I realized that I would need to find the river. It was the only place that I knew, that would let me orient myself. I made the decision, and started walking, I shouldn't stay in one place for long.

"Saia, you there?"

"Feedback: Affirmative."

I sighed in relief. "Do I want to know all that happened last night?"

"Feedback: The Host's mental state deteriorated, leading to a primal and instinct based behavior."

Yeah, that was about right. I started walking.

I kept looking around me, the shadows looking far scarier than they did at night. I knew that it was just the side effect of feeling like a human again, but it didn't mean that it also wasn't true. [Lesser Strength] gave me a slight boost during the day, but otherwise I was almost helpless.

I found a tall tree and decided that I should risk climbing it. If I could see the terrain, maybe spot the river, I would at least know if I was going in the right direction. Climbing was . . . easier than I thought it would be. My nails were still as sharp and tough as they were at night, and with [Lesser Strength] I could pull myself up with ease. A few minutes of careful climbing, and I pushed above the treetops to look around. Again, a sea of green and blue met my eyes. Then I noticed something in the distance, a massive red wall with lightning flashing through it, so tall that it towered over even the mountains in the distance. The blight. It took my breath away with its majesty. It also reminded me of the vision. Of the feeling I felt . . . I remembered, what I felt with the beast, sikiri, it was the same feeling I experienced in the vision, the touch of wrongness that the monsters held.

I was a fool. Some things were greater than me and my wants.

I gazed at what Shimi had called the mist wall. It looked different during the day, more impressive somehow. I tried to remember where it had been when I had first seen it, and then I used it to give myself a rough direction. After one last look, I started my climb down and the search for the river.

I found the river a few hours and one near-death experience later. A bird half my size had attempted to swoop down on me. I was lucky that I heard it coming at all, let alone had the time to evade. I managed to land a solid hit with a rock throw, which made it leave me alone. I was probably too alien and too much of an effort to pursue, for which I was thankful.

The first thing I did was wash myself as best I could. I had already asked Saia to consume all the blood from my body, but I still felt dirty. Then I headed upstream, hoping to find the waterfall with which I could orient myself, and find the ruins. I kept my head on a swivel looking for threats. As the sun started to set, I reached my destination and started my way back to the ruins and camp. Night had fallen before I reached the ruins.

I hesitated before the crack in the ruins, I hadn't found Shimi's body near me, but that didn't mean that I couldn't have done something before rushing away. It was all a blur. With a deep breath, I entered the ruins and was met with the pale light of the sphere protecting the camp.

"You are back," Shimi said from near the campfire.

I closed my eyes and whispered a silent prayer of thanks to the God that I had turned my back on. I walked forward and saw Shimi tense; he held a dagger in his hands.

"I . . . I'm sorry," I said slowly.

He tilted his head at me.

"It was the **thirst**," I said quickly. "When you used the potion, I think that it spent all of my stored reserves, and it made me hungry. I'm good now."

He looked at me for another few long seconds and then sighed. "I guess now we know how it affects your kind," he said. "It was my fault; such tests should be done with greater care."

I opened my mouth to disagree and then . . . I sneezed. Then, the Shimi that was sitting slowly turned to mist, and I felt cold steel at my neck. I froze and turned my eyes to the side where the real Shimi stood next to me. "I apologize," he said as he pulled his weapon away. "I had reason to be careful."

I swallowed and nodded, the sensation of the weapon on my throat a painful reminder that I could've died without even realizing it. I knew that Shimi was powerful, even weakened as he was, but I somehow always had this idea inside of my head that I could've fought him, or at least that if we ever fought it would be head on. I was on the lowest step of the ladder in this world. And I had to finally admit to myself that I needed help; it was long overdue. I knew why I tried so hard to do everything on my own, why I nearly deluded myself into thinking that I could compare. Living a life where I had no choices of my own shaped me, and this place was my first and probably only chance of a change.

The vision, being chosen as an Exemplar and brought here in the first place. It made me feel like fate was on my side, like this was what I was supposed to do. But now I understood that I had just stumbled onto something that I probably shouldn't have. I had no right to think of myself as some kind of a savior, someone who was going to prevent what I saw in the vision.

Slowly we made our way to the campfire, which somehow wasn't making any smoke. It was a testament to how exhausted I was, that I didn't even question how he had managed that. We sat down, and he provided a new set of clothes. Then after a while he broke the silence.

"How is your arm?"

I glanced at it, knowing that it should've still felt sore but was now perfectly fine. "All healed up."

"Good," Shimi said. "Though, I think that we should test the potion on you during the day as well. Just so we know how it affects your changes then, if at all."

I wasn't quite sure if that was smart. "Not without blood on hand, I don't think," I said.

Shimi nodded. "Yes, that would be prudent."

"I got another Carving, no skill again," I told him.

He sighed. "Seventh Carving, it was to be expected. You are unlikely to gain another skill until your First Investment."

We settled into an awkward silence. I felt like some of the trust between us was broken, and I decided to try to mend it.

"I am sorry for attacking you," I apologized again.

He nodded, but didn't say anything. Instead he turned to look at the fire softly crackling. I looked at him, seeing this alien being illuminated by the soft light of the fire. It cast him in shadows, accentuating his features. Nine fox tails, fuzzy ears on top of his head, blue skin, and orange eyes. A long pointy nose and wide mouth. In the faint light he looked like something out of a story, a trickster demon waiting to steal your soul. No one would ever mistake him for a human. By all rights, I should be afraid of him, I should recoil from what was alien. I didn't. He had saved my life, twice. And I had saved his.

This world was filled with dangers, I knew that. There were secrets and events happening all around me that I didn't understand. I was overwhelmed. Saia, the message, Kirios, the Grand Spell, all of these things were weighing on me, fighting for my attention when all that I should be doing was thinking about surviving. Planning what I would be doing once I got back to Earth. Would I spread what I knew to others? Should I prepare them for what would happen once our protections were lifted and Earth became a full part of Kirios? Or should I look only after myself, prioritizing my own survival?

"There are things that you should know," I started.

He looked up from the fire to meet my gaze. "I understand the importance of secrets; you don't need to share anything that you don't want to."

I shook my head. "I do want to. I . . . I need to, I think. It is important. I've not had an easy life, I've never had choices of my own. I don't trust easily, nor do I like serving others. This place, this world, I felt like it was my chance to be free for the first time in my life, that it was an opportunity. I don't want to die," I admitted. It was harder and easier to admit than I thought it would be. I wanted to live and experience a life on my own terms. I met his eyes.

"This place is a deathtrap, and I, we both, need help if we are to survive. So . . ." I paused, taking a deep breath. "As a child I was sold to a powerful man, and I had served him every day since. This"—I raised one hand to touch the raw wound around my neck—"this is from when the people I served, who I considered my family, decided to execute me, to hang me. The Master, the man who ruled where I came from had decided that I failed. I had killed the people that had executed someone under my Master's domain, a young child, and in doing so I had started a war and caused the death of one of our own. Someone important. My years of service meant nothing compared to that one mistake."

I closed my eyes, thinking back on my last day on Earth. I'd spent it in the dungeon, too drugged to do anything to escape. The Master had made his decision. He hadn't even listened to me. I was sentenced the moment I returned and said what happened. I didn't understand exactly why, but then again, I didn't want to. They had thrown me aside.

"I am sorry that happened to you, Marianna," Shimi said softly.

I met his eyes, and I could see the compassion in them. "Thank you for saying it, but I didn't tell you to seek sympathy. I just wanted you to know some of my past, so that you understood who I was."

Shimi looked away, then after a few seconds back to me. "I was seven years old when the Grand Spell brought my world here. I grew up surrounded by conflict, by death. I lived at Mother's side, learning from her that power was the only thing that could guarantee survival. My mother is not a kind person. I did not learn about love and compassion from her. I have done many things in my life. I have been a soldier, a scholar, a leader. I was . . . lucky, lucky to have met the right people at the right time, lucky that I had been given opportunities that granted me great power. Once, I had tried to use my power to do good, I tried to make the world a better place, a more peaceful place. I failed, and I retreated from everyone, so I became an adventurer, seeking knowledge that was lost."

He grew quiet for a few long seconds, and then spoke.

"In YoKai-ni culture, a name is one of our most important possessions. You must understand, it is not something given out lightly, even when the other person already knows it. To repeat it is to remind the one you are conversing with about who you are. Our true names are only ever used when the situation calls for it, when something of great importance is taking place. Because our names change with us—they tell our story, they reflect our lives and who we are at the moment. The names we have are given to us by others. Sometimes it is by someone close, making it a private and intimate thing. Sometimes, an influential figure would get a name from the people around them, their followers or even enemies. At birth, every YoKai-ni is given a single descriptor. It serves as what we call the *beginning verse* of our name and stays with us for the rest of our life. The name of our family, what we call the *end verse* is added to it, given to us by one or both parents. But all that comes in between has to be earned. The name my mother gave me at birth was Shadow, for I was born in the Shadow of the Old Tree. With my mother's *end verse* I was once the Shadow Beneath the Light of the Broken Moon. That name has changed many times in my life, as I grew, as I changed, as I made friends and enemies."

He kept his eyes on mine, and I could feel the weight of what he was about to share with me. It was an important part of his world, of his culture and people.

"My name is The Shadow That Quells Empires Stands Grinning and Triumphant Beneath the Light of the Broken Moon."

I inclined my head. "It is a pleasure to meet you." I paused, then tilted my head. "Shadow?"

He smiled. "That will do."

I glanced down at my wrist, the silver brace on it. It was time. "If we are doing introductions, Saia, why don't you introduce yourself."

"Feedback: This Unit's designation is Self-Replicating Autonomous Interface Armor Unit, Prototype Mark 3, current designation: Saia."

Shimi, or rather Shadow, looked at my wrist with wide eyes. I rolled my eyes. I held up a hand then cleared my throat. "Shadow, this is Saia, Saia this is Shadow. Why don't you, uh, introduce yourself in person. We organics like to talk to things that at least appear lively."

"Feedback: There is no difference between my forms, all of them are *drone* forms. However, this Unit understands your meaning."

A moment later she shifted over my arm, and I rotated my hand to put out my palm. The goo arranged itself in the shape of the dragon. She looked at Shadow and tilted her head. "Statement: Greetings."

Shadow stood, his tails freezing behind him and his ears twitching. Then his eyes widened, and I saw fear in them. No, not just fear, but terror.

"Statement: This Unit's designation is Self-Replicating Autonomous Interface Armor, Prototype Mark 3, current designation: Saia," she repeated.

"Marianna Rojas," Shadow said slowly, his body completely still and his eyes glued to Saia. "Why do you have what appears to be a dragon hatchling on your hand."

I blinked. "You know what she is?"

Shadow's eye slid up to meet mine, then they narrowed. "Explain, everything," he said tersely. Then, he pulled himself back. "Please."

I explained, telling him how I explored the ruin, and how I found the rift. I told him about what I had encountered in there and then how I found Saia. She chirped in with a few clarifications. His expression once I came to bonding was . . . dangerous, but he didn't interrupt. Once I finished the story, he looked down at Saia, deep in thought.

"A piece of land, floating in space?" Shadow asked. I had just finished describing what I saw.

"Yes," I answered. "It was as if someone had just scooped up a hill and a few buildings. It all looked abandoned, though."

"These monsters that you described," Shimi started. "I recognize them. Deep dwellers, they live mostly in caves on Du'Vir. They came along with the Dwarves, though the ones that I am familiar with are a bit larger and stronger than what you described."

"What I saw in their memories made me think of something," I started. Shadow tilted his head, and one of his ears twitched. "To them it was as if they were in a cave, and then they were there. The light that they saw was the same as what I saw when I was brought to this place. If they are from the same time as the Dwarves, then I think that the Grand Spell just kept a few of them somewhere, and then dropped them there when it needed them."

"Why do you think that they were just not brought there from Du'Vir?"

"The fact that you say they are supposed to be larger and stronger. You said that when the Grand Spell takes a world, it floods it with Source, mutating all life?"

Shimi nodded. "Yes . . . they could have been the same animals, only they had not gone through thousands of years of living on Kirios, adapting to these Source levels. And that place . . . it could have been a piece of land that the Grand Spell didn't use."

"Statement: This Unit did not perceive any change in the state of its existence. However, it had become apparent that something had occurred to change the nature of reality while I was abandoned."

Shadow was pacing about. "You don't understand what this represents," he said at last.

"What do you mean?" I asked.

He grimaced and paused; he opened his mouth but didn't speak. Then after a moment he continued pacing. "Dragons are some of the most dangerous beings on Kirios. Only a few are known about, the great dragon of the Storm Peaks on Elvaros, the Deep Terror of Du'Vir, as some examples. They do not interact with people often, and most of those interactions end in blood. Armies went after them and were wiped out to the last man, rearranging the landscape in the process. Most people leave them alone. The few times they acted, it shook the entire world. We always assumed that dragons lived in the times of the Ancient Ones. But now . . . what you told me," he shook his head. "If they had no connection with the Ancient Ones, if they are . . . artificial lifeforms like the stoneforged of the Dwarves . . . Saia—"

"Not necessarily," I interrupted, shelving the knowledge that there already were artificial lifeforms in this world. His ear twitched as he turned his attention to me. "Well, Saia was made in the image of Ke Erzi, so the dragons that live here could be their remnants."

He closed his eyes. "Possible," he said. "But even that would mean so much that you cannot properly understand. We believed that the Elves were the first race brought here since the creation of the Grand Spell, but if they were not, then how many cycles has this world gone through? How many Great Expansions? So much was lost to the ages that we have no idea about the distant past. We have the remnants of the Ancient Ones, but most of our knowledge is us filling in the gaps based on what we know, or what we think we know. This can change so much."

He grew quiet, and then glanced at Saia. "Tell me, dragon," he said slowly. "Do your creators have the same markings as the ones you have on your skin? The hexagons?"

Saia tilted her head. "Feedback: Negative, the appearance of all Self-Replicating Autonomous Interface Armors is the result of our Structural Biomass."

Shimi grew quiet.

I spoke. "Why did you ask that?"

Shimi met my eyes. "I met a dragon, once, long ago when I was a child. My mother wanted to . . . it is not important." He closed his eyes, his chin turned upward, and his expression turned wistful. "It was as green as the deepest forests, as large as a hill, towering above me, its eye as large as my entire body. It was so long ago, but I still remember, it was covered in the same type of markings."

I glanced down at Saia, at the hexagonal shapes all over its silver surface. That would mean that dragons were probably all artificial. Or the dragon was actually wearing the armor like Saia.

"The truth *is*. It cannot be changed, only our understanding of it." Shimi sighed. He turned to look at the corner where the rift used to be. "Dwelling on this will not help us survive the jungle. And I fear that the Grand Spell has new things in store for us. This rift, for one, I have never seen anything like it before, and I suspect that it is not a trap of the Ancient Ones. No, I fear that it is a spark of change, and that always brings turmoil and death to the world. The last time the Grand Spell introduced something new was when it made the ancient lands soaked with Source wake up, creating the Elementals." He closed his eyes, almost in remembrance. "Millions died, and the world lost much. It has taken us hundreds of years to recover. This time it has added something new at the same time it is bringing over another world. I fear for our future."

I grimaced, then decided that I shouldn't delay much longer. "There is something else that I've got to show you."

He tilted his head and looked at me with an expression that almost made me want to keep my mouth shut, but I had decided on this course. I would be trusting. I would put good into the world and see if it would reward me with the same. If I was going to live free, I would do it on my own terms.

His expression turned pained, and then he motioned for me to go ahead.

I stood and had him follow me. Saia sat on my shoulder as I led him through the corridor, then down the stairs and over the sinkhole into the small room with the crack leading to the hidden area.

We entered in silence, and he looked around with his eyes wide. "This is incredible, and so preserved," he said as he looked at mostly ruined furniture. He noticed what had once been a bookshelf. "Blights, books?"

"It's too bad that they are completely ruined," I said. There was nothing but dust.

"Ruined?" He asked, his eyes meeting mine. "No, not ruined. It is all here." He pointed at the bookshelf. "There are people who have skills that can repair them, this place has been sealed. There are no pieces missing. I need to gather this, take it to the people who can restore it. So much knowledge."

I blinked. I hadn't realized. There wasn't anything on Earth that would be able to restore something so clearly broken down. I was impressed. I glanced at Saia, wondering if her creators could've done it.

"There is more," I said then led him to the other room. He froze once we entered, staring at the statue on the other side. Slowly, he walked forward, glancing down at the remains of Kolan Shuk. He stood there in silence for a long time.

I walked up to stand next to him.

"We never knew exactly how they looked," Shadow said, then bowed his head. "Those images," he said, turning to look over my shoulder behind us. "It looks like the Blight War."

I didn't say anything. I didn't know. Instead, I reached for my belt and a small satchel with a crystal inside of it. I opened it and pulled out the white crystal then placed it on the table in front of Shadow.

He frowned at it.

"What is—" The message activated.

"Hello, friend from across time . . ."

I watched him as his expression went from shock to disbelief. He stood motionless and listened to the message that probably filled in many blanks about the history of his world. Once Kolan Shuk's message finished, he glanced in my direction, then looked at the crystal.

"Touch it," I told him.

Hesitantly, he did as I asked. His eyes closed, but I could see them moving behind the eyelids. It didn't take long for him to step back, his hand pulling away from the crystal as if he was burned by it.

He looked at the crystal for a long moment, not saying anything. I let him digest what he had just experienced. I remembered the feeling all too well. Then, I felt something inside my chest expand. The impression was revealed in my mind, a feeling given meaning.

Ornament of the Revelator — No Investment; Second Carving

[One Truth Verified] skill gained.

Future

We returned back to our camp in silence. Shadow had offered the crystal back to me, which surprised me. I figured that he would want to keep it. Once back, we sat around the fire in silence. Saia jumped into my lap, and I patted her absentmindedly. Her skin, or hull, or whatever it was, actually felt really nice. It was smooth, and felt like it would be soft. Somehow the motions of petting her made me feel a bit better. I couldn't help but worry about what Shadow was thinking. What he had just seen would be a lot, or I thought as much at least. I didn't know if he would even believe in it.

As the silence stretched, I decided to speak first.

"That monster I encountered in the jungle, that made me feel that terror," I started. He raised his head to meet my eyes. "I remembered, it felt like what I experienced in the vision. Less intense, a lot less intense actually, but still the same."

He nodded. "A sikiri is a monster, blight infected. I had suspected when you said it. I just didn't want to believe it. Monsters don't leave the Blight Curtain, not since the Blight Wars. Some remnants are encountered from time to time across the world. But we were very thorough during the war."

I didn't say anything, I had nothing to say. He turned back to watching the fire. After a while he spoke again.

"We have no real seers you know," he started. "We have people that had tried, and many nations of the world keep trying. But to my knowledge no Seer Mask had ever been able to gain enough Investment. We don't know how. A few times, someone got lucky, gained a Carving or two. Rarer still they gained a skill. Something to let them glimpse into the future. Every time though, when they use it, they go mad."

I blinked. "Was it something that they saw?"

Shadow shook his head. "I don't know, no one does." He raised his head to look at me again. "If I am right, the vision showed us the past, the time when the

Ancient Ones—the Vim—ruled and expanded. And then when they encountered the blight. When that battle happened I thought . . ." He paused, then
grimaced. "At first, I thought that vision was about the Blight Wars, again something in the past. That perhaps it was all an allegory, because what they fought
did not look like monsters I am familiar with. Then once I realized what I was
looking at, when I saw the horrors in that square . . ."

He grew silent, his eyes going back to the fire.

"You think that it was true, that it happened?" I asked, hoping for him to
laugh at me. Somehow, his expression told me that it was a hollow hope.

"Monsters that we fought were always animals corrupted by blight," he
started. "Later, some of our people got corrupted too. They were harder to fight,
but we did as we had to. What I saw in that vision, it was nothing like the war.
Those monsters did not look like any animals. They looked like people unlike
anything that I had ever seen. And the people that fought them, whose memories
we have seen, those could only be the Ancient Ones, the Vim."

I remembered what I saw in the recording, in the vision, the memory seen
through the eyes of one of them. I nodded.

He closed his eyes. "Yes, I think that this happened."

"Do you believe it?" I asked.

"It is a message from an Ancient One," he said slowly. "They still hold secrets
that we have not even begun to scratch. Knowledge of the Source that we can
only dream about. Seer Masks exist, even if we have never been able to make
them work. The message gives a warning about the blight, or at least what is
behind it. I . . . I don't know yet if I believe it. I need to think about it."

I could understand the need to think. I'd had a while to dwell on what I had
found too. I let him think, and pulled myself into my soul space.

The now very familiar room appeared around me. Saia was again standing
next to me. I looked around for any changes. Behind the Mask, there were two
new additions, two small pedestals with not bowls, but icons on them. I walked
over and looked at them more closely. One was an open book, made of stone, the
other a seal—like an old one that was pressed into wax on letters. One was my
[A Lesson Remembered] skill, and the other my new one, [One Truth Verified].
I leaned down, reading the plaques beneath them.

[A Lesson Remembered]

Remember any lesson you've learned.

[One Truth Verified]

Verify the truth of any single piece of written word.

[A Lesson Remembered] was straightforward, though it had not yet become available again. The other one was harder to be used, I felt. I would need to experiment with it, once I had the chance. I glanced at Saia.

"Any changes, with how you feel when you are in here?" I asked.

"Feedback: Negative, however this Unit has observed that following a visit to this space, the synchronization with the Host increases slightly. Current synchronization at 15.5%."

"What does the synchronization actually mean, and do?" I asked.

"Feedback: Many of this Unit's systems are currently unavailable because of the low synchronization rate. Like the direct neural communication link, status display, and others. The rate is low because of the incompatibilities caused by the fact that the Host is not Ke Erzi. This Unit has been trying to compensate."

"Ah," I said. It did make sense, of course. Saia was not made to be bonded to a vampire. But we were stuck together now. I could not remove her without a chance of killing myself, and I would get her basically erased if that happened. It was just another thing that was now my responsibility and that I had somewhat ignored. There was just too much to do.

I turned and walked to the corridor of doors. I could see that it had deepened and that new doors were now present. There were eight doors in total now, each different from the last. I walked over and immediately recognized what had to be the door of the reaper, just next to the one of the mature ferrorn. There was a quality about those doors that stood out from among the others. There were two more doors. The first was made out of wood with patches of blue fur on it and a hoof print in the center—the door of the okolon most likely. The next one was adorned with feathers, the door to the cresser, I suspected. The other was unfamiliar to me, a wooden door with two strange paws indented on it—the animal next to which I woke up after the **thirst** took over. I didn't know what it was. I didn't remember the fight, and the corpse was ripped apart beyond recognition.

I glanced at Saia and then had her shift into blade and chain. I rolled my shoulders and then opened the door leading to the okolon. It wasn't aware that I was there. I had ambushed it, and this place reflected that. The area was the thick jungle and the riverbank where I had attacked it. I moved slowly, taking care not to alert it. I knew now just how dangerous the creature could be.

I didn't want to risk death. I had a different plan this time.

Once I got close enough, I pulled out the knife that was always on my waist, then aimed. I waited as the okolon bowed its head to drink, and then I hurled it at the beast with all of my considerable strength. The knife spun through the air and hit the okolon on the side of its neck. It burst into mist immediately, jumping away, the knife going with it. I didn't move from my spot as it ran away. Instead I stood and waited. Soon it rounded around a tree in the distance, and then I could hear it from behind me.

This place was not the jungle, this was inside of my soul, a small area that bent on itself.

I let my blade and chain down and started spinning. The okolon heard me, but I still sent the blade flying at it. Of course, it turned into mist and jumped away. There wasn't much room in the jungle to really use the chain, but I still swung it around, creating noise, forcing the okolon to run. It re-formed, and I could see that the side of its neck was soaked in blood. I followed after it, slowly. I couldn't keep chasing it, I would tire long before it did. Instead, I kept scaring it, forcing it to run.

It didn't take long for the wound and its own tiredness to catch up with it. I walked behind it as it stumbled trying to get away from me. As it slowed I still kept my distance, swinging my chain and then lashing out from a distance. I was not getting close to it again.

Over the next few minutes, I stabbed and slashed it enough that it collapsed, and I finally decided that it was safe enough to walk up to it and slice its throat. The animal collapsed into particles, and I gained a new skill orb. I picked it up, wondering if it was what I needed. Shadow had said that most animals would have a handful of active skills, but that most of them would be passive. He was also certain that there was some logic behind how and which skills I gained. If what he thought was right, for the blood I got from my own kills, I should be getting their best skill.

I walked back to the main room and placed the skill on a shelf.

[Mist Step]
You may turn to mist and execute a step in mist form.

I smiled as I saw that it was the correct skill. From what Shadow told me, I should be getting the base version of the skills. It meant that the skills would, or at least should, improve with me as my Mask advanced. I turned and walked back into the corridor, and then to the room with the cresser. The bird died as easily as it had died the first time. Though it had nearly ruptured my eardrums with a screech that I was pretty sure was a skill. Once I brought its orb to the shelf, I was proven correct.

[Sonic Screech]

Release a powerful sonic screech.

I assumed that the power of the screech would rely on the power of the person using it. If someone had stronger lungs and vocal cords, they would probably be able to do more damage. It fit with what Shadow explained to me: my [Lesser Strength] did scale based on my own physical strength.

I returned to the doors and hesitated before the one of the unknown animal. I had killed it while in the thrall of the **thirst**, so I didn't know what it was or what it was capable of. If I died inside of here, I would die in the real world too. Still, I was curious and sure enough that I could defeat it. I entered its room. It was the jungle again, and nearby I found the animal. It was short, had an almost boar-like look to it, coupled with curved tusks. It snorted in my direction and charged me. I was taken aback by its speed, but I gathered myself quickly.

I stood my ground and waited for it to get closer. It leaned its head down, pointing its tusks in my direction and got ready to gore me. I jumped to the side, but its head blurred, and its speed increased, taking me off guard for a moment. I managed to put my left hand out quickly, leaning on its head. The animal's attack was powerful enough that I was picked up from the ground as I let myself be pushed, guiding the force of its attack with my hand on its head. Its attempt at goring me threw me up in the air above its head. I took advantage and threw my blade with my right straight down, piercing the top of its skull.

I dropped down lightly and walked over to the animal as it twitched on the ground. I grabbed the dagger and twisted before pulling it out. It died, and I collected another orb, which I returned and placed in a bowl.

[Lesser Impale]

Execute a quick impaling motion.

Again, it wasn't anything really powerful, but still, another skill. With three new skills I had access to four on the shelf, and two slotted into my slots, six skills. I glanced at the pedestals, thinking, then I reached over to the shelf and picked up [Mist Step]. It was the strongest skill I had access to, and I had seen just how effective it could be. In a place where everything wanted to kill me, I felt like I needed more options to escape. I walked over to the two pedestals, trying to figure out which one I should switch out. In the end I decided on leaving the [Lesser Strength] active, It gave me an overall boost, while the [Debilitating Wave] was a one and done skill that had a long cooldown. [Mist Step] was better in every way. I switched out the two skills, feeling the loss. It would take time for [Mist Step] to activate, but there wasn't anything that I could do about that.

I looked around the room, then with a thought brought myself out of it.

I opened my eyes in the real world, Shadow was still deep in his thoughts, and I didn't want to interrupt him. I stood, Saia cradled in my arms and walked to the other side of the camp, where he had his rack of weapons. As I looked them over, Saia spoke in a low tone.

"Statement: This Unit has detected an increase in the synchronization rate of

7%, as well as a strange phenomenon. This Unit is still in contact with the drone unit within the soul space."

I blinked. "What, you are still in there?"

"Feedback: Obviously not, this Unit's core is nestled against the base of your skull."

I took a deep breath. "You know what I mean."

"Feedback: Clarity in communication is preferable."

"Fine." I rolled my eyes. I wondered what that meant. Was it just because of the synchronization rate? It was the only explanation that I could see.

"Statement: Communication with soul space lost."

I grimaced. It seemed like it wasn't permanent just yet. I shook my head and turned my attention to the weapons. There were a lot of different ones, though most were some kind of sword variant, and all oversized, too big to be wielded comfortably at least by me. Granted, I knew nothing about the styles and people of this world.

After a while I returned to the campfire. Shadow still seemed deep in thought, and his expression didn't look like he was getting anywhere. I figured that perhaps a distraction was in order. I walked over to where my sleeping area was and retrieved my glaive, then walked back over and sat next to him.

He turned to look in my direction, and I placed the glaive and the knife I got from the chest next to his feet, then I pulled out the two pouches from belt.

He raised an eyebrow, one of his ears twitching inquisitively.

"What is it?" he asked.

I pointed at the objects. "I got this from that rift, in the chest at the end."

I reached over for one of the pouches, then offered it to him. He opened it up, then spilled its contents on the ground.

All three of us peered at the seven gemstones on the ground. Gleaming in four colors, two of each, giving off a faint light, at the start at least, minus one now since Saia had *assimilated* one. Shadow, just like me, could feel something from the gemstones, so he let them lay on the ground without touching.

"They definitely have Source," he said, leaning down to look at them from up close.

"Statement: This Unit concurs with that statement," Saia chirped from my shoulder. "Though, this Unit has no records of anything similar on Erzi."

Shimi glanced at the tiny dragon, but then turned his attention back to the gemstones on the ground.

"Any idea what they are?" I asked.

"If it is not native to that world, and . . ." Shadow frowned. "It came with these other items? Inside of a chest?"

I nodded. I had wanted to see if he knew what the gems were before letting him see the other items. I reached over and nudged the three items in front of Shadow. First, I offered him the other pouch, the one filled with silver.

"This is currency," Shimi said slowly as he let the coins drop onto his bare palm. I tried to suppress a wince and failed.

"What is it?" Shimi asked.

"They are made out of silver," I answered after a moment of hesitation.

Shadow glanced down at the coins. "And that is . . . bad?"

"Yes."

He paused to see if I would say anything else, but even with trust, there were things that I had trouble revealing. "Well, they are no currency that I am familiar with," he said, "though that means little. There are countless kingdoms and nations in the world that have their own." He glanced up at Saia. "They are not from your world, are they?"

"Feedback: Negative."

He nodded. "As I thought."

Next, I offered him the dagger. He took up the sheath gently, his brow furrowing. "This is familiar."

I tilted my head, that wasn't the response I had expected. "Familiar how?"

Shadow raised his head, and his orange eyes met my own. "This is definitely a dagger of YoKai-ni make. More precisely, this is a Tengu-gi style dagger." He gestured in the direction of my other dagger, tucked at my waist, the one I had taken from his rack. "If you will?"

I pulled out the dagger and passed it over. He unsheathed the other one, then put them next to one another, looking them over for a few seconds. "This one." He raised the one that I had taken from him. "This is an old blade, crafted by a master of his craft. Perhaps one of the best in the world."

I blinked; I hadn't realized that his weapons were so valuable.

"This one that you found, is inferior in every way. It is not expertly crafted nor put together. And it is made in an old style," he said, then his eyes narrowed. "And yet, that is strange, because the blade was made in the crafting style that is no longer practiced. A style that has been irrelevant since our world was joined with Kirios."

I tilted my head. "Isn't it possible that someone just experimented with that old style?" I asked.

Shadow nodded. "On its own, it is not that strange, you are correct. But this . . ." He tapped the handle. "This is what makes the blade strange. This thread here is called liksan, and it can only be made by harvesting the excrement of a particular animal. An animal that no longer exists. The transition is not kind. The Source mutates life in many different ways. The consequence of my world arriving here was that this animal was hunted to extinction by its natural predator, whose mutation made them far more aggressive. Liksan is beyond precious, it cannot be replicated, it is used in only the greatest of works. For someone to place it on a dagger such as this one, it is unthinkable."

I grimaced. I had my suspicions, and it seems like I was somehow right. I grabbed the last item that I found, the glaive, and then offered it to him.

He put the daggers aside and accepted the glaive. He took a long look then nodded. "Likewise, this too is of a poor quality. Though I am not familiar with this style." He leaned down to look at one of the screws that were holding the haft and the blade in place.

Yes," I said. "Take a look there, behind the blade, the text."

He did as I asked. He found the text easily enough on the decorative part of the haft. "Made in . . ." He frowned as he tried to read what had to be an unfamiliar word to him. It seemed that the translation of the Grand Spell wasn't exactly perfect.

"It says, *Made in China*," I told him.

He raised his eyes to meet mine. "I assume that you know what that means?"

I nodded. "China is a country from my world. That means that the weapon was made there."

He tilted his head, then glanced back at the glaive. "From your world?" His eyes slid to the two daggers next to him. "Oh."

"I think that these . . . rewards, were put there by the Grand Spell. That it took them from the other worlds. Yours and mine. Or perhaps they are just copies. I don't think that it matters."

His eyes narrowed. "The Grand Spell possesses godlike power—no, it is as a god. Its reach extends beyond this world, touching many others. This . . . it is not beyond it, not by any stretch of imagination."

"Yeah," I said slowly. "But why introduce something like that? A rift in space that leads you to a what? A piece of another world, where you need to fight a monster to get rewards and leave?" It was all so familiar to me. Which made me wonder if perhaps the Grand Spell got the idea from us, from Earth.

"There is no point in attempting to understand the Grand Spell. Its designs are far beyond comprehension. One thing is for certain, this will cause a lot of . . . chaos."

He shook his head, then put the weapons aside and returned his attention to the gemstones. Seven of them were on the ground in a pile, four colors, orange, light blue, brown, and light green. "Then, are these from another world as well? Or are they something else entirely."

"Statement: The gemstones appear to be elemental in nature, and they contain a minuscule amount of Source Weave along with an engram that is beyond this Unit's ability to comprehend."

Shadow's eyes narrowed and he picked up one of them. As he was picking it up, I noticed that the light of the gemstone in his fingers and one of the ones on the ground dimmed as it was raised away from the other gems. Just like when I had done it before. Shadow noticed it too. He brought it close to one of the other gemstones and nothing happened. He frowned then pressed it closer to the one that was of the same color, and both started to glow faintly.

I told him about what I found out before, that they glowed next to the ones of the same color and next to two other colors as well. Saia repeated what she discovered or at least what she believed about the colors corresponding to fire, air, earth, and water elements.

He glanced at the gemstone in the palm of his hand. "I see that why they say the wisdom of dragons holds true even for hatchlings."

Or alien intelligent computers made out of metallic sludge that can take the shape of a dragon, I thought, but didn't say out loud.

"Do you have any idea what they are?" I asked instead.

"I can feel it tugging at my Mask, as if it wants to touch my power."

"Do you think that there is danger?"

"There is always danger, Marianna. You should learn that lesson before life forces you to," Shadow said, then opened his eyes and looked at the gemstone. "Well, I do like to be on the forefront of new discoveries."

With that he raised the gemstone and pressed it against his chest.

Nothing happened.

Both of us frowned. "This is strange," Shimi said. "It almost feels like . . . Ah." He made a pulling motion over his chest and manifested his Mask. The blue and white Mask appeared in his hand, and Saia immediately perked up.

"Query: This Unit requests that item for assimilation."

I turned and glared at the dragon on my shoulder. "Saia!"

Shadow's ear twitched and his eyes glanced at me. "Assimilation?"

"That means that she wants to eat it," I clarified.

"Respectfully, no," Shadow said to the dragon.

"Statement: Regretful."

"May I?" He gestured to the gemstone. I waved him to go ahead. He placed the gemstone against the Mask, and it flowed into it then disappeared.

"Oh," Shadow blinked. "So that is what this does."

His Mask winked away, and he grabbed one of the daggers and unsheathed it. Then, he swung it, his hand blurring in a slash to his side. The air wavered, and I heard a hiss, saw sparks flash through the air where the blade went through.

"Well," he said, studying the edge of the dagger as it went from bright and heated back to normal color.

"What is it?" I asked.

"The gemstone altered, or maybe upgraded my skill," Shadow answered. "When I pushed it against the Mask, I felt like I could push it in the direction of one of my skills. Not all of them, I don't think that all of them were compatible, I assume. I chose one of my oldest and weakest skills, [Slash]. It now seems to have some elements of fire, a very weak effect, but still it is there."

He manifested his Mask then placed a palm over it. He closed his eyes and then I heard a crack of breaking glass. Fragments of orange crystal fell from his Mask. "Hm . . . it looks like you can remove them from the skill, but that destroys them." He grimaced and then looked at me. "Apologies, I did not intend to destroy that which is yours."

I waved my hand. "It's okay, at least now we know. You never saw anything like this before?" I asked.

He shook his head. "No, it is something new. And I doubt that this is all there is to it. New additions by the Grand Spell are never so simple. Once everyone finds out about this, if those rifts start appearing everywhere . . . Blights."

"Should I try one?" I asked.

Shimi glanced at the gemstones. "I wonder how they would affect your skills. Would it impact your base skill, the [Empty Skill], or the skill that you slotted in, or both?"

I was eager to find out as well. I reached for the brown gem, then manifested my Mask and brought the gem near. I felt the pull and then . . . nothing. The pull was there, but somehow I instinctively knew that the brown gem didn't fit.

"I don't think that this one is compatible with anything that I have," I said.

Shimi tilted his head, and one of his ears twitched. "Hm, if we are correct in our assumptions, then that one is Earth attuned. You have [Debilitating Wave] and [Lesser Strength], I don't see how that could impact either of those skills. Try another."

"I've switched out [Debilitating Wave] for [Mist Step]," I said as I reached over for a green one.

"Smart choice," he said.

I repeated the process and felt the pull again, then as I touched my Mask, again the same instinctual sensation appeared. This time I knew that it would work. I felt like it could make a connection with only one of my skills, the [Mist Step], so I pushed it in that direction. The gemstone melted into my Mask, and the pressure inside of my chest pulsed.

[Mist Step] skill upgraded.

"It worked," I said then stood up wanting to try it out. Then I stopped as I realized that the skill was not yet active. I returned to my seat with a grimace on my face. "It attached to [Mist Step], but the skill isn't active yet. I have a cooldown when I replace skills."

He nodded, but his attention was on the gemstones.

"This is amazing," Shadow said. "I can only imagine what more there is to discover about this."

I nodded, though to me it was just another new and strange thing among an entire array. For him this was something truly new, in that at least we were equal. With nothing much to do, we both turned to our own thoughts, the night came to an end, and with it came sleep. I was exhausted. I closed my eyes, and dreamed.

Bond

omething is missing here," I heard Khalil say and raised my eyes to look at him.

"Missing where?" I asked.

"Everywhere." Khalil grimaced. "According to my research, the vampires are . . . hiding something."

I chuckled. "Oh really? What was your first clue? That they hid in the shadows for a few thousands of years?"

Khalil glanced in my direction and gave me a smile. "That was not what I meant. I am referring to their origins."

I tilted my head. "It is just a story, like the ones in your holy book."

Khalil glanced down at his cross, his thumb gently rolling one of the beads on the chain. "It's not the same."

"Isn't it?"

"I invited the talk about the vampire origins, not my own faith," Khalil said.

"Sorry, Ali." I raised a hand. "What did you mean?"

"Their origin speaks of a great calamity, a fleeing people that believed that their gods had abandoned them," Khalil said. "This is not that strange. Many holy texts have similar stories. Some believe that the reason many religions stories have similar themes like the flood or an exodus is because of something, an event, that is shared in all of our history. Though that might also—"

I cleared my throat, and he paused, then coughed uncomfortably and blushed. "Right, back on track. Their origin speaks of a hundred people venturing into a forbidden valley, seeking aid from a dark god that had predated their own. They drank from an ancient pool that they believed would let them contact this ancient being, and almost all of them died. Only three of them survived. The original vampires. On the surface, there is nothing strange in that story. Until you take into account the actual science."

"In what way?" I asked.

"*The vampire biology is based on the symbiotic relationship between the sanguinium bacterium and a host. The change is complete and permanent, and their origin myth plays into it too closely. The pool is obviously the place where they found the bacterium, the people that died were the ones who didn't survive the infection, the three that survived were the first vampires. Subsequent infections, the turnings, were then done by the bacterium already acclimated to their new hosts, and therefore easier. The myth checks all the boxes.*"

"*And it shouldn't?*"

"*Where is the allegory?*" Khalil asked. "*Where is the grandeur, the acts of God?*"

I tilted my head at him. "*What do you mean?*"

"*First, the story was written down during the times of ancient Greece. We know that the oldest vampire remains are at least ten thousand years old. Why nothing before then? There is . . . so much missing. Everything is missing!*"

"*We have accounts of vampires from as far back as we have of the human race.*"

"*That's my point exactly,*" Khalil said. "*We have human accounts; the vampire records are barely existent. And no records reliably confirmed to have been written by a vampire exist beyond three thousand years ago, the start of the Bronze Age at the earliest. What about before? There is nothing, it is as if vampires just came into being right then and there. Or rather they just decided to start recording then. And yet, we have stories about monsters in the night stretching far beyond that, cave paintings, tablets with written warnings. They existed before, but we have no evidence from the source itself.*"

"*That's easy,*" I said. "*Vampires are long lived. They would see little need in recording their history. Why bother when your sire had lived through it all, and they seldom died. And they always lived among the humans, so they left no remains of their own settlements.*"

"*Nothing? Not even one instance? The myth too is . . . it is as if it was invented based on what the genesis stories of other more popular religions at the time were.*"

"*You are reading too much into it, Ali,*" I told him.

"*They are hiding things. They told us that they have four stages in their life. The young or Fledgling vampire, those that were just turned. Adult, which they become once they mature—most often it requires at least a hundred years to reach that stage. The Elder stage, once they get older than two hundred years, and the Ancient, those older than a thousand. Can you imagine living for that long, Mari? How much time would you have to alter history? It would be easy with their influence.*"

"*You are not going down the conspiracy theory route, are you?*" I asked.

Khalil grimaced. "*It isn't a conspiracy if it's true.*"

I laughed. "*Next you are going to tell me that vampires sank Japan.*"

Khalil grew quiet, and continued reading, doing his research.

This was the second dream I'd had since coming here. The state of stasis that the day brought put a vampire into a dreamless sleep. Now that had changed, and I wondered what else would change for the vampires as well as other races on Earth.

I was aware that I was dreaming, even though I could not change anything. It was as if I was experiencing the past. I sat in the college library, a passenger in my younger body. Across from me at the table sat Khalil, my friend. He held a cross which was attached to a chain of praying beads wrapped around his hand as he read from a book on the table. The scene had played out exactly as it was in my memories.

I remembered thinking that I shouldn't have said that last part. It had hurt him. He had always taken his research into the vampire history seriously, as well as his skepticism toward them.

Then, the dream changed. Khalil raised his head.

"What do you want to do with your life Mari?"

Khalil had never spoken that question to me. Somehow, I could feel the dream shifting around me, and I raised my head, now in control of my dream-self.

"I . . ." The words were at the tip of my tongue. That I wanted to do good, that I wanted to make sure that what I saw in that vision didn't happen again. That the darkness frightened me more than anything else ever had. What I had seen in the vision, the horrors that those monsters committed, it was as if I felt the presence of pure evil.

The world had changed, things would never again be the same. I witnessed the power that Shadow held, the godlike power of the Grand Spell. What did being good mean compared to something like that. What would doing good even look like. I'd spent my whole life being used. I had no agency of my own. Not until I stumbled onto the message from the past.

I had given Shadow the knowledge. Perhaps that was enough. He was far better equipped to deal with all of that than I was. No, my goal should be fixed on Earth, and helping it survive what was going to come. I had no friends to look for, no family. My sire had watched as they put a silver rope around my throat. I was alone. But I still loved my world. It was the only thing that I had ever known. I wasn't going to let it suffer. I remembered old stories my mother used to tell me, the books my father used to read me. The smiles of a young girl dreaming about dragons.

So, I would survive and return to Earth. Do everything I could and use what I had learned to help them. Not for the greedy who stood on top, not for the nations and politicians, not for the vampires or shifters or even humans. But for those little girls and boys, and their dreams.

* * *

I opened my eyes as the sun moved behind the world. I sat up and looked around, finding Shimi on the other side of the fire, talking with Saia.

"Well slept?" Shadow asked.

I nodded.

"I have just been filling in Saia here regarding the nature of Source on this world. She finds it very . . . fascinating."

"Statement: That is correct."

I smiled for a moment, and then turned my eyes on Shadow. "Can we talk?"

His ear twitched, and a few of his tails swayed behind him. "Of course, about what?"

I stood and walked closer, taking a seat on one of the stones next to the fire. My eyes were drawn to the flames as they danced across the logs.

"Did you think about . . ." I trailed off, we both knew what I was talking about.

He nodded, then tapped a chest next to him. "I've gone back to the room and gathered everything that I think can be salvaged. I need to bring it to someone who can restore it. Perhaps there are more clues in what the Ancient One left behind. For now, I cannot ignore it, I must act as if that vision was true. The Blight Curtain is clearly connected to what happened back then. We need to come together and discover how. Our survival has become a lot more important, Marianna," he told me with a sigh. "Alone, I have no chance of reaching the coast, especially not if a monster sikiri is around. I am going to need to rely on you."

"I'll do my best," I told him. A part of me felt relieved that the message was not going to be my responsibility. It was better that way. He could talk to the right people in this world, spread it better than I ever could. My small part to play would be keeping him alive, helping him leave this place. That was good, it was enough.

"We need more than just your best, Marianna," Shadow said then stood and walked over to me. He knelt in front of me. "I need to prepare you better, to train you as much as I can, and we just don't have enough time." He sagged, as if a great weight had just been laid on his back. And it had, I had put all that I found on him. I reached over and placed a hand on his shoulder.

"I'll do anything that you think I need to. I don't want what we saw to be the truth, but more than that I don't want to live with the knowledge that perhaps I could've prevented something terrible in the future and I just didn't do enough."

Shadow smiled at me, the nodded to himself. "May I know what your profession was, before you arrived here? Do you have any formal combat training?"

I blinked; that was not what I had expected, but I nodded. "Yes, I do."

"The way you attacked me before was interesting," he said. "And I have watched the manner in which you move your body. It speaks of someone who has had some training, not nearly enough, but some. Except that something does not seem quite right to me."

I raised an eyebrow but then decided to just tell him. "I was . . . an enforcer I guess you could say."

"You served a Lord?"

"In a way. A warlord is a better word for it perhaps. I worked for an organization that dealt with some . . . unsavory things."

Shadow must've noticed my hesitation because he didn't press to learn everything. "But you were trained in how to fight?"

"I was trained in how to enforce, in how to use firearms, and yes, I had some martial arts training." If you could call a few years of learning from my sire training.

"Martial arts, that sounds like you learned a fighting style?" Shadow asked, surprised.

I nodded. "Yes, from my sire, the man that turned me into a vampire."

"Ah." He scratched at the base of his ear with two fingers. "Can you show me?"

I blinked, but then moved to do what he asked without asking why. I would trust him and do what I could to help our chances. I showed him what I knew.

I went through the motions, demonstrating a couple of basic stances of the martial art that my sire taught me to Shadow. He had never told me what the art was called, and now I realized that I should've asked. I wasn't very good, I could admit, I had always relied more on my superior physicality. Shadow sat and watched as I executed a few techniques against phantom opponents, then he joined me and asked for me to demonstrate on him. We continued for a while, well past the point where I thought we should've stopped. I was embarrassed to speak as it became apparent that he was a lot more skilled than I was. The silence between us stretched save for a few questions that Shadow had about the reasons why I would do something, or the positioning of my body—questions that I had very few answers for. But I was emboldened to push through. We were bound in purpose now, had shared and trusted each other.

"That is enough." Shadow called our sparring off. "I see now."

I tilted my head. "You see what?"

Instead of answering, he went back to the fire and sat down, clearly near exhaustion. He motioned for me to join him, and I did as he asked.

"Can you tell me about this . . . **thirst** of yours? What does it feel like?"

I started at the change in topic. I wondered why he wanted to know, but then decided that he had the right to it if he was going to be spending time near me. Slowly, I started to explain.

"The **thirst** is like a . . . ravenous maw, always hungry. It can be sated for a time with blood, but never fully suppressed. It is always here." I placed the palm of my hand over my stomach. "Always waiting in the background. It amplifies all that we are, our emotions and our desires. Ultimately, it wants to ensure its and my survival, at all costs."

"A survival instinct," he said thoughtfully. "How do you learn to control it?"

"Control comes with age," I told him.

"You were not taught any ways of controlling it?"

"No. When I was a Fledgling, I was just kept away from people and given blood daily. Then I—" I stopped and remembered what it was like when I was first allowed back into the world. The first place I was taken was my sire's cabin, and the first thing he did was to start teaching me martial arts and the art of tea brewing, *chadō*. Now that I thought about it . . . that had helped center me. I hadn't even realized it at the time. "Maybe I was, actually."

Shadow nodded. "My kind, or rather, my father's race, the Tengu-gi have something akin to your **thirst.** We call it the Way of the Mind. It allows us to enter a state that increases our physical attributes and gives us a pure and unbreakable single-minded focus. But it is hard to control, and often young Tengu-gi lose themselves in it. To combat it, the Tengu-gi of old had developed several different schools of teachings. Some are combat-related teachings, others are meditative techniques refined over thousands of years."

He paused, his eyes holding mine. "This art that you've been taught, it was not developed for your kind."

I blinked, then tilted my head in confusion. "What do you mean?"

"It was not made for someone who is as strong and as fast as you are. Your movements, even if they are unpracticed, reflect a wastefulness in execution. It is not refined. Perhaps the intent was not to teach you to fight, but to control this **thirst** that nearly consumes you."

I opened my mouth to deny it, but then I paused, thinking. I was not at all familiar with martial arts before I was turned. I wouldn't know the difference, but the little things that my sire did were starting to make sense. The way that he spoke, tried to teach me calm, precision, and control. We never trained at our full vampire speed, only as fast as a human could move. Was that because what he was teaching me was indeed a human martial art, or had I missed something? My sire's gaze at the end came to me again, the disappointment that I saw.

What Shadow said was interesting. I didn't know if a vampire martial art even existed. I learned nothing of anything like that in my classes, nor had I heard anybody talk about it. If a martial art developed for a vampire existed, it was kept a secret. Or perhaps there was none, Elder Vampires hardly had a need for it. They stood at the top of the food chain on Earth. I glanced at Shadow, thinking. The people on this world would have a lot more to train for, both physical improvements and skills.

"You might be right," I said finally. "But what does that have to do with anything?"

He didn't answer immediately. Instead he looked down, almost ashamed.

"I must apologize again," he started. "What happened before, with the healing potion, was my fault."

I frowned. "No, no," I started. "I shouldn't have let the **thirst** take control like that."

Shadow smiled. "I am much older, and much more powerful." He looked away. "I am supposed to be wise. I knew that healing potions had side effects, and I decided to use it still. Not because you needed it. Your own healing capabilities were sufficient to handle it. I wanted to speed it up, in part because I was selfish. I need you." He turned to look back at me. "I need you in order to survive this place. And I decided that having you whole was worth whatever side effects you might suffer. It was a miscalculation on my part, a most grave one. I know what you did, I saw how you fought your deeper nature and ran into the jungle to get away from me. You decided to go out there where you knew danger existed, danger that could kill you, just so that you could minimize the chance of hurting me."

"That's . . ." I trailed off as his smile turned sad. He inclined his head at me, which made me feel embarrassed for some reason.

"Thank you for what you did, Marianna," he said. "I owe you a debt. You remained by my side when I was injured. You decided to stay with me when you could have left and hid alone. With your skills you could've survived in this place for thirty days and then gotten back home safely. Blights, you could've just stayed here, in this ruin, and you would've lived."

"You saved my life too, and I didn't know anything about this place," I told him.

Shadow nodded. "You could have left after I woke up, after we talked at any point. Once you knew what was out there. No, you repaid me when you saved my life in turn. Now, I owe you twice over for what you did. And now, now there is more here than either of us understands. A message from the Ancient Ones that ties the blight to the creation of the Grand Spell. Dangerous history and a vision. It is not fair, but it has fallen on us to make sure that the message doesn't die here with us. I had stepped away from the world for too long. If I had a choice I would've ignored this. Perhaps if I was alone . . . No, the Grand Spell has initiated another Expansion, and your people are arriving. We must do our part. And there is something that I can do to repay my debt and perhaps give you more tools to help us now. Give you the tools to survive what your world will have become."

Shadow stood, and I could see how shaky his feet were, how tired he was just from the short exertion of light sparring and demonstration. "I lived this life for a long time Marianna. I have witnessed the arrival of other worlds and races, two times before. I have seen the upheaval and turmoil that such events bring. And I have lived through all this alone, scorning companionship save for just a few brief moments burning in my memory. I am an outcast, a man of no people, a Tsu-gi. A freak of nature in eyes of many."

I could feel the passion, but also the pain in his voice. Something about it called to me, to the parts that made me feel like he was a kindred spirit ever since I met him, though I had no way of putting it into words. I had spent my life feeling much the same.

"You Marianna Rojas, risked your life for me when you had no need to. You took it upon yourself to stay by my side, something that many others would not have done. You are owed for that, but even more than just a simple debt, I feel . . . a *tsinju!shi*." Shadow said a word that I didn't know. In my head I saw images instead of words. It didn't take me long to realize that it was a word that did not have a direct translation into a language I was familiar with. What I saw was a bond forged in fire, camaraderie, friendship, partnership, love, all these things and more beyond anything that we on Earth have a word for. An unbreakable bond forged in a short time, a spark that moves mountains, that reshapes the world. A moment that changes a direction in one's life by pulling them onto a path they never would've trodden otherwise.

"For that, I would offer you something, and I hope that you accept." Shadow paused, then took a deep breath and looked me in the eyes. "Out of all the YoKai-ni races, that of my father's side is the rarest. My father's race lives in the mountains of Asha Kai-ni, beneath the shadows of the Old Tree. And they rarely come down from their hidden libraries and archives. Very few people ever meet one of the Tengu-gi, and even less so their young. All the Tengu-gi children inherit the **Way of the Mind** from birth, the ability that grants strength and unyielding focus. They are not allowed to climb down the mountains that are their home until they master it, for that is just how dangerous it can be. There are many different ways and teachings that help in mastering it, and many are similar to what you were taught, based on calm and control," he said.

He made an effort to stand straighter even though it obviously hurt him. "I was not born in the mountains shrouded in mists, and though I never knew him, I inherited my father's blood's gift—the **Way of the Mind**. I had no teachers to help me, no ways of mastering myself. And my mother, she meant well, in her own way at least. But, she fueled many of what I would consider my worst appetites."

He turned around and started pacing. "I was not a force for good in my youth, Marianna Rojas. And yet, I have done good. I have used my might for the good of all in this world. Once, long ago, when war threatened to consume us all, when I saw how we could destroy our civilization and fall, I acted. I brought empires to their knees, I stopped countless slaughters and forbade wars of annihilation. I forced the entire world to a table and under threat had them all sign an agreement in blood. I gave them rules for war, no use of weapons that cause suffering in their victims, no weapons that razed cities with both innocent and the guilty. I made rules for the exchange of prisoners and their treatment."

I blinked. That sounded like the Geneva-Budapest Conventions, the treaties written after the Great War, agreed on by the vampires, the shifters, and the world powers.

"The Shadow's Peace they called it," he continued. "And even now, thousands of years later they still abide by it, because they are so terrified of me returning. But I have never wanted to be that thing that they fear in the shadows. I wish that they could have put aside their greed and been better. But we must all accept the reality of the world. I learned a lesson when I forced those rules on them. It only made them find different ways to get what they want." He shook his head. "I was wild back then, but those experiences helped anchor me, and they helped me to fully master the **Way of the Mind**. Because of that past, I devised my own school of being, my own way of life, one that differs greatly from that of my ancestors who keep to themselves. It is a way of life for a half-Tengu-gi who does not live amongst his kind in the mountains, but who is in the world among the other races. It is not a school of calm and control, of meditation on the mist covered peaks. But that of passion, power, and pursuit of overwhelming victory in all things. It is a way of having power so that you would never be subject to the influence of another. I am the only user of it, I have never had a student, never passed on my teachings."

He closed his eyes for a few moments, and I remained quiet.

"I have always thought myself invincible." He opened his eyes and smiled sadly. "These last few days have made me think again on my belief. I find that I regret it, not leaving something of what I have gained over the years, something to endure even after I was gone. The Shadow's Peace is a mockery of what I intended it to be." He bowed his head, and then whispered. "I want something that could be good, even if it is on a smaller scale. Would you accept this? Would you listen and learn what I have to teach?"

I looked into his eyes, and I saw my sire, my teacher. I had always looked up to him, even though I could reflect enough to know that I was not a good student. My sire was a quiet man, very much unlike the cartel's Master. He had tried to teach me, and here and now I understood just how many of his lessons I had not learned. I failed and for that I was set to be executed. If I had been a better and faster fighter, perhaps Pablo wouldn't have died. Or perhaps if I had more control, if I had left that warehouse, perhaps everything would've been different.

But none of those things were true. I was here, and the past was the past. It was only chance that I still lived. This was a second chance, a gift. An opportunity to be better than I was.

"I accept."

Woe

call my school of being, the **Heart of Azure and Scarlet**," Shadow started, using a stick to draw a circle with a crack in its side in the dirt. We had moved back to the fire and sat down next to it. He started by explaining what a school of being was. Which was exactly what it meant. A way of life, a teaching. What bushidō would be on Earth, or a life lived through strict religious practice. It encompassed everything.

"Named so for the two moons that circle our world. The azure moon is called **Hinda** in the elven ancient tongue, the broken watcher. They say that the moon broke on their arrival, and that it was the act of their goddess attempting to fight the Great Mistake, the Grand Spell that brought them here. They say that their goddess followed them here, and that now she lives in their lands, keeping the worst of this world at bay. There might be some truth to that. The elven continent of Elvaros is the safest continent in the world. Monsters are rare there, and animals are not highly Invested."

His hand moved, and he drew another circle, this one smaller. "The second moon, one that is scarlet, is called **Nonda**, the hateful eye in the elven tongue. The Elves thought that it was the hidden home of the evil god that brought them here, what they later learned was the Grand Spell from the ruins of the Ancient Ones. Meanings and understanding changed over the years, but the names remained. All races call them the same thing, though each has its own ideas about their meaning. For the YoKai-ni, what matters is the color. We place great importance on such things. Azure is the color of ruthlessness, of indifference and solitude. Scarlet is the color of survival, of fervor and righteous fury."

I tilted my head at that, and I saw Shadow's smile turn almost embarrassed.

"Yes." He cleared his throat. "As I said, I was not a good person when I was young. The prime principles of my school are those of survival at all costs, of leveraging all at your disposal to eradicate your enemies and walk your own path.

I have known people, great mages or warriors, who believe that there are wrong or evil Masks, evil practices or teachings. I have never subscribed to that, though I do give room for some of it to be true, in unique cases. My belief had always been that there are no evil teachings, only evil people. A Mask, or a teaching, just *is.* What you do with it is what gives it morality. There have been times in history when necromancer Masks were forbidden, when all people holding them were hunted down and killed. And there have been times when nations rose on the backs of undead cultivating the land. It is all matter of perspective and the morality of the person using the power." He paused, his eyes holding mine. "Do your martial arts have rules?"

I thought about it. I wasn't quite sure, but I had heard of many ways of life on Earth that had rules, that had oaths or vows. I nodded.

"You said that your world has no magic," Shadow continued. "Which confuses me, yet . . . Suffice to say that magic, the Way rather, is a big part of a *school of being.* Everyone in this world has Masks and skills, but there are other ways of achieving power, far more difficult paths. Such as this." He looked at the campfire that had started to die down and threw another piece of wood at it, then he reached out with his hand and flicked a finger at it. A small plume of fire left his finger, igniting the piece of wood. I blinked at that, then gaped at him.

"That was a cantrip," Shadow told me. "There are ways of learning how to use smaller Weaves without a skill, though it is hard to learn and even harder to master. I myself only know two. I am showing you this to make you understand that there are different paths to obtaining power. A **school of being** is just one, and it is part of the Weave itself. Like all things that you do, it will influence your Mask, and it will influence the way you live your life. The Source around us enforces those who live in accordance with a code at the very center of their way of life. It is the Esoteric part of the three attributes. Physical is self-evident, improvements of the body. The Weave is the cantrips and spell skills, ability to command the Source. Esoteric is . . . you could call it the *perfection in all things.* A farmer after a lifetime of work, every action done with purpose and understanding. Imagine a blade master that had spent his entire life trying to master a cut. The moment he achieved it, he would gain a waybound skill that would tap into that perfection." He raised his hand then dropped it fast toward the ground.

[*Azure Moon Style;* Ruthless Palm]

The skill echoed in my mind. I felt it impact the world around me. And just how he said, there was a perfection there. His palm stopped just shy of hitting the ground, but a ripple of air surged around it, blasting the dirt and dust away in a perfect expanding circle.

"There is greatness in the perfectly executed actions that resonates with the world around us, beyond just bending the Source to your will," he said, and I could do nothing but agree.

I listened attentively; it seemed like there was a lot more to all of this than I thought.

"For now, you don't need to bother yourself with understanding. You should focus on learning the base tenets of the **Heart of Azure and Scarlet**. When I say learning, it is more than just knowing it intellectually. You need to align and embody them; only then will you be able to touch the Way in a manner that will allow you to gain these skills."

"That does sound a bit . . . extreme?" I said slowly.

He nodded. "It is. There is great power to be found in a way of life. Being certain of one's path. But it also requires sacrifice. Perhaps, it would be best if you tell me what you want your life to be like? What are your goals?"

I opened my mouth, then closed it. A week ago, the answer to this question would've been that I wanted to serve the cartel well. To make my sire proud. I'd failed in that desire and nothing would ever make it right. Even if I returned back to Earth and found them, what was done was done. They would hunt me down, attack on sight. They were about to execute me after all. No, I was on my own, and I had already decided what I wanted to do. Help Shadow survive so that he could search for the truth behind the message. And help Earth get through the integration as best as it could. I was a vampire, and I had gifts that many coveted. Shadow had said that he did not think that there were evil powers, only evil people. He said that he had tried to do good, that he had lost faith in the world on that path. I got to choose what to do with what I had. Perhaps I was a fool, and perhaps the world would disappoint me like it had him, but I would try nevertheless.

"I want to do good with my life," I answered. "I want to help you survive, and then help Earth survive the integration. Create something that is fair for all."

Shadow's eyes sparkled with the light of the fire. "Ah." His expression turned somber. "To do good. Perhaps it is fate that the two of us met. Perhaps life plays its games, and we all dance to its tunes. Many great things have come of me following a similar path, and many just as terrible. Forgive me, I am cruel. You are young to bear the weight of choice, I should not have asked. You would not have even been considered an adult by any race on Kirios save the Harpiem. And yet . . ." He trailed off.

I took a deep breath. "Do you think that trying to do good is wrong?"

Shadow turned his head down, looking at the ground. "Trying to do good is never wrong, Marianna. It is just that you must be ready and strong enough to bear the consequences of such actions. Perhaps I have been alone for too long, perhaps I had my heart broken too many times. But it is your path, and I only hope that it takes you farther than it has me."

He turned his face back, his eyes sad and filled with age. "It is funny, that we are so similar. Looking at you is as if I am looking at a mirror image from so long ago. Life has taught me many terrible lessons that you are yet to experience. What do you consider to be good, Marianna, is not what everybody else will consider to be the same. You could wish for peace, but what if the world is so filled with differences that only conflict can resolve them? What if the world itself was built to thrive on it? What would you do if your good, the peace in the entire world, stifles it instead of saving it? What if to save a people you have to kill another? Or what if someone else has the same dream, yet their methods and vision differ than yours? Will you fight for it? Let conflict arise between what you believe to be good and what somebody else knows. Will you listen to the thoughts of others, even those who are not qualified to comment and give such opinions. I have tried so many different ways, and all ultimately failed. Inevitably, desires such as ours create discord, chaos, unless your desire is so shallow and weak that you would settle for it to be limited. A city, a kingdom, there it might work."

I opened my mouth and then closed it. It was telling that his mind went to such things. I hadn't thought about it in that manner. I hadn't thought about how or where, but I saw now just how old he was that he had experienced all of that. I knew what he was talking about. The cartel was . . . not a force for good. Yet it did good things. The villages in the mountains that the government had ignored and forgotten survived because of the cartel. They had protection, they had food on their tables. The police and the government were the enemies in their eyes, and the cartel were the good guys. It was the same on a larger scale, countries and corporations.

"The tenets of the **Heart of Azure and Scarlet** are ultimately built on selfishness," Shimi told me.

I blinked at that. "Selfishness?"

"To desire good, is ultimately a selfish goal, when you take it to its logical conclusion. You believe that your vision of good is greater than the price those around you must pay for it. And you are willing to do anything to see it through. It is what I based the tenets of my school:

"Ambition is the drive to achieve Greatness.
Emotion is the fuel that grants me Purpose.
Calm is the surrender to the will of Others.
Control is the shackle that robs me of Ambition.
I do not conceal my Ambition, I Relish.
I do not suppress my Emotion, I Embrace."

I frowned at that. "That sounds a bit . . . tyrannical."

Shadow nodded. "And yet . . . You must hold true to it in your heart. Otherwise, those who have no care for any kind of morality will tear you down. There are many paths that lead to power. This is mine. What you do with power defines you. All those who wish to bring goodness into this world must be stalwart in their belief and power, for you will always have those who are envious, who covet what you have. I do not know what kind of a world you come from, but here, power is the ultimate currency. Without power, you are nothing, and your desires worth less than dust. To bring about an age such as the Golden Age of the Bond of the Leaf of Elves long since passed, you need to have the might to make it happen."

He shook his head. "Perhaps you are too young to understand, still filled with hope and light. It is unfortunate that such is the way of things, that choices come to us when we are most unprepared. It was the same with me. And now here we are, in this wretched place filled with danger and death. Making choices that might not matter beyond tomorrow should we end up in the bellies of some blighted beast. Tell me, Marianna Rojas, would you pursue this goal of goodness to the very end? Stand as a shield against those who would tear it all down?"

I thought about it, but I couldn't really give an answer. I did believe that I could do good, that I had been given an opportunity to gain power. I had an obligation.

"Perhaps you should think on it for a while. It is a great responsibility," Shadow said. "More than most ever consider or are ever faced with. If you get to live to be as old as I am, you will perhaps feel the full gravity of choice, the knowledge that most lives beside yours are but a flicker in the grand wildfire of life, and that your every decision can shape the direction that fire spreads. I have done my share of fighting for the good I believed in, and it has left me filled only with doubt and regret. Yet now"—his eyes got a faraway look to them—"when I think about it all. I do not know if given a choice to go back and do things anew, I would do anything different at all. I saved lives, I created a room where happiness could grow. I don't know."

I didn't give him an answer to his question. Instead, a deep quiet settled over us. He went to sleep, and I kept looking at the fire, thinking. Vampires look far into the future, as we live for longer than a human ever could. Many vampire texts are filled with the references to the low worth of human life. Of their willingness to impose their beliefs on the world.

I remembered Khalil's and my discussions. Ultimately, even before I was a vampire, I had believed that they had done net good for the world. Many of the traits that made humanity great had been the traits that the vampires had encouraged in them from the shadows, or at times from atop their thrones. The great deeds that they had achieved had come with a price, often one heavy in lives, and yet, now we look upon the great pyramids and we marvel. They inspire greatness, despite the price in blood that it had taken to build them. We reached for the stars, for the light, inspired by the deeds that had their roots in suffering and darkness. Some said that was all just vampire propaganda, and I wouldn't know if it was. I only knew what the humans knew and what the vampires released in the public. But I have always believed that we have done good for the world.

I lived a hard life. I knew that there was always a price to pay.

I wondered what the world was going to be like now once it was integrated. How many of our great feats would get erased in the chaos that would follow. Shadow had told me only a little of it, but I knew that we were going to tear ourselves apart long before the denizens of Kirios got the chance for it. I had seen how people stabbed each other in the slums, how we clawed and schemed. How we executed little girls just to provoke. There was goodness in the heart of man, but so often we let evil win.

What Shadow was offering was a lifeline, and a path that led to power. I felt it in his tone, saw it in his eyes. To learn what he had to teach would put me on the same path that he walked. I did not know the details, but his words were plain.

I wondered if I could do that. I had always dreamed of being important, but I never had the chance. I cowered, and followed others, taking only what small pittance they deigned I had earned. But I understood power, I knew that all the people in the world who had the means to change things, had it. That they could stand in a room and have everyone quiet down in awe of their sheer presence.

Great leaders of nations were like that, humanitarians, heroes who jumped into fire, people who I saw on the tv from afar who made you stop in that awe of what they had done, what they were doing. Those that made you think that perhaps there was goodness in the world.

I understood then what Shadow was saying about selfishness. I wanted that; I wanted that power, I wanted to be able to change things. On Earth, they would've tried to teach me that it was wrong to want it. That I should suppress it, that there were people whose job it was to do what the rest of us couldn't. That we should all be meek and just follow. But Shadow offered another path. I did not think that he was evil, not that I had ever considered myself wholly good. Unlike my dear friend Khalil, I knew that pure good and pure evil were a lie—the world was filled with the shades of gray. Doing good did not mean that you yourself were good.

I made my decision.

I glanced over the fire to see that Shadow was still asleep. For a moment, I debated waking him up, but decided that he probably needed more rest.

I glanced at Saia who sat next to me, motionless. If I didn't know what she was, I would've thought that she was just a statue.

"You know," I whispered. "You might want to try to appear more lifelike."

Saia's head turned in my direction. "Query: For what purpose?"

"I mean, it doesn't bother me, of course. But if we survive all of this, eventually we are going back to Earth, and that means other people. If you at least appear as a living thing, you might not freak them out."

"Query: And this is preferable?"

"Not freaking people out is preferable, yes," I answered.

"Feedback: This Unit will take that under consideration."

I narrowed my eyes at her. "You can just say that you don't want to."

"Query: Elaborate."

I closed my eyes and took a deep breath. I had a tiny voice in my head telling me that she was messing with me, but I couldn't be sure.

I was just about to respond when I felt something in my chest. I stood up immediately. "The skill is ready."

Saia tilted her head, and I smiled. I wanted to try it out immediately.

I took a step and turned to mist. Using the skill was intuitive, I felt as if I had always known how to use it, even though I didn't quite understand how it worked. For the duration of a single step, I was a vaguely human-, or rather vampire-shaped mist. While I was mist, I still could see, though the color of the world turned monochrome, muted. The sound became muffled, and scents disappeared, while my sense of touch became a sensation that I didn't quite know how to describe. If I had to, it would probably be something like saying that I was feeling stretched. I did some limited tests, though Shadow had already told me all that he knew of the skill. The skill worked for a single step, and there was a minimum distance that would be considered a step, as well as a maximum one. A half step was still considered a step, but anything below that wasn't. That meant that I could do a few shorter steps in quick succession in order to get it off cooldown, though I had to actually move some distance and not just attempt to run in place.

On the other side, taking a leap still counted, allowing me to extend the duration I was in the mist form. That had its own disadvantages, of course. Anyone could see the mist and know where I would land. The speed of the mist was equal to the speed I had when I used it, and since vampires were able to move extremely fast from a standstill position that gave me a bit of an advantage. Another important thing to know was that the skill took everything that I carried with me. My clothes, my weapon, and Saia as well. There were limits to it, but Shadow didn't know them exactly, though he was certain that I wouldn't be able to grab someone's hand and pull them with me too. Not at my Investment tier at least.

As I re-formed after my step, I felt a gentle breeze expand out of my landing point. Dust and dirt flew away in an expanding circle. I frowned, I had not seen anything like this when the okolon used it, but then remembered that I had added a green gemstone to the skill.

"Wind," I whispered to myself.

"I see that your skill is ready." I turned to see that Shadow had woken up.

I winced. "Sorry, I didn't mean to wake you up."

"It is fine, I am as rested as I can be under the circumstances," Shadow said. "Did you test out the cooldown yet?"

I shook my head, then started making steps, counting them as I went. On my eighth step I felt the skill become available again. "Eight," I told him.

"Base version, not surprising," he said.

I leapt across the room, turning to mist and flashing across the several meters distance in less than a second. It was such a great skill, I couldn't help the smile on my face. I played around with it for a few more minutes, Shadow watching me from his cot.

Then, finally, I decided that we should finish our conversation. I walked closer, taking a seat on one of the stones next to the fire. My eyes were drawn to the flames as they danced across the logs.

"What will happen to Earth?" I asked finally.

I didn't look at him, but I heard him shuffle. "I already told you. Your world will be integrated, flooded with Source, changed forever."

I shook my head. "That's not what I mean. You said that we will have a year of being isolated, that six months into that year, portals will open that will allow small parties from the rest of Kirios through. You said that they will try to take advantage of us."

"Yes," Shadow just said.

"What will happen afterward? Once the isolation is over, once anyone can reach us?" I turned my eyes from the fire and met his.

Shadow's ears twitched and his gaze held mine for a few seconds. "You misunderstand, your population will be reduced greatly, it always happens. It is not that they will come into direct contact with you. It is just that you will be so weakened that they will just claim land that is empty, or that has few survivors. The nations of the world will send expeditions. They are forbidden from waging an all-out war of extermination by the Shadow's Peace, but there will be conflict, even among themselves. Your world's survivors, them they will bully, they will exploit, they will bribe. In the end they will split your world amongst themselves. Your kind will fight for a time, but ultimately they will lose. There are individuals on Kirios who hold more power than you can imagine, skills that can level mountains. And there are more of us than there will be of you. You will lose. Some of you will be accepted as citizens, a gesture meant to show that you can live in harmony and peace; most will accept the life of the second-class citizens in hope that their children or their children's children will rise to be equal—and they will. Some will adapt and make a new life in the untamed places of your world, delaying the inevitable. Eventually, some hundreds of years from now, maybe a thousand, a nation of your own will arise with enough power that they will try to take back what you lost. Perhaps they will succeed for a time. In the end, your lands will be as those of other continents. Split amongst all races."

"That happened to other races too?" I asked him.

"The Elves were the first," Shadow answered. "They were uncontested for a long time. The Dwarves arrived later, and while history talks of conflicts, the elven kingdoms and the Dwarves found a balance. The dwarven republics care little for the surface world, and the Elves hate their halls of stone and fire. They each have kingdoms on the other's land. The YoKai-ni, my kind, are the most warlike of us. The Shadow's Peace is the consequence of the war they caused and the wars that followed. Those who remain on the home continent often raid other nations. But there are some nations that had adopted other races, who have lands on Elvaros with the Elves, and Du'Vir with the Dwarves. The Naga-shan live underwater and don't care for anything above. They hold little of their own continent's land, as their land was settled by other races, and they pushed into the oceans. The last to arrive were the Harpiem, the ones that we call the Wandering People. But they weren't the wanderers when they arrived. They are the weakest of the races, and they did not hold up nearly as well as the other races did. Their land was taken from them, and now they are a nomadic people. We drove them from their cities and made them into what they are now. The conquest of your world will not be filled with an ocean of blood, though some rivers might flow. Instead, they will take through word and power that you cannot match, through numbers and just being there when you cannot. They will claim it by taming the wilderness that will rise. There are just not enough of you to be a real threat. Perhaps once, if you had arrived long ago when there were fewer of us on Kirios. If you fought with all you had . . ." He shook his head. "Conflict and blood accelerate Investment. It might have been enough. But now? One race against hundreds of nations? Even united, you would still be outnumbered and overpowered."

Shadow's eyes seemed sad. He opened his mouth to speak, then closed it as if he had thought better of it. Finally, he added. "I am sorry."

I nodded. It wasn't his fault. "Can I stop it?" I asked. I wanted to do good.

His eyes narrowed at me. "Stop everything? No." He shook his head. "But there are ways. If you make it too costly for them, perhaps you could carve a place for your people. A place that could be strong enough to resist, give your people a safe haven to grow and adapt to the new world."

"The message, the vision," I started. "If they knew, could they be persuaded not to come? Can you unite the world?"

He looked at me with a sadness in his eyes. "I know of only a few people in the world who would believe me. Even if they see it with their own eyes, they will not trust it. To them, a real seer does not exist. If the threat still exists, if it even is real, I will need to work from the shadows and prepare. Discover what the Blight Curtain really is."

I glanced at my palms. I could still see faint traces of blood on them. I was made to kill, to destroy. I was a vampire.

I remembered a quote from an old vampire, Sikmeh, living in the times of Rome.

"Woe to the conquered, for might is all that matters. I find it resonates with me, and I wish I was there when that Gaul cur uttered it. Perhaps I would've turned him. As it stands, his words speak to the nature of the world. Strength is paramount for a leader. And so it is the right of the vampire to stand above the mortal, for we have the power and foresight needed to ensure the prosperity of all. Perhaps one day they will realize that."

I was one of the quotes that Khalil would often point to when we were debating whether vampires could be benevolent. The more I look back at those times, the more I realize that I knew nothing. It had taken experiencing the change for me to understand the power that a vampire could wield. That it so often corrupts was no surprise to me now, and yet . . . they had done good, they had built monuments that stood the test of time. They had inspired greatness and when it was necessary stood against evil.

And now we will be faced with people who held even greater might. It was the natural order of things—the vampires were right. Shadow knew it too, this world had people that were too strong. Earth would be conquered.

"Woe to the conquered," I whispered to myself.

Shadow tilted his head and frowned. "Woe to the conquered?" he repeated, questioningly.

I didn't respond. Earth needed power, it needed champions that could stand and help us hold off what was coming. It needed people who could survive this threat to live and stand against the greater one yet to come. Thirty of us were sent here, and I wondered just how many would see the dangerous avalanche rolling down the hill straight at us.

I hadn't seen it either. Not until the rift, not until I realized just how alien our new reality was. I glanced at Saia, a tiny dragon, but also an achievement that made Earth's look so small. And I had seen the remains of that world. I was not someone great, I was not a good person, though I did want to be. I was arrogant to think that I could do anything to help. But the memories of my sire came to me, his teachings, his kind eyes from before. Khalil and the skepticism that he used as a shield. Stories of great people who made the world a better place. For the first time in my life, I felt like I had something unique to just me. I wasn't just one young vampire among hundreds. I had a Mask, I had my own power. I could feel the **thirst** pulse inside of me, almost in beat with my Mask. I could tell myself so many lies, but in the end I was just as flawed as the vampires that Khalil often warned about. I was arrogant, and I was greedy, but Shadow's words echoed in my mind. It was what we did with that power that mattered.

He was right, I wanted to do good, and for that I needed power.

I held Shadow's eyes, feeling determination seep into my expression, my Mask and the **thirst** thrummed in rhythm. "Can you teach me how to do it? How to keep that from happening to my world?" It was such an arrogant thing to ask, but I was a vampire, it was in our nature.

Shadow's orange eyes narrowed, and he walked over to me, towering over my sitting form.

"You said that you wanted to do good." His eyes held mine, looking almost sad for a moment. Then they changed, and an expression I had never seen on his face appeared. It was a terrifying look of someone filled with more emotion than they could express. Almost a grimace of rage and hate that burned out from his eyes, sadness and happiness that twisted his mouth into a grin that was both mocking and pitying in the same breath. His tails spread out behind him like a fan, swaying as if they were in the wind. "If you want to walk down this path, I can teach you. You will suffer. You will endeavor to take their pain on your own back, I can see it in your eyes. They will not thank you for it, but that is the price we pay. If you want to do this, you will spill blood in the name of protecting, in the name of good. You will face evil, and be branded a tyrant, a conqueror. They will call you evil to justify tearing you and what you try to build down. It is in their nature. You need to be stronger than them, to be a ruthless monument that will not bend or break in the face of everything that they throw at you. You will need to understand the **Heart of Azure and Scarlet**."

I stood up and spoke, giving voice to what I felt inside.

"Vae Victis." *Woe to the conquered.*

Interlude
The Terror in the Stormlands

Knight Mage Herim of Roughrock walked behind his escorts, a pair of **Royal Guardsmen**, as they led him through the corridors of the Stormgarden Fortress. The vibrant moss on the gray stone walls shone with light, illuminating their path. The way the moss was grown and tended was exquisite, but Herim could not bring himself to admire it in the way that it deserved. His mind was on his task, and his failure. Two more villages had been struck by calamity, their people murdered. They—he—had failed in stopping the monster, or whatever it was. It had gotten smarter; there was less evidence than there had been the first time. Only one thing linked the villages now: all the dead were found with their bodies drained of blood.

As they came to stop next to a large stone door covered in elaborate carvings, Herim took a deep breath, trying to calm himself. It would not be courteous of him to show his irritation before the Storm King. He had been called to Stormgarden abruptly, and with little reason given, though Herim suspected that it was because of his failure. Perhaps the Storm King wished to chastise him in person, or perhaps he simply wanted to hear what excuses Herim had.

He would've gladly submitted to any punishment. He deserved it. Four dozen people were dead, and worst of all, a child. The Stormlands were howling for justice, and Herim had been unable to provide it. Yet, he burned with the need to be out there, to finish what he started. The summons only served to delay his hunt.

Still, Herim knew that he had no choice in the matter. His escorts instructed him to wait as one of them entered the room, then came back a minute after, bidding him to follow. Herim entered the throne room behind the **Royal Guardsmen**. The first step into the Storm King's throne room took his breath away. The domed room was built of gray stone, with six pillars leading up to a tall staircase that contained a white throne at the top, a throne he knew had been carved out of quartz. A glass dome was above them, showing the raging storm outside, the majesty of the sky. The Stormlands were a reminder that even in the harshest of places, nature could still thrive. The Storm Kingdom might not have the great forests of the Forest Kingdoms, but it embodied the Way of Nature just the same. With its sprawling fields of lush grass, with mighty rivers and great stone hollows. The storm outside flashed, lightning illuminating the sky. The sight of it from beneath the dome was . . . it was an awe-inspiring room, made to impress, and to oppress in equal measure.

Herim had entered through a side door, and as he was led forward he saw people being led out of the room through the main entrance. That left only five people in the room, Herim and his two guards, with the three people at the top of the staircase.

Two women stood on either side of the throne; their face-paint as thunderous as the storm raging outside marked them as Lightning Warriors. Oathbound women in service to the Storm King. Herim had never had the honor of meeting one before, since they rarely left Stormgarden, but he had heard tales of their might. They said that only those women who knew the loss of a child were allowed into their order. Herim didn't know the truth, but that would explain why their numbers were so few.

Their armor was slim, and at a glance immediately recognizable. It was made out of the white wood of a stormcatcher tree, the only trees that grew in the Stormlands. They were towering and solitary pillars that drew the lightning to them. Flash counting was a game that Herim used to play when he was young. Sitting beneath the cover of a storm shelter and gazing out in the distance, counting the lightning as it crashed against the trees near his village.

They each held a klek-ur in their hands, tall weapons with three blades at the end that looked like claws of a bird of prey. Their gaze followed him as he was led before the stairs to stare up at the throne.

Herim knelt, one knee on the ground and both hands on top of the other, his head bowed and eyes closed.

"My king."

"Knight Mage." The king spoke in a slow but firm voice. "May you always weather the storms."

Herim raised his head and met the eyes of the monarch. "Only to welcome the one that comes after," he finished the saying.

"Rise," the Storm King said, and Herim did as he was told.

Jaun El Annur, the Storm King, was wearing the elaborate black and yellow robe of his office, designed to look like a storm cloud in the night. His crown was stone, with seven uneven prongs tipped with different crystals. Each crystal represented one of the provinces in the Stormlands. It was not a comfortable looking thing, which was also by design. Life in the Stormlands was not soft. It was as hard as the stone they built their houses with, as hard as the life that weathered the storms.

His hair was fair, his gaze golden, and he had the bearing of the ancient rulers who held the elven race together as they faced the calamity, who kept them alive through their arrival to Kirios. None of it changed what anyone who looked at him could see. The king was young, his eyes gave him away.

Barely three hundred years old, he had taken the throne upon the untimely death of his father. Herim did not envy the young king, surrounded by kingdoms whose monarchs were thousands of years his senior.

"We are told that your search did not produce results," the king said.

Herim suppressed the desire to grimace and bowed his head. It was his failure. "Yes, my king," he responded.

"Three of our villages," the king continued. "A child."

The words were uttered in a calm and measured tone, but Herim heard only condemnation. He raised his head, bearing the responsibility as befit a member of a Knight Order.

"It is my failure, my king," Herim said.

The king's golden eyes bore into him, the power of his Investment heavy in his gaze. Herim knew that he was not as highly Invested as his father was. Perhaps he wasn't even as Invested as Herim himself was. It didn't matter. His Mask was that of a king, and it was a heavy thing.

"Matters have come to our attention that you are unaware of. We wish to make them known to you."

"My king?" Herim blinked. That was not what he had expected.

"A new age is upon us all," the Storm King said. "A new Great Interval is here. The Great Mistake has found another suitable world to bring across the ocean of stars."

The words struck Herim. Hearing them from anybody else would have him dismiss it as the ramblings of a madman. But the king held no madness in his gaze. Herim was a Knight Mage, one of the higher ranking members of the Knights of Stormpeak Keep, among all the Tempest Orders, and the Stormlands in general. That position was not one entrusted to him lightly. It was his job to seek out and deal with threats to the people of the kingdom, be they from within or without. For the king to share that information with Herim meant many things. First, the king had undeniable proof of his words, and second, he believed that the information was relevant to Herim's quest.

And that meant that . . . the threat he was hunting could be something none of them had ever encountered before. Herim had not been alive during the last Great Interval, and he did not know more than what he had read in the scrolls in the Stormpeak Keep libraries. Each event was described as world shaking, but the actual arrival of another world was meant to be something that no one could miss. The records said that the sky would change color and that Source would wash over the world. Herim didn't remember anything like that happening, which meant—

"Exemplars," he whispered, mostly to himself.

"It is so," the king said, his voice bringing Herim's attention back to the throne.

"Pardon my question, my king. But any Exemplar who arrived, they would be of low Investment. Even if they had unparalleled talent and managed to advance rapidly." Herim shook his head. "The dead include two individuals of high Investment, both in their Fourth. No Exemplar should be capable of that."

The king's expression didn't change as he nodded his head. "We have one of the Exemplars here. Through a lapse in judgment, the Exemplar has overheard of the events you are investigating. He believes that he might be of service. This new world might prove a great threat to the tenuous peace we now enjoy." The king suddenly sagged, almost as if holding some incredible weight on his back. He raised a hand and covered his eyes, rubbing at them gently for a moment.

Then, he raised his head again, and locked eyes with Herim. "You will be allowed to speak with the Exemplar. You will not speak of this to anyone, you will not repeat what you learn from him, nor will you even suggest to anyone the existence of the Exemplars or the coming of the Interval. The Crown has plans, and we do not need any disruptions."

"Of course, my king, you have my word," Herim bowed his head.

The king looked at him for a long moment, and then he stood. "Leave us," he said to his guard.

Herim saw their confusion, but they obeyed instantly. Soon, everyone exited the room, leaving Herim alone with the king. It was highly irregular, but it also warmed Herim's heart to know that his king held such trust in him to allow him in his presence alone.

The king walked down the steps from his throne, to stand before Herim.

"There is one more thing," the king said slowly. This close, Herim could see the tiredness in the king's eyes. "This will not leave your mouth, ever—you will take this to your grave. I speak only to inform you of certain signs you should watch for."

Herim was confused, but he nodded his head and waited.

"We have been made aware of something peculiar happening. Two weeks ago, just before the arrival of Exemplars, a prophecy was spoken."

Herim blinked. "A prophecy? But, there are no—" He paused at the look in the king's eyes.

"The crown must look for advantages everywhere, even storms that are not easily navigated," the king said. "We've been trying to learn more about Seer Masks. One of these . . . attempts . . . bore some fruit. The Seer is mad, as all of them are. But for the first time in years, his ravings changed. Two weeks ago, he spoke something new. It is as follows:

"Howl in agony, blood bathed comes, the Deceiver will take all that we've built. Howl in suffering, blood will rain, the Conqueror walks the land. Howl in despair, the Seeker soars, and all quake beneath the shadow of dark wings."

It was nonsense, as all prophecies were.

"My king . . ."

He raised his hand. "It will make more sense once you hear what the Exemplar has to say. We do not know if this is related, but we must be vigilant. Something is changed."

"I understand," Herim said, bowing his head.

"Good," the king said, then waved his hand. "My Guardsmen outside will lead you to your meeting. You have until the end of the day."

Herim knelt again. "I will not fail you, my king."

"May you weather the storm," the king said, then after a moment, "may we all."

"You will enter. The conversation will end once you leave the room," the Guardsman explained. "You will keep yourself from making inquiring questions into the Exemplar's world—only matters concerning your task may be explored. Be thorough, as you will not be allowed to speak with him again."

Herim nodded. "I understand."

He looked at the simple wooden door in front of him, collecting his wits. This was not what he had imagined when he was summoned before the Storm King. He marshaled his thoughts and took a deep breath. The Guardsman opened the door and led him in.

Inside was a small room, occupied by a single person sitting at a table. Two goblets and two pitchers were placed on a tray next to them. Herim paused as he beheld the Exemplar, noting immediately both the similarities and the differences to his own people. The Guardsman had mentioned that the Exemplar was a man, and that his people were called human, but little else beyond that. At a first glance one might confuse the Exemplar with an elf, but it was an impression easily dispelled.

The Exemplar's skin was rougher, more weathered it looked like, with a lighter tawny skin tone the color of the fallen leaves often found on the trees in the far north where the desert heat dried them so. It was so unlike any elven skin tone that Herim was struck for a moment—his people's skin tended to be in the ranges of pale green for the people of the forests, and shades of gray for those like him who lived in the Stormlands. The ears, likewise, were different, smaller and without the narrowed points extending upward. His face was covered in hair as well, in a manner that resembled what one might expect of a dwarf—a beard. An elf had no hair on their face aside from eyebrows. He was taller than a dwarf, not quite as tall as Herim himself at a glance, though it was hard to tell with him sitting.

The clothes he wore were all black, and robe-like, though made of what looked like quality materials of expensive make. He saw no traces of stitching, and the threads were exquisite and fine. His arms were on the table, elbows resting on it with his hands closed in a fist. A golden chain with black beads was wrapped around his fingers, and a strange symbol hung from the end, resting on top of the knuckles of one hand. The symbol was gold in color as well, though it looked painted. It was two lines, one horizontal one vertical that crossed, with some elaborate carvings on the ends of the lines.

The man's eyes were closed, his head bowed over his hands, seemingly unaware of their intrusion. The door closed behind Herim, and the man raised his head and opened his eyes to reveal strikingly blue gems staring back.

"Ah, pardon, I was praying," the man said in a rough and deep voice. So much so that Herim almost heard it in his chest. It reverberated strangely. *Curious*, Herim thought to himself. Elven voices were higher pitched, and more musical in nature. This sounded more like grinding of stone.

The Guardsman approached and spoke to the human as he stood up. "This is the man I told you about; he will hear what you have to say."

Herim stepped forward and introduced himself. "I am Knight Mage Herim of Roughrock, in service to the Stormpeak Keep of the Storm Kingdom's Knightly Order."

The human inclined his head. "It is a pleasure to meet you, Knight Mage. My name is Khalil Abd al-Nur, Knight Priest of the Order of the Dragon, based in Constantinople, at your service."

Herim tilted his head. Many of the words the man said had meaning, but they were not spoken in a way that he understood their gathered intention. Still, a few did stroke his curiosity.

"A fellow knight? Your world has them as well?" Herim asked, intrigued.

The man's lips curved into a smile. "The meaning of the word is similar enough that the Great Mistake translates it in that way, or so I am told at least. I have not been allowed to learn much about what it means to be a knight among your people."

Herim opened his mouth to speak, but the Guardsman cleared his throat from behind the human. His glare was enough to tell Herim that he should follow closely the instructions given to him.

"Right," Herim said, then gestured for the man, Khalil, to sit. Herim walked over to the table and took a seat opposite the man. "How much do you know about why I am here?"

Herim wondered how the man could help. He still didn't believe that an Exemplar could be responsible, especially not now when he had met a human. He didn't have an [Inspect] skill, but highly Invested people had . . . an aura about them that he could recognize. He felt nothing like that from the man. Nor did he think that the human was particularly strong without a Mask. Still, he had been summoned here by the Storm King, and there had to be more that he did not know.

The human took a deep breath and placed the chain in his hands over his head so that the strange symbol rested on his chest. He then spoke. "I've over-heard a few of my . . . minders, talking about massacres in your lands. I am filled with sorrow to hear that. No people deserve such deaths, especially a child. I pray that God will shelter their souls." He inclined his head, in what Herim assumed was respect, then made a strange gesture with one of his hands, touching his forehead, his stomach, then each breast before touching the symbol on his beaded chain.

Herim nodded in return. It was a good sign for the human people that he felt that way. Herim knew that a YoKai-ni or a Naga-shan would not have cared. The mention of a god was interesting, but the look from the Guardsman behind the human warned Herim not to deviate from his task again.

"Thank you for your words," Herim said. "Yes, it is a tragedy, a threat that is my responsibility to find and punish."

The human met his eyes. "Tragedy, yes. I do not know much of what had happened. The only thing that caught my attention was hearing that all the vic-tims were drained of blood, is that correct?"

"It is," Herim answered. "The first village had more carnage, people torn apart. But the attacks that followed were far cleaner in a way. With little signs of fighting, only people found dead with wounds on their necks and missing blood. There is no beast in these lands or any that I am familiar with that attacks in such a way."

The human closed his eyes and grimaced, almost as if in pain. "My under-standing of Masks and the power that they grant is not complete. I am learning, but I am told that races on this world have different natural gifts, yes?"

"That is so." Herim allowed him to continue.

"My world has more than just people like me." The human pointed at his chest.

"Several races?" Herim asked, intrigued. "Like the YoKai-ni?"

"From what I understand, no, not like them," Khalil responded. "I guess vari-ants, or sub-races, is the right term. Cursed as well, perhaps. The most numerous are those like me, human, but there are two more variants that we call shifters and vampires."

Herim frowned. The word *shifters* he understood, though he did not know its meaning within the context of the human knowledge. The second word was unfamiliar to him. He waited a bit to see if the Grand Spell would show him impressions to better understand. When nothing happened, it became apparent that it was just a name and not a word that conveyed meaning or idea. "And you think that one of them might be responsible?"

Khalil nodded in agreement. "The vampires of my world feed on blood— they need it to survive."

Herim leaned forward across the table. "How strong is a *vampire*," he said, testing the unfamiliar word on his tongue.

"That is a more difficult question than you realize," Khalil said, then he stood slowly and reached over the table for the pitchers. He gestured, asking Herim which one he would like. From the look of it, one of it was filled with blue liquid, probably lipis—a spirit, the other was clear, filled with water. Herim pointed at the one filled with lipis, and the man poured him a glass, then put the pitcher down and poured water for himself. His movements were slow, and Herim could see the slight shiver in his hands. The man was scared. From the way he moved, Herim could also tell that the human wasn't particularly strong, no stronger than a Maskless elf at least, and far less coordinated judging by the spilled water. Perhaps as strong as a Kitsu-oi.

"Vampires are a delicate issue on my world. They are very secretive, but very powerful. My order's guiding principles are to stand in the light and curtail the vampires' more savage instincts. All vampires are stronger than humans, a lot stronger. Enough to do the things you describe, to rip people apart, yes. Though the degree of their strength varies."

Herim subdued his instinct to interrogate. The Exemplar was clearly a *guest* of the crown, but he saw no signs of mistreatment. He did not know the plans of the king, and did not wish to overstep. He could also see that the human was willing to share, perhaps even felt compelled to.

Khalil took a sip of water, then licked his lips before meeting Herim's eyes again. "I've had the opportunity to see a demonstration of one of your high Investment people. A Knight in his Third Investment," the human said. "The feats of strength that he demonstrated for me were beyond what most vampires would be capable of."

Herim grimaced. That did not bode well. The gulf between a Third Investment Mask and a Fourth was wide. It was the breaking point in power.

"There were two people that were in their Fourth Investment among the victims," Herim explained. "They had been a lot stronger than a Third Investment Knight."

"I don't know if a vampire could defeat someone like that," the human said. "Perhaps with the help of their own Mask."

Herim doubted that any of the Exemplars would've been able to advance their Masks even to the First Investment, not at the time of the first attack. From what he had been told the Exemplars arrived barely a day before the massacre. "What can you tell me about them?" Herim asked. "Their strengths and weaknesses, how I can find them?"

"There are several different types of vampires." The human reached for his water again, and Herim waited patiently for him to finish, struggling not to rush the human and aware of the watcher in the corner who was able to end this meeting at any point. "They are several times stronger than a human like me, their senses are better in every way, and their wounds regenerate faster. They are immune to disease and most poison. They don't age. A vampire is not born, but made from humans by another vampire, turned. At the time of their turning, they become Fledgling Vampires. At this time, they are not in control of their emotions and need blood constantly. From what you have said, I would've expected it to be an out-of-control Fledgling. But I do not think that Fledgling would've been able to kill a Masked with as much power as your people seem to wield. They are erratic, not in full control of themselves. Prone to violent outbursts."

"The first village was—" Herim trailed off as he remembered the carnage. "No, even though it was violent, it was not mindless, not even there."

The human nodded. "An Adult Vampire is more in control of themselves. They are all usually more than a century old, more accustomed to their power. Though some could get arrogant, entitled. Still, even with their experience, I don't think that they would be able to kill an entire village of people, especially if there was someone that strong among them."

Khalil glanced at his cup, saw that it was empty. "The attack, it happened at night?"

Herim inclined his head. "As far as I am aware, all of them seem to have."

Khalil nodded. "Vampires can't stand in direct sunlight; it is certain death for them," he said. "Or at least they can't on Earth. With Masks and this new world, I don't know if that changes things."

Herim blinked. That was actually very important. It changed his entire tracking process. He had kept the range wide, but if his target couldn't move during the day, that narrowed the circle significantly.

"I," Khalil started. "It would have to be an Elder Vampire. They get stronger with age. And Elders are their oldest, thousands of years old. I don't know why one of them would do this though. They are very careful with their actions, preferring to act out of shadows, behind the scenes. And no Elder Vampire would lose their control and go on a killing spree. They police their own. An insane Elder Vampire would've been killed a long time ago."

Herim reached over and poured more water for the man. "You think that one of these Elders would be able to match someone as strong as the knight you met?"

Khalil grimaced. "Maybe? I don't know. I've never faced an Elder Vampire myself, I only know the stories. We have records of some being killed, but it is usually in fights against other Elders. Once, it took an army to take one down, and still they couldn't kill him until they ambushed him during the day."

Herim had already gotten more than he had expected out of this. He had a new direction for his investigation. "Tell me, how long or far can these vampires fly?"

Khalil's head swung up from the cup to lock onto Herim's eyes. "What?"

"Fly? The victims, most were dropped from high altitude. We believe after they were picked off and their blood drained."

The human's hand moved to his chest where it grasped the symbol on the chain tightly. "That's impossible." He shook his head. "This can't be a vampire then."

Herim frowned. "You said that they drink blood, and that they can only act in the night. That fits with all the events."

He shook his head again, and stood up. "No, you don't understand. A vampire looks exactly like a human, like me. They don't have wings."

Herim stood as well then made a step toward the man. "What is it?"

"It's not possible. Only thirty Exemplars were sent here from my world, thirty! There were less than a handful of them. The chances that even an Elder Vampire was chosen are astronomical!"

"So there are vampires that can fly?" Herim asked.

"I don't know for sure. They are so rare that I've only heard stories. Some do mention that they can change into different forms, even appear as demons with great wings."

"Would a vampire like that be strong enough to kill a Masked knight?"

Khalil didn't answer immediately. He took a deep breath, then walked back to take a seat. "Listen to me. You need to find him and put him down immediately. You need to gather an army, the strongest people you have."

Herim's eyes narrowed. "You are afraid."

"Yes," the human said. "If what you said is true, then you are dealing with an Ancient Vampire. The oldest of their kind, so old that no one knows their origin. Some think that they are a myth, the progenitors of their race. The few records we have of them speak of calamities when they appear, great floods, volcanoes erupting, empires falling. They are so powerful that the stories say they can't stay awake for long. That they sleep in a kind of stasis. And that when they wake they are often so hungry that they lose themselves. There have been no stories of one in thousands of years, most people think that they are nothing but a fairytale. But if those stories are true, then the Ancient Vampires are the most powerful beings on my world. And I don't think that your Masked can match their power, not from what I have seen. If one of them was brought here while asleep?"

That did not sound good. The human bowed his head. "May God preserve us and shelter us, if they got a Mask of their own," he whispered, then met Herim's eyes. "If the Great Mistake pulled a sleeping Ancient Vampire, then they would wake up hungry. Hungry and in a strange place, a new world. They would be confused and feel threatened. They would not be in their right mind. God, they wouldn't have the frame of reference for so many things. Coming here was strange for me, but the current culture of Earth at least is filled with things that give me the ability to understand. We had postulated about the existence of other races, other worlds. We have stories about magic and . . ." He shook his head. "An Ancient Vampire who has been asleep for thousands of years would have none of it. If they woke up without any sense of self but the hunger? Then it is an Ancient Vampire controlled just by their **thirst**. Pure instinct and predator, with no human emotion to temper it, no compassion, no guilt, nothing."

"How do I stop them?" Herim asked.

"Gather as many powerful people as you can," Khalil said. "And silver, all the silver you can get."

Herim narrowed his eyes. He didn't know if he trusted the words that the human spoke. He couldn't quite imagine any Exemplar could be that powerful. The response he was asking was equal to what would be required for the strongest Masked in the world. The world shakers who might as well be gods. But, he looked into the human's eyes and saw true fear. And that, that he believed.

Through the Jungle

spent the next day learning more about Shadow's school of being. We didn't have the time for him to do more than just teach me the basics. Still, there was a lot to learn. The most important part was perhaps the three principles behind the **Heart of Azure and Scarlet**. We were having a short break, which I used to review the lesson with [A Lesson Remembered]. Even though I didn't yet understand everything, I wanted to learn. The lesson flashed inside my mind, the skill helping me remember it in great detail.

"A way of life requires dedication," Shadow said as he began his instruction. "All things that grant power do. You cannot gain anything great without showing the Last Intent your willingness to sacrifice."

I listened attentively again. In the memory Saia was sitting on the ground next to me and doing the same.

*"To master the **Heart of Azure and Scarlet** you must fully accept its tenets, you must live and breathe them, embrace them fully," he said, reiterating what he had already told me.*

I only nodded. I had already made the decision to follow this path.

"In order for you to be recognized as a follower of this way of life, you must abide by its core principles, of which there are three. The first principle is the tenets, what I have already shared with you:

*"**Ambition is the drive to achieve Greatness.***
Emotion is the fuel that grants me Purpose.
Calm is the surrender to the will of Others.
Control is the shackle that robs me of Ambition.
I do not conceal my Ambition, I Relish.
I do not suppress my Emotion, I Embrace."

He repeated the tenets. I still thought that they were somewhat tyrannical, but the more I thought about them, the more I could see a deeper meaning within them.

*"The meaning of the words is for you alone to discover. How you understand them will shape your relationship with the **Heart of Azure and Scarlet**. The second principle is the rules, a sacrifice for the world. The Way, or perhaps the Grand Spell itself, recognizes when we make such offerings to the world. This is your personal sacrifice, and as such it should remain private. To give you an idea of what kind of a sacrifice I am talking about, it can be anything, from deciding that you will never again speak, to deciding that you will never again wear blue-colored clothes."*

I blinked; that sounded like a vow. "That seems, I don't know, easy?"

Shadow shook his head. "Some sacrifices are greater than others, but do not mistake them for being easy. The Way knows your heart. How powerful the school of being you adopt ends up being will depend on your dedication to it. Let us use my previous idea as an example—you decide not to wear blue-colored clothes for the rest of your life as your rule, but you already hate the color blue. Well, then the world will recognize the depth of your sacrifice, and your connection to the Way and your school of being will reflect that. Obviously that was not a great sacrifice, and with such shallow rule you will never scratch more than the surface of the school of being with it."

"How do I decide something like that?" I asked.

"You just make a decision and start doing it until it becomes second nature," Shadow answered.

I nodded, trying to think about something deeper that I could do. I would need to think about it a bit.

*"You need not decide now, nor do you need to start with a great rule. You can decide on something smaller and easier, then just add more rules as you go on," Shadow said, interrupting my thoughts. "It will take you a long time to learn enough of the basics in order for the Way to recognize you as someone who follows the **Heart of Azure and Scarlet**."*

"Wait." I tilted my head. "How is this going to help us survive, If it will take a long time for me to learn anything?"

"I am preparing you not just for surviving the coming days, but also for the return to your home. The truth is that you will need to teach yourself based on what you learn from me now. I am no Teacher, *but I hope that your* Student Ornament *is enough to help you learn better. As far as helping us survive now, well, you are already very strong, you just don't know how to effectively use what you have. Which brings us to the last principle of the **Heart of Azure and Scarlet**: the two combat styles, and what I will focus on teaching you."*

I came out of the lesson and shook my head. Shadow sat on the ground, his eyes closed, still napping. I had seen just how exhausted he had gotten from just a few hours of physical activity, so I decided to let him sleep. I took advantage of the time to mentally review the rest of his instructions the old fashioned way.

After his talk about the principles, the lesson had turned more practical. We had spent most of the last day practicing the two styles. Shadow had started by describing to me the Azure and the Scarlet styles of combat. Both were focused on channeling emotions and not suppressing instinct. Transforming feelings into a source of strength and trusting natural instincts. It was a stark contrast to what I knew from Earth, the teachings that said that I should always seek to be calm and master myself. In a way, what Shadow taught was liberating—his approach was one of validating emotions.

The *Azure Moon Style* was, like the symbolism of the moon above this world, rooted in ruthlessness, indifference, and solitude, drawing on the wielder's emotions to fuel their power. Shadow created the *Azure Moon Style* in a way that was characterized by powerful, heavy counterstrikes and a solid defense, focusing on slow, deliberate, and highly controlled movements. It was based on fear as a natural instinct. Fear was an emotion that was experienced in response to a perceived threat, danger, or harm.

And as he described what it was meant to achieve, I could see how it could apply to me as well.

Fear was an innate response that was hardwired into our brains, and it triggered a range of physiological and behavioral responses that are designed to protect us from harm.

From an evolutionary perspective, fear played a crucial role in the survival of our ancestors. The ability to detect and respond to potential threats allowed them to avoid danger and increase their chances of survival. Fear helped our ancestors to recognize and respond to predators, avoid dangerous situations, and escape from harm.

Fear was also closely linked to the fight-or-flight response, which is a physiological response that prepares the body for action in response to a perceived threat. This response involves the release of hormones such as adrenaline and cortisol, which increases heart rate, breathing rate, and blood pressure. This prepares the body to either fight the threat or flee from it.

True, a vampire's response was slightly different. The **thirst**, or rather the sanguinium bacterium, was the one in charge. Its responses to threats had saved my life on numerous occasions. My sire had taught me that the **thirst** was something to be kept in check, always controlled. Yet . . . its purpose was to survive, the same as mine. Perhaps there was more to my own existence than I had previously believed.

Still, the *Azure Moon Style* relied on instinctual movement to draw the opponent out and force them to overextend, then ending the battle with a single powerful counterattack. It was brutal and efficient in a ruthlessly pragmatic way.

The ***Scarlet Moon Style*** was rooted in survival, fervor, and righteous fury. It emphasized the importance of channeling one's emotions to enhance their combat prowess. The ***Scarlet Moon Style*** did not control or suppress emotions, but instead embraced and harnessed them, using those feelings to fuel a relentless aggression.

It relied on anger, and rather than focusing on defense, the ***Scarlet Moon Style*** aimed to dominate the battle by relentlessly attacking, wearing down adversaries, and exploiting any openings to inflict critical damage with no regard for defense.

I understood anger; you couldn't live without knowing it, not in the place I had lived most of my life, having the life that I had. I'd seen its power, how motivating it could be, how it turned small villages forgotten by their governments into a force to be reckoned with. I saw how anger could be a catalyst for change, how it could motivate individuals to address the source of their frustration and injustice.

I had also seen the anger of others used by those who had seen the opportunity for their own gain.

Anger was a powerful emotion, one that I had experience with. I'd had anger overwhelm me before, and had acted without thinking. I felt the power it could give me. The now faint pain around my neck and the scar that would remain there perhaps forever was a constant reminder of what could happen when one just acted out of anger.

Yet, I couldn't deny that anger was a big part of what motivated me now. I didn't want to get rid of my anger, didn't want to suppress it, I only wanted to learn how to channel it properly.

Shadow had gone through and showed me the basic stances along with the ways one had to move while practicing these styles. We had to adjust the styles, of course., Neither style was made for a vampire but a Tsu-gi, someone who had tails, and his center of balance was a lot different than mine was. And that wasn't even accounting for the way that his Mask and skills differed from mine. He had developed the two styles when he had already been an established fighter, honing his skills to near perfection.

He had demonstrated only two techniques for me, one from each style, which had exhausted him so much. And even though, according to him, what he had showed me was not the full demonstration of what the ***Azure Moon*** and the ***Scarlet Moon Styles*** represented, I was . . . awed.

His skills allowed him to create illusions of mists, or even full copies of himself that were indiscernible from the original. Coupled with his natural ability to make anyone hallucinate, it was a terrifying combination.

But what truly impressed me was the way he was able to immediately adapt his styles to something that I could use. I didn't have skills that allowed me to create illusions, but I was a vampire with near perfect coordination, incredible regeneration, and great physical control over my body. And Shadow had leaned into those aspects to devise a way for me to learn.

So, the *Azure Moon Style,* the more defensive one, based on using his illusions and pheromone tricks to draw an opponent out for a counterattack, became something else. Using my coordination and control, I too could trick my opponent by letting them win trades that were inconsequential to me. Instead of using illusions, I could just allow my opponent to wound me in places that I could heal from with ease, making them grow bolder and overextend in order to crush them when they made a mistake.

The *Scarlet Moon Style* relied on speed and attacks, creating illusions that constantly forced the opponent to back step, hammering in at their defenses and piercing through them through sheer overwhelming offense. Shadow relied on his copies to attack from several directions, and used his tricks to fool his opponents into misjudging his attacks. Again, the way that he adapted his style was based on my main strength, my regeneration. I could allow myself to disregard wounds and focus on offense, mimic what he accomplished with illusions.

In the end, the *Azure Moon Style* ended up being difficult for me to grasp. And while both styles had overwhelming the opponent as the ultimate goal, the *Scarlet Moon Style* was the one that suited me far more. The *Scarlet Moon Style* was a death by a thousand cuts, compared to the single monstrous strike of the *Azure Moon Style.*

Next to me, Shadow stirred, and I got ready to continue the lessons.

"That is looking good," Shadow said as he walked around me then took a position directly across from me. "Your stance is passable. Now let me see what you have learned."

I resisted the urge to glare at him and focused on the matter at hand. I had taken the opening form of the *Scarlet Moon Style* technique he was teaching me, the **Veiled Mist Assault.** My body leaned forward with most of my weight on my right leg, which was in front of the left, bent and with the knee hovering over my toes. My hands were crossed in front of my face, my fingers bent into claws. It was an aggressive position, and one that allowed me to leap into action in a moment.

The **Veiled Mist Assault** had three forms, or Katas. The first Kata, and the one I was in was called: *From the Mist, Strike,* was meant to be used when attacking from an ambush. It was designed to present a smaller profile, while still keeping your muscles tense and ready for action. The technique aimed to catch the opponent off guard and create a favorable advantage from the onset of the encounter. Of course, that wasn't the case here, but I still executed it.

With a sudden movement, I leapt forward, lashing out at him with my claws in a one-two strike. He dashed back, evading, and I followed, moving into the second Kata, *Tempest in the Mist.* I never stopped moving as I entered the second form, letting my emotions guide my attacks, rapidly spinning and attacking from multiple angles, creating a flurry of attacks that carried explosive power and seamlessly chained multiple rapid strikes. With my physical attributes, that came easily to me. I let my instincts and emotions guide me, which made my body move in a wild manner that allowed me to unleash a torrent of devastating blows. It was meant to be a follow up to the first Kata, a devastating attack following the emergence from an obscured position, like a tempest appearing from the mist.

He didn't block. Instead his body weaved, evading my strikes. I still couldn't catch him, so I moved to the last Kata, *Advance, Whirling Mist.* I lashed out with my right hand, a spinning strike that Shadow moved to evade. Just before my strike finished its full range of movement, I threw myself at him and *stepped.* [Mist Step] turned me to mist, and my momentum carried me forward at an incredible speed, bridging the gap that Shadow's evasion created. My step finished, and I re-formed in the same position as before. My attack finished its arc, with almost no time left for him to react. My claws swiped across his chest, and he dissolved into mist.

I caught myself and stopped, too surprised to do anything but glare as his body disappeared in front of my eyes.

"That was . . . passable," Shadow said from behind me, and I whirled around to look at him. "Let's go again," he just said.

I opened my mouth, then promptly closed it. I ignored the beads of sweat on his brow and did as he said, settling again in the starting form of the technique.

We moved through the jungle at a quick pace. And I kept my eyes open for any threats from my position at the front. Which was how I saw the threat long before it noticed us. I knelt quickly behind a large root, taking cover and then gestured behind me. I looked ahead at the dark shape milling around the base of a tree. Its snout was low to the ground, sniffing, and then it stabbed its tusks into the root. It raised its head, breaking the root apart and making room to put its head beneath and retrieve whatever it was that it had found. I watched as it ate the mushroom-like plants, then slowly started meandering about. I gripped the glaive in my hand tightly and got ready just in case it noticed us. It sniffed around a few more times, and then, thankfully, wandered away.

I released a sigh as it left, then turned and glanced at Shadow. He was hiding just behind me, holding the serpent-tongue spear in his hands. The big trunk that contained most of his equipment and supplies was placed on the ground next to him, and his eyes were on the jungle around us. The animal was the same as the one that I had killed while consumed by the **thirst**. The animal itself wasn't strong enough to really pose a threat. It was something that I was confident I could've handled, but we didn't want to fight anything if we could help it. In fact, we had been avoiding most of the wildlife as we made our long trek through the jungle. Aside from the few hunts to gather blood for myself. And those consisted of mostly of me climbing through the trees looking for nests to grab birdlike creatures while they slept.

"Let's go," I said and he nodded, following after me. I knew that we couldn't afford to stay in the same place for too long.

We set out again, moving as quickly as possible through the jungle, while also remaining as stealthy as possible. We wanted to avoid making a noise and drawing attention, or getting delayed by unnecessary obstacles. We had left the ruins days ago, after Shadow spent a week teaching me about his way of life. My Student Ornament had improved up to the Fifth Carving, though I haven't gotten any new skills from it yet.

I had learned as much as I could. He taught me two techniques from each of the two styles, for a total of four. Of course, I hadn't gotten really proficient in anything that he taught me, but at least I understood the basics. I lacked a lot of the tools that made those techniques complete, like the skills that he had, but he assured me that over time I would find my own to replace them. And that if I followed his school of being fully, eventually I would earn skills of my own. By executing actions that were perfect and resonated with the world, whatever that meant.

I had no choice but to trust him.

As we walked through the jungle, I turned my eyes to the sky. We'd reached an opening in the big canopy, which let me see the clouds above. It was early morning, so my strength was lessened, which meant that we didn't want to get involved in any fights.

I kept my head turned up, scanning the skies.

"She should have been back by now," Shadow commented.

I grimaced and nodded. Saia had been scouting for us. I wasn't really worried, since the little dragon part of her wasn't really her, it was just a drone. Her real body was inside of mine, though with our synchronization so low she could only communicate with me through her drone. Which made things a bit more difficult. If anything had happened there was no way for Saia to let me know.

Before I had a chance to think on it further, I saw a small shape above the tree line. Immediately, I released a sigh of relief as Saia made her way down. I put my hand out, and she landed on my palm.

"What took you so long?" I asked.

"Feedback: The interference caused a confusion with the drone's sensors, resulting in the drone unit heading the wrong way for several leagues."

I tsked to myself. We didn't know what was causing that interference, but it had happened before too. Once her drone was sufficiently away from me, she got some kind of a phantom signal that told her that I was in the wrong direction.

Which frustrated Saia to no end. It should be impossible according to her. After all, she was nestled inside of my nervous system and was directly controlling the drone at a distance.

"What about our friend?" Shadow asked as he stepped closer.

Saia turned her tiny head to look at him. It wasn't an action that was necessary, but I had noticed that Saia had started to do it more often after I suggested that it might make her seem more alive.

"Feedback: The sikiri is following, at its current pace it will catch up to us in three days."

Shadow's eyes narrowed then turned to look at me. He didn't say anything, there wasn't a need. I already knew. The beast had been following us since we left the ruins. We hadn't been certain at the start . . . Saia had kept an eye on its movements from the sky—it wasn't that hard to keep watch over a giant snake—but it quickly became apparent that it was somehow following after us—tracking us.

"It will catch up with us before we reach the coast," Shadow added slowly.

We had known that it was a possibility ever since Saia noticed the sikiri. We had tried to change direction, but always the sikiri had adjusted and followed.

"We can increase our pace again," I suggested.

"Even this is pushing me to my limits." Shadow sighed. He paused for a moment, then continued. "We both know that it is coming after me."

I grimaced. I didn't want to say it, but it seemed like the most likely explanation. The sikiri hadn't noticed me when I was near it the last time I encountered it. It couldn't be following me.

"There is still a chance that all of this was a coincidence." I tried to hold on to some hope. After all, it hadn't started moving after us until we left the ruins. There were things here that we weren't aware of.

He shook his head. "No," he said. "It is clear that it has a skill that lets it detect me somehow, a skill that tells it where the greatest threat is, or one that helps it detect high Investment." He sat down on his trunk, his head bowed. "I could . . . leave in another direction, lead it away."

I narrowed my eyes at him. "Can you avoid it?"

"Of course," he said, and I heard the lie in his voice. "I might be weakened, but I do not need to fight it. I can just hide."

"That would leave us both alone in the jungle. You said that there are dangers here that could kill us both."

"We have gotten far enough away from the inner ring that it is unlikely you will encounter anything that can really threaten you. And besides, you can just hide as well and run out the clock."

"Which would leave you weakened and alone in the jungle without a way to the coast," I added.

He waved his hand. "I will manage."

I knew what he was trying to do, of course I did. So, I walked over and knelt in front of him. "We made an agreement, remember?" I said gently. I had learned a lot about him over our short time together. Enough to know that he was a man filled with regrets. Somehow, I knew that he didn't want me to be another one of those regrets. "I'm not leaving you to die, I'll honor my words."

He opened his mouth to argue, but then paused at the look in my eyes. He held my gaze for a little while, then nodded. "Then, we need a plan. It will catch up to us one way or another. Better that we dictate where that happens."

That I could agree with wholeheartedly.

The Ambush

"Are you afraid?" Shadow asked, his voice a whisper behind me, as the two of us walked through the jungle. I didn't answer immediately. Instead my hand reached for my wrist, not finding what I was looking for. I caught myself. Saia was of course not there. She somewhere ahead of us, scouting for a good place to make an ambush. The fact that my hand moved almost unconsciously to try to touch her spoke volumes about how important she had become to me in such a short time.

My first instinct to his question was to say that I wasn't afraid, but that was a lie. The tenets of the **Heart of Azure and Scarlet** taught me that emotion was not a burden, that it was not to be suppressed. So I answered truthfully. "Yes," I said, not even trying to mask the fear in my voice.

I remembered the feeling I got when I looked at the sikiri the last time. The aura that gripped me, that sent me to the verge of panic. The memory of that encounter with the sikiri still haunted me—the chilling terror I had felt in the presence of the massive creature, the sinister hiss that had reverberated through my bones, and the sheer size and power it had displayed.

I remembered the feeling of helplessness as I hid in the hollow between the tree roots, the way the sikiri had effortlessly lifted the body of the okolon and made it disappear. I shuddered at the memory of its enormous, snakelike head looming above me.

"And what does your fear tell you?" Shadow asked.

I stopped and turned to look at him. I thought about it, letting my emotions flow through me. They were a natural response, my instincts giving me a warning. Humans had evolved over a course of millions of years, the evolution that had honed our bodies for one trait above all others: intelligence. I was no longer a human, but I shared a lot of their base qualities. What I did have now was the **thirst,** and it too had evolved over its existence. Its history might not be as explored or known, but I knew what purpose the **thirst** served. It had evolved for survival over everything else. It spoke to me through my human emotions, and my intelligence allowed me to understand and gain insight from it. The **thirst** sought the same goal it always did. To feed and to be the biggest predator around. That I felt fear, meant that even the **thirst** understood the danger that the sikiri presented.

I remembered the tenets: Emotion is the fuel that grants me Purpose. Our purpose was clear, to survive the jungle and reach the coast. Fate had taken the decision out of our hands, The sikiri would catch up to us, it was inevitable. The sikiri was in the way of us achieving that purpose. We would need to confront it, one way or another. The thought of facing the sikiri was terrifying, but not surprising, my fear did not mean letting it rule me.

"The sikiri is the most dangerous thing I have ever encountered," I answered Shadow's question with a conviction. "We shouldn't face it head on. If we could, we shouldn't face it at all. My fear tells me that fighting it head on is death."

Shadow nodded, his eyes piercing into mine. What he saw there, I couldn't know, I could only hope that he approved. "An ambush, *From the Mist, Strike*," he said, quoting the name of the **Veiled Mist Assault**'s first Kata. "One should always strive to end the conflict as fast as possible, with overwhelming might if at all able."

I agreed. It echoed some of the teachings that my sire tried to instill in me, what now seemed like it was in another life. "So, how do we do that?" I asked.

"We are likely facing a young sikiri. A mature one would have caught up to us by now. That is a boon for us, otherwise we would have no chance. From the way you describe the encounter, there are two possibilities. One, it has a terror skill, which will be an issue to deal with but not an insurmountable one. Or two . . . it is blighted, a monster."

"Which is worse?" I asked, already suspecting the answer.

"If it is a monster, then it will be stronger than its Investment might suggest. Though it will also be . . . erratic. The blight is . . . it affects the mind and it feeds on negative emotions. Its presence will make you feel more deeply. If we encounter it, do not try to fight what you feel."

I raised an eyebrow.

He heard the unspoken question and answered. "Hunting monsters is a difficult profession. Only a few ever become any good at it. This is because of the effect that monsters have on people, the way that they influence emotions, it plays tricks on the mind. To resist one needs a stalwart mind, forged by discipline practiced for decades. All monster hunters are taught how to control and suppress emotion. It is how they resist the effect the blight has on a person."

I blinked. That sounded very different than what he had just told me to do.

He saw my expression, and one side of his mouth lifted into a wicked-looking grin. "You noticed that this is almost an exact opposite of what I and my school of being teach?"

"I did," I answered. "I assume that there is a reason for that?"

He nodded in response. "What the blight does is not innately wrong. It just amplifies what is already there. It fans the flames of your emotions. Suppressing and controlling them works, but it also keeps so much more of it chained up inside. When such control slips, the outcome is far more destructive. My way is more dangerous, but if you learn to channel your emotions properly, then you will never have anything to fear from the blight. And we have no time to teach you how to guard your mind. So, let your emotions flow through you freely, feel deeply, but do not let them control you."

I nodded. It wasn't like I had much choice. "How do we fight it?"

"The first step in any battle that you can choose, is picking the battlefield."

The ground trembled, and I grabbed hold of a nearby tree to steady myself. It ended as quickly as it started, and I glanced behind me to check up on Shadow. His head was turned to the sky, looking through the gap in the canopy. I knew what was in that direction, what it was that he was looking at. I could assume what he was thinking about.

"You think that it's connected to the tremors?" I asked as I grabbed a gourd from my waist. It was filled with blood of a birdlike creature I had hunted the day before, the same species as one of the first beasts that I had hunted in this place.

Shadow turned to look at me as I drank, then he sighed. "I do not know," he answered. "We had never thought about it. The Blight Curtain existed here forever, as far as I know. And so had Ish Vimza suffered from the ground itself shaking. Yet, it has gotten worse of late. I assumed that the new Expansion, your arrival, had something to do with it. Or perhaps that it was a side effect of something that the Grand Spell is doing. But now . . . after what I saw in that vision . . . We are wrong about the nature of the blight. Perhaps there are things that we do not yet understand."

There wasn't anything for me to comment on, so I simply nodded and returned my eyes to the ground and the task at hand—preparing the quicksand trap. Saia had spent a day scouting ahead of us until she found the spot. According to Shadow, the quicksand was the best chance we had of taking the sikiri down.

We had spent almost an hour checking out the location afterward, and Shadow had finally agreed that this spot was the best we could hope to find before the sikiri caught up to us. It was a narrow stretch of path filled by the treacherous quicksand. We had been lucky in our search—we found a spot with the not only right kind of terrain, but also some natural cover.

The path was surrounded by dense foliage that would force the sikiri to slow down and give us the advantage in combat. We grabbed as many vines and leaves from the jungle floor as we could, setting aside any stones and dirt to fill in the gaps. With Shadow's help, we used these items to cover up the quicksand patch.

It had been a day since we started preparing, and the sikiri would've taken that time to catch up quickly. I just hoped that we had timed things properly.

Shadow was very good at making improvised traps. He had me felling a tree and cutting out a large piece of its trunk as a trap. It had been a bitch and a half to move, but between the two of us we managed to wrap it up with vines and rope that he had among his gear, then pull it up into the air, setting it up hidden behind one of the larger trees overlooking the quicksand. We also made sure to hide the rope so that the sikiri wouldn't notice. I didn't know how smart the monster was, but Shadow was taking no chances.

We continued working all around the ambush spot until even a seasoned eye would struggle to spot where danger lurked beneath our feet, or above our heads. We also hid away a few of his weapons, just in case we had to grab a new one quickly.

As I worked, my mind wandered to the sikiri. Would the trap be enough? I wondered. I couldn't help but feel a sense of unease about the upcoming confrontation. I didn't know how strong the sikiri actually was, but every instinct that I had screamed at me that facing it was death. I tried to push the fear aside and focus on the task at hand.

"Are you sure this will work?" I asked Shadow, looking up from my work.

He nodded confidently. "Yes. One does not survive for as long as I have without knowing how to hunt properly and adapt based on his prey." Then, he hesitated. "That being said. The sikiri is an apex predator. They are smart, and if this one is a monster . . . then our success will depend on the skills that it has and how good our ambush is. We need to make sure the bait is convincing enough, then strike fast and with no hesitation."

I nodded, remembering the lessons. "*From the Mist, Strike,*" I said.

Shadow raised his head and met my eyes. The side of his mouth rose in a half smile. "Yes, exactly. If we execute the plan well, we can kill it before it has the chance to do anything. Otherwise . . . I do not think that I could do more than use one of my stronger skills once. Perhaps a handful of my weaker ones."

The plan was made without needing to rely on Shadow and his power. I had seen how tired he got when he demonstrated skills for me when he was teaching me. If he was forced to do that, he was not going to be able to do much else after.

But, at least we had a plan in place. It was better than trying to outrun the monster when we had no hope of doing so.

As we finished setting up the trap, we waited for Saia to return, I had sent her ahead to keep an eye on the sikiri and let us know when it got close.

As we waited, I couldn't help but feel nervous. This was it, my first real encounter in this new world. A fight against an opponent that was powerful and had skills. I knew that Shadow was experienced, but I couldn't shake off the feeling of dread that weighed heavily on my chest.

Nightfall approached, and some of my tension bled away with the setting of the sun, as my true nature awakened once again. We'd tried to time it so that the ambush happened at night, when we would have the element of surprise on our side, and when we were at our strongest.

We knew that the sikiri would be heading straight for us. Saia and Shadow had tested it out, and it was as he had suspected. The sikiri was following him. As he said, it was most likely a skill it had.

Then, a glint of something reflective caught my eye, and I raised my head to see Saia drop down through the trees.

"You're back," I said in relief. I was getting worried.

"Statement: The sikiri will arrive within the hour at its current pace."

"The time has come, then." Shadow's voice vibrated with intensity as he spoke. He approached me and firmly grasped my shoulder, his gaze piercing straight into my soul. His words penetrated deep within me, conveying a warmth that brought tears to my eyes. This man had been in my life for only a short time, yet he had become a teacher, a mentor. Circumstances forced us to work together, and somehow a trust was born between us.

The world was cruel, that we'd met here in this place filled with so much danger.

With emotion swelling in his voice, he whispered, "No matter what lies ahead of us, I am thankful that our paths have crossed."

I gave him a small smile. "And so am I." In just a few days, he had given me lessons that I felt like I would be unraveling for the rest of my life. I didn't know if he understood exactly what it was that he had given me, the **Heart of Azure and Scarlet** was a step that had cemented my desire to discover my own purpose in life. To be something more than a servant of the cartel.

I didn't know what sharing his way of being meant to him fully, but I could tell that it had meant a lot to him as well.

He nodded, then turned his head to look in the distance, at the dark jungle ahead. "Let us begin, as we agreed," Shadow said. "I will go and lead it back here."

I took a deep breath. This part of their plan was the most uncertain. Shadow was weakened, and they didn't know how the sikiri would react if it saw him. But they also had to make sure that it fell into the trap, and Shadow was its target.

"I'll be ready," I told him, and he walked away, quickly disappearing into the jungle.

I waited for what felt like eternity, time enough to reflect. My life was never perfect. It was always filled with strife. If I died today I would lament not getting a chance to do something with my life. But, at the same time, if I had to die, doing it on my own terms felt . . . good. I was dealt a bad hand, but I was the one who was playing it.

I looked around one last time, making sure that everything was ready. Saia was hidden above among the branches, waiting to strike. And I was kneeling next to the rope that held in place the giant log above me.

The silence of the jungle was broken by a low rumble that made my heart beat faster in anticipation of what would come next. The quicksand trap was nearly impossible to detect until you were right on top of it, I hoped that the sikiri would not have the time to notice. I waited silently, watching from my hiding place deep in the foliage as the sounds grew louder.

Then, finally I saw movement. Shadow ran through the jungle at a pace that was faster than even I could manage. I could barely track him, though what I could see clearly was what came behind him. A giant snakelike monster was crashing through everything in its way.

Seeing it immediately brought the same reaction as I had experienced last time. The all-consuming terror that made even the **thirst** hesitate. This time I was ready for it. I didn't fight it, I accepted the fear for what it was, a warning from my instincts.

The sikiri's scales hit the dirt like a constant drum roll. In the silence of the jungle, it was a death march. A deep, rumbling shriek that was like the sound of a volcanic eruption. The monster's hiss was a reverberating rumble that circled through the trees and came back to me, like the echoes of a thousand slithering tongues.

The moonlight above illuminated its passage, and let me see its form more clearly.

The sikiri was a giant serpent made of scales and muscle, with two tendrils swept back and dangling off its head. Its body was almost twice as wide as I was, and sharp sharklike teeth filled its mouth. It was gray like dirty snow, with dark green and brown patches. Its four eyes were the color of gold, bulbous and large, and it was hard to pinpoint where they were looking.

Then I caught traces of red over its scales. From what Shadow had said, that meant that the sikiri was blighted, but not yet fully a monster. If it was a monster, its eyes would've turned red. Still, it was a dangerous beast.

Shadow ran ahead of it and over the quicksand. Even knowing the plan, I felt fear rise up in me for a moment. There was of course no reason to. The sikiri followed Shadow as he whirled around and raised his serpent-tongue spear and yelled, challenging the beast. The sikiri hissed and snapped forward, I felt the move imprinted in the fabric of the world around me, in the Way. I knew that it was a skill, and I saw how quickly it moved. Its maw opened, and it flashed across the distance taking a bite out of Shadow. Its mouth engulfed him, and the teeth snapped closed around his waist.

For a moment, I almost stood up, but then I saw Shadow's body fall apart into mist. An illusion.

The attack carried the sikiri forward, straight into the quicksand. It sank in, pushing the quicksand out of the pit in a small geyser of mud. It let out a hiss of rage and thrashed, but it was too late. The treacherous ground had taken hold of it, trapping the monster in place.

The real Shadow appeared at the other end of the trap, his weapon raised and ready. "Now!" he yelled, and I turned. My dagger slicing through the rope tied to the root next to me.

A groaning sound came from above me as the tree log was set free, and it swung through the air. The sikiri raised its head above the quicksand as its lower body, the part of it that was out of the pit, tried to wrap itself around a tree and pull itself out of the trap. Just in time for the log to come swinging straight at its head.

The bark shattered like glass as it splintered upon impact, sending wood chips shooting all over. I twitched my head out of the way as shrapnel flew in my direction, I felt warmth on my face and knew that it had cut me. I ignored it, quickly sliding my dagger into its sheath and puling the glaive from my back.

The sikiri was stunned, one of its eyes was a bleeding mess, and it kept shaking its head as if in a daze. It thrashed and pounded, trying to find a way forward, but was quickly being swallowed up by the quicksand. Shadow jumped forward, leaping over the pit and the beast.

His movements were graceful and precise, as if he had done this a thousand times. His nine tails fluttered behind him like ribbons as he soared through the air. He extended his arm and with a single, swift motion, unleashed his serpent-tongue spear. I felt an imprint on the world, a skill activating, but I didn't hear what it was. My attention wasn't on that, but instead on what was happening in front of me.

His attack cut into the sikiri's head with dizzying speed, piercing its scales and gouging out a deep gash from the side of its snout to the rim of its eye. The creature let out a loud screech of pain and confusion, now blind in another eye, making its left side completely dark. Then Shadow somersaulted over to the other side of the trap, landing on solid ground with a loud thud. But before he could regain his balance, his legs gave way beneath him and he collapsed onto his knees.

The sikiri released a sound, a cross between a hiss and a roar that made my knees weak. I trusted my instincts and our plan. I acknowledged my fear and used it as fuel to fulfill my purpose, the death of the sikiri.

Without a moment of hesitation, I ran forward, then leapt into the air as the sikiri remained still in confusion. Its thick hide shimmered beneath two moons as I raised my glaive high above me. With all my strength and skill, I aimed for the gap between two scales on the base of its head that Shadow had instructed me to watch out for.

My blade connected with a dull thud, sinking in barely a handspan deep. The momentum of my attack thrust me forward and onto the beast's neck, where

I attempted to drive it deeper. As my arms strained against the creature, I felt vibrations begin to resonate through it, then beneath my feet. I suddenly realized what was happening too late—the beast was activating a skill. Its scaly hide began to vibrate faster and faster in a span of less than a second, with an intense hum that threatened to make my ears bleed. I didn't even have the chance to react before my glaive shattered in my hands as it jerked away from me. Something struck me hard as the sikiri sprung into motion and sent me tumbling backward, a wet sound of an eruption echoing in my ears. I gasped as I landed heavily on my wrist, feeling it snap in two.

I caught myself and pushed to my knees, holding my side. Sweat broke out all over me as pain throbbed through my wrist. I grabbed the gourd on my waist and quickly drank what little was left inside. The sweet, thick fluid made me forget the pain for just a moment, but it wasn't going to heal me. It wasn't going to make all this pain go away, or anything else. It wasn't that potent, but it couldn't hurt.

Shadow was near me, leaning against a tree with one hand while keeping himself upright by clutching its rough surface. His face was pale and streaked with sweat. He was breathing heavily.

The sikiri was out of the pit, and what was left of it was just an empty hole in front of us. The quicksand had been thrown all around us, it was streaking from the trees and across the ground. The beast was wrapping itself around a tree on the other side of it. I noticed that one side of its head was drenched in blood and blind: we had hurt it. Then, it turned its good side toward us, and two golden eyes glared at us.

In the faint light of the moons, I could see the red on its scales, it looked like . . . like it was growing, expanding. The two golden eyes had a tint of red in their depths now.

I felt Shadow stir, and glanced at him. He was looking at me, his eyes wide. "It is—"

He didn't get to finish whatever it was that he wanted to say. The tree the sikiri was wrapped around shattered as it squeezed then launched itself across the pit. It was so fast that I barely had the time to turn and look in its direction, and I knew immediately that I had no hope of getting out of the way.

The world turned on its head as I was thrown to the side just as it was about to hit me. A rush of air blew past me as the sikiri struck, the ground cracked and exploded, and trees were felled by its passage. I could barely react as I hit the ground, then rolled trying to avoid the falling trees around me.

I raised my head just in time to see that the sikiri had turned around. I still couldn't believe that it could be that fast, and was looking for us. I saw no sign of Shadow, but with his skills he was likely invisible.

My heart was pounding so hard I thought I'd pass out, but somehow I managed to stay conscious. I should've used my [Mist Step] skill, I realized. I shouldn't have needed Shadow to push me out of the way, but skills weren't second nature to me yet, and in the chaos I had forgotten. The sikiri had seen me and was coming my way. It was obviously exhausted, its movements jerky. We had hurt it, just not enough.

It reared up then lashed down with its head. I jumped to the side, knowing that even if I used my skill I wasn't going to be fast enough, and it . . . missed?

For a moment there was silence, then the noise of cracking branches echoed around us as they began to fall from the force of the sikiri's attack. It took me a moment to realize that Shadow had to have used his pheromones or a skill to make it appear to the sikiri as if I was in a different place. It took the sikiri a moment more to realize the same.

The sikiri flicked out its tongue and then it shifted toward me, ready to attack. Before it could, Saia swooped down from her hiding place above, her claws outstretched to reach for the creature's head.

She scratched the beast's eye, her powerful claws doing damage, but I didn't see or hear what I expected. She hadn't been able to do damage to the reaper; I doubted that she would be able to harm the sikiri, not on her own at least. She didn't have my strength, even if her drone body was sturdy.

The sikiri shook its head, then turned and opened its mouth in the direction of Saia flying above it. A skill blasted out, hitting Saia and sending her into a tree with a thud. I took a step forward and pulled out my dagger with my good hand, steeling myself as the sikiri turned back around.

The fight wasn't even close to over.

The Taste of Death

The first time I encountered death, it was when my grandfather died, my mother's father. I was very young; I didn't understand what had happened. And for the longest time, all that I remembered was the smell of death.

To me, it was the scent of polished wood, the casket they placed him in. The scent of the freshly cut flowers that made up the funeral wreaths which surrounded the casket. The scent of too many people in our small home, as they came to pray by my grandfather's side. Then, it was the smell of wet soil, lingering in the air as we buried him. That was what had remained etched in my mind, what I associated with death.

I had forgotten that when I was turned. From that moment on, death took on a new meaning for me: it was the end of all things sweet and good in this world. The decay of hope, the darkening of one's future. Tasting death, for a vampire, meant experiencing a life. It is the loss of salvation, of succor, absconding with all that was once sweet and never to be felt again. It was like biting into something delicious and realizing it wasn't food at all, but rather something unique that could never be savored again.

Now, when I looked into the single whole eye of the sikiri, as the gold in it slowly bled into red, I learned a new meaning of death. It hissed, and in that tone, I heard death. It was deafening, so loud that it could deafen you forever. The sikiri's cry was a hiss like a hot steel blade drawn across a stone, or a river of molten lava crashing into the sea. I heard its scales grinding against each other as the muscles beneath moved, a melody of violence and power. In those sounds, I heard death.

The sikiri coiled itself, its eye never leaving mine. Then, it launched itself forward. It was so fast that I barely had a chance to react. This time though, I remembered my skill. Its maw opened up to swallow me whole, and I stepped to the side, turning to mist.

The color bled out of the world and sounds quieted. I wasn't fast enough. The sikiri's teeth passed through a piece of the mist that corresponded to my right arm. Immediately I felt a sensation unlike anything I had felt before. It wasn't exactly pain, but it felt like a thousand needles had just been pushed through every single part of my arm.

My step finished, and I re-formed as the rest of the sikiri's body flew by me. My arm felt numb, and my knife slipped from my fingers to the ground. I tried to move it, and realized that sensation was coming back swiftly. I knelt, trying to pick the knife back up when the sikiri's tail lashed out and I dashed out of the way, cursing. It smashed into the earth where I stood just a moment before, sending debris flying everywhere, and I lost sight of my weapon.

Cursing, I took more quick steps back, putting a greater distance between myself and the beast, but also running down the cooldown on my skill.

Shadow was nowhere to be found, and Saia had recovered near the base of the tree she was thrown at. The thundering of the sikiri landing after its attack rumbled through the forest, shaking trees and rattling leaves. I ran to Saia and grabbed her.

"Chain," I said, and she transformed without delay. I took the blade part and put it in my broken left hand. I'd healed enough that I could somewhat close my fist, but I knew that wasn't going to be enough. So I used the chain to wrap the blade around my hand, hoping that I could keep hold of it. All the while I kept an eye on the sikiri, as it recovered and coiled to turn its attention on me again. Before I could finish wrapping the blade, Saia shifted, the chains I wrapped around my arm and the blade melted in my fingers, engulfing my hand and wrist then solidifying into a kind of a gauntlet with a chain attached at the bottom and a blade sticking out straight out of my knuckles.

"Thanks," I managed to say before I had to move again. The sikiri had recovered and was turning my way, this time slowly. I ran, moving around the hole where the quicksand used to be and putting it between us.

There was no use running, I couldn't outlast it, and even if I could, the sikiri was much faster than me. From what Shadow had said, the sikiri was in the Fifth or Sixth Investment, which made it incredibly tough. And I could see that. I hadn't been able to scratch the reaper corpse, and that one was on the Sixth. The sikiri's scales were tougher than the reaper's, though it did have some weak areas. The fact that Saia had managed to wound its eye and that I managed to even scratch its hide proved that true. That limited the ways I could hurt it.

The sikiri watched me with one good eye, its forked tongue slithering out every once in a while. I could see red lines crawling over its scales, and the gold in its eye was now almost completely overtaken. The sikiri raised its head, slow and wavering. It was hurt, I could tell, still dazed from the log crashing into its head.

It straightened and headed in my direction. Then, suddenly it paused, its eye moving to the side as if tracking something.

"The blight is taking it."

My hand whirled around at the sound, my hand nearly taking Shadow's head off. Thankfully, I stopped just shy of his throat.

The sikiri hissed, then jumped forward, smashing its head into a tree.

"I'm making it hallucinate." Shadow answered my silent question. "It won't last long, not with its Investment."

I glanced at him, seeing that he was breathing quickly, his hair matted with sweat. His blue skin was looking paler than usual.

"It is turning into a monster," Shadow wheezed.

The red lines, the blight spreading across the sikiri's body was moving faster now. From everything that he said, once it turned monster, we were screwed.

Shadow grimaced. "We cannot let that happen."

"How?" I asked. Our plan was as perfect as it we could've made it, and it had gone off as well as it possibly could, yet it was still not enough.

"I have one more skill in me," Shadow said with a wince. "I need you to distract it."

My fear spiked, the **thirst** quieted down, almost cowed by the prospect of facing the death in front of us. I accepted the fear, took it in, and wielded it like the tool it was.

I nodded to Shadow, then took a step forward. With a deep breath, I let the chain and ring drop from my right hand, then I started to spin it underhanded. I settled into the second Kata of the **Veiled Mist Assault,** *Tempest in the Mist,* skipping the first one. One leg in front of the other, my balance shifted forward, as if I was in the middle of a step. I spun the chain, faster and faster, until the shrill sound of it spinning drowned out everything else. The sound was like a mountain being torn apart by a storm. A melody of violence.

The sikiri snapped its head back, as if to rid itself of the trance-like state that Shadow's pheromones brought, then it slowly shook its head. Then as the sound of the chain rose, it froze. I had shifted around so that now I was on its blind side, yet it could still sense me. Before it could bring its eye on me, I wound up and threw the chain and ring with all of my vampire might. It flew through the air, thrown by a vampire's strength. It hissed through the air with a thunderous whoosh that braced me for what was to come.

The ring smashed into its snout with a loud crack and made it rear back. The scale on its snout wasn't damaged, but the speed of my throw was enough to startle it. Before it recovered, I jumped forward, spinning and pulling back the chain and wrapping it up around my left forearm as I ran.

As soon as I got it back to a manageable length, I whipped the chain above my head. Again, the sikiri started turning in my direction, and once again I let the chain go, this time aiming more closely. The ring hit the sikiri in the eyes, or rather the ruined wounds that were left of them. A low whine escaped from the creature as it veered away from me, but I quickly followed, spinning the chain above my head once again.

I wasn't fast enough to taunt it and then evade its attacks. I wasn't strong enough to seriously hurt it. I could only attack, give myself over to the **Scarlet Moon Style,** and distract it with continuous assaults. I pushed all thoughts of defense into the back of my mind, and let my fear come forth. I let it guide my actions.

With every beat of my heart, I discerned what it was that my fear was telling me. The sikiri was powerful, but we had denied it more than half of its vision. It could still hear and use its tongue, if it worked in any way as a snake's did, and it could still smell me. But I feared it laying eyes on me again, so I moved in concord with that fear. I kept myself on its blind side, running around it and sending the chain flying at it as fast as I could.

The strikes didn't do much when they hit the scales. They couldn't even crack them, but when I hit its wounded eyes, its reaction was clearly pained.

The sikiri began to lash out with its tail in an attempt to ward me off. I evaded, not by getting out of the way, but jumping forward, getting closer and attacking again, faster and stronger. Every time my fear pulsed inside of me, warning me of shadows and danger, I attacked. The sikiri began to hiss louder, then I saw its tail swipe and a long arc of something black headed toward me as if its tail had turned into a whip spinning in circles around its body.

My eyes widened and my blood boiled as adrenaline surged through me and my fear spiked. I stepped to the side, turning to mist. The whiplike extension of its tail snapped at the ground behind me, and I finished my step. My chain re-formed alongside me, still mid-spin, but now closer to the sikiri's head. I twisted my wrist, rippling the chain and sending the tip faster. It smashed into the sikiri's ruined eye, the speed and the strength of the ring punching through the wound, sinking into it. Immediately, I wrenched the chain back, pulling it out violently. With it followed gore and the ruined eye that had been stuck inside of the socket. It ripped out of the wound, and came to rest on the sikiri's scales, still connected by the blood covered nerves.

The sikiri roared its fury, and the black extension of its tail started smashing into the ground wildly. My breath hitched as I stepped in to meet it. I felt a strange sense of confidence wash over me, like I already knew what I needed to do. Without thinking or hesitation, I ducked and dodged every strike from the tail almost flawlessly, never taking a step backward when a step forward would suffice, not letting my fear drive me away, but using it to know when to move. Not worrying about where my next move should be taken from there on out, I danced in front of danger passionately instead of fleeing for safety.

My chain was now an extension of my body, an extra limb that obeyed each motion centered around the sikiri's head as if it had become a part of this fight. For a moment, I wondered if Saia wasn't helping me somehow, but that thought faded into the background almost as quickly as it came, left to be dwelled on at another time.

Amidst the chaos and destruction, one thing remained unchanged: my fear was still present with each movement, cautioning me whenever I stepped too close or hesitated too long but propelling me forward at just the right times as well.

With every forceful spin and strike that impacted against its scales, deadly sparks leapt, though still I did nothing more than annoy the beast. The red lines of the blight were advancing faster now, and almost all of its scales had turned crimson. I kept dancing, taking quick steps and feeling [Mist Step] become available again.

Then the sikiri's attack smashed a fallen tree, and it exploded into debris. Wood pieces flew in all directions, but I paid them no mind. I couldn't focus on defense. Not when a piece whistled by my ear, clipping it, not when it ripped my shirt and opened a gash on my shoulder. Not when a piece of wood stabbed into my kidney. I felt the burning pain of the wound in my side, but I ignored it; I needed to focus on the task at hand.

The familiar hum of the sikiri's scales vibrating reverberated through my body like a wave. I could feel it in every bone, but mostly my ears throbbed with pain. It was an intimidating sound that rattled the air and shook the ground beneath my feet.

The sikiri blindly lunged forward, not caring for anything other than reaching me. Its tail smashed into trees, dragging them along as if they weighed nothing at all. I moved to meet it, and as I did so, I felt as if I had started to understand the true core of the **Scarlet Moon Style,** the true meaning of a disregard for defense, just pure offense.

I saw the air shimmer as a sound wave exploded out of its body just on top of me. I stepped, turning to mist. The blast smashed through me a moment before its body followed. The mist stretched, blasted apart, and my mind went white with agony. For a moment I felt stretched to the point of breaking, as if I was on the cusp of forgetting who and what I was. And then the mist moved back, coalescing, and my step ended. I re-formed and tripped immediately. The momentum of my chain carried me forward as it wrapped around a tree and pulled me aside. I collapsed, twisting and falling on my back, hitting the ground hard, my body completely numb and unresponsive. I couldn't feel any part of my body; instead all I felt were needles that stabbed every part of my existence. My lungs were locked, unable to take a breath, my muscles as if they didn't even exist.

A dark shape rose over me: the sikiri, its one remaining eye staring at me and its maw opening up to swallow me whole. The **thirst** raged inside of me, and my fingers twitched. It wasn't enough.

Then Shadow flickered into existence above us, his serpent-tongue spear raised above his head for a strike. One moment he was alone, and then six more of him appeared as if made out of the mists. Three holding the same weapon glowing azure, and three glowing scarlet. Shadow's weapon turned black. He swung, and I heard it inside of my mind. Unraveling with control yet somehow hurried and filled with pain. It rang like the sound of a thousand cut strings.

[Song of Seven Mists, Quell Them All]

Then the world went insane. My eyes couldn't follow all that happened, only that the sikiri was thrown back as seven arcs of light the size of its entire body slashed into it. It moved out of my view, and I pushed against my body, willing it to move through the numbness as I heard the sounds of crashing.

After a few seconds, I managed to push myself up, and Saia flowed back into her dragon form. I saw Shadow kneeling on the ground in front of me, and a bit away from him the sikiri. Blood was splattered everywhere, and the ground had deep gashes cut into it.

I half crawled, half stumbled my way to him.

"You did it," I managed to say, my throat threatening to seize up on me.

Shadow's eyes were closed, and his face turned into a grimace of pain. He didn't respond, and I saw that he was shaking.

Then, before I could say anything else, the sikiri stirred.

I turned my head toward it in disbelief as it rolled slowly, turning around, its scales now fully crimson. Its head rose from behind its body, and I saw that half of its face was gone, Shadow had sheared off half of its head, along with the wounded eyes. The scales all around its head and neck were cracked, and many gone. I could see the bones sticking out through the flesh. Its head lolled, barely holding on.

"Marianna," Shadow whispered. "I can't move."

I glanced at Saia. "Blade," I said, and she flowed back into my weapon without question. My wrist was recovered enough that I could use my left hand, though it still felt stiff.

The sikiri turned its head toward me enough that it could point its remaining eye in our direction. A single ruby the size of a head glowed in the dim light of the jungle. It glared at us for a long moment, and then its mouth opened up, one cheek completely gone. It hissed, and then the hiss turned into something else. The sikiri spoke.

"A THOUSAND . . . TIMES . . . YOU . . . TRY . . . KHANUM . . . A THOUSAND . . . TIMES . . . YOU . . . FAIL." Its words resonated in a way that made my skin crawl. I stopped, struck with terror. My breath came in ragged gasps, fear consuming my every thought as I tried to make sense of what was happening. I felt a fire raging within my chest, and my heart boomed like a drum, threatening to rip through me. Then, an eruption of pure, scorching hate consumed me, a savage anger toward the injustice of the world around me that no words could describe. White-knuckled, I grasped the chain with unrelenting force, until my nails pierced my flesh. The sound of rage roared in my ears, and I heard it beckoning me to join its chorus, singing anarchy to anything that crossed my path. Anything that pretended to be order, that bowed to the will of others. Furiously, I shook my head, trying to push the rush of emotion back.

"Don't fight it," Shadow whispered. "Let the emotions flow, know and understand that the emotions are yours, but do not let them control you. You use what you feel, not act on it. You act based on what you want."

I closed my eyes, remembering the lessons of the **Heart of Azure and Scarlet.** Emotion is the fuel that grants me Purpose. I was feeling these things, but they were there to fuel me, not control me. Calm is the surrender to the will of Others. I would not push my feelings out; I would not surrender my will.

"It speaks?" I said incredulously.

"Do not let your emotion overwhelm you, and do not listen to its words," Shadow said. "It speaks blight madness, nonsense that takes root in the mind. Do not think about what it says. That's how the blight infects."

I opened my mouth to ask more but realized that this was not the moment. I just nodded then focused on the monster. It had an aura of red, thin ribbons of red mist rising from its scales. The wound was terrible, blood spilling everywhere, the monster was on its last legs, yet somehow, I felt more fear now than I had before.

"ALWAYS . . . A THORN . . . KHANUM . . . A THOUSAND TURNS . . . AND STILL YOU . . . TRY . . . ABANDON THE FALSE . . . WAY . . . ACCEPT . . . OUR . . . GIFT." The voice wormed its way into my mind, and I glanced at Shadow, wondering what the monster meant. How many times had he fought the monsters that they taunted him like that. I shook my head, pushing all thoughts about that aside, trusting in Shadow's warning.

"It needs to die," Shadow wheezed out. "Now."

I stepped forward, my stance that of *Tempest in the Mist.* I started spinning the chain, in front of me. The monster wavered in front of me, then hissed. The emotions hit me like a truck. They were coursing through me like an avalanche, threatening to swallow everything in its wake. I focused on them, let me carry me forward, used them as fuel for what I was about to do. The ground rumbled and shook beneath me, but I ignored it, my steps sure as I ran forward. The monster's scales started to vibrate, red mist coalescing around it.

It reared up, then snapped at me. I swung the chain toward the ground then I stepped forward, turning to mist.

My step ended on top of its head, the chain continued and bit into its wounded side, the ring hitting bone and bouncing off. I changed my stance into the last Kata, *Advance, Whirling Mist*. My balance shifted forward, and I bared my fangs as I let all the emotions pulsing through me out. I roared my anger and fear, and let everything go. I attacked as I fell on top of the sikiri's head. I whipped the chain wrapping it around its head and grabbed the ring in my hand, then I dropped on top of it and stabbed with my blade.

The edge slipped into its head, sinking in, but not deep enough. Its flesh was too tough for my meager strength to penetrate. Not deep enough to hit the brain. The sikiri rampaged, trying to throw me off, but I kept my grip on the ring, keeping myself wrapped around its head.

Its scales started to vibrate, and I let the tenets of the **Scarlet Moon Style** guide me. I let my instinct guide me: I let the **thirst** take the wheel.

I leaned down and bit at the exposed flesh on top of the sikiri's head, my fangs barely pushing into the tough meat. But blood flowed, and I tasted it on my tongue. The power of it nearly sent me into a frenzy. Strength filled me, and I started stabbing the blade again, and again, each time pushing it deeper.

The monster's skill activated, and my body shook, my bones shattered and healed just as fast as the blood flowed down my throat, as the **thirst** took the monster's essence.

Pain and pleasure mixed inside of me, bringing me to heights unlike anything I had ever experienced. It was life, it was delirium, it was death.

My blade came down again, my muscles screaming as I tore them apart, pushing them beyond anything I have ever done before. I felt the blade slip through, I felt it sink into something soft, and I felt the sikiri's death on my tongue. The churning ocean of my emotions stilled, and I knew that the monster's influence was gone.

The taste of death was like the knowledge of a ripening fruit plucked too soon. It was the taste of the loss of potential, like a sweet, succulent flavor stolen away. It was the taste of victory and fulfillment, like an exotic dish savored with relish.

And then I felt the memories of the sikiri come, flashes of the battle. Immediately, I knew something was wrong. The images were swallowed up by a red cloud swelling up inside my head. It filled every part of my mind, so much so that I could no longer feel my body.

The cloud pulsed, and then it spoke.

Invoker

As the blazing crimson cloud swelled around me, a voice echoed all around.

"SEIZE THE ONLY TRUE WAY. PANDEMONIUM, FREEDOM."

The cloud was reaching out to me, and each heavy, clinging strand seemed to yank at pieces of me buried deep inside. An intense surge of fear and anger pulsed through my veins as if I had been injected with a powerful drug. My heart began to soar, and I was filled with an inebriating euphoria. As if I had finally been given leave to enjoy life to its fullest. My emotions were calling out to me, tempting me to dive deep into their depths and finally experience freedom for the first time ever. They held the promise that I could be strong and true to myself. That all I had to do was take the plunge and free myself from the shackles of my thoughts.

A voice inside my head screamed at me to take the plunge, to finally relinquish control and accept the inevitable. I could feel my internal struggle spilling out as if it were a volcanic eruption, threatening to consume me. I had been living my life on someone else's terms for too long, and this was my chance; this was my time to seize the reins and become my own master.

Yet I knew that this was the trap that Shadow warned me against. I knew that I had to resist, but it was so hard. I could tell that trying to suppress what I felt would be an impossible task.

It is telling me to accept what I feel. Was that not what Shadow taught me? ***I do not suppress my Emotion, I Embrace.***

I heard my own voice echoing inside my head. Then I shook my head. *No.*

The tenets of the **Heart of Azure and Scarlet** were never meant to be a surrender. Embracing one's emotion wasn't about giving in to it, but rather using it to guide your actions, so that you could accomplish what you set out to do without being overtaken by it. But this . . . it felt like surrendering. To give in would be contrary to the message of the **Heart of Azure and Scarlet;** embracing was not surrendering.

I let myself feel, embraced those feelings, and the cloud pulsed around me. **"RENOUNCE THE HERETIC CONSTRUCT THAT BINDS YOU. REJOIN THE WAY."**

I realized my mistake then. The emotions that the blight made me feel were too strong for me. I wanted to fight against the surging emotions, but I knew that it would be too much for me to bear. The temptation to give in was strong, and I could feel myself slipping away. Though I tried to embrace them, I felt myself being trampled. I fought against the urge, knowing that if I succumbed I would lose all that Shadow had taught me.

My heart and my mind were battling one another, trying to outdo each other in a desperate and silent power struggle. My heart screamed for freedom and the chance to be true to myself, and it listened to what the blight had to say; my mind argued for control and stability—it argued against what Shadow taught. It wanted to fall back on what I had been taught my whole life, to suppress emotion. It felt like a waking nightmare, one where I would never have a chance at winning unless I chose a side and made it through the ordeal alive. What I learned from the **Heart of Azure and Scarlet** was still too recent. I did not understand it fully enough for it to provide enough protection against the blight.

Red was filling my mind, and I could glimpse in it the freedom that it offered. For a moment I understood. The madness of what Shadow called blight was freedom from all restraints, from all morality, from all concepts such as good and evil. Acting solely on what you felt in the moment. It resonated with me, resonated with the **thirst**.

I felt the blight find purchase, then I felt it start worming its way in—

The world around me shuddered, and the red cloud pulled back. For a moment there was silence, and then the blight's voice boomed all around me.

"KHANUM." The red cloud trembled, it tried to get closer to me, but something held it back.

In this strange place that was in between a memory and imagination, I turned and saw something step in front of me. A person, shrouded in a black mist, nine tails waving behind them.

"Shadow?" I whispered, and was surprised when I heard my voice.

The person glanced back at me, but all I could see was the black mist waving around. It did look vaguely like Shadow; it even had ears on top of its head.

The red cloud bulged and churned. **"A THOUSAND TURNS, AND STILL YOU REFUSE YOUR NATURE."**

"I am nothing like you, Voice," Shadow said in a deep and distorted voice. **"YOU KNOW THAT YOU ARE. YOU FOOL YOURSELF KHANUM."**

"Enough," Shadow said, waving a hand. **"This is not the moment you tempt her. Begone."**

The cloud surged forward, then, as if it hit a wall. It scattered and it broke, flowing away.

Immediately, I felt all the pressure building inside of me drain, and I sagged to the ground. I managed to raise my head, and see Shadow standing over me. I opened my mouth to speak, but he did before I could.

"Wake."

[Empty Slot] skill gained.

Mask of the Drainer — No Investment; Tenth Carving
Mask of the Drainer > Mask of the Blood Invoker

Mask of the Blood Invoker — First Investment; No Carving
*|**Potential Augmentation**| trait unlocked.*
[Swap Profile] skill gained.

Ornament of the Student — No Investment; Seventh Carving
[Practical Learning] skill gained.

I opened my eyes and was welcomed back to the world of torment. The smell of blood and sweat assaulted my senses. Sunlight pierced through the branches above me to stab straight into my eyeballs, immediately igniting the worst headache I had ever felt. Everything was so raw, that for the moment I didn't know what was happening. Then the rest of it hit me. Every single part of my body hurt, as if my bones had been pulverized repeatedly. I opened my mouth to speak, and the only thing that came out was a groan filled with agony.

"Slow now," a voice whispered from next to me. I tried to turn my head, and pain shot through my neck.

I grimaced, my vision darkening for a moment. When it cleared up, I saw Shadow leaning over me.

"I'm alive," I said. I glanced around, seeing that we were nestled between a boulder and a few trees. I saw no signs of the sikiri or our battle.

"You are alive," Shadow confirmed with a smile.

Then memories flashed through my head. The fight with the sikiri, me drinking its blood, then the blight.

"Oh no," I whispered. "Am I infected? I drank its blood, it spoke to me—"

"No, no," he said hurriedly. "You are not blighted, that is not how the blight infects. It is a disease of the mind and Source, and yours is clean. You fought it off, and I am proud of you. Many who are stronger would've succumbed, and many have."

I remembered the person shrouded in a black mist. "You helped me," I said slowly, though my throat hurt. "I would've succumbed if it wasn't for you. It spoke to me, and then you . . . you kept the blight away. But, how did you—"

"Do not," he said quickly. "Push it out of your mind, do not think of what happened, do not think about what you heard. The more you think of it, the more power you give it. It is madness. Nothing that it says ever makes sense, yet if you think about it, it will start to make sense to you, and it will drive you mad."

I swallowed, hard. Just remembering the red cloud and how I felt . . . It was overwhelming. I did as he asked and closed my mouth.

"You resisted on your own." He glanced away, almost as if he was ashamed. "I just gave you the tools you needed to do it."

I opened my mouth, then closed it, deciding to follow his advice and not think about it again. It was an easy decision. What I experienced was not pleasant at all.

"How long was I out? And where are we?"

"A day. Your body was almost fully pulverized at one point. If you were anybody else I would have written you off for dead. But your healing saved you, though it slowed down considerably with the arrival of dawn," he said.

I grimaced. That explained why I was still feeling like shit. It was daytime, but somehow I felt almost as if it was night. Or at least my body did—my senses felt closer to what they were normally, without the sun's suppression.

"We are near where we fought the sikiri," Shadow said in answer to my second question. "I was not well enough to carry you far. Now that you are awake, we should find better shelter. The jungle is still full of danger, and neither one of us is in any fighting form."

I nodded, then paused. "Wait, where is Saia?"

Shadow glanced away. "She was destroyed in the fight," he said slowly. "I am sorry."

I opened my mouth, then closed it. "Oh, that's okay," I said. Saia's drone wasn't her. She was inside of me.

"You are reacting a lot differently than I expected," he commented.

"Because she is fine. Her real body, or I guess you could call it her core, is inside of me," I told him. "I'm going to need to get her more mass to rebuild, but that shouldn't be an issue."

As long as I could figure out how to do that without her drone around.

At his blank look, I gave him a short explanation. I knew that we touched on some things concerning Saia, but I didn't think that he really understood everything.

"The wonders never cease." Shadow shook his head.

I smiled, and then felt a pressure in my head.

Ornament of the Revelator — No Investment; Third Carving

I blinked, and remembered what happened when I woke up. "I've gained more Investment," I said slowly. "A lot more."

Shadow perked up at that, and one of his ears twitched on top of his head.

I grimaced, then groaned as I pushed myself up into a sitting position, with Shadow's help. I glanced down and saw that I was wearing different clothes. The last thing I remembered was the sikiri using its skill and it breaking my bones. If Saia was destroyed, then I could assume that my clothes were as well.

"What did you gain?" Shadow asked, bringing my attention to him.

I relayed what I woke up to. His eyes widened, and his tails twitched behind him.

"Four Carvings? So, you do get more Investment if the blood comes from a live target. Perhaps it was because you landed the killing blow? Or because you drank while killing it? The sikiri was at least mid-Fifth Investment. The disparity between you and it could have garnered you a significant amount of Investment, regardless of my involvement . . . Hmm . . . you will need to do more tests to figure out what exactly you gain your Investment from, though the Mask name change does suggest blood as the main source."

"Why did my Student Ornament jump that much?" I asked. It had gotten even more Carvings than my Mask.

Shadow waved his hand. "Combat is the great teacher, and those who survive it learn much about many things."

I nodded slowly, looking back. It did make a lot of sense. I've learned how to set up a trap for a much stronger opponent, and I could definitely say that I learned a lot from the fight itself. Like how much I still have to grow.

"What is a trait?" I asked.

"It is the core of every Mask," Shadow answered. "Once a Mask reaches First Investment, it gains a trait. It consists of a passive and an active effect which you trigger by wearing your Mask."

I blinked, I had tried wearing my Mask before, though only in my inner space, and it hadn't done anything.

"All Masks increase their wearers attributes significantly while worn, and usually grant a unique benefit," Shadow continued. "Though how it does that differs depending on Mask type. They can also not be worn for a long period of time, as they are very draining, and they almost always have a very big drawback to their use."

"So, it basically gives you a temporary boost?" I asked, then something occurred to me. "Wait, why didn't you use your Mask when we fought the sikiri?"

Shadow sighed. "I am in no state to bear the fatigue that comes with my Mask, nor would we be able to . . . handle the drawbacks of it. The sikiri was, as wrong as it seems to say, the lesser threat. Putting on my Mask would've meant certain death for us both."

I frowned. I wanted to ask more, but I also knew that it was a private thing, and I didn't want to push unnecessarily.

"Do you think that it's safe enough for me to see what it is?" I asked.

Shadow glanced around them, then nodded. "We should be safe until nightfall. Hopefully you will be well enough by then to move."

I tried to move my legs and felt stabbing pain shoot through me. Yeah, hopefully.

Without a delay, I focused on my chest, and pulled myself in.

My soul space manifested around me. The wooden room with empty shelves on three walls and pedestals in the center. Now, there was something new on the far wall. I started toward it and was interrupted almost immediately.

"Statement: This Unit is pleased that the Host survived."

"Saia," I yelled, kneeling down and picking up the tiny dragon. "I wondered if you would be in here."

I was immensely relieved to see that she was fine. The dragon had grown on me, both literally and figuratively.

"Statement: This Unit is bonded with the Host," she said simply, as if that explained everything, and perhaps it did.

"I was a bit worried since I got pretty torn up from what I remember, and from what I can tell by how I feel," I said.

"Statement: The Host's injuries were severe, the [Repair] engram has been working beyond current peak capacity. The effectiveness has increased to 10.2%."

I smiled. "That's great, thanks for the help."

"Clarification: Of course. This Unit's survival depends on the survival of the Host."

"You do know that you can call me Mari, right? I think that we've been through enough together for that much."

Saia looked up at me for a long moment, and then responded. "Report: This Unit will oblige, Mari."

"Now." I turned my eyes toward the changes. "Let's see what's new."

I approached the center pillars where my Mask and Ornaments were displayed. The first thing I noticed was that my Mask was slightly different. The teeth were longer, more savage looking, the horns sharper, and the jade had spread somewhat over the black, obsidian-like, surface. The tiny etchings that I had seen had also cleared up, leaving the Mask feeling as if it was a smooth piece of art.

It seemed like the Carvings would be starting again from scratch with each Investment tier. Next, I also noticed that physical was added to the other two attributes next to my Mask name. From what Shadow had said, that meant that now I would be getting a slight increase to all of my attributes with each Carving, instead of just two. The second big change was another plaque beneath the main one. I leaned down and read what was written.

|*Potential Augmentation*| *trait*

Wearing the Mask of the Blood Invoker grants a significant increase to all attributes. All cooldowns are greatly reduced, after the Mask is removed, all used skills are put on a long cooldown.

Slotting skills of the same type grants bonuses.
Current bonuses available:

<u>Beast:</u> Slotting in skills that all contain <beast> type increases their effectiveness and reduces cooldowns. All physical senses are heightened.

<u>Movement:</u> Slotting in skills that all contain <movement> type increases their effectiveness and reduces cooldowns. Air resistance of your body is reduced.

That was very interesting, though I didn't quite understand everything. I raised my head and looked over the pillar to the far wall. There were some changes there too. I walked over to what was now three pedestals. I approached the [Empty Skill] pedestals and took a closer look. Each of the pedestals now had two bowls instead of the usual one, and the second bowl on each pedestal was gray and inactive.

I glanced down and saw that there was an extra grayed out plaque on each one. Then I noticed another change on the skill plaque.

[Mist Step]

You may turn to mist and execute a step in mist form.
<beast> <weave> <survival> <movement> <mist> !wind!

There were what appeared to be tags on the skill, written down on the bottom of the plaque. It was the only way that I could describe them. I glanced at the other skill I had slotted in and saw that it was the same.

[Lesser Strength]

Grants you a passive increase in strength.
<beast><physical>

That was very interesting. Though . . . [Mist Step] had a tag that was marked differently, !wind!. It clicked nearly instantly. I had used one of the gemstones on it to upgrade it. That had to have added that tag. That was something that I would need to talk with Shadow about.

I glanced at the last pedestal, but just saw that there were two empty bowls. I continued to the side of the wall where my other skills were and looked the new ones over. The first was a symbol of two arrows chasing each other in a circle. It was obvious which this skill was immediately.

[Swap Profile]

Instantly swap to the second set of preset skills.
<weave><esoteric>

I glanced back at the pedestals and the extra bowls on each pedestal. I had already figured out that it was something like that.

"Well, Saia," I started. "It seems like we have a lot more options now."

"Feedback: The intricacies of the Mask system and the designs of the Great Spell are remarkable. It rivals the greatest deeds of Ke Erzi."

I smiled at her but didn't comment. Pride in one's creator was understandable.

I took a look at the last new addition. It was a plate with an image of what appeared to be myself in the process of swinging a long stick.

[Practical Learning]

All learning through practical means is accelerated.
<learning> <physical> <esoteric>

That seemed like it could be very useful. Finally, I walked over to the shelf and took a look at the skills that I had stored there. All of them had tags added now, and all of them were tagged as <beast>. Which, if I thought about it made sense. They came from animals in the first place. I looked over the skills available to me and found that I had only one more <movement> skill, the [Lesser Leap] skill, not enough to slot all three for that bonus. Though, I wondered if it would work if I slotted just two. Regardless, I wasn't about to experiment right now, not after the sikiri. I needed as many skills as I could get. Then I paused, as I remembered something. When I woke up, I had felt a bit more . . . awake, for the lack of a better term. And by that I meant that more of my vampire side felt awake, and it was during the day. The Beast Bonus did say that all physical senses were heightened. Perhaps it did work with only two.

Still, though a Movement Bonus would be nice, I preferred more skills. I picked up [Debilitating Wave] to round out my three, then went for the last three skills to set up my second profile. Then something occurred to me.

I put the skills back on the shelf then walked into the hallway of doors, as I started to call it. I walked down the ones I had already entered and gotten a skill from, and found the new ones. There were a few. I had hunted a couple of birdlike animals over the weeks to sate my **thirst** and to gather blood to have on hand.

While I was debating going in to get new skills, I noticed the last door. It was made out of red stone shaped like a snake twisting around the door frame, with a wooden door etched with an image of the sikiri. Just looking at it made me feel anxious. I was definitely not entering that place. I had barely survived with Shadow and all the prep we did. I stood no chance on my own. There were three doors that I had no intention of opening anytime soon, the sikiri's, the reaper's, and the mature ferrorn's. I knew the advantages that being a vampire gave me, but I also understood how lucky I was to have survived all three of those encounters. If Shadow weren't there, I would've died a long time ago.

I shook my head, then turned my attention to the three doors occupied by birdlike animals. I glanced at Saia and raised my eyebrow.

"You up for some hunting?" I asked, and she shifted into a weapon.

Together, we made quick work of the animals inside. Not like they were any challenge, at all. One of the doors had belonged to another of the cresser birds, which did give me an answer to the question I had since all this insanity started. My doors weren't race specific, but rather source specific. I could have duplicates of the same race, as long as I drank the blood from a different source.

The three skills I gained were nothing special, as I had expected. The animals had been barely in their First Investment.

The first, and the most useless one was [Peck], which allowed me to "peck" something with my beak, which I didn't have. The last two were a bit better.

[Quick Claw]

Execute a quick attack with your claws.
<beast><physical><offense>

[Sharp Eye]

Focus on a faraway target.
<beast><physical><esoteric>

I wasn't quite sure what the difference was between using a skill and just executing an attack on your own without it. That was another thing to discuss with Shadow. Either way, I now had seven skills on my shelf, and six eligible for use. I'd decided to use [Debilitating Wave] in my main profile, so that left five for the other three skill slots.

After some debate between me and Saia, we settled on [Sonic Screech], [Lesser Impale], and [Quick Claw]. All three were offensive in nature, and I felt like we needed that. And there was still a lot to test out, I had no idea how the switch worked.

I walked back to the pedestals and slotted the four skills in. The three in the secondary bowls were inactive, looking the same as they did when placed on the shelves, which I had expected. They would probably activate once I used [Swap Profile].

With all of that done, I turned to look at Saia.

"So," I started. "How do I get you biomass to create a new drone?"

"Feedback: This Unit currently has a swarm spread throughout the Host body, making repairs to broken biosystems."

I nodded. "Right," *Because all of that made complete sense to me.* I closed my eyes and took a deep breath because I realized that I wasn't even joking. "And that answers my question how?"

"Feedback: The best manner of providing biomass would be through ingestion."

I blinked, then narrowed my eyes. "You mean you want me to eat it."

"Feedback: Yes." After a moment she added. "Mari."

I closed my eyes. Of course it did.

"That is an amazing trait," Shadow said as we walked through the jungle.

The night had fallen, and we had started on our journey again. After I had tried to eat pieces of the sikiri. It didn't go well. I had nearly chipped a fang. I've only managed to drink its blood from the wounds that Shadow had caused. Though, I also doubted that Saia would even be able to consume sikiri's biomass. She wasn't able to do it to the reaper's remains.

I was going to need to find some weaker prey.

"You think so?" I asked through gritted teeth as we walked. We were making abysmal progress; neither one of us could move at anything like our usual pace.

Also, the Beast Bonus did work, as I had found out when the night fell and my already heightened senses got even more so. It turned out that having your sense of touch be more sensitive when you were injured wasn't a good time. I was having to suppress a wince with every step, partly because I felt so raw I could barely force my muscles to move, and partly because I could hear my bones groaning in my eardrums with each step.

"Some Masks get special skills that they can only use when their Mask is worn; others improve their existing skills. Being able to use your skills faster is very good. Though you will need to test out just how long this 'long cooldown' actually is."

I grimaced and resisted the urge to curse. I would've liked to test it all out now, but I also couldn't afford for us to be caught with me not having access to skills.

"Yeah," I said instead. "How long have we been walking again?"

Shadow glanced up at the moons shining above us. "It is not even the middle of the night."

This time I did curse. Shadow chuckled but didn't comment. Rest would be a long time coming, I gritted my teeth and kept going. There wasn't much else to do.

Adult

"U

gh." I grimaced as I bit into the almost charred meat stuck on a stick. Luckily, I had gotten rid of most of the burnt part before biting down, but the meat was still tough. I tore it apart with my teeth and then pulled it apart in pieces and swallowed them quickly. "This is disgusting," I muttered after swallowing.

Shadow laughed from his seat across from me. "Fascinating is what it is," he said, then shook his head.

I looked in his direction and bared my fangs at him. Then I burped, and black smoke burst out of my mouth. "Oh God." I groaned as if I was going to be sick. The taste was, as it always was for a vampire, bland. What was really bothering me was the sensation of ants crawling around my stomach, and the black smoke that left the taste of something rotten in my mouth. I wished that I didn't know what Saia was doing inside of me right now, but sadly, I did.

"Do you know how much you are going to need?" Shadow asked.

"She said that"—I had to pause as another burp interrupted me, sending one more plume of black smoke out of my mouth—"this should be enough."

It had been a day since I first woke up after our fight with the sikiri. And I had recovered enough to be able to hunt some of the birds that called the jungle home. My body still felt sore, but I was overall healed, though I still felt aching in my bones. The bones were the hardest to regenerate for a vampire, and sadly Saia's [Repair] engram wasn't enough to actually help heal bones. From the few short discussions I had in my soul space with Saia, her engram worked by helping the body mechanically. If I had a cut, Saia's nanites, as I understood it, in my blood would try to push the wound closed, but they couldn't really heal it, not yet anyway. The body itself had to close the wound. Saia didn't understand my physiology fully, and our synchronization rate was still too low. Though it was climbing rapidly, and was now close to 20%.

I paused as I felt a strange sensation in my stomach, as if something was moving inside. Before I could even react, I felt it rising through my chest and then in my throat. As I doubled over and retched, a blob of silver goo spilled out. It fell to the floor and wriggled, twisting and bubbling before forming into the shape of a dragon.

I blinked and shook my head trying to dispel the terrible taste out of my mouth to no avail.

"Hey, Saia," I said, then narrowed my eyes. "You are smaller."

"Feedback: This Unit's biomass conversion rate of the matter available in this place is still low. With time and understanding that shall improve."

"Right," I said. "But you can grow more, right?"

Saia tilted her head. "Feedback: Affirmative, with the increase in the synchronization rate between us and the increase in your ability to provide power, this Unit is able to operate a larger drone form. There was no need to leave the biomass within you."

I blinked, then nodded. That made sense. With every Carving, as I got stronger, my body was able to provide more energy to Saia.

She then proceeded to "eat" the rest of the bird in front of me.

"Fascinating," Shadow whispered as he watched gray goo writhing and consuming mass.

"Yeah, that's a word," I added. I did agree with him though. I just couldn't shake the knowledge that Saia was inside of me, or that she had tried to do that to me when I first found her.

I reached for my flask and took a sip of the blood that I had drained from the sikiri's corpse. I'd started to get a feel for the power of the blood I tasted. I could almost tell what Investment it was. The sikiri was definitely the strongest, but tasted close to what the reaper had. I wasn't quite sure how the food chain worked when one accounted for Investment, though I hadn't really observed anything that suggested that it differed greatly from a similar example on Earth.

Once Saia was finished, her size hadn't increased that much. I would need to go hunting again to get her more biomass, as unfortunately she wasn't large enough to turn into a weapon for me just yet. She had to grow for that.

I finished downing the rest of the blood in the gourd and wiped my mouth. The power of it made my tongue tingle, but I was starting to get accustomed to how the blood here tasted. What I couldn't shake was the strange feeling I's had ever since I woke up. At first I'd thought that it was a side effect of my injuries, or of the sikiri's blood. But I was mostly healed now, and I still felt something. It was like a faint buzzing that spread through all of my body. Like something inside of me was expanding. What frightened me the most was that I felt different. I just didn't know how. My entire body seemed more sensitive. Like every inch of my skin could feel every twitch of muscle underneath. The best way to describe it might be over stimulation, like touching everything you see to try to understand what makes you tick. At first I thought that it was related to my trait, as the Beast Bonus did increase all of my physical senses, and I had noticed the difference, but this was something more. All this, I knew, must've something to do with the **thirst**, because drinking blood made it worse for a little while. It wasn't really bad, it just made me feel strange in a way that I wasn't accustomed to.

"You are certain that this blood can't get me infected with the blight?" I asked Shadow for what was probably the tenth time.

Shadow shook his head. "It cannot, people regularly consume monster meat. Whatever the blight really is, it leaves the body on death. And even if it did not, we have never seen it infect anyone through touch or any similar manner. The blight only infects if you allow your emotions to take hold of you, if you accept its madness."

I grimaced. I had no choice but to trust him on that.

"Something is wrong?" he asked.

For a moment, I debated not saying anything, but then I told him everything about how I hadn't been feeling the same since I woke up.

"I'm not saying that I feel wrong, it's just a weird feeling, I'm sure that it's nothing," I said.

"Statement: This Unit has not detected any anomalies in the Host Source Weave signature."

Shadow turned to his chest and rummaged through it, pulling out a familiar object, the Reader.

"We should've checked to see if there are any changes," Shadow said, offering the crystal to me. "Perhaps what you are feeling is a change in your attributes? I am not sure if that would account for everything you described, nor do I think that it is likely for you to have gained an increase after just one Investment tier, but we should check and make certain, yes?"

I hesitated for a moment, and then reached out and took the crystal in my hand. He placed the piece of paper over the top and it started to glow, writing out my Mask's abilities.

There were no unexpected changes. My attributes were the same as they had been before, the only changes being my Investment and my new skills. Though, curiously, the Reader didn't show my second set of skills.

"Well," Shadow started. "I guess that we can rule out attribute issues. Though, I do think that you have gotten stronger, just probably not enough to transition into the next tier."

The sensation was fading away as the **thirst** did its thing and feasted on the blood.

"Query: This Unit requests that item for assimilation."

I blinked at her. "Saia!"

Shadow did the same, then glanced back at me. "That means she wants to eat it, right?"

I nodded. "We talked about this Saia. I'll find you something to consume later."

"Wait," Shadow said after a moment. "Saia, you are supposed to be able to use Source Weave, yes?"

"Feedback: Correct. The change in the nature of it has made most of my engrams inoperable."

Shadow narrowed his eyes, then glanced at the Reader still in my hands. "And at its core, the Reader is a Weave. Why do you want it?"

"Feedback: I detected the use of the Source when you activated the item. I want to attempt to replicate the engram that powers it."

"Saia, you can't just ask to destroy other people's property," I told her.

Shadow raised a hand, his eyes still on Saia. "I am very much interested in seeing if she could do it. The crystals you found in that rift were beyond her, but this is something far simpler. And the Reader is not really valuable, I can always get another once I return home."

I opened my mouth, then closed it. It wasn't my decision to make. I offered him the crystal back, and he took it and offered it to Saia.

The dragon looked at it for a moment, and then surged forward, turning into liquid form and swallowing the rock entirely. I watched in fascination as the goo released black smoke, assimilating the item.

"Well?" I asked once she had re-formed back into a dragon.

Saia remained stationary for a few seconds, her blue eyes flashing. And then she moved, turning her head in my direction.

"Feedback: I believe that I was successful. I have been able to replicate the engram of the item. I am not yet certain how to activate it."

I took a deep breath and realized that I was exhausted. I still had to heal. "Well, you figure it out, I'm going to go and sleep."

Shadow leaned down next to Saia, and I left the two of them to it. I walked over to a bedroll and lay down. I was asleep in moments.

"The vampire life cycle has three stages," Professor Harkins said, pointing at the images of vampires on the holographic projector. I kept my attention firmly on him and the subject matter. Most of what I knew came from the stories around the hacienda and the villages nearby. And all of that came from either humans or wolves. Neither was really the source. The professor on the other hand was a vampire, and I was almost foaming at the mouth to learn more.

"The first, and the most feral is the Fledgling cycle. It is our birth cycle, and every vampire's birth reflects the way it was brought into that life, namely blood and

emotion. At this stage we are unable to control ourselves for the first seven months up to a year of our life, depending on who our sire was. During this cycle, a Fledgling is the charge of their sire. It is the sire's responsibility to make sure that the Fledgling is well fed and kept away from humans. Because, as all you obviously know, a vampire endangering humans has severe consequences."

I shivered. I knew that the vampires had the death sentence. I had grown up in a place filled with violence, it was not a stranger to me.

"After the Fledgling has acclimated to their new life, and has achieved rudimentary control over themselves, they are allowed to prove that they are no longer a threat, and only then are they allowed to rejoin society in a controlled environment. Only around ten percent of all those turned ever make it out of this stage. Most never grow beyond the feral state they are born into, and of those who do, many lose control later in life and are executed by the Red Corps. It takes, on average, a hundred years for a vampire to grow out of the Fledgling stage and become an Adult." I shivered, I couldn't even imagine living for that amount of time while having an axe hanging over your head.

*"An Adult Vampire is a vampire that is in full control of all of their faculties. They are not driven to fits of emotion, and they have a firm grasp on their **thirst**. They are stronger, faster, more capable in every way than a Fledgling. And finally, we have the Elder Vampires. The oldest and wisest of my kind. Who we will not cover in this class." The professor smiled at the collective cry of dismay from my classmates. I smiled too, knowing that while vampires do share a lot, they keep just as much hidden.*

"Excuse me, professor." One of my classmates raised his hand. I glanced and saw a young man with a neatly trimmed beard and a cross hanging around his neck. "What about the fourth stage? The Ancient Vampires?"

The professor tilted his head and then chuckled, his eyes flashing with gold in the dim light of the classroom. "There is no fourth stage in the vampire life cycle, young man. Some stories, are just that, stories. You are far too old to still believe in fairy tales, especially if you want to pass my class."

The rest of my classmates chuckled at that, and the man put his hand down, turning to the book on his table.

I turned my head back to Professor Harkins and saw him keep his eyes on the student who asked the question for a few seconds more, his gaze filled with intent. Then his expression cleared up, and he smiled, continuing the lesson.

I woke up, the dream still fresh in my mind. Or rather, the memory. It was one of my early days in America, when I had been so eager to learn about anything and everything. Back then, vampires fascinated me, and I hadn't even had an idea that I would one day become one of them.

I took a deep breath, then sat up, remembering what Professor Harkins taught us. He taught Introduction to Vampirism, a basic subject that had lasted for only one semester. I frowned, thinking that I had to be remembering it wrong. He had said that the Fledgling Vampires remained sheltered for months up to a year. That . . . That hadn't been what had happened to me. I hadn't spent anywhere near that time under guard.

"You are awake," Shadow said from nearby, interrupting my thoughts.

"Yes," I said, shaking my head from the sleepiness and standing up. "Did I miss anything?"

"Feedback: I have succeeded in activating the [Mask Reader] engram."

"Really?" I asked as I took a seat on the rock next to Shadow.

"Feedback: Affirmative, I can already read yours."

"You don't need the paper?"

As a response, Saia's eyes flashed, and then I yelped and jumped back, sliding off my seat and falling to the ground.

"Marianna?" Shadow called, and I calmed myself.

My hand moved in front of my eyes, trying to grasp something that wasn't there.

"Statement: I have projected it directly through your optical nerve."

I nodded as I looked at the words floating in my vision. "You can, uh, do that?"

"Feedback: Of course, I am attached to your nervous system."

"Right," I said. "Maybe give me a bit of a heads-up next time."

I shook my head and pulled myself back to my seat, then I focused on the text in front of me.

Marianna Rojas

Mask of the Blood Invoker (Physical, Weave, Esoteric):
First Investment; No Carving
Ornament of the Revelator (Weave, Esoteric)
No Investment; Third Carving
Ornament of the Student (Physical, Weave, Esoteric)
No Investment; Seventh Carving

Attributes:
Physical: C
Weave: F
Esoteric: C

Skills:
Profile 1:
[Mist Step]

[Lesser Strength]
[Debilitating Wave]
(Beast Bonus Active)

Profile 2:
[Sonic Screech]
[Lesser Impale]
[Quick Claw]
(Beast Bonus Active)

[Swap Profile]

[One Truth Verified]

[A Lesson Remembered]
[Practical Learning]

"Statement: I have taken the liberty of adding the missing information, since I am already aware of which skills you have slotted in."

"Thanks," I whispered. Sometimes, I forgot just how scary the entire concept of Saia was. I shook my head and looked over at Shadow. "Did she read yours?"

Shadow chuckled, then glanced at Saia.

"Feedback: I was unable to accomplish that task."

I frowned. "Why?"

"I expected that," Shadow answered. "I have protections in place against such things. Even if I didn't, the Reader works based on the Investment of its user. It cannot read someone who is much more powerful than the one who uses it. Saia probably shares your power, which means that she can't read mine."

That made sense.

"You can see it in your eyes?" Shadow said then, leaning forward to look at me closer.

I blinked. "Uh, yeah," I answered. "Saia is projecting the text in my vision; it looks like it is floating around a hand's length away."

"Fascinating," Shadow said, then blinked. "Oh, I never noticed the way your eyes were shaped, or that green in them."

I frowned. "What?" My eyes were hazel.

"The way that your pupil is cracked?" Shadow added.

I froze. "That's not possible," I whispered. "Do you have a mirror? I need to see."

Shadow's ear twitched, and he raised a hand, then grimaced as I felt a faint imprint on the world, on the Way, around him. A moment later mist shaped like a person appeared in front of me, then quickly turned into me.

An illusion, a mirror copy of myself stared at me, and I saw my state. I wore Shadow's clothes, covering most of me, but my neck and hands were free. My nails had caked blood stuff under them that I had long since forgotten about. My skin was dark, perhaps a shade darker from being in the sun again. My hair was wild, unkempt, and spreading around my head like a mane. But I had little attention for those details. Instead my gaze found my eyes.

My eyes were transfixed on my own reflection in the mirror image. They were still hazel, mostly. But there was a change, a big, significant change that left me breathless with wonder and curiosity—and fear. The border of my pupil was cracked, like shattered glass, and from the black nothingness in the center of my pupil, emerald green was leaking through. It was just a tiny trickle, barely visible to the naked eye. It weaved through the cracks and into my iris, just a tiny bit, sending a small web of lines through my eyes. It was so faint that I could barely see it. But it was there, unmistakably.

"Marianna?" Shadow asked.

I turned my eyes to look at him. It took me a moment to find the words. "That should be impossible."

My eyes now marked me as an Adult vampire, and that should be impossible. I wasn't even a decade old; it took Fledglings at least a hundred years to turn Adult.

Shadow tilted his head inquisitively, and I explained. I told him everything about how the vampire stages worked, and what the change in my eyes signified.

Once I was done, I asked him a question.

"Could my Mask, the Investment, somehow had accelerated it?"

Shadow shook his head immediately. "No," he answered. "The Great Spell does not interfere with the natural flow of life, not for beings like us at least. Investment enhances what is already there, it does not work such changes. Not at your tier of Investment at least."

I narrowed my eyes at the last sentence. There was more there to unpack there, but I trusted his opinion. I frowned, and thought about it more, remembering my dream, and the thought that I had when I woke up.

"It took me less time to leave the feral state than it was supposed to," I said, mostly to myself. Then more memories came back to me. The day when I was hanged, the fight with the wolf and the vampire, an Adult vampire, one that I had matched in power. I . . . never had the chance to properly think about that. Everything that I knew told me that that was supposed to be impossible. Yet, I had done it. The blood one drank and their sire was supposed to play a role in the development of the vampire, which left only one explanation for it. My sire, Akatsuki Jin. The cartel's Master hadn't turned me himself; he had asked my sire to do it. I had never really wondered why. The stories about vampires being in thrall to their sire, unable to disobey were just that, stories. So, in practice it didn't really matter who turned a vampire. The differences were supposed to be minute. And yet . . . Here I was, with eyes of an Adult Vampire.

Now, the strange sensations I had since I woke up, since I fought the sikiri and drank its blood, made a lot more sense to me. I . . . wasn't feeling as deeply as before. And the **thirst** didn't howl at me whenever I smelled blood. Experimentally, I picked up one of the gourds that I had filled with blood from the bird I hunted for Saia and opened it up.

I took a sniff and felt not a stir from the **thirst**. Part of it could be that I was sated, but, it had always at least rumbled whenever it could sense blood.

I turned to Shadow and told him my suspicion. It wasn't like he would have answers, but I felt the need to say it to someone I trusted. To work through it all myself.

"So, you think that your . . . *sire?* Is the one responsible?"

"I'm not sure," I answered. "I don't know much about him. Only that he is older than the Master of the cartel. He's a very private individual."

"Well, there is nothing that you can do about it other than accept. The world is as it is, and we have a lot more pressing things to worry about. We are still days away from the coast."

I took a deep breath and then sighed. He was right, I pushed all those thoughts away.

Then something flashed inside my mind.

Ornament of the Revelator; No Investment; Fourth Carving

I blinked, then told Shadow about what happened.

"Well, I guess that we know now what gives you Investment for that Ornament. Revealing things that the other party has no knowledge about."

"That seems about right," I said. At least it felt right to me.

"Of course, there is still a lot of nuance there. Not all knowledge is weighed equally," Shadow added.

I would figure it out eventually, I had no doubt about it.

The day was getting late, so we packed up our camp and prepared to set out. We still had days of trekking through the dangerous jungle in front of us. And I fully intended on living long enough to return to Earth. The world had ended, but I still wanted to find answers.

The Blood Dance

I gazed down at my own reflection in the shallow pond, watching the faint light of emerald swimming through my eyes. The crack in my pupil was still small, unchanged from the last time I had looked, but just the fact that it was there at all was incredible. I kept thinking that it was just my imagination, yet I could feel a shift inside me. Emerald green spilled into my eyes, marking me as an Adult vampire. A full member of my kind under the rules. If I was back on Earth, this moment would've been a big deal. Vampire adulthood was something that most Fledglings never lived long enough to achieve.

The color of my eyes told more than that, of course. It revealed my bloodline for all to see. There are three vampire bloodlines: Sea, Sky, and Desert. Named so for the color of their eyes. Emerald like the seas, cerulean like the sky, and golden like the deserts. From everything that I have learned, there are no differences between the three bloodlines, though I have heard stories, rumors, and straight up racist remarks over the years. Not even vampires are immune to being assholes to one another.

For the most part, vampires didn't separate themselves by their eye color. You could find vampires of all three bloodlines working together with no issues. The color of one's eyes was cosmetic, as far as I knew.

Most of the vampires in the cartel had the blue eyes of the Sky Bloodline, the same as the Cartel Master. The only Emerald vampire in the cartel was my master.

I didn't know what or how my eyes had changed so fast. But I was grateful for it. I could feel the **thirst** being a lot more under control. I hadn't felt my emotions spike for little reason in days. It was a mystery, but one that I would hopefully have the time to figure out eventually.

"Still thinking of your eyes?" Shadow called from behind me.

I turned, trying not to look too embarrassed. I had been spending a lot time looking at my reflection.

"You rested enough?" I walked over to him.

He sat near the fire with Saia, as she tried to convince him to allow her to consume his relic item. The head of the rod that created the spherical shield that they had been using to keep the signs of their presence and the wildlife away.

"My body is rested," Shadow said, then glanced at Saia. "My mind though is getting more and more tired by the moment."

"Statement: Adding the engram of this item to my list will increase my contribution to the team significantly."

Shadow narrowed his eyes at her. "And what am I to do once I am back on my own?"

"Feedback: This Unit is sure that you will be fine," Saia answered.

Shadow narrowed his eyes at her. He opened his mouth to respond but didn't get to. Before he could utter the words, the ground below them began to quiver. I quickly grasped onto the trunk of a nearby tree, bracing myself against the violent trembling of the earth, riding out the quake.

"Am I wrong, or are they getting more frequent?" I asked after the shaking subsided.

Shadow glanced in my direction and grimaced, his tails waving around widely. "I am not certain," he answered. "If I had the time and the means, I would have ventured deeper into the jungle, to the inner ring, tried to see if there is a cause." He shook his head. "There is so much happening in the world, and so little time."

There wasn't much that I could say about that. We gathered our camp in silence, then continued on our way. We were, according to Shadow's reckoning, at least two days out from the coast. Thankfully, we hadn't run into any problems, no monsters that could seriously threaten us, aside from a pack of kiji, the reptilian wolf-like animals that I had seen at the river what seemed like a year ago. Saia had scouted them a few days ago, though the pack didn't seem interested in us. We spent the days mostly just walking, as much as Shadow's state allowed, and training. And by training, I meant Shadow sitting on the ground and yelling at me. But, he had taught me two more techniques, one from each style again. I was still far more comfortable with the *Scarlet Moon Style,* but Shadow insisted that I should learn both. He had also told me that there were seven techniques total for each style, which seemed like a lot, but then again, Shadow was very old, and he probably had time to develop all of them properly.

We were within reach of the coast, and I couldn't help but feel the anticipation building. We were getting close to the end of our journey, and we had survived.

I knew that I made a mistake the moment the thought entered my mind. Some on Earth would say that vampires were cursed, that they had turned away from God's grace and therefore the world rejected them, that that was the reason we couldn't walk in daylight. It was moments like this that made me think that there was some truth to the cursed part.

The sky split apart, as if it wanted to prove my thoughts wrong, then blazed with light cycling through all the colors of the rainbow, so bright it tickled the back of my eyes. The flashes came from the east, far in the distance and so high up that I wondered if that lightshow was happening beyond the atmosphere. It looked like an aurora ramped up to a hundred. Each burst felt like a punch, splashing across my retinas and leaving white spots wherever they touched. They illuminated everything below them in blazing detail, like the world had been set on fire. And like a curtain of lights, it was coming down to the ground.

"We are out of time," I heard Shadow say, and turned to look at him.

The light reflected in his orange eyes, making them look like a fire burning steadily as it settles into the coals.

"What is it," I said as I turned back to look at the display in the sky.

"Your world is arriving," Shadow whispered.

I looked at the light, trying to equate his words with the meaning behind them. That was an entire world, my world, coming down and . . . merging with this one? I didn't even know how to wrap my head around it.

"East," Shadow said. "It looks like your world will settle north of the Hallowed Plain continent."

I remembered, vaguely, that the Hallowed Plain was the home of the Harpiem. I didn't understand what that meant for us.

I turned back to ask him what that would imply for Earth. As I turned I froze, my hand rose almost of its own volition and pointed above Shadow's head, behind him. "What is that?" I managed to ask, and he turned to look at the second wall of light, coming down in the distance.

Shadow frowned. "Split?" he said slowly, then shook his head. "No, two. Two worlds."

"What do you mean?" I asked, not understanding.

"It is a second world. The Great Spell picked two at the same time," he said, his voice filled with emotion that I couldn't identify.

And then the jungle around us went crazy, and the sounds of animals filled the air: roars and growls, screams and squawks, a rumbling beneath our feet.

"We must find shelter. *Now.*" Shadow moved.

"What? Why?" I asked as he pulled me with him, his eyes scanning our surroundings.

"The Interval, the arrival of another world. It is an event that causes a great surge of the Source. It is a time when many great feats that usually require an immense amount of power are possible with far less," Shadow explained as he moved, but in his eyes, I saw something that very much looked like panic.

He opened his mouth to continue when howls filled the air, and they sounded like they were very close to us. Immediately, my thoughts went to the pack of kiji.

Shadow glanced in the direction the howls were coming from. "It can also drive the wildlife into a frenzy."

Finally understanding the gravity of what he was saying, I snapped into focus, looking for a place where we could hide. If the pack was going to come after us, we needed either a place where we could hide, or one suitable for fighting.

We ran as fast as we could as the howls followed us, getting louder and louder behind us. I pushed Shadow, having to pick him up a few times when he stumbled. Saia flew ahead, scouting, searching for anything that could be of use. As we ran through the jungle, I started to get desperate. There were no caves or ruins that we could hide in. After almost an hour of running I saw something in the distance.

"There," I said, pointing at a small hill.

"That's not a shelter," Shadow said breathily. I glanced at him, noticing just how quickly he was breathing. His ears were slumped on top of his head; I could see the shaking in his limbs. I had moved as fast as I could to stay ahead of the pack, I had pushed him just as fast. I knew that he was weak, and that the fight with the sikiri had taken even more from him. I hadn't noticed it much immediately after, as I had been injured too. But once I had healed, I saw just how painful it was for him to follow at any type of faster pace. He hadn't used a skill since the fight, and I knew that even if he wanted to, he wouldn't be able to.

I saw that in his eyes now, the defeat, and the frustration at his own weakness. I had felt that before, I recognized it.

"We won't find shelter," I told him. "I'd rather fight on top of a hill, take the high ground."

It was daylight, I was weaker now. The sun was coming down, but we still had at least an hour before nightfall.

"Marianna," he said slowly. "I cannot—"

I raised my hand, interrupting him. "I know," I whispered. I would have to fight on my own.

He bowed his head and followed me up the hill. Once there, I looked around. It was clear of trees, giving me a good vantage point to see anything coming up at me. There was one large rock in the middle where I instructed Shadow to go.

"Climb up there, use your bolt launcher to give me cover, or at least distract them." He dropped the chest from his back and nodded, opening it up and pulling up his rack with weapons.

I waited as it grew then approached and picked up his big serpent-tongue spear. It was the largest weapon, and the one I was most familiar with. Saia had gotten some biomass, but she hadn't gotten back to her previous size. At best, she could turn into a smaller knife.

I took a deep breath and got ready as Shadow climbed the rock. There was no time to prepare any traps, or to think of any kind of a plan. I let myself accept the reality of the situation, acknowledging my anger at the turn of events and that I could do nothing to change it.

I settled into the opening stance of the **Scarlet Moon Style** technique, **Veiled Mist Assault**, *From the Mist, Strike*. Then I waited.

Saia returned first, the howls following her.

"Statement: The kiji pack is close," she reported, not that it was necessary, I could hear them coming up the hill.

"Distract," I told her as the first dark shape climbed up to the top of the hill.

In the light of the day, the animal looked a lot more dangerous, as if a komodo dragon had a baby with a wolf. Long, slender legs with an elongated head and jaws filled with sharp teeth. It looked somewhat like the ferrorn, which I realized made sense. The two species were probably related somehow, what a jaguar was to a lion perhaps.

I didn't hesitate, I let my instincts guide me and jumped forward, deciding to strike first. I turned into mist, crossing the distance with [Mist Step] in a flash. The animal didn't expect it, and I re-formed a step away, my swing reappearing just above its head. My spear split its head open straight down the middle, killing the animal instantly.

Two more kiji rushed from behind it, and I jumped back, using quick steps to create space and also use up the cooldown on my skill. The two kiji rushed me, and I danced to the side and swiped at one of them, surprising it again. It had probably never encountered anything like me before, and my strength was deceptive. I didn't look as strong as I was. It tried to dodge, but I cut open its side, from shoulder to rear.

More kiji climbed up, bringing the number to almost a dozen. I didn't know how many there were in the pack. We had never gotten close enough to count, but from what I could see and hear, there were a lot more of them still coming. I switched to the second Kata, *Tempest in the Mist*, and I advanced straight into them.

The second kiji's claws started to glow red, and it jumped on me, swiping at my side. I ignored it as my focus sharpened on the one already injured. I stepped closer to the retreating animal, and the claws from its comrade burned across my back shallowly. I ignored the wound and stabbed, piercing through the animal's throat, then I cut upward, slicing through its spine.

The kiji weren't highly Invested—from what I remembered they should be around the same level as the young ferrorn that I fought when I arrived. If I was facing the pack back then, I would've had no chance. But now, I had changed a lot, and I felt secure in my power.

The kiji behind me advanced, I could hear its footsteps, and those of a half a dozen other kiji rushing me from the side. I took a step, throwing myself on them and triggering [Mist Step]. I reappeared in the middle of them, and pulled at the sensation of the [Debilitating Wave] skill inside of me. I felt it swell up through my chest and into my throat, forcing my mouth open in a soundless cry that released a ruby wave of energy.

As the wave hit them, they stumbled, stunned. Saia swooped down as I lashed out, never stopping, just moving my spear in a circle around me dancing like a storm. My anger swelled, and with it my attacks. I cut, spilling blood in all directions as Saia mauled the kiji, going for their heads and eyes with her claws.

I didn't bother to see if my attacks were lethal, I just went for doing as much damage to as many of my foes as I could. Blood splashed in all directions, spilled over me, and soaked me in it, I tasted it on my lips.

I was smiling, feeling alive as I unleashed a flurry of attacks. Kiji around me fell, but always there were more to take their place. Saia swooped down, distracting my opponents for me, and I heard the air whoosh as a bolt flew and hit one of the kiji in the side. The kiji howled, and I felt a skill, but I didn't know what it did. They jumped forward with greater fervor, became even more aggressive, the bodies of their packmates ignored.

I felt claws cut into my thigh and reacted, bringing my spear down blindly to cut the beast. With the daylight, I wasn't healing as fast, but I didn't care. I ignored the injuries, I gave myself over to offense, taking on wounds if it meant I killed another kiji. Wounds didn't matter to me, if I killed them all before they inflicted enough wounds to kill me. When the night fell, I would heal.

With [Mist Step] I flanked two kiji, moving through them. They snapped their jaws on mist, then shook their heads in confusion. I re-formed and lashed out, cutting them apart.

Two died in a span of seconds, but more were coming. I wished that I had a moment to grab one and drink, but they were attacking so fast.

Another snapped its jaw around my calf, preventing me from moving. I stabbed toward it, but another kiji jumped at me, hitting me in the chest and taking me to the ground, its jaws around my shoulder. I roared and grabbed my knife, pulling it out and stabbing its side as another kiji pulled me by my leg. The one on top of me let go as I opened its stomach, and I was dragged beneath it, stabbing all the way as blood showered on top of me.

Two kiji had me by my legs, their teeth sinking deep as they pulled me across the ground. Other kiji moved for me, probably intending to rip me apart on the ground. My [Debilitating Wave] was on cooldown, and I had lost my spear. I gripped my knife tightly and used [Swap Profile].

I felt the change in skills wash over me, and immediately I lashed out. I opened my mouth and a [Sonic Screech] blasted out. The kiji around me all screamed in pain, and the two dragging me let go of my legs. I rolled and launched myself low at the closest kiji. With [Lesser Impale] I stabbed my knife and felt it sink into its side then keep going, my arm pulling me forward and impaling it all the way to my wrist.

I knew that I had no choice now, so with my free hand I swiped at its throat with [Quick Claw], opening it up. I reached down and placed my mouth over the wound, pulling the dying kiji on top of me and drinking. The other kiji recovered enough that it attacked, biting my hip and swinging its head trying to pull me away. Blood spilled down my throat, and I felt the **thirst** waking up, my body trying to heal, even though the sun weakened it.

With a mouthful of blood, I pulled out my knife and started to swing it widely around me. I felt it connect, but I didn't know how much damage I was doing. I rolled, trying to get out from beneath the kiji, and saw red glowing claws heading for my face. I twisted and slashed at the claws, redirecting them to the ground next to my face where they sank into the dirt like it was clay. Then I pushed off the ground and bit down on the kiji's leg, pressing down with my teeth until I felt bones crack then splinter in my mouth.

The kiji above me howled, and I got a knee beneath me, then managed to push up. Saia fell on another kiji that was about to take a bite out of my face, and another was distracted by a bolt hitting it in the shoulder.

My breaths were quick, my heart was pounding in my rib cage, and I was tired. I reached for my chest and pulled, manifesting my Mask into the real world. Shadow had warned me about using it—it would grant great power, but it also would drain quickly, especially at early Investments. According to him, he had barely been able to use it for more than a few dozen seconds before it wiped him out when he was on my Investment. I had no choice. I looked around and saw that there were still shapes moving around me in the dim light. They were as shadows. And then the last of the light grew even fainter, I placed the Mask on my face and felt the power surge through my body. The sun was fully behind the horizon, and I awoke fully.

I felt my smile widen behind the Mask on my face, as the **thirst** growled in my stomach, as blood fueled me, as my wounds started to close faster. As my Mask burned on my head. Wearing it was unlike anything that I had ever experienced before. It was as if liquid lightning was coursing through my veins—it was the worst and the best of the **thirst** all merged into one. It was heavy, a weight that gave me so much, but was also dragging me down with it. I knew that I didn't have a lot of time.

I took a wide stance, settling in the last Kata: *Advance, Whirling Mist*. Then I advanced.

Marianna was overwhelmed. Shadow fired another bolt, trying to distract a kiji that was preparing to leap at her back. The fight was bloody, and he had been losing hope that they would get out of this. When Marianna went down, when the kiji got on top of her and he heard the tearing of flesh, he thought that it was over. He still fired bolts as fast as he could, lamenting his weakness. His body was burning from the effort of just standing upright. Desire to use his skills burned inside of him, but so did the knowledge that if he even tried his body would give out on him. He had exerted himself too much against the sikiri, and he had nothing more to give.

And then, somehow, Marianna crawled out of the pile of the kiji, and she got back up on her feet, her dragonling swooping down to help as much as possible.

Then, he realized that shadows had lengthened, that light had dimmed and that the moons shone above. He looked at Marianna, saw her clothes torn to shreds, blood dripping from her, her hair matted and soaked with it, plastered to her face. Her wounds were clear even from a distance. Her calves were torn up so much that he could see bones, and her side was missing a piece where a kiji had bitten off her hip. Then she reached for her chest and pulled out her Mask. As the light of the two moons hit her face, he saw her smile widening. It was a mad grin that reminded him so much of his old self that it hurt his heart. Shadow watched as she put the Mask of jade and obsidian on her face.

The wounds on her body started to heal at a rate unlike anything he had seen before. Through the Mask, he could see her eyes blazing with emerald light. In them, he saw a complete surrender to herself as she took a position of the last Kata in the **Veiled Mist Assault.**

Then she moved, attacking in a whirlwind of death and blood, dancing around and sending showers of gore and carnage in all directions. A knife in one hand, and claws in the other, she moved in a near perfect way of his school of being. All anger properly directed; all thoughts of defense abandoned. She ignored wounds and killed her foes, soaking the ground in their blood.

She grabbed the beasts and peeled their skin back in feats of strength rivaling someone of much higher Investment, ripped limbs from bodies and bludgeoned others with them. She cracked bones and pulled spikes of broken ribs to impale those still alive.

When she was done, when there were no more enemies to fight, she stood in the center of that carnage, her head tilted up at the moons and her eyes closed. She was breathing heavily as she reached up and pulled the Mask off her face, blood dripping down her cheeks, but still smiling.

In that moment he felt both pride and fear, for he knew that he had found someone who would continue his legacy, who would understand his teachings.

But Shadow also saw more than most could discern. He saw through to the core of who Marianna was. A moment later she collapsed on the ground.

He glanced up at the two moons above and made a decision.

The Connections That We Forge

Shadow guided me with his arm around my back and mine around his shoulders as I walked with him to a small rock. Wearing the Mask was . . . bliss, it was a taste of power on the same level as tasting my sire's blood on the day I'd been turned. With that Mask on, I felt invincible, like I could do anything, like I had all the power I wanted in my hands. I had also finally been able to figure out what exactly my Mask provided me: my healing skyrocketed. Saia's estimation was that it increased by just over 100%, which was insane.

I vaguely remembered getting injuries during that last part of the fight that healed before I even registered the pain of them. On the downside, the moment I took it off, I felt a wave of exhaustion that drained me completely, so much so that my body barely responded to me. Shadow had said that if I had kept it on for even a few seconds longer I probably would've passed out, maybe even died.

And all of the skills that I used were still on cooldown a day later. And I had used nearly all of them. With my Mask on, [Swap Profile] had its cooldown reduced enough that I had been able to use it once, which meant that it too was now no longer available along with all the skills I had slotted in both profiles. Though, on the bright side, I now knew how shorten the cooldowns for all of my other skills. When I wore my Mask, their cooldown was nearly instant. Though I had felt myself being drained the more I used the skills. That power didn't come without a cost.

I had no idea what a long cooldown meant and for how long I would be powerless, but I was going to find out. At least we haven't run into anything dangerous so far.

Shadow set up our camp, as I sat on a ledge and watched the distant skies. We were on a high cliff, one that had a great vantage point. In the distance I could see the ocean, blazing with light reflected from the cacophony of the aurora above it. My world, coming down. It seemed far too peaceful for what it implied, just a light filling the horizon that was changing the very structure of an entire world.

Saia jumped into my lap and looked ahead with me. It was something new for both of us. I could smell the ocean, the taste of freedom and an endless expanse.

We had reached our destination, and it was beautiful. And soon I was going to return to Earth. I hadn't even begun to think about what I was going to do, aside from knowing that I wanted to help people survive.

A few minutes later, Shadow took a seat next to me on the ledge, holding one of the empty gourds in his hands as he stared out at the sea with me. For a while we were silent, just enjoying the sights.

"It will not be long now," he said after a while. "Our journey is coming to an end."

"I wouldn't be here without you," I said. "Thank you for everything, for teaching me."

Shadow smiled. "We helped each other, tsinju!shi," he said and I again saw images in my head, the translation of the word that I was still not fully familiar with. We had a bond between us, that of a student and a teacher, of two people who survived death together, camaraderie. An unbreakable bond. Tsinju!shi, as he said.

"Will I see you again?" I asked.

"Survive your world," Shadow said. "And I promise you that you will."

"I won't die," I promised, and fully meant it. I was prepared to do everything to survive and help as many people on Earth do the same.

"I have something for you. Gifts," Shadow said. I blinked and turned to look at him. His eyes were still on the ocean in front of us. "But I need to ask you something before I give them to you."

I tilted my head, wondering what this was about. "You can ask me anything," I said. It wasn't like I was going to keep secrets from him now.

"I know that you do not care much for your family, the one that sold you away," Shadow started, and I was taken aback. I hadn't expected that to be the topic. "I wondered if you know why your family gave you your name, what it means in your world?"

I frowned, it was a . . . touchy subject for me, but what I said before still held. I trusted Shadow more than I had probably trusted anyone else in my life. It felt so paradoxical—we'd known each other for barely a month, and here I was feeling so connected to him. Yet, a part of me felt that it was right. We'd gone through more than most people go through in a lifetime.

"My name is two names, Maria and Anna. Together they have a few meanings," I answered slowly, turning my eyes to look at the endless water in front of us. "I don't know if my parents had any of those meanings in mind when they named me. They never told me, or I don't remember if they had. What I know about my name I learned in school, more out of personal curiosity than anything else. Rojas, my family name is a derivative of 'red.' I don't know if it means anything else. And Marianna can mean 'bitter grace' or 'sea of bitterness,' but the one meaning I like the most is the 'star of the sea.'"

"*The star of the sea,*" Shadow repeated.

"Why do you ask?" I glanced back at him.

"I have been thinking about what I could give you that could reflect the amount of gratitude that I feel. Not just for helping me survive the jungle in my state, but for being who you are, for talking with me and trusting me. For showing me that I have fallen into a hole of my own making. You helped me reawaken something that I thought I lost long ago. For this I wish to give you something, if you agree, of course."

I looked him in the eyes, seeing a kindred soul. Which terrified me. He was older than any vampire I had ever heard about. He had done so many things in his life that having him look at me and see himself instilled a sense of fear. It made me wonder if I was on the same path. Yet, a part of me invited it, it wanted to be someone who could stand alone in the face of everything the world could throw at me and weather it.

"What?" I asked finally.

"I told you that YoKai-ni culture values names greatly. I would like to give you a name," Shadow answered with gravity.

I blinked, remembering what he had said about names in his culture, the true name that was only ever used in important situations. It was a name that changed with the person, that grew and evolved over time, a name that was a private and intimate thing.

"I . . . I don't know what to say." His offer surprised me.

"There are only two people in my family, myself and my mother. I am her only child, and I have never had children myself. Usually, what I offer is a grand affair for the YoKai-ni. My mother gave me the right to do so long ago, so it is within my rights to give you this invitation. I wish to give you my *end verse*, have you join my family."

My chest tightened, and I felt my face flush in surprise. I hadn't expected to be offered such a gesture of kindness, but as I let it sink in, I realized that yes, I truly wanted this. A deep sense of loneliness had taken root inside of me years ago; my own family had sold me, and the cartel hung me. I had bad luck with family, yet Shadow had done more for me than any of them ever had. With a sudden surge of emotion, I managed to utter, "I would love that," a smile spreading across my face.

He turned so that he was facing me, and I did the same.

"Ordinarily, this would mean a big ceremony, a feast. Introduce you to the family. But my family is small, and my mother is . . . she is not the most social of people. So, forgive me for doing this in such a humble manner," he said with a smile.

I didn't care about those things, just the fact that he asked meant the world to me. "I don't need that."

He nodded. "Then, I give you my *end verse*. May it mark you as part of my family, for better and for worse. It means that we stand together in all things, united as a family always should be. All that is mine, is yours, and all that is yours is mine."

I didn't know the customs, I didn't know if there was anything that I should say or do, so I simply bowed my head.

"As for your name, I have witnessed who you are, and so I grant you the *beginning verse* to your name, Star, for the meaning of Marianna in your tongue. And I add to it, to give you your full true name. From this day until the day your verses grow, you shall be known amongst the YoKai-ni as *The Star That Dances in Blood Beneath the Light of the Broken Moon*. Know that all are bound by honor to give you their own name should you ever introduce yourself fully. Know that by exchanging names you are afforded the rights of the Old Tree's Hearth. A day of peace, to talk and find common ground. May your name be a guiding light to you in the mists that surround life."

I closed my eyes and turned my face from him, trying to hide the tear that rolled down my cheek. I felt it when he said the name. Like a skill almost, an impression in the Way, as he called it. I didn't understand how, but it felt fitting. It felt beautiful.

"Thank you," I whispered, my head still bowed. I felt him put a hand on my shoulder as he knelt next to me. I felt the courage to raise my head and meet his gaze—our eyes locked in an intense stare that could not be broken. Nothing was spoken, yet a deep connection was made; more was said in that moment than any words could ever describe.

"I have one more thing for you," Shadow said slowly. He leaned back, then raised the empty gourd that I had seen him holding before. He pulled the cork out of it, then had me hold it. I frowned as he pulled out a knife, and then started rolling up his sleeve. My eyes widened as I realized what he was about to do.

I grabbed his hand. "You don't need to do that," I said quickly.

He smiled. "I want to," he told me. "I don't know how it will work, but from what you have told me a piece of my essence will be locked within you. I don't know if it will be a copy of me as I am now, with my thoughts and reasoning. I don't know what limits the Grand Spell will place on it. Perhaps it will be just a simple obstacle to overcome, but perhaps it will also help you along your journey. We are family, and I will arm you as best as I can, give you all that I can so that you can survive your world."

I didn't know what to say. The name was more than I had ever expected to get out of life. This—this was far more than that. I watched as he made the cut on his forearm, then filled the gourd with his lifeblood. The smell of it hit me, thick in my nostrils. It made me imagine what it must taste like, I couldn't help but feel the anticipation build. The power of it was tangible in the air.

The pink liquid fell, each drop spiraling down to the gourd, poured with great precision. I heard it splashing inside as it filled up, and it echoed in my ears like whispers. The **thirst** woke up, and I grabbed hold of it, kept it from pushing me to raise the gourd and down the blood like a monster that I was.

I almost didn't hear him when he spoke, but then his words pierced through my haze, and I raised my head to look at him.

"I offer this gift freely," he said, gesturing for me to take it, to drink.

I swallowed, my tongue feeling heavy in my mouth. I craved it, the taste of it, the power of it. I licked my lips as the desire to drink it took me, the **thirst** aligned with my will, I felt its power stab through me along with a deep desire. I wish I could say that I was composed, but I didn't even remember raising the gourd to my lips. Instead, the next thing I knew was the explosion in my mouth as it hit my tongue.

The blood filled my every thought; it was a deep rich taste of a life well lived, the taste of the morning mist, the taste of elusive power. It tasted of all the food I've ever eaten, all the drinks I've ever drank, all of it soaked in blood spilled by the source of the life I was tasting. It was greater than anything I have ever experienced. I gulped it down like it was my last hope, my salvation, my everything. The sound of it flowing down my throat filled my ears, the noise of a waterfall falling against the rocks.

Then it hit my stomach, and everything went white. Memories flashed through my head, so fast that I couldn't understand a thing that I saw. All I understood was feeling. Fear, rage, glory, they filled my mind with flashes of images I could get a glimpse of. A giant city with ringed walls, with towers as tall as skyscrapers. A tree that rose from a mountain, its roots twisting around it as mist surrounded the base of it, the shadow of its branches casting everything in darkness.

A golden throne, swallowed by vines, with dust covering the floor.

And then it was over, and I had drunk the last drop.

I came to on the ground, Shadow kneeling above me.

"Are you okay, Little Star?" he asked.

I opened my mouth, and only garbled speech came out. I shook my head and forced myself to slow down.

Mask of the Blood Invoker — First Investment; Fourth Carving

Three Carvings? Just from his blood? It was a lot more potent than anything I had encountered before.

"I'm fine," I answered. "I . . . didn't expect that. It was unlike anything that I have ever tasted."

"Well." The side of Shadow's mouth raised in a half smile. "I assume that it tasted good?"

"I . . . yes," I said, suddenly feeling a bit shy.

"Good." He nodded then raised his eyes to look at the sky. "It is almost time."

I glanced in the same direction, saw that the light was growing brighter. Before I could ask how he knew, it happened.

Light started gathering around me, and I sat up, startled.

Shadow put his weapon, the serpent-tongue spear in my hands, and reflexively I closed my hands around it. The light expanded to hold it too. Saia, or rather her drone form jumped on my legs and was covered too.

"My last gift, for you, Saia," Shadow said and ripped the small stone from the head of his rod, then placed it in my lap as well. "Be vigilant," he added. "Survive."

"I will," I told him. I tried to find the words to express the depths of my gratitude, but none came. The light grew so bright that I lost sight of him, and then I felt a sensation I had felt once before. I felt as if my body grew and contracted all at the same time as the light swallowed me whole.

I was going home.

The Shadow That Quells Empires Stands Grinning and Triumphant Beneath the Light of the Broken Moon had to look away as the Grand Spell took *The Star That Dances in Blood Beneath the Light of the Broken Moon* away, back to her home. He could not even begin to describe the way that he was feeling in that moment. There was a lot of worry, yes, an emotion that he was not very familiar with, or hadn't been for a long time at least. He worried about what awaited her back home. By now it would have changed completely. The geography, the wildlife, everything would have become alien to her. And also, far more dangerous.

Her struggle here, on Ish Vimza, would provide a great deal of experience. But Shadow knew just how much danger a newly integrated world faced, and not just from the changes and wildlife. As always, it was other people who were the most dangerous.

He took a deep breath, taking comfort in the realization that he had done all that he possibly could for her.

He stood up, his legs still shaking from the effort. He glanced back, into the darkness beneath the trees of the jungle. He wondered if he would live to worry for much longer.

"Show yourself," he called. His body was barely holding him together, and he knew that he wouldn't be able to use any of his skills. But at least he would die on his feet.

He had felt something in the jungle for weeks now. Something that he couldn't quite put his fingers on. Something had been stalking them.

At first, he had thought that it was an animal, but the more time passed the more he became convinced that it was not. The fight with the sikiri had sealed it for him.

When Marianna drank its blood, he had felt the blight take hold inside of her, and he had known that she had lost the struggle. Then, he felt a skill being used from somewhere near them, and a moment later the blight was banished from her body as if it was never there in the first place.

Shadow had never seen anything like it, and that alone was what made him hopeful that he was going to live through this.

The stalker stepped out of the darkness, peeling out of it like a wraith. Black mist surrounded them. It was shaped like a Kitsu-oi, with nine tails made out of mist swinging behind them.

That made Shadow frown, all Kitsu-oi had tails, but nine was the rarest number. The fact that there were two nine-tailed people on Ish Vimza at the same time was . . . unlikely.

What was even more unlikely was that he recognized the skill that shrouded them, it was as familiar to him as breathing.

"Who are you?" Shadow asked.

The figure stepped closer, and he saw their glowing eyes pierce out of the mist shroud, two jade jewels. Then the shroud receded, and he blinked as he saw their face.

"That's impossible," he said. "You . . ."

The figure just smiled. In that moment, Shadow realized just how little he actually understood. And knew that everything that he had held as truth was about to change.

Moments and Tears
of the Stormlands

Oluwatobi Musa sat back on his haunches, watching over his family playing by the pond. He was fortunate, he knew, to have found such a place in the middle of nowhere. He'd brought his family here in search of a better life, and so far, it had been kind to them. He thanked God every day for his blessings, and for allowing his children to experience the joys of this life.

Around him, the desert stretched on, vast and silent, and yet here he and his family were safe and secure, and the future looked a little brighter. As he watched his children continue to play, staring down at the monitor lizard that was hissing at them, he was filled with a deep sense of peace and contentment, and prayed that this feeling would never end.

Both his son and daughter were in their true forms, free from all human concerns. It was liberating, and moments like these were what made him believe that he had made the right decision by taking his family out of Lagos and into the desert. Oluwatobi found solace in the vast expanse of desert around him. Here, he was not only surrounded by nature, but connected to it. He could see it in the sand, feel it in the air, and hear its call in the wind. It was a kind of communion with the world that he had never known before. Better that they were here, alone, than among the so-called civilized people. With their never-ending greed, the overconsumption of everything in their way, the technology that robbed them of all connections with the natural world.

He took a deep breath and allowed himself to relax into his environment. As he did, something inside him began to stir: a longing for what this place revealed to him about himself and his family's journey out here; a reminder of why they had chosen this road less traveled by most people; a reaffirmation of why this was where they belonged as part of something larger than themselves, as part of Nature itself.

Oluwatobi had hated walking down the streets seeing them staring at their wrist screens, letting pixels consume their lives. Mother Earth had so much more to offer.

This was right, he thought to himself.

The air was fresher here, uncontaminated by the toxic fumes of a large city. Here, in this serene setting, he could finally feel like himself again and not be judged for who he was. His family had been persecuted in their home city, where those around them feared what they didn't understand. People had called them "wolves" and were afraid that their presence would bring harm to their city. But Oluwatobi had never felt more in touch with nature than he did now, standing out here in the open desert, with its wildness and its vastness.

It saddened him sometimes. He had to admit, technology had so much to offer, even to his kind. Through it, they had learned who their ancestors were, how they had become who they were. They were descendants of the mighty Andrewsarchus, and even though they had changed, adapted to their dual lives, all shifters felt the call of nature. Technology had given them that, yet the humans and the vampires used it only to exploit.

Oluwatobi felt his mate brush his shoulder as she came to sit next to him. He glanced in her direction, saw the pale dust color of her short fur, the thick brown mane around her neck, the muscles that bulged beneath, the earthy scent that clung to her.

Life was good.

The sun had already begun to sink in the sky, and its last rays spilled a warm orange hue across the desert expanse. Oluwatobi and his mate sat in silence, watching as creatures of all sorts made their way home for the night or out for an adventure.

The stars began to twinkle above them, and Oluwatobi looked up at them with admiration. As he did so, he thought back to how far they had traveled and how much they had endured together since then. He thought of how far they could still go if only they stayed true to themselves and followed their own paths instead of trying to follow those set by society—the ones that weren't meant for them. His heart swelled with pride knowing they chose a different road—one less traveled, but more rewarding—a journey that led them here and opened his eyes to a world he would never have known before this night.

Suddenly, his mate turned her head to the sky, and light reflected in her eyes. Oluwatobi turned and followed her gaze, just in time to see white light high up in the sky, getting stronger, a wave of it spreading in all directions.

He heard his mate growl, and he yelped at his cubs, calling to them. The light was too fast. It hit the ground and washed over them all. His world became blinding white, a loud noise filled his ears, and it was as if everything had just ceased to exist. It lasted only for a moment, and when Oluwatobi opened his eyes, his mate was missing. He turned around looking, his ears twitching on top of his head as his cubs yowled in fear. He sensed no sign of his mate, only the fading scent of where she used to be.

He raised his head and looked up. Lines of all colors filled every part of the sky, like a giant web of a million auroras. And they were coming down.

Oluwatobi moved quickly, leaping to his children. He grabbed his son by the scruff of his neck and ushered him back to the crude shelter they had made. The lines of light were falling faster now, and he feared what was about to happen.

His children hid behind him as a wall of twisting light hit the ground, and then . . . then the world went mad.

Andrew Carter sat at his workstation. The holotable projected the protein and several working versions of molecules that could bind with it. The processor was currently running down more molecule variations. He could feel it, they almost had it, a universal cure. Soon, diseases of all kind would be a thing of the past. Soon, humanity would enjoy the same strengths that the shifters and vampires did. The vampire protein floating above his table was a terrible thing, but they had stripped it of all its nasty tendencies. But it still remained a weapon, a delivery mechanism that could push past any defense. A weapon of the sanguinium bacteria, one that would answer to whatever programming they wanted.

"It is close," Hannah said from his left.

"It is more than just close," Andrew said. "This will work, I know it will."

"We need more testing," Hannah said. "Years of trials."

Andrew rounded on her. "This can work! It can save people now!"

"You don't know that." Hannah shook her head.

Andrew opened his mouth to argue, and then he stopped.

"This is wrong," he whispered. Something at the back of his head was nagging at him. "You weren't here."

There was light coming in from the window, and he walked over and looked. A familiar light was coming from the sky.

"This is a dream," Andrew whispered. "I was alone when it came for me."

Hannah looked at him as if he had lost his mind, and he remembered. She and the rest of their team had left him, had gone home for the weekend. They didn't think that what he was doing was right, they had an argument. Andrew alone stayed; he had fallen asleep at the table. The light woke him up. Now as it came for him again, he closed his eyes, welcoming it.

Andrew Carter woke up on a small straw cot. He grimaced, the pain of his burned face aching through his head. The headaches had been nearly constant, but he pushed through it. He had learned to live with it these past few weeks.

How long had he even been here? It had to be close to a month. He knew that his time in this world was expiring. That soon he would be returned. He had learned so much, and soon he would be able to help humanity in ways that he never before could.

Slowly, he stood up and walked over to the small bowl filled with water. Gently, he unwrapped the bandages around his face and cleaned his wounds before rewrapping them. Then, he put on his work outfit, the thick leather gloves and apron, his goggles, and the breathing mask. Then he left his small shack, carefully. He had grown accustomed to this in the weeks since he had been brought here. He grabbed the hanging rope outside his home, and then Andrew stepped onto the line rope, slowly and carefully, feeling for a balance point.

His eyes scanned the horizon as he made his way along the tightrope, then someone flew by him, yelling as they passed.

"Well woke, Andrew!" The Harpiem greeted him as he passed.

Andrew waved, recognizing Jass by his bright blue tunic and the red feathers in his hair denoting him as the commander of the city watch.

Andrew took a deep breath, taking a quick glance down. He never really got used to living in a city built on the side of a cliff. Especially one that had been set up in three days. He didn't know how Harpiem did it, but he was amazed when he watched them drop down the shacks and ropes over the cliff to set up a temporary settlement. He shook his head as he fought against the vertigo, and then he started making his way across the rope line that connected the shacks.

With two hands on the top rope, he carefully slid his legs against the one on the bottom, making his way to his lab.

He reached the isolated hut and entered the lab with his limbs burning from the effort. He quickly shook them off and then walked over to his worktable. The first thing he did was check his work list again. He didn't know how long he had left. He had lost a few days on his arrival, before the Harpiem found him half dead on the plains.

But he knew that he had to do as much as he could for his new friends. Equip them as best as he knew how, he owed them that much at least.

With an increased sense of haste, he started his work. He took up his simple mortar and pestle, getting to work.

He was so engrossed in his work that he didn't even notice when a Harpiem came into the lab. "Teacher! You are early!" Andrew raised his head to see his student, A Harpiem with red feathers on his wings, skid to a stop with an amazed look on his face as he gazed at Andrew's work.

"Wow!" he exclaimed breathlessly. "You have been busy."

"Careful," Andrew said as Brin rushed ahead. "What did I teach you?"

"Never rush." Brin caught himself and Andrew nodded.

"What do you have there?" he asked.

Brin smiled and pulled over his satchel, showing him the assortment of plants he had gathered.

"You found more brown weed?" Andrew asked, surprised.

"Yes, teacher," Brin said. "I had to fly far down south for it, near the old trails."

Andrew smiled for what felt like the first time in ages as he walked over. "This is good. With this we can get your people more healing salves."

The name of the weed was mundane, but it was a very potent ingredient in the healing salve that Andrew had developed. With this he would be able to set up his hosts with enough to see them through the next leg of their journey.

"Good, good," Andrew murmured. "Let's start working on this batch. We don't have much time."

Their work continued into the night, but by the end of it they had made two full crates of healing salve. Enough for the entire tribe.

"That was amazing, teacher," Brin said. "I even got a Carving from it!"

Andrew smiled. His own Mask had hit a plateau it seemed, after the rapid gains he got at the start. But that was to be expected from everything that he had learned. So much was new to him back then, an entire new world to explore, with ways of doing things that were foreign to him.

He looked at Brin, at his carefree smile of contentment and pride. He knew how hard life was for the Harpiem in this world, how harsh it could be. He had seen the beasts that harried their path. Andrew glanced at the chest in the corner of the room and debated with himself.

In the end, responsibility won against morality.

"Brin," he said slowly.

"Teacher?" The young Harpiem tilted his head.

Andrew walked over to the chest and knelt down to open it. Inside he looked at the wrapped package, and then before he could change his mind, he picked it up. He carried the package to the table and unwrapped it, revealing three small vials, their contents glowing faint blue.

It was an abomination, created by his superior knowledge and aided by the cursed skills he had gained in this world. And yet, Andrew couldn't bring himself to throw it away. It had a use.

"What is this?" Brin asked.

Andrew raised his head, his heart started to beat faster, the light outside of the lab got brighter and brighter.

"I want you to take this, and give it to your alchemists once you reach Par Nata," Andrew said, naming the large gathering of Harpiem tribes, the place where his rescuers had been heading. "Don't use it, not unless you have no other recourse, and if you must, give it to one of the guards."

Brin's thick brow furrowed.

"Teacher," he said slowly.

Andrew looked down on his creation. Working with Source was such a . . . it was going to change everything. He could already see all the terrible things that humanity would do with it. Like he had done.

"It's a drug," Andrew said. "It will make anyone who takes it strong, but the side effects . . . I didn't have the time or the equipment to test it properly." He suspected only. His [Document Trait] skill told him . . . terrible things. "Give it to the alchemists, and let them test it out. They will do better than I ever could."

His Mask was not yet on the First Investment, he just knew that Harpiem had people better than him, at least as far as matters of the Source were concerned.

Brin nodded. "I will do as you ask, teacher."

Andrew nodded, feeling relieved. At least he would leave the Wandering People with something to repay them.

The light grew more, and he felt a familiar sensation. The Grand Spell had come for him.

The bearer of the Mask of Malefic Alchemist was going home.

Knight Mage Herim of Roughrock coughed, and blood spilled out of his mouth, falling to the shattered cobblestone beneath. He glanced at his hand, seeing that only the hilt remained of his weapon. The blade had shattered, and he didn't even remember when it had happened. His thoughts were filled with a fog, something that he recognized from experience. Head wound, a concussion. He would have to push through it. The air around him was thick with smoke. It was hard to see, and even harder to breathe.

He could make out the shapes of people running about in confusion, but he could not tell who they were or what they were doing. But he could hear screams—screams of terror and pain alike—coming from all directions.

He tried to stand but found himself too weak to do so and stumbled back to where he had been before half crawling half dragging himself across the broken stones toward a nearby alleyway. He pushed himself up against the wall and leaned his head back.

Above, the light of the sun shone through the clouds, streams of it stretching to touch the ground as if it was a sign. And it was. It was providence, the light that so rarely shone on the Stormlands had come when they needed it the most. There would have been no victory without it.

The entire night and the morning that followed felt like a nightmare, an illusion cast by the fiends of Asha Kai-ni. In his wildest thoughts, he couldn't have imagined it going this way. Their enemy was dead, burned a hundred times over, its body dismembered, and bones pulverized to dust, flesh torn and scattered. They had to be sure, but even now, Herim feared that it wasn't enough, that he would hear that laughter in the air, and that the violence would start again.

He shook his head. *No, the vampire is dead.* Such a monster should never have existed. Two whole Knight Orders had come after it, and now . . . Herim couldn't even bring himself to look and see who else had survived.

He had watched the Storm Knight, the Knight Commander, the leader of his order, face the vampire in battle, and he had seen him fall. A man who had lived for thousands of years, who had reached the Sixth Investment, one of the highest Investment people in the whole world. And the being from another world killed him.

It was madness. Even with all the preparations they had done, they hadn't accounted for the sheer cunning, the intelligence that lurked behind those golden eyes. The brutality.

The haunting cries of the people filled the streets as they emerged from their hiding places. Herim's heart raced with fear and shame as he watched them hobble across the cobblestones.

Herim had no right to meet their eyes, filled with shame as he was. They had hunted the monster. Cowardice kept him on the ground. The monster was gone now, killed by them all at a terrible cost, but Herim could not shake his guilt.

Herim sat on the ground, drained completely. A part of him blamed himself, yes, for surviving, for the little voice in his head that told him that the dream of his life was finally accomplished. His Mask had advanced, Sixth Investment, an accomplishment that put him in the upper echelon of all the Masked in the world. Yet he cursed his Mask, cursed himself for being weak. There was no joy in his accomplishment. Two hundred knights had met the monster in battle, and he had seen them fall like trees before a high storm. He was afraid to go out and search, fearing that he was the only one left.

The city was in ruins, and thousands more were dead. They had won, but in his heart, all that Herim could think was that he had failed.

The battle had been the hardest thing he had ever been a part of. The monster just kept healing, no matter what they did. It knew that they had silver, and it destroyed their preparations before even engaging them in battle. It had ambushed them a day before they planned the attack on its lair. It had to have known, somehow. Herim couldn't get the memory out of his head. Mortal wounds closing instantly, a monstrous strength that let it pull armored knights apart as if they were made out of clay. The wings that could blast air with such force to pick up entire wagons and send them spinning down the streets. All of that with no skills.

And its Mask . . . No being of such strength should ever have a Mask. It was an abomination.

Something caught his eye, and Herim raised his head. Light was filling the horizon, and immediately he knew what it was.

Only one thought filled Herim's mind at that sight; that there was an entire world out there, filled with the same kind of monsters.

Khalil Abd al-Nur, Knight Priest of the Order of the Dragon, looked on at the carnage in front of him as the sky blazed with light. Buildings were razed to the ground, streets filled with craters, fire blazing as Elves ran down the streets throwing water at it, trying to quell the flames.

Carriages drawn by beasts native to this land carried more water, or just people who rushed to clear the rubble and try to save those who were buried beneath.

Khalil was in a state of shock. What he had seen that night was . . . unlike anything he could've ever imagined. He had been called up to speak with the knights on the eve of their planned assault against the vampire. He had thought that they were prepared, that they would be victorious. And ultimately, they had been. Yet there was so much death, so much carnage.

All the stories he heard on Earth echoed inside his head. He had even laid eyes on the vampire himself. He had seen the image of evil with golden eyes and the unshaken knowledge of superiority that they held. Today, he had seen what the worst of vampire kind was capable of. He had seen why his order was necessary.

And he had learned that even here, in this new world, God could still hear his prayers.

When the morning came, the battle had continued under the overcast skies filled with storm clouds. It had given the vampire protection, hid it from the sun. Khalil had prayed as he had never prayed before. He had reached out for the strange new force that his Mask of the Believer offered, and he asked with his [Act of Faith].

The skies parted, and the sun shone down, at last.

The vampire had not been burned as Khalil had expected, but the effects were immediate. It had recoiled from the light, almost seemed confused to see that it hadn't died from its touch. At least he now knew that the stories that spoke of Ancient Vampires were true, they could walk in sunlight. And that had given the remaining knights an opening to strike.

Khalil had never seen such might wielded by the righteous, but seeing it, he knew that everything would change. No longer would humanity cower in weakness. This world offered power to all who were willing to reach out and take it.

Khalil stood alone, forgotten amidst the chaos, as light started to surround him. In moments it engulfed him, and took him back to his world, his faith and resolve firm in the knowledge that he would help humanity survive the darkness ahead.

A New Dawn

The light dimmed, and the disorientation vanished in an instant. I opened my eyes and saw a sight that was both familiar and not.

"You all right, Saia?" I asked the little dragon next to me.

She had the stone in her mouth, the gift that Shadow had given her.

"Feedback: Affirmative," she answered, the sound coming from her entire body. One of these days I need to ask her how she did that. A moment later her head morphed, and she swallowed the stone whole, consuming it. I hefted the serpent-tongue spear on my shoulder then left her to it and started looking around.

We were back on Earth, in the same place I was taken from, the courtyard where I had been hanged. I saw the wall where I had been pulled up, and my fingers touched the scar on my throat, and I felt a phantom pain, an aching there even though the wound had now healed.

There were changes all around that were obvious. The hacienda I had once called home stood before me, and the sight of it shook me to my core. A thick vine curled up the side of the house. It was covered in dead leaves. Wildflowers grew between large cracks in the stone path leading to the front door. For a moment I thought that it had been years since I had been here, but then more things started to stand out.

The trees were thicker, their leaves bigger, and all the plants looked slightly different than what I remembered them to be. As if they were mutated, and from what Shadow had told me, I knew that was exactly what had happened. The Source had changed the Earth completely, and the changes hadn't even run their full course.

It was night, and the two now familiar moons shone from above. My world was now part of Kirios, a planet that had magic.

I listened closely for any signs of life, and heard only the sounds of nature. That didn't mean that there was nothing nearby.

Carefully, I stepped inside the house. The light from outside carved through the darkness to show that the house was abandoned. Dirt spread from the open door inside across the carpet. It was as if a storm had passed through the home. I walked around, inspecting each room. Everywhere I looked there were signs of being quickly vacated: a half-eaten meal in the kitchen, piles of clothes strewn about bedrooms and dust invading even deeper parts like closets. There were also signs of battle. I saw bullet holes in the walls, casings on the ground, pictures knocked down, furniture moved around.

Whatever happened, happened quickly. People weren't prepared for it.

I knelt and picked up one of the casings, noting the dark smudges on its surface. I rubbed it with my finger, and some of the residue flaked off. It looked like rust, but I knew that was unlikely. Casings had little iron in them. Then as I pressed gently on it, the casing cracked in my hand. I frowned, then picked up another, only to see the same thing happen.

The blood soaked into the Persian carpets like a watercolor painting. The stain lines stretched and marked the carpet, indicating that something large had been dragged away. I could smell old, coppery blood everywhere in the room.

I made my way to the armory in the basement, taking the stairs down into a hallway that brought back memories. It was cleaner down here, but still covered in dust. The paintings on the walls were as I remembered them, all telling the story of the Cartel Master's arrival in the Americas and his conquests.

Seeing them made me worried—it was as if I was looking at images of the future. Earth had six months before portals opened and allowed other denizens of Kirios access to our lands. That was how long I had to create something that could fight back, something that could endure and protect what Earth was supposed to be.

Shadow had prepared me as best as he could, but ultimately it was going to be on me to make decisions. And I barely had an idea how to start. Earth had been ravaged by Source for a full month, I shuddered to think what had happened in that time.

There were signs of struggle down here as well, casings and bullet holes, drops of blood. No one was killed here, but they had bled.

I reached the armory and saw it was mostly empty. The racks that used to be filled with rifles and guns were bare, the lockers where Kevlar vests used to be kept were open and empty too. I walked through, and saw a few boxes of ammo on the table, I didn't even need to glance at them to be able to tell what state they were in, I could smell the rust in the air.

I looked anyway and saw that all the cartridges were covered with dark red substance. I pulled one out and pressed it. The metal splintered as if it was made from cheap plastic, and powder spilled onto the table. I scrunched my face as the smell hit me. Something was wrong with the powder too. I didn't have an in-depth knowledge about the propellent used in bullet cartridges, but even I could tell that it wasn't supposed to look like that. It was clumpy, as if it had melted into clay.

I turned and searched the rest of the room. One shelf held machetes and knives, and all of them had the same rust-like substance covering them.

I glanced at the weapon on my shoulder, and its almost pristine look. It was made on Kirios, with a metal alloy that I wasn't familiar with. But I was pretty sure that it still had the same metals. I brought the blade close and licked it, then nodded to myself. It did taste like iron. Shadow had warned me that there would be a lot of changes to Earth, and this one seemed to be part of it. Except . . . It seemed like a big oversight not to mention that our metals would change properties. All the remaining weapons in the armory were useless, they had turned brittle.

I didn't know how or why, but I did assume that the Source was to blame. I shook my head and walked over to the safe in the back. It was open, and most of the stuff inside was gone. I remembered there being Claymore mines and other explosives inside, but those had obviously been taken. I still checked it, though it seemed like most everything was taken. I had to assume that whatever had happened to the weapons wasn't an immediate change. The people would've had the use of such weapons, for a little while at least.

I sighed and made my way back, stopping to check on other things in the house such as technology. The TV's and computers were dark and with no power, I had no way of checking if they still worked. Though, anything that had metal was affected on various levels. Not everything was fully brittle, but almost everything looked affected. From the few picture frames that were made out of metals to kitchen tools and water taps.

I walked through the entire house, until I reached the bedrooms. There I took the time to look through the closets and pick up some clothes. The first room I checked belonged to the Master's mistress, though there wasn't much there that I could, or rather would use. I didn't think that walking the wilderness around in expensive dresses was the right move. I eventually found a few pants and shirts that fit me well enough, along with a big backpack to keep all of the extra stuff in. I still wanted to check my room and take my own clothes if they were still there, but I didn't have much.

I even went through the drawers, taking a look at the jewelry. Gold and silver was mostly okay from what I could see. I stayed away from the silver pieces and took the gold ones along with any pearls and other precious stones. There wasn't much. A lot had obviously been taken when the house was abandoned.

Then I returned to the kitchen and rummaged through the pantry, taking a few bottles of water and some food. I didn't need it, but I might encounter human survivors, and I had to be prepared for that.

Saia found me back in the living room, kneeling on the floor and trying to figure out what had happened.

"Query: This was your home?"

I glanced at her and shook my head. "No, it was my master's home. I lived in a shack on the other side of the estate."

Saia tilted her head, but didn't respond to that.

"Were you successful?"

As a response Saia's eyes flashed, then a wave of light expanded out of her until it covered us both. I looked around at the familiar sphere.

"It works," I said, excitedly.

"Statement: The engram is operational, though I can detect that it isn't operating in the manner it was intended."

I tilted my head. "Really?"

"Feedback: Affirmative, but it will still aid me in making my own engrams work. I have started rearranging the priority list on engram reconstruction based on what I learned from using this one."

"Does it have a name?"

"Feedback: Shadow referenced it as [Threat Reduction Field]."

"That's a mouthful," I said.

"Feedback: It is an apt name, for its purpose."

I nodded. She was right. The sphere did make it less likely for animals to come near it. It had a mental effect that made them more likely to turn away from the direction of the sphere. I was sure that it was going to be useful to us.

"How long can you keep it up?"

"Feedback: This Unit takes power from the Host. It will remain active as long as you can provide power for it."

I frowned. "It is draining me right now?"

"Feedback: Affirmative, this Unit estimates that it will take several hours until the drain becomes noticeable. The Host's body should be able to provide enough power to run it for a bit over a full day. Assuming a recent feeding."

I didn't know if I would ever get over the fact that I was what powered her.

"Well, we don't need it now," I said, and she turned the engram off. Together we made our way out of the big house and into the courtyard.

Suddenly, I heard something above me move. I jumped forward and spun around swinging the weapon from my shoulder. The blade cut through the neck of the snake that had just lunged at my head. I stepped aside as the head hit the ground and the rest of the snake tumbled down from the rooftop to hit the stone with a heavy and wet sound.

I tilted my head and listened for signs of more danger. Saia took to the air and flew a few loops around me before landing next to me again.

"Statement: I see no sign of more threats."

I nodded, then allowed myself to kneel and take a look at the dead snake. It looked like a boa, but also it did not. Or at least it was changed. The creature was massive, probably twice the length of any normal boa constrictor. Its head was as long as my entire arm, with bone-white ridges above its eyes. The most distinctive feature was the three extra sets of fangs in its mouth. And its body was thicker, almost as thick as my waist. There was also something strange that I only now realized. It had no scent. I knew that Source was involved with that.

I had known that animals would change with the Source, but I hadn't really imagined what that would look like.

"We are going to need to be very careful, Saia," I said. The snake had died quickly. My weapon cut through it easily enough. It wasn't anywhere near the strength of the beasts I fought during my month away, but I still didn't have access to my skills. And that made me extremely paranoid. I had only had my skills for a short time, but I found that I now felt naked without them.

I looked around, seeing the overgrown lawn and the forest nearby. The estate was out of the city, in the wilderness. It was an hour away from the closest village, two from the city, and that was by car. I didn't see any cars around, so I had to assume that they had been used when this place was abandoned.

What I couldn't tell was why they left. I could imagine their confusion when the Grand Spell took Earth. What Shadow had described sounded so apocalyptic. Earthquakes, mountains torn apart, rivers and oceans siphoned. The weather was supposed to have changed too, though I didn't see much evidence of it now, but then again, I had come after everything had settled. I shuddered to think what I was going to discover.

I went back inside and found an empty bottle that I then filled with the snake's blood, taking a bit for myself to quench my **thirst.**

Then we headed to the other side of the estate. I found the shacks where the staff lived easily enough. What I encountered was similar to the main house: blood everywhere, but no bodies. I could only assume that they had been eaten by the animals. I kept my guard up, but I still searched through it. I found nothing that I could use, a few decade-old phones that didn't work, clothes, and daggers that were rusted over.

I could feel the sun coming, and I knew that we should find shelter. I didn't think that there was anything in the jungle that could threaten me, but I didn't want to go exploring during the day without my skills. Hopefully, they would return soon. I approached the small shack that used to be my home and entered.

It was as I had left it. No one had disturbed anything. Which made sense—they wouldn't have had the time to clear it out after my imprisonment and execution. It was a simple room, with just a table, a chair, and a bed taking up most of the room. I had a radio on top of a table and a small chest where I kept most of my clothes. I opened it up and took out a few of my own clothes: pants and shirts, and my spare vest. My best set of clothes was the one that had been torn up in Ish Vimza's jungle. I had never had many possessions. My phone wasn't there, but that had been taken when I was imprisoned.

I walked up to the table and tinkered with the radio. It was one of those old ones that still ran on batteries, which was a pain in the ass since batteries it used were rarely produced nowadays. Thankfully, I had a set of rechargeable ones. I opened the back and saw that the batteries seemed in good condition; I saw no sign of any degradation. I turned the radio on and was surprised to hear static. I wheeled through the frequencies but didn't hear anything.

Then it sputtered and died, a spark flashing from inside and smoke starting to leave the cheap plastic.

"Damn." I shook my head and put it back.

"Query: What was the purpose of this device?" Saia asked.

"It could receive . . . communications, I guess. Though I used it mostly for entertainment." I tried to explain a bit about how it worked, but as it turned out Saia understood radio waves a lot better than I did.

"Statement: I am fully capable of monitoring such transmissions. I shall alert you if I detect anything."

"Thanks," I said, I didn't have a lot of hope that she would find anything.

I reached down and picked up a pair of dark sunglasses from my table. I used to use them often when I walked amongst the humans, as a way to blend in more easily. I had learned how to move my body in the more relaxed manner of humans, but a vampire's eyes often unnerved humans. I've heard the term unblinking often when I was growing up. Now I figured that they would come in handy hiding the color of my eyes. Anyone taking a look at me would realize that I wasn't human, and as Shadow had taught me, knowledge was power.

I walked back to the chest and rummaged until I found a small black cloth face mask that covered my nose and mouth. Humans used to use them often after the last big pandemic, so seeing someone with one wouldn't be that strange, it would also make it, so I didn't need to be that careful with hiding my fangs when talking.

I wanted to help my world, my people, but I also knew the reality of what happened when disaster struck. I had grown up in the poor barrios. I had seen how human baser nature could swim to the surface when times were rough.

If I was going to accomplish my goals, I had to be smart about it. Find a place that can be defended, a base of operations, then find survivors and bring them there. Expand and take back the wild.

I had an advantage because I knew what was coming, and according to Shadow I was probably the highest Invested person on Earth right now. It would be harder for me to gain Investment now, since the quality of blood here was nowhere near what I had to drink on Ish Vimza, so people would catch up to me, but for now I was ahead. I had to take advantage of that.

I equipped myself as best as I could, a backpack on my back with clothes and supplies, Shadow's dagger at my hip and his serpent-tongue spear in my hands. I put the glasses and the mask in the pocket of my vest, easy to grab but not in the way for now.

Then I looked down at Saia. "Let's go. There are two more places I want to check."

Together we made our way into the forest. It was silent, but for the sound of the wind passing through the trees. The change in nature was making me have a strange sensation of wrongness. It was as if I couldn't convince myself that I was home, and in some way that was true. I would never be home again, it would never be as it used to.

After a short trek, we found our first destination. A tall wooden wall barred my way, and I jumped, soaring over it with ease. I landed inside the courtyard of the shifter compound. The training yard was as I had remembered it, if a bit overgrown. It was the place where I first learned how to throw a real punch. The shifters had taken me in, though they had kept me at a distance. I wasn't one of them, but they had helped a young and angry little girl find a place for herself in the cartel.

I sniffed the air and detected the scent of shifters. They had a particular scent that was easy to detect, but it was faint. They hadn't been here in a while.

The shifters served as the main enforcers for the Lágrima Sangrienta Cartel, so this was where I hoped to find weapons, if any remained. I walked through to the main house, noting that it too had been left in a hurry. There were no cars, just like at the main house.

I made my way to their armory, keeping an eye out for anything interesting. The armory was unlocked and open, and I entered to find that it too had been stripped mostly clean. There were a few Ka-Bars around, but they were affected just like the other items that had iron in them. As I studied them a bit closer, I saw that these seemed in better state than most others I had seen, though they were still affected.

"Any idea what is causing this?" I asked Saia.

She tilted her head. "Feedback: The effects are consistent with the corrosion effects on certain metals and alloys on Erzi."

I nodded. "I assume that it has something to do with the Source."

Saia tilted her head. "Feedback: Insufficient data, Ke Erzi never considered a possibility of a world without the Source. I cannot ascertain if that is the cause, but it is likely."

"You aren't going to start corroding right?" I narrowed my eyes on her.

"Feedback: Negative," Saia responded. "This Unit is made out of ferosim, also called the living metal. It does not corrode."

"But you did have metals or alloys that didn't corrode?" I asked.

"Feedback: Affirmative," she answered as she landed on the table near one of the weapons. She placed one paw on the blade, and I saw it flow to cover it for a few seconds before re-forming. "This item contains higher amounts of a material that Ke Erzi used in most of our alloys. It does not corrode."

"Carbon probably," I said. It would explain why these weapons weren't as corroded as the other ones that were predominantly steel. That gave me some hope. Even if a lot of our technology was affected, we could still recover it. We would just need to find different alloys and materials that worked better in a world filled with Source.

I continued my search until I found a half-opened locker in the corner of the room. I pulled it open fully and saw a case on the bottom shelf. The symbol etched on the plastic case immediately made my heart beat faster.

I pulled the case out and placed it on the table. The etched symbol was simple, a hammer on an anvil, with H-tech written below it. Hephaestus Technologies was a vampire led company that specialized in making equipment for both the shifters and vampires.

I clicked the latches up and opened the case to find the weapon still inside. It was a modern revolver, and a model that I recognized. I had used it only once, and that was in practice. It was designated for military use by the shifters in the UK's special forces. I knew that the Cartel Master had managed to procure several of these for his enforcers. I didn't know how they left his one behind, but I was lucky.

It didn't look like it was corroded at all, and that was probably because it wasn't made with metal at all. It was dark green and black, made out of ceramic and carbon composites.

I pulled it out and pushed the cylinder out, noting the eight chambers waiting to be loaded. The H-tech Rhino Model 3 was a big weapon, slightly oversized for my hand, but I could manage it. It resembled a hand cannon more than it did a regular handgun. I knew that it had a kick that would shatter a human hand easily, and it probably had something to do with .600 caliber bullets that it used. I glanced down at the small ammo box in the case and opened it only to be immediately disappointed.

The bullets had corroded, useless.

"Damn," I cursed. Saia leaned down to inspect the bullets, and I sighed. It was too good to be true, and by now I was sure that I just had rotten luck in life. I should've known, there was no reason for its bullets to be still functional. I had already seen that even the powder in the cartridges was affected.

Still, if someone ever figured out a new type of propellant, the weapon would be useful. Just as I was about to put the weapon back in its case, I got an idea.

"Hey Saia," I started. "What are the chances that you could have your drone make me ammo for this thing?"

Saia took a look at the ammo in the box then answered. "Feedback: The shape would be easy enough, though I do not understand the way that it was meant to be used."

Quickly, I explained how the guns worked, and what a bullet needed in order to be fired.

"Feedback: I can create this ammunition, but it would be useless. I cannot recreate this propellant."

I grimaced, then thought about it for a bit. "So, if you made me an arrow, I could obviously fire it out myself?"

Saia nodded, but I wasn't really paying attention as I was thinking of the ways that we could make it work. "Hey," I started. "How do you move, or rather how does your drone move?"

"Feedback: This drone moves mechanically, through the use of limbs and wings. It is analogous to the way your own body moves. It has artificial muscles that enable movement. In the relaxed form, it flows through the use of nanosized individual units."

Though I didn't fully understand, I did get the picture. "But you can't just shoot yourself in a direction, right?"

"Feedback: Not without leverage, and not as fast as this weapon of yours requires."

I shook my head. The sun was nearly out, and I had one more place to visit before daylight arrived. *I'll need to think some more about this.*

I stored the weapon back in its case, and then put it away in my backpack. Then we headed back into the forest, heading toward my sire's old home.

We found the cabin with relative ease. The leaves of the trees were beginning to turn a deep crimson here, and they crunched under our feet as we walked along the overgrown path leading from the estate. Tall weeds grew in waves in front of us, and when we pushed them aside, thick clusters of red berries appeared on spindly stalks. No one came this way often, even before the Grand Spell arrived. I could smell my sire's scent in the air—wild and old, like the scent of the mountains and incense mixed together.

The cabin peeked out from the foliage. The vines had grown over time, covering the walls, and then wrapping around them to cover even more of the wooden structure. Overgrown bushes blocked the doors and windows, making it impossible to see what lay beyond them. There was no indication that anyone lived here anymore.

I walked up to the home, Saia trailing alongside me. Memories of my time here came to me, unbidden. This was the place where I had spent my first moments as a newly turned vampire. This was the place where I had known the first moments of peace and quiet in my life. The place where I had learned how to be a vampire.

Looking back on it, there was a lot that I had missed. Much that I wasn't taught. I didn't know the reasons for it, but my sire had always been somewhat distant from me. Once, I had simply looked at him as a wise and old mentor that knew better than me. Now, I wondered.

Things stood out now in retrospect, inconsistencies with what I had learned about vampires in school. There was much that I had to get answers to.

I slid the panel door open and stepped into the home. I walked down the hallway to the main room. It was as I remembered it. A simple home, one with few commodities. A home that was a snapshot of an earlier time. I noticed a lantern on the floor that had fallen from the ceiling where a branch had punched through the roof. Other than that, there were little signs of disarray here. I walked through it, not even knowing what I was searching for. I entered my sire's bedroom, noted the open closet and drawers. He had packed before leaving. It seemed like they had all decided to leave the estate. Whatever happened for them to make that decision had to have been significant. This place always felt important to my sire.

I was about to leave when something glinted in the corner of my eye, drawing me to one of the open drawers. I knelt down and peered inside. The backside of a rectangular frame caught my gaze, and I grabbed it with one hand and cautiously flipped it over. My eyes widened as I recognized the photo made by an old style camera.

For a moment, I stood frozen, gazing at a moment that I had forgotten. My eyes were drawn to the picture, and my heart thumped as a rush of memories flooded back. I was wearing a deep blue kimono, embroidered with tiny cranes in flight. My sire wore a black kimono with simple lines and gold accents. There was a ritual involved, just before that picture was taken. We sat around a small table, steam rising from two delicate cups of tea resting between us. My sire had sat me down and served me tea, the first time he had done so. He had looked at me levelly and spoke slowly about our obligations: that we must seek progress above all else; that our longevity made us guardians of this world, tasked with watching over it and ensuring its welfare.

Those words had always stuck with me. They were partly why I wanted to try to save as much of the Earth as I could. I felt like it was my duty, the reason I was gifted with as much power as I held.

My face looked the same as it did now, it had been years since then, but I hadn't changed. *No, I am different,* I corrected myself as my fingers rose to touch my neck; there was no scar in the picture. And my eyes, those were different too. The Marianna in the picture had hazel eyes, ones that still looked human. Mine were now filled with emerald lines.

I looked at my sire, his dignified appearance, and I felt only anger. I remembered my sire standing as the Master gave the order for my execution. I remembered those emerald eyes looking at me with disappointment. It felt like a betrayal by a parent, something that I had some experience with. It was as if that was my life's story, to always be betrayed by those that were meant to protect me.

The picture was left behind. I meant nothing to him. I let the anger flow through me, it was righteous, it was my entire being telling me something. It was the fuel that granted me purpose. And right now, that purpose was to be better than they had been. I had an entire world to look after. I had no time to spare for myself.

"Query: Are you all right, Mari?"

I glanced at Saia. I had forgotten that she was even there.

"I am," I said, turning my eyes back to the photo. "It's just . . . memories."

I almost threw the picture back into the drawer, but then I hesitated. Before I could change my mind, I pulled the backpack from my shoulder and slid the photo in one of the pockets.

Then, I walked out, heading to the back part of the house. I entered the training room. The roof was broken, and the tatami was ruined by the elements. It had rained it seemed. The training weapons were still on the walls, most of them at least. I walked over and looked at them. Just like what I had found on the estate, anything with metal was corroded. But there were a few weapons that were made just out of wood. Training swords and staves. I debated taking some, but ultimately decided against it. I had the long spear, the dagger, and Saia, it was enough.

The sun rose above the horizon, even inside I could feel it. Weakness spread through me, and I sighed, rolling my shoulders as an ache spread through my body. A ray of light pierced through the crack in the wall, and I approached. Slowly, I put my hand in its path, It didn't burn me. I had expected that, Earth's sun no longer shone on these lands. But I had to check. I was weakened, and without my skills. I needed a place to stay, for a little while at least.

"Saia, can you use the field please. We'll stay here until nightfall."

Saia did as I asked, and a sphere of pale light surrounded us in a moment.

This place had never been my home, not really. But it was the closest thing I had to it. I realized that I had never truly belonged anywhere. I resolved myself to change that. I wanted someplace that was my own. I wanted people that saw me as more than just a tool.

I had to rest. There was a big day ahead of me tomorrow. I didn't have a concrete plan, but the first thing I had to do was find survivors, and that meant settlements. I settled down on the floor, my weapons within reach, and allowed myself to close my eyes.

Tomorrow I would start exploring my new world.

About the Author

Ivan Kal is the author of *Vae Victis,* an apocalypse LitRPG series originally released on Royal Road. He has been writing for over a decade and, in addition to producing his web serial, has published more than thirty books on Amazon. His other interests include martial arts, computers, and gaming. Visit his website at www.ivan-kal.com.

DISCOVER
STORIES UNBOUND

PodiumAudio.com